Praise for Richard Hall and *Fidelities*

"[A] rich, poignant collection . . . The ruminations in *Fidelities* are remarkably palpable, utterly believable. Enlivened by precise flourishes of description, they touch directly on the reader's empathy button, and hold."   —*San Francisco Chronicle*

"Many of these stories are light in tone and charming in manner, but the relentless presence of AIDS and its consequences animates them. . . . Hall excels at depicting how to go on."
—*The Washington Post Book World*

"Beautifully controlled . . . arresting . . . insightful . . . pungent . . . diverse . . . [and] keenly observed."
—*Publishers Weekly*

"Hall writes . . . in a measured, often moving voice that explores the difficulties of grief and commitment."
—*Kirkus Reviews*

"The elegance and refinement of Hall's prose have once again marked him as one of our most distinguished writers."
—*Gay Pride*

PENGUIN BOOKS

FIDELITIES

Richard Hall was a novelist, an acclaimed short-story writer, and a widely produced playwright. He was book editor of *The Advocate* from 1976 to 1982 and the first openly gay critic to be elected to the National Book Critics Circle. His landmark essay, "Gay Fiction Comes Home," was the front-page article in *The New York Times Book Review* in June 1988, and his reviews have also appeared in *The New Republic*, the *San Francisco Chronicle*, and *The Village Voice*. His *Family Fictions: A Novel* is also published by Penguin. Richard Hall died of AIDS-related complications in October 1992.

RICHARD HALL

Fidelities

A BOOK OF STORIES

PENGUIN BOOKS

PENGUIN BOOKS
Published by the Penguin Group
Penguin Books USA Inc., 375 Hudson Street, New York, New York 10014, U.S.A.
Penguin Books Ltd, 27 Wrights Lane, London W8 5TZ, England
Penguin Books Australia Ltd, Ringwood, Victoria, Australia
Penguin Books Canada Ltd, 10 Alcorn Avenue, Toronto, Ontario,
Canada M4V 3B2
Penguin Books (N.Z.) Ltd, 182–190 Wairau Road, Auckland 10, New Zealand

Penguin Books Ltd, Registered Offices: Harmondsworth, Middlesex, England

First published in the United States of America by Viking Penguin,
a division of Penguin Books USA Inc., 1992
Published in Penguin Books 1993

1 3 5 7 9 10 8 6 4 2

"Death Writes a Story" first appeared in *Finale* edited by Michael Nava,
Alyson Publications; "A Faustian Bargain" and "Avery Milbanke Day"
in *The James White Review*; "Country People" in *The Advocate*; and
"Good Deed" in *Tribe* and later in *Editor's Choice III: Fiction, Poetry
& Art from the U.S. Small Press* (1984–1990), The Spirit That Moves
Us Press.

THE LIBRARY OF CONGRESS HAS CATALOGUED
THE HARDCOVER AS FOLLOWS:
Hall, Richard Walter.
Fidelities: a book of stories/Richard Hall.
p. cm.
ISBN 0-670-83785-7 (hc.)
ISBN 0 14 01.4797 7 (pbk.)
1. Gay Men—Fiction. I. Title.
PS3558.A3735F5   1992
823'.8—dc20   91–45376

Printed in the United States of America

For Marny, again

CONTENTS

A Simple Relationship   1

The Jilting of Tim Weatherall   21

Diamonds Are Forever   35

Silence   63

The Temple of Aphaia   77

Death Writes a Story   93

The Cannibals   115

A Faustian Bargain   135

The Language Animal   163

Manhattan Transfer   189

Country People   209

A Good Deed   227

Being a Baroness   247

Avery Milbanke Day   257

AUTHOR'S NOTE   277

A Simple Relationship

When Terry talked to Bill Crossette they always had three conversations at once. First, there was the ordinary one, audible and connected. Above that were the overtones and implications heard only by the two of them, including attitudes, histories, old jokes, politics. At a third, lower level there was a cultural ground music—all the books, movies, plays, operas, concerts they had read or seen or heard.

A conversation with Bill was so exhausting for Terry that it could only be sustained for an hour or so. By then he was worn out from the weight of their cross-references, allusions, subtexts, and had to take a break. It seemed that deconstruction—a word they never used—had been invented especially for them. Sometimes, after a really good talk with Bill in his floor-through on Grace Court in Brooklyn Heights, Terry would have to go home and lie down. In his own small apartment in the West Village he would replay their conversation, exhume leftover meanings, invent addenda and glosses.

Because of all this, Terry's meetings with Bill were rather rare. Usually they talked by phone. To get together they both had to be in prime condition, like prizefighters before a big bout. It was no accident, Terry realized, that Bill shared his life with someone of a different background entirely. Roberto Fegato was Portuguese. Bill had met him at Fire Island ten years ago, soon after Roberto arrived in America. Roberto, still in his twenties then, knew very little English. He worked at the Pines Pantry. When he turned up with a delivery order, he was invited in and didn't ever really leave except to pick up his gear and his last paycheck. This was exactly what Roberto had dreamed of back in Braga.

In the years Terry had observed the two of them, Roberto's English had become fast and serviceable. However, there was no way he could possibly hold three conversations at once with Bill. Sometimes, in the early days, Terry wondered how Bill could stand it. Everything with Roberto was very simple and direct. Who took the dogs out. Whether Roberto should make one of his codfish specialties for dinner. What happened at the Banco de Santander where he worked on lower Broadway.

But later Terry came to know how Bill stood it. This was because of Alex, whom Terry met a few years after Bill met Roberto. Terry had been sitting in a cubicle at the Everard Baths, just before the famous fire, worried that at forty-eight he had lost his charms, when a tall, balding man of about fifty peered in. Terry smiled. The man entered. They both undid their towels. Then, to his surprise, the man whispered, "I live near here. Would you like to come home with me?" This had never happened to Terry at the baths before, but he said yes at once. Not only was the man hot, he was looking for something more than a quick fuck. Terry had broken up with a long-term lover several years before and was beginning to doubt he would ever find a replacement.

As they walked down Seventh Avenue toward Alex's apartment on Twenty-third Street, just a few blocks from the baths, Alex spoke of himself in a mild, pleasing way. He was a textile artist. He sat all day at a board in a studio on Madison, painting florals. He didn't design these himself; he detailed and elaborated designs his company bought in Europe. He called them knockoffs. He had worked for the same studio for twenty-five years. "I hate my job," he remarked as they passed the Fashion Institute of Technology.

"I want to free-lance, design my own stuff." Terry glanced at him, expecting some sign of anger or bitterness, but Alex's expression was as mild as his tone. It was a pleasant face seen under the light of streetlamps—craggy, benign, with a generous nose, wide-set eyes, rosy skin, and a soup-strainer mustache. The bald head, which reflected the gleams overhead, was nice too. "You see," it said to Terry, "I'm not a fancy guy at all."

As they walked on, Terry wondered if Alex, whose last name was Conlin, really wanted to free-lance. Maybe he liked painting other people's designs and not worrying about a paycheck. Maybe he'd chosen security over freedom without knowing it. He started to point this out, to remark that the first syllable in *free-lance* is *free,* but stopped himself just in time. He hardly knew the guy, after all.

Just before they reached Alex's apartment, Alex told him he had been married until last year. He had lived in the suburbs with his wife for twenty-six years and left her to live a gay life in Manhattan. "How do you like it?" Terry asked. "It's easy to find sex but not so easy to make friends," Alex said. Terry felt his pulse jump when he heard this. "The best thing is to combine the two," he replied. Then he told Alex a little bit about Jack Smallens, his previous lover. He made it sound happy and idyllic, even though toward the end it had been a nightmare.

Alex lived in a small room in a building that had once been a hotel for merchant seamen. When they walked in, the track lighting overhead was giving out a low rainbow of colors. "You always keep those on?" Terry asked. "Just when I go to the baths," came the reply.

They had a very good time. Alex was a considerate partner, scaling his reactions, adjusting to what was wanted. Terry liked Alex's body—long, with stringy muscles and hair nicely distributed all over. He had spied weights in a corner of the room when he came in. But rather to his disappointment, Alex didn't care about getting off. After half an hour Terry said he couldn't hold back anymore. Alex told him to go ahead, don't worry. Terry held Alex's slim, conditioned body in his arms and shot onto his ridged tummy. When he came, Alex's face under his own took on the soft contours of a much younger man.

After they washed, Alex took out sheets and blankets and made up the platform bed. Terry liked the assumption that he would spend the night, and stretched out contentedly. This reminded him of the old days, when going home with someone always meant an extra pillow and a decent breakfast. He thought vaguely of the new velocity of sex—something he'd discussed with Bill Crossette—but didn't mention it now.

The next day, in his own apartment, Terry decided that Alex's unselfishness in bed was probably the result of a long marriage. He'd trained himself to hold off, women's orgasmic rhythms being what they were, and hadn't gotten into the gay swing of things. The idea was pleasing to him, as pleasing as Alex assuming he would spend the night. He could almost feel ties forming. Alex, unlike most of the people he'd met in the last year or so, had a long training in intimacy.

During the next few weeks they got together at one apartment or the other, though Alex obviously preferred that Terry come to his place. Terry could see he felt more comfortable among his own tapes and machines and glass sculptures and leather chairs, even though Terry thought it rather crowded and cluttered—not least because of the drawing board by the window. Still, since Alex preferred that, he went along. Maybe it was another reflex of family life, something about providing and sheltering. Alex had raised two children also.

Terry found Alex's company pleasant without being exciting. He wasn't full of words and ideas. If Terry wanted an opinion, he had to ask for it. The opinion, when it came, was always fresh and insightful, but it was never volunteered. After a while Terry stopped asking; it was enough just to be in Alex's company. He always felt calmer and his mind stopped jumping around. He knew he ver-balized too much—a bad habit left over from college days, when he had discovered conversation after a repressed adolescence—and

New York had made it worse. The people around him seemed to be assisting at an eternal *conversazione*, as Henry James had said of the Venetians. Now, with Alex, he could take a break from all that. He could shut up, listen, and look.

Terry Sennett worked in the public-relations department of a midsize chemical company. His job consisted of digesting a large amount of information and regurgitating it quickly into speeches, press releases, articles, and annual reports. He had learned to do this, had mastered the spurious rhetoric of corporate narration, but his work had repercussions in his free time. Some nights, he couldn't clear a space in his head. The day's words kept jumping around, an alphabetic sludge he couldn't evacuate. Then he'd have trouble settling down, sleeping, even talking to his friends.

Alex helped him with this without intending to. When he was with Alex, Terry found himself speaking more simply, more honestly. Alex set up a frame of reference and he had to stay inside. Not that Alex would fail to understand any of the tangles at the office if they were explained—Terry just didn't feel like explaining. They didn't seem important.

However, one night at a Chinese restaurant, Terry started talking about the president of his company, whom he'd just gone to Shreveport with. Before he knew it, he was launched on an intricate description of Mr. Gormon, the new plant, the press conference, the South, and everything else that popped into his mind. He knew he was irritating Alex, but he couldn't stop. His mind was spinning; the words had to get out. Finally, when he paused for breath, Alex snapped, "Why are you making such a big thing out of it? What's the difference if they're jerks in Shreveport?"

Terry stopped, suddenly deflated. Then he began to feel irritated himself. Alex didn't enjoy the pleasures of language, the play of ideas. Terry's own neediness had locked him into an unsuitable relationship: being with Alex was the next thing to having a lobotomy. Defeat and depression swept through him, and his forehead went cold. They'd never really connect, never have the kind of total rapport he needed, the kind that he and Jack Smallens had had until everything went sour.

He didn't say much for the rest of the meal and neither did Alex. But when they got back to the little apartment on Twenty-third Street and sat together on the bed watching TV, Terry pushed his disappointment aside. Maybe all his talk was merely a demand for attention. It was good to be here, to know that Alex expected him, had made a place for him. If he was dull sometimes, at least he wasn't a prima donna. Terry had certainly had his share of those. When a commercial came on, he gave Alex a big hug. "What's that all about?" Alex asked, pushing his glasses up his nose. "That's for being nice," Terry replied, wondering if he sounded hypocritical.

But despite his belief, that first morning, that Alex would soon be reaching orgasm, it hadn't happened even after several months. Alex was as considerate as ever, doing everything Terry wanted and then some, enjoying Terry's climaxes when they came—but not getting there himself. After a while he stopped trying. When Terry finished, Alex would lie back—by now they had experimented with baby oil, cowboy getups, and porno tapes—and get ready for sleep. If Terry asked, he'd say, "What's the difference whether I come or not—you enjoyed it, didn't you?" Terry would try to explain, but Alex would get agitated and the conversation ended. They had reached an impasse. Terry tried to remind himself that it wasn't important, that if Alex didn't care he shouldn't be bothered either, but he was. In the morning they never discussed the subject. Terry always told himself, Maybe next time.

But as more months went by and they settled into habits and routines they both liked, Terry's frustration in bed increased. He knew he shouldn't make comparisons, but he couldn't help thinking about Jack Smallens. He and Jack had had wonderful sex. They used to refer to the bed as another room. Now, getting into bed with Alex was almost a strain. And for both of them—he could see it in Alex's clenched muscles, his tight shoulders, his wary remarks.

At last, after about six months, Terry decided to get some professional help. He knew a therapist who was occasionally hired as a consultant by his company to help with personnel problems. She might see him for free. One Saturday in April, he called and was invited to her apartment for tea.

Dr. Jean Horstmann had a young-old face and wore her hair in a faded blond braid around her head. She looked a little like Irene Dunne in *I Remember Mama*, except that she was heavy. She was quite different at home, Terry found—more motherly, less authoritative. After serving tea in her living room, which was full of sepia photos in silver-gilt frames, she settled back on her couch. "I'm glad you have a friend, Terry." Her right cheek dimpled, reminding him that his grandmother always said a dimple was where an angel kissed you.

"Yes, we met about six months ago. His name is Alex Conlin."

As he began to talk he felt a slight quiver of treason. He hadn't told Alex he was coming here. Alex had never gone to a therapist, and when Terry told him he had spent five years in analysis when he was in his twenties, Alex had said, "What in hell did you find to talk about for five years?" Now he was about to discuss their sex secrets—Alex's especially—without permission. He took a deep breath and kept going.

Dr. Horstmann listened, her eyes half closed, her horn-rims halfway down her nose. From time to time she took a Milano cookie from a plate.

"The underlying cause of this is helplessness," she said when Terry finished and she had asked a few extra questions. "The fear is that he will lose control, his world will collapse, if he really lets go. Karen Horney pointed this out a long time ago. Do you know *The Neurotic Personality of Our Time*?"

Terry didn't.

"It's a defense for people who believe they're weak and have to be strong."

Terry mentioned Alex's long marriage, job stability, raising two kids. "So, I don't know if he's really all that weak."

Dr. Horstmann nodded. "Of course, the important thing is how he sees himself." She paused. "Let me ask you, Terry—if this . . . blockage . . . is never cleared up, would you want to continue with Alex?"

Terry drummed on the arm of his chair. He hadn't thought about that. He could imagine their nights continuing, Alex always with-holding, his own release becoming more selfish and solitary. "I . . . don't know." And he didn't. He couldn't bear the prospect of going back to his old life, his old weekends, but he didn't know how long he could take the tension of their nights together. Finally he said, "I guess I wouldn't give up the good things just for that."

"All right." Her tone was brisk. "We're making progress. The next thing is for you to decide that this problem doesn't matter. Your new attitude will communicate itself to Alex. He'll relax, trust you more."

That was good to hear. Once Alex realized he didn't care about a mutual orgasm, he'd be able to have one.

But Dr. Horstmann was ahead of him. "I don't mean you are to stop wanting the orgasm because you think you'll get it that way. That never works. You must really not care."

She went on to describe various techniques, including back rubs, massages, temporary exits from the bedroom. "But none of that will help," she went on, "unless you take the pressure off him. Unless you really don't care."

Terry nodded. It would work, he just knew it. And once they'd found the missing piece in bed, they'd find other things, too. More talk, more sharing, more rapport. Everything connected, after all. He passed on his new enthusiasm to Dr. Horstmann, who warned him against expecting rapid results.

But as he started walking downtown he didn't let her words of caution dampen his spirits. Though he'd come across a great many sexual hang-ups in his time, he'd never dealt with this one before. But now he could handle it. He had misjudged Alex right from the beginning. Far from being simple, he was terribly complex. He was living on top of a volcano of unexploded emotions. Terry would help him with some of those—that's what lovers were for, after all. Jack Smallens had actually rescued him from his own analysis when it had reached a dead end, when he was going over and over the same old woes. And now he could do the same for Alex.

As he walked he recalled they were invited to a dinner party that night with some friends of his. It would be an evening of supertalk, not only with Bill Crossette but with some Jesuit priests and an NYU professor. Alex would be lost; he'd probably spend this evening like the last one, when he hadn't opened his mouth. But now Terry knew that Alex's surfaces were misleading. Inside all that mildness, he was seething with anger and helplessness. The proof of this would be apparent later in bed.

By the time he got to Alex's, he'd decided. *No dinner party tonight.* The next moment he realized it would have to be a mutual decision.

Alex opened the door with his usual offhand greeting. They hugged. Alex's slim, hard body felt good. After a while Terry brought up their date that evening. "Do you really want to go to Ernie's tonight?"

Alex studied him with his wide-spaced and very beautiful hazel eyes. "You want to, don't you?"

"I can see Ernie anytime."

Alex laughed his little laugh. "I don't know. I thought we made the date."

"You know Ernie—lots of people, buffet, no sweat."

Another laugh. "Well, it's up to you."

"No, it isn't up to me." Terry tried to keep the irritation out of his voice. "I want us both to decide."

Alex studied him some more. "If we don't go, what'll we do?"

They discussed various ideas. Alex watched him closely. *He wants to find out what I want so he can agree,* Terry thought. This irritated him further. If Alex wouldn't assert himself, how would they ever solve their problem?

At last they decided to go to a movie. Terry insisted that Alex select it, which he finally did.

In the theater they sat with their thighs and knees touching. It gave Terry a good feeling—Saturday-night date at the movies, one of the things he'd missed when he was growing up. And knowing that they were going home to spend the night together added to his comfort. He let his thoughts circle ahead, recalling some of the suggestions Dr. Horstmann had made. At this point, sitting next to Alex—a whole system of contradictions and complexities—they seemed a little pat. Still, he'd have to try.

When they got home they smoked a joint, which Alex prepared in his usual deliberate way, with his leavings, his strainer, his rolling machine. They finished and lay back on the bed. Alex ran his hand over Terry's chest, lingering at the nipples. Terry had very sensitive tits. "Wanna get undressed?" Alex whispered.

This was it. Terry turned on his side. "Would you like me to give you a massage?"

"What for?"

"Relax you."

"I *am* relaxed."

"Lemme try."

They stripped. Alex lay on his stomach and Terry started kneading his shoulders and latissimi, which were full of tension. Alex moaned once or twice. He seemed to be enjoying it. Gradually Terry worked downward, then started pulling and pushing the muscles of his ass. He wondered if he should offer to fuck Alex. They'd done everything but that. Was it possible he wasn't in touch with Alex's deepest fantasies? Hadn't insisted enough? He stuck his finger in gently.

"Leave my asshole alone," Alex growled.

"I think we have some unexplored complexes here."

Alex sat up quickly. "Are we going to have sex or aren't we? If not, I'm going to sleep."

"I'm just trying to turn you on." His voice sounded a little whiny. He certainly didn't want that.

Alex was looking at him suspiciously. Terry knew what he was thinking. "I have an idea!" A fake enthusiasm altered his voice. "I'll go in the bathroom for a while and then come back and surprise you!"

Alex was glaring at him now. "What the fuck for?"

"Well . . . maybe I . . . um, inhibit you. So if you pretend I'm not here and then I come in when you're not expecting it . . ."

Alex let out an ugly snarl and got out of bed. He had caught on. It had been too crude or too obvious or too God knows what. "Are you on that subject again?"

Terry lay back. It would never work. He should have known. Now everything was worse.

Alex sat at his drawing board and stared into space. The area between them felt broken to Terry. He had a sudden glimpse of the fragility of their bond. It could end anytime—tonight, for instance. His belief that he could clear up the problem was arrogant, condescending. The next moment he had the clear impression that his affair with Alex was a mistake. They'd never connect at the levels he wanted. They were mismatched all the way.

He lay without moving for a long time. He heard Alex strike a match and then he smelled smoke. Alex rarely smoked real cigarettes, but he did now.

After a time Terry asked, "Are you going to sit there all night?"

"I'm going to sit here till you stop that bullshit."

"I'll stop."

Finally Alex got back into bed with tense, jerky movements. He turned his back to Terry and kept to the far side. Only after a while did Terry stretch out one arm. Alex wriggled away from it.

It was hard getting to sleep, and he knew Alex was having trouble too. At last, as Terry started to drift off, he saw a strange picture. He and Alex were throwing things at each other. When he looked closer, he could see they were throwing letters of the alphabet, which neither of them could catch.

The next morning they gave each other plenty of room. Alex fixed French toast and they read the Sunday paper without comment.

They had made plans to visit the Brooklyn Botanical Gardens —the cherry trees were in bloom—but they got ready without saying much. Alex's silence was irritable and Terry kept his thoughts to himself. His doubts of last night were still crowding around.

The cherry trees looked like giant strawberry ice-cream cones, though Terry refrained from saying so. They walked around for a while; then Alex nodded at a bench. He had brought his sketchpad and colored pens.

Terry sat quietly, noting the trees, the children, the couples picnicking. From time to time he glanced at Alex's pad. He wondered if Alex had made a career out of flowers and leaves because of his personality problems. What was more soothing than roses and mums, two of his specialties? Drawing figures or landscapes might require him to face . . .

Terry dropped this train of thought. Who was he to judge? To feel superior? A few months ago he'd found Alex's company refreshing because it stopped his mind from jumping around. Now he was using Alex as a new jumping-off place.

He forced himself to keep quiet, soaking up the sights all around. At last he remarked on the beauty of one particular tree, labeled *Prunus pilosiuscula,* whose limbs scraped like elbows along the ground.

Alex eyed it over his half-moon reading glasses, then nodded. "It's really something."

Terry felt himself come down, condense. *It's really something.* There was nothing extra in that remark, nothing from which to launch a reply. It was like a minimalist painting. And then he saw what his choices were. They were not those Dr. Horstmann had promised with time and patience and trickery. He could accommodate himself to Alex, to the shape of his mind, to the shape of his sexuality, or he could not. There was no middle way.

Terry wasn't eager to have dinner at Bill Crossette's the following Thursday, but he couldn't think of a good excuse. Bill saw through his excuses as through a pane of clear glass—it was one more burden of their friendship. So when Bill said Roberto would be working late and they could have a talk, he agreed, though he knew that Bill had heard the reluctance in his voice.

On arriving in Brooklyn Heights—he'd brought a Pouilly Fumé—Terry began to feel a stir of the old excitement, however. And when Bill admitted him to the spacious apartment, and he saw the elegant things Bill liked—a partners' desk, a *Ganymede* from the school of Rubens, the Empire pieces with their striped silk fabrics—he expanded even more. Bill was a designer/architect, but his interests didn't stop there. He had just signed a contract for a book on Edith Wharton's landscape art. He was doing a new translation of Catullus. Other projects were in the works, including a country house just outside Doylestown.

Bill investigated him with bright blue eyes behind aviator glasses when he entered. He was tall, with lank chestnut hair, exactly ten years younger than Terry. "You look tense," he announced. "I have just the thing." The thing turned out to be Kir, which Terry didn't much like, though he drank it. They sat in chairs on either side of the fireplace and surveyed each other. Terry had the feeling that the curtain was about to go up on a play that would make enormous demands on him. At the same time, he was stimulated by the idea.

After some preliminary remarks (the curtain raiser, Terry thought) Bill swirled the ice in his glass. "Well, my dear, how are things with Father of the Year? We missed you at Ernie's last weekend."

"Everything is fine."

"I'm delighted to hear it."

But Bill didn't sound delighted. He was really hoping for some bad news, Terry thought; then he and Roberto could discuss it in bed. And what a juicy tidbit he could offer them—including advice from one of New York's best therapists, a relic from the age of Horney. "We didn't go to Ernie's because . . ." He might as well tell the truth. "Because Alex doesn't like that kind of thing. It's better if I go alone."

Bill absorbed this. "His wife never threatens to sue for alienation of affections? Demand enormous sums of money? Where is she anyway?"

"Gainesville. He sends her presents five times a year. It's practically a part-time job."

A ghost of a smile. "What does he send? Costly little baubles from Tiffany's?"

"It depends on the occasion. At Easter he goes down to Ferrara's and orders a coffee cake with a hard-boiled egg in the middle."

He shouldn't be saying these things, shouldn't be holding Alex up to ridicule. It seemed that Bill and this apartment existed on one side of his life and Alex on the other and there was no way to bridge the gap. Tonight, he knew, Alex was working at home on a free-lance job—a pattern featuring Scooby-Doo, a cartoon Dalmatian. He'd been excited at the idea of painting an animal for a change. But who the hell was Scooby-Doo? What kind of work was that? He could imagine Bill's reaction if he told him. And then, quite suddenly, he noticed that Bill was looking at him with something like tenderness. He had misinterpreted Bill's motives in asking about Alex: he wasn't being critical—all the criticism had come from inside himself. Bill sensed everything he was feeling now too, all the conflicts and crosscurrents. That was another burden of their three-level friendship. Terry decided to relax. He would just talk to Bill.

The evening went well after that. Bill had made a *navarin au printemps*, and the wine was excellent. They both let go. Bill spoke of his problems in translating Catullus and what views of power and sexuality lay behind the verb forms *pedico, irrumo,* and *futuo.* Terry developed a notion he had played with recently, that there was no future for the human race unless childhood was abolished. They talked about the egoless state sought by Buddhists and how it could be attained only by people with egos strong enough to be safely put aside; they discussed whether it was possible to outrage the American moviegoer anymore and the relation of admission prices to the need to be outraged; they wondered whether Jean Cocteau and Jean Marais should be compared to Hadrian and Antinoüs; they decided that human faces were critical components in a vocabulary of signs that rewords itself according to status, culture, occasion, and age. Their ideas were silly sometimes, or arch or merely pointless, but they both enjoyed them. Terry felt marvelously close to Bill as they talked, and he wondered if sharing the excitement of their thoughts wasn't a form of making love.

At last, when they both reached bottom, Bill threw a weary look at him. "Number five, darling."

"Right, number five."

It was their shorthand, swiped from a novel, for the final, unanswerable question: "Where will it all lead us?" It signaled the end of the visit.

By the time he said good night, Terry was exhausted but elated. Heading for the subway, he recalled that when he was ten or twelve and unable to speak his thoughts, he'd gotten in the habit of screeching wordless tunes that drove everybody crazy. His parents told him to quit that noise, but he couldn't. The need to express something, to communicate, even without words, came first. There was a lump in him, a dark shape, that couldn't be ignored. If he tried to ignore it, if he pretended it wasn't there, it would grow and grow until it suffocated him.

A few weeks later Alex suggested they take a trip to Williamsburg. He'd been given a few days off from work; they wanted him to go down and memorize the colonial wallpapers. Then he'd come back and do some knockoffs.

They hadn't spent a night together since their quarrel. Alex hadn't suggested it, and Terry went along. The one time they had dinner together hadn't been successful. They seemed to have nothing to talk about. Terry didn't want to ask about things at the studio—he knew the whole cast of characters by now but wasn't really interested—and Alex asked nothing about Terry's office.

They had never really shared their friends, so there wasn't much overlap there either. In fact, sitting across from Alex, watching him munch his Greek salad in his usual deliberate way, Terry recalled his impressions of their last night together. No, they'd never really bond, never share things. How could they?

Still, when Alex called to suggest the trip to Virginia, Terry agreed. He had some extra days coming at work and he liked bus trips. Besides, he was touched by the invitation. Alex was still trying, still offering something. Comfort, maybe, or companionship. Neither of them number one on the agenda, but still better than staying home with the TV.

By the time they met at the bus terminal, Terry was in good spirits. He and Jack Smallens had spent a year in Europe at one point, the high tide of their love affair. Maybe traveling with Alex would have some good effect, bring them together, loosen things up.

Alex insisted that Terry take the seat by the window. It was, Terry knew, one of the small courtesies that Alex specialized in from long habit. Still, it made him feel good. There wasn't a hint of competition in their relationship.

As the bus rolled off, through the tunnel and out into the industrial wastelands of Jersey—his own company had a gas storage facility here—Terry began to feel almost elated. It was a beautiful day in May, and soon they'd be surrounded by the flowering trees on the thruway. He could feel freedom running through his veins, the old illusion of escape that came with the start of any trip. He glanced at Alex, noting the highlights on his bald head, his strong hands with their spatulate fingers, the mild, good-humored expression on his face. Their eyes met. Alex smiled tentatively. He was waiting, Terry knew, for him to say something. Something to reestablish their bond, to bridge over the division of the last few weeks. But he wasn't sure what to say, what to hope for. At last, with the feeling he shouldn't be doing this, he plunged in. "I went to see a therapist about us. A woman I work with sometimes."

Alex focused his beautiful eyes on him. "When?"

"A few weeks ago. Just before our . . . um, experiment." He permitted himself an ironic sputter. "The one that didn't work."

"Why did you do that?"

"Why do you think?"

Alex looked down and away. He's embarrassed, Terry thought, the pleasures of the highway now evaporating. "What did she say?"

Terry shrugged. "It doesn't matter. The whole idea was stupid. I shouldn't have gone." He looked to his right, at the racing scenery, then let his thoughts curl around. Maybe he wanted too much from the relationship. Maybe there was too much left over from the silence and screeching of his boyhood, from his days with Jack Smallens, from everything else. A new thought struck him. Maybe there was no bridge between Bill Crossette and Alex Conlin, between his two halves, because there was no need for one. Who said the two sides had to join up?

He looked at Alex. He was staring straight ahead. Terry started to speak, to ask what he was thinking, then closed his mouth. Let it alone, he thought, let it alone.

Terry didn't like Williamsburg much, but then he hadn't expected to. Alex found it interesting, though. Not only the wallpapers, which he studied methodically, making drawings on his pad when they got outside, but also the craft displays—glassblowing, wig-making, forging. He lingered at each demonstration, asking questions. Terry didn't mind waiting while Alex peered and questioned. He was glad he was enjoying himself. He even found himself responding a little, thanks to Alex's interest. What he might have dismissed offhand—how they used a miter box in the old days—now looked quite clever. He began to redefine the word *technology*, though he didn't share his thoughts with Alex.

When they got to the House of Burgesses, an elderly lady in a hoopskirt greeted them in the name of the governor of the colony and insisted they make a leg. She showed them how to do the bow and the hand motions. Everybody in their group, including Alex, followed instructions. Again, Terry found himself resisting—this was too corny for words—but at last he gave in and did it. The movement felt very odd and kind of elegant. He had a flash on the eighteenth century—it could be defined as a set of body motions determined not only by manners and custom but by clothing. When they went downstairs to the garden, he was quite tickled by the whole thing, though he kept his reactions to himself.

That night in their motel, in separate beds, he reviewed the day. He had stopped disliking Williamsburg. So what if it was all ersatz? Who had decreed reproductions were no good? Actually, the town was very beautiful, with wide spaces, fine trees, elegant homes and shops. He had opened his eyes and accepted it as it was.

"You going to sleep?" The voice, so light and undemanding, arched over the space between the two beds.

"Why?"

"I thought I'd come over and say good night."

"Come on."

He heard a light step. Alex, who always slept in the nude, slipped under the covers with him. He made low cooing noises. They were meant to be funny, so Terry chuckled. "I really enjoyed today," he said.

"Yeah, it was really something," Alex replied.

That phrase again. Terry recalled the last time he had heard it, in the Botanical Gardens. This time it didn't bother him. Alex was in bed with him and they had been traveling together. He felt a looseness moving through him, a liquidity. He would simply have to learn to speak another language or, at times, no language at all. He reached down and gave Alex's cock a friendly tug. A sound of assent emerged from Alex. Terry slipped out of his underwear and turned off the light.

It was almost like a reunion. At one point, after Terry had finished, it seemed that Alex was going to finish too. He pounded away, his face crimson, his shoulders sweaty, his pectoral and stomach muscles straining. But the climax eluded him and finally he stopped.

"That's okay," Terry said, "it doesn't matter. Let's go to sleep."

He felt marvelous. The looseness, the liquidity, was in his voice, too.

The next instant Alex doubled in on himself, straightened up, then collapsed again. He came in spasms and waves all over the sheets. When he was through, groans and sobs sounded for several minutes more. Terry held him tightly.

At last, when Alex had subsided, Terry reared back and looked at him. "You okay?"

"I'm fine," Alex whispered. "How about you?"

The Jilting of Tim Weatherall

He didn't know if Mark would come, even after the nurse told him about calling New York. You never knew with Mark; he might change his mind. He liked to brood on his wrongs. Sulling—that's what Betty called it when they were touring Spain, all three of them in the little FIAT. "You're sulling!" she would screech in her funny-angry way, and he'd stop. Betty always knew how to handle him, but Tim had never been able to get Mark to stop sulling. It was manipulation, revenge, control, and he'd never been good at countering those. Still, Mark had promised to come, and he usually kept his word.

Two days here, two days of pure whiteness—curtains, uniforms, walls, sheets, pisspot. Where had all the colors gone? His eyes skimmed down. His body so white too; didn't even seem like his own now, just something he was attached to. Mama in the nursing home had been all shrunken and withered too, but not white. No, nut brown from all those years in the garden and the Texas sun. So many gone ahead of him—Mama, Daddy, Pernell, the Old Gent, Pat, Mr. Sam. With all that company he wasn't afraid. He'd never been afraid of anything much except being alone and going crazy. "The potent poison quite o'ercrows my spirit." No one here to quote *Hamlet* to—he'd have to wait till Mark came. Mark was good at quotations; it was a game they both enjoyed.

The nurse had popped him full of Valium again, over his signs and signals no. She said it was to keep him from shaking the IV loose, but it was just to make her work easier. No sass from the patient. He looked at the contraption, the Septra dripping in. It wouldn't work. None of their measly drugs would work, he knew that. They probably knew it too. *I've led a perfectly trite gay life, right up to the end.*

Mark would come for sure. Too squirrelly to stay in New York and feel guilty. To think he'd hooked up with Mark all those years ago. Now there was no escape, the two of them due to orbit space together, just as they'd wandered around Europe and America, tied together and tied apart. A life sentence, after all.

Last time he'd gone home, he'd made Jimmy drive him to the baths in Dallas. "This is your coming out," he'd said as they drove off in the big Imperial. Jimmy had taken it pretty well, picked him up later, even listened to an expurgated version of what had happened. They took him as he was down home—another crazy Weatherall. At least everybody pretended. Underneath, of course, they were all fearful and tight-assed and born-again. All but Mama. He was descended only from Mama. *I don't care what you do, Timmy honey, just be the best and have yourself a time.* She didn't care what the rest of them said, but deep down there was sorrow, disappointment. It almost killed him when he thought about it.

Rob woke him up. A cutie. "Would you like a back rub, Tim?" It was against hospital procedure—nobody was supposed to touch him without gloves—but Rob didn't care. Rob's cool palms on his back felt great.

"Just what the doctor ordered," Tim whispered.

"When's your friend coming from New York?" Word got around. And they liked him. He was from the heartland, a small town. They'd forgive you anything in San Francisco if you came from a small town. He'd told Mark once that even if you were from Cleveland or St. Louis, you had to invent a small town to come from.

"Pretty soon."

"We want to have you looking real good."

"Last time . . ." It was hard to talk; he had to take extra gulps of oxygen through the tubes in his nose. "I got a perm." He tried to laugh, but his lungs wouldn't move. He'd gone to Western Hairlines on Polk and gotten himself curled and set and dried. It shook everybody up. His students had loved it the most. It set them free to do crazy things. That's what they wanted from a teacher, courage and contempt; they searched your eyes, your words, looking for that. The dates and names they could learn for themselves, but not how to be free. That had to come from somebody ahead of them in line. Funny about freedom, though—it came and went. One day here, next day gone. A fear that you could overcome sometimes, other times not.

Rob helped him into a clean robe, fussing and clucking. Now he was embarrassed, his cock and balls shriveled away to nothing. The next minute he didn't care. He'd been handsome for a long time—*a face prettier than most,* who'd said that?—and now it was over. No use sweating it.

Mark would come or he wouldn't, no use sweating that either. Maybe he was still sulling about the article. He hadn't been able to help it, that attack on New York publishers and Mark in print. If he hadn't written it, Mark would have had the upper hand forever. Smug, superior. Maybe he was wrong to write it—a little wrong—but it was done. He couldn't make amends forever. Daddy had never apologized for anything, just kept his mouth shut. The Weatheralls were arrogant, everybody knew that, but for him the arrogance was like the freedom. It came and went. Some days, he felt just the opposite—a clap of air, a vacancy, a piece of shit.

He wished they'd turn up the oxygen. They said it was high as it would go, but he didn't believe them. Maybe Mark would make them turn it up. Mark was good at intimidating people, that executive manner of his. All front, of course, but always on tap. But he himself only had it on his good days. Sometimes, when things were bad, he even got flustered with waiters and doormen. He thought they could see right through him, to Mama in her straw hat and housedress, topping onions, to Daddy with the road-building team and a couple of mules, not even called mister. Sometimes the waiters gave him so much attitude he couldn't even ask for a glass of water.

Why was he thinking about Mark? He knew how he'd feel when Mark walked in looking sleek. He'd resent him. God, it was impossible. How could two people love each other when there was so much resentment? Maybe it wasn't even love, just a silent burning slavery like Mama to her garden and Daddy to his mules.

A stir outside in the hall, then a baby crying. They said they had a baby here in the ICU—what a way to start your life. Hard enough with three older brothers, every one a terror, but at least he'd been healthy. Paul said the line got itself played out with Tim, but that was Paul being mean.

Another noise. Was that Mark? He'd written some poems about Mark, but they weren't good. Too complicated. The best poems came out easy, dropped from the sky, borne on the beat of a drum. Mostly when he'd been in love with someone sweet and new, Joe or Richard or Doug or Gary. Flames leaping, wings spreading, the poem delivered whole and perfect. Or the lines came out of old tears, Texas, Ticky Branch, Mama's ranunculus, the Old Travis graveyard, where he didn't want to be buried. He'd tried to capture his feelings, let the world know. Not that many people listened. He'd ended up publishing both books himself, giving most of the copies away. He even snuck into a couple of bookstores and slipped copies on the shelf, just to be there, so he could go in later and look. Of course, Mark could have changed all that. *I'm sorry, Tim, we don't publish poetry anymore.*

Another noise, now the door opening. He knew that voice, the easy, cultivated tone, East Coast, Ivy League. He'd wanted to talk like that once, when he got out of North Texas State, but later he didn't care. He found his own voice, a mix of drawl and twang, flat California and Boston nasal, in all the places he'd lived and taught. It came together in a sound that was his own. He'd never borrowed anything he couldn't return.

"Here's your friend from New York!" The nurse was Inez, from her name tag, just like his mother. He could write a poem about that.

"How are you, Tim?" The voice heavy, sorrowful, the familiar head bending over. Of course, now that the time was here, he couldn't answer properly, couldn't repeat all the things, almost choking on what he wanted to say—his students, the nurse named Inez, his poems, getting out of Texas, love, anger, resentment.

"I'm fine."

What was the use of giving twenty-five years to someone if you couldn't say what was on your mind?

"You look good."

Lies and more lies.

"How was the trip?"

A dim recital, he didn't listen, just something to fill up the space, the time, while they both thought other things. The chance to speak the truth was gone now, both of them too hurt, too wary, to take a chance. *That's what happens; don't sweat it.* But he wanted more, always more, not settling for platitudes, politeness. That's who he was—inflamed, pissed off. If he wasn't that he was nothing.

"You can only stay ten minutes. Just leave your robe in the basket there." Inez pointed, then left. Mark was wearing that bedsheet but not the gloves. He should have refused to abide by the rules. They might have lasted longer, might still be together, if Mark had been more of a fighter.

No, not true. They were opposites, air and earth, fire and water, and that's what had kept them together.

Mark sitting on the bed now, sloping it, looking at him with dark, all-registering eyes. He could feel the old pull, the old surrender. Let go, relax, turn it over to Mark. Mark was Paul's age, three years older, and Paul had always known what they should do. He'd always followed Paul's instructions, no matter how hard, how scary. He hadn't gotten away from Paul till he left for college. And here he was, still with Mark.

I'm sorry, Tim, we don't publish poetry anymore. Mark beside him, taking his hand, but the words burning in his head, flaming in front of his eyes. Mark could have talked them into it, a senior editor, convinced them these poems would sell, would make a stir, but he hadn't wanted to. No, deep down he wanted to hold Tim back, a hick teacher, a dependent. Mark liked that; it made him strong, superior. He'd quoted Maugham at Mark once—"For you to be happy, it is not enough for you to succeed, your friends must also fail"—and it had stung. Yes, by God, it had stung because it was the truth.

"I'm sure you're going to be okay."

Lies, more lies. He would never be okay, but that didn't matter anymore. What mattered was to tell the truth. But how could you do that when everything was so complicated and it was almost impossible to talk? *You should have published my poems, Mark, gone out on a limb. It wouldn't have cost you much, and it would have meant so much to me here, now, one last thing . . .*

No, he couldn't say that; he never complained, never whimpered. He'd learned that from Daddy. *I'm going to whup you, Timmy, and if you cry I'll whup you twice.* And from Paul, *Don't let him see, Tim, whatever you do; don't let him see.* But still, it was hard, just like lying here with Mark alongside and not being able to tell him anything.

"The hospital wants me to call Jimmy and Fay."

What did he say?

"They think they should know about your . . . um, condition."

"No." He tried to shout but he couldn't. But Mark understood. It was the last thing he wanted, his sister and all of them in Texas. It was just what they were waiting for, proof that everything they said about him was true.

"No," he said again, trying to impress Mark. They mustn't hear he was sick, mustn't be given the chance to cluck over him. He'd always been off to one side, and now this, so shameful they'd never tell a soul outside the family. Partly he didn't care, he'd always liked to shock them, but partly he could shrivel up from humiliation. Too complicated to understand, just like with Mark.

"Don't worry, Tim, I won't."

Mark would keep his word, but maybe the hospital would call Texas anyway. Last time, Fay had said she didn't want him in the house. He'd gone to a fleabag motel off the interstate, feeling like he'd been run over by one of the trucks going past. They couldn't face the truth, none of them, even after Jimmy had been nice about taking him to the baths and listening to his stories afterward. But when it hit close to home, they couldn't take it. Mark looking at him hard now, trying to read his face, but Mark knew everything anyway; it was written down between them with a powdered ink called Instant Truth. *As far as we're concerned, Timmy, you're dead.* That's what Jimmy had said, the hardest thing he'd ever heard. He'd called New York and told Mark what happened, even though his hands were cold and the sweat of madness was dripping from his forehead. And then he had broken down and wept, wept across the continent, as Mark tried to ease him, help him forget. But you could only forget for a while, and now it was back.

It was Stewart who'd wanted to talk to him, following him around for days, looking for a chance to talk to his uncle about school, dating, his mother and father, all the things kids want to talk about. And Tim had loved it. His nieces and nephews were like his children, his best students, like looking into a mirror. He wanted to draw them out, educe, instruct. There was a miracle involved. And at last, through Stewart's jokes and hesitations, his bravado and shyness, he had heard the question. Stewart was worried about being gay. He wanted Uncle Tim to listen, advise, deny. But it was his job to teach, not deny. And so he had described his own life in San Francisco—the good things, the dangers, the fellowship and hate—but it had been too much. Stewart's face, like his, sharp-featured and strong-chinned, had closed down, the words stuck in his throat, the old stutter coming back. And of course, Stewart told his parents, expressed the fears. And so Jimmy and Fay had blamed him for everything, accused him of converting the boy to his own wicked ways, asked him to leave the house. He'd driven to the motel, sick with rage and despair, and called next morning. *As far as we're concerned, you're dead.* He'd heard everything in Jimmy's voice when he said that—his father drawing out his belt, Paul twisting his arm, the trouble in the navy, all the sadness and pain.

And now the hospital wanted to call them, say he was sick, fulfilling the prediction they'd made since he was a kid. No, no, they mustn't do that.

Mark's hand pressing his own, the dark eyes sending a clear message, sorrow piling up in the corners of the room, white like everything else.

"We don't need them. I have your power of attorney."

Yes, he'd made that out giving Mark full authority, even before he was certain he'd be here. Who else was there? It was so fucking hard, but Mark was the only one in spite of everything. Yes, hard. How could two men make it? Everybody telling you to be the best, beat the other one, except the other one is in bed with you, kissing and hugging and promising eternal fidelity. How in the name of God could you fit it all together?

And if Mark loved him so much, why didn't he publish the poems? Why did he leave him at the church door, month after month, while he fiddled and diddled in that skyscraper office of his? And why did he wave it off so coldly, so imperiously, knowing how much it meant? *I'm sorry, Tim, we don't publish poetry anymore.* He didn't exist, he was wiped out, just a blank in the great drama of Mark Deerson's career!

Mark was like the others, like Jimmy and Fay and all of them in Texas. They wanted him to be little Timmy. Maybe there was some profound littleness to him, a Timminess, that he couldn't hide, no matter what. They all saw it, smelled it, and took advantage of it. But that wasn't true. He'd fought back, found his own strength, gotten his revenge over the years. He'd made a joyful noise, the clamor of truth and honesty, and they respected him for that. Who could say? There was no way to make sense of it all, and it was too late anyway.

Mark moving to the window now, turning so that his streaky face was hidden. Sorrow radiating from everything, from the machines, the pisspot, the IV tubes, the curtains. He'd have to go soon. Mark always obeyed the rules, and his time was almost up. And then Tim remembered. "There are clean sheets and towels in the bureau." He'd managed to speak, important to tell him this, even though it took so much effort. And Mark turned, breaking into a beautiful smile, a gift of home he understood. Towels and sheets, books and pictures, walls and a roof. They were both terrified of being homeless; it was the curse laid on them at an early age. They carried that fear around with them—eternal vagrancy, nowhere to lay their heads. There was Mark's fear of abandonment, parents divorced, a broken home, and his own terror of poverty, eviction, Mama coming in and saying the sheriff was outside with a notice. But they had found the missing home together—or rather a list of homes, a succession of places where they could be safe, washed, fed, stored. The first one was the apartment in New York, and after that Valencia and Rhinebeck and Paris and New York again and San Francisco—the last split that had landed them on opposite sides of the country. But through it all, country and city, abroad and here, they had carried home around with them, home being the place they created when they met. And now he could lie back, rest for a minute, because Mark knew where the clean sheets and towels were, would believe that his mother and father were together again, that the sheriff wouldn't barge in with a notice.

Mark leaning over him, soaking up the message, bathing in that sweet truth, the bond between them so strong he could reach out and touch it. Was it possible that it was home that had kept them together all these years, nothing else? That they had put up with the hurts and betrayals because they couldn't let go of that one idea?

" 'The potent poison . . .' " It came out so faintly maybe Mark couldn't hear it, but he took it up.

" '. . . quite o'ercrows my spirit.' " A slow smile of satisfaction, a tremor of completion. "Nonsense, Tim, you're not overcrowed at all. You'll be okay."

No answer to that. There were other poisons too, not just the one in his lungs. There was being afraid—that was deadly—and depending on Mark too much. He'd had to struggle against those venoms for twenty-five years, half his life almost. But he had, yes he had. His teaching, his students, his poems, his lovers, proved that he had struggled and won.

He hadn't seen Inez come in, but she was swabbing his arm. My mother's name, he said, but she didn't look up, must not have heard. Mark moving off, talking to two men, doctors from their jackets, one with eyes like blue taws. He tried to speak, rise up, but Inez wouldn't let him, saying stupid things, This won't hurt, you'll feel better, just you wait. What were they going to do to him? Not another drug! They were going to put another poison in his system. And now the doctors coming forward, killers both of them, something in their hands, an iron cock. We're going to help you breathe, Tim, this won't hurt, please try to relax. *Mark, where are you? Stop them, Mark.* The needle jabbing, Mark disappearing, the doctors holding him, and the iron cock forced between his teeth, down his throat, plunging until he can't breathe at all, and the doctor with the blue eyes saying, "Don't fight it, Tim, don't fight it."

But he has to get the thing out of his mouth, spit it out before he chokes. *If you let them do this to me, Mark, I'll come back and haunt you.* But Mark doesn't hear and they're still holding him.

But they wanted it, all of them, Jimmy and Fay and Paul and Daddy, wanted to keep him small and afraid, Mark too, and he has this one last chance to fight them, fight this terrible thing, and then the needle jabbing him again, the furrows of his body opening and the deadly plow stays down, and he is alone, alone, the iron death in his mouth, while his mind ebbs, falls, and Mark bends over whispering, and the doctors leave and there is nothing in the room but a foul wind blowing Texas clay and California dust and the unfairness gathers into a monstrous pain in his gut and he hates them all and he is going to die.

"I think he's doing better."

"He's a darling; we just love him."

Cool hand on his forehead, a cobweb brushing, as he wakes with the good news that all times exist together, there is no morning and evening, no yesterday and tomorrow. Whom can he tell? But there is no one, and the stranger in his mouth, his throat, won't let him anyway. But he knows. There is no past, no future, only one sentence waiting to be written, the sentence that winds around the world with his name on it, Tim Weatherall, master of sentences.

"How do you feel, Tim?"

A familiar voice but the light has changed, shadows on the ceiling, everyone looks different now. No way to tell them, the foreign thing inside him has swallowed his voice.

"Doctor says you're doing better, coming around, the stuff is working."

They don't understand, they're too far away now, just shadows on the ceiling. But he could have told them the good news, that everything is a single poem—the chaparral cock that Daddy is training, the board-ark trees in Sister Grove, the bus to Potrero Hill, the light on the bay, Mark's hands, Jimmy laughing when they drove home from the baths, the court-martial at Pearl Harbor, all of it fine forever.

Cobwebs on his forehead again, too far away to matter. They won't find him here, but they don't know that yet. Not yet. He's gone off by himself, bound for glory, going to show some ass to God. He wasn't afraid, not at all. They thought you had to abide by their rules, let the judges set your style, but they were wrong. He had found the place marked free. Mark wasn't there; nobody was there but him, with a red rose growing from his cock and a poppy from his belly and yellow fields of mustard all around. It didn't matter about the poems; Mark hadn't jilted him after all, nobody had jilted him, because he wouldn't allow it.

"Listen, Tim, we can't find your will."

A thin ray of sound meaning nothing.

"We looked everywhere but we can't find it. Can you remember where you put it?"

Something white waving in front of him, a hand, a piece of paper, he didn't know. *Together we make one person.* That's what Mark had said, and it was true for a while, but now he knew it was dangerous. Important things got lost, separateness and self, one person gained and the other lost. That had started the bad times, thinking he had to be part of a pair, doubleness, when all the time, he was reaching for the place marked free, and he only found it now, after all these years. He didn't need a big brother, that had been a mistake, a wrong turning, he had always been free and strong but he wouldn't let it come out.

"They're going to bring a lawyer up tonight; they'll cut back on your medication."

But he wouldn't be here tonight, didn't they know? They couldn't catch him if they ran all day. He was finished with little Timmy, with nodding and smiling, saying yes ma'am, no ma'am. He felt sorry for them, not understanding, playing by the old rules. It was a shame about Mark, still plotting, grabbing hold. Why didn't Mark understand how easy it is to be free? Too bad they hadn't seen it before; they wouldn't have crowded each other, jilted each other, set off fires and rages that made the earth smoke. But no use crying about it, no use feeling sorry that Mark is still plotting and grabbing even though nothing will come of it. *Let go, Mark,* but he couldn't say that, couldn't speak, because only truths were possible now and the real truths can never be spoken out loud.

"If there's no will, Jimmy and Fay and Paul and all the rest will get your house in the Haight. You don't want that, do you?"

No, they didn't understand. It didn't matter about the house. The house was like the book of poems, earth-crossed. He was finished with it. Home was okay, but you had to be ready to fly away.

"Tim. Tim."

Noises in his ear but it didn't matter. He could see something coming, a red Dodge van. *Doesn't that frost your balls, a red Dodge van with Daddy at the wheel. Better than those mules, Daddy, come and get me.*

Cobwebs on his forehead, noises in his ear. When would these people learn? The prisons of the earth had been built hand by hand, brick by brick. They huddled inside when they might have stepped out into the light. Stepped outside and let the stink blow off.

The van is so close I can see the chrome shining. Oh, let me ride in a Dodge van with Daddy at the wheel, so slick and high up off the ground.

There were times when he thought he was going crazy. In the navy when he got caught and the court-martial board gave him a Section 8, and later when Mama died, and then again when he heard he'd gotten infected. But now he knew he had just been looking for the exit door. He'd always known it was there, not like the people huddling in the dark.

Give me a lift up, Daddy, away from all these people. I never thought this would happen, not in a million years.

If only he could tell Mark that life isn't a battle, that next time it'll be better, they'll just touch hands and move on.

Start this old thing, Daddy; that's right, get it going. We're heading for heaven in a red Dodge van.

Yes, tell Mark. Don't you see, Mark? Don't you see?

Diamonds Are Forever

She had a headache, the kind she called a sinker. The top of her head, toward the back, collapsed. Some people might tolerate this, but she had a low threshold of pain.

She knew the immediate cause of the sinker, as well as its ancient, irremediable origin. The first one had hit her in the kitchen of her childhood home after she made a jelly roll exactly as Miss Axley had taught them in home ec, using a clean dish towel for rolling it, sprinkling confectioner's sugar on top, cutting off the crusty ends so the thin spirals of grape jelly peered out like capillaries. A professional job all around, but of course, she always took pains. And then *he* had turned up. Yes, Lester had walked into the kitchen at the very moment her creation sat in gleaming perfection on the table, and asked, "Can I have a piece?" He couldn't—it was for her girlfriends who were coming over—but he had given that smirk she knew so well and raced upstairs to Mother. That was when the first sinker had started, the ursinker, the protosinker, the very same that had affected Cain when he caught Abel taking something that wasn't his and punished him for it, even though it meant being branded as a criminal forever. But she knew why Cain did it. It was etched in her mind from Sunday school, though nobody seemed to pay much attention. "And the Lord had regard for Abel and his offering, but for Cain and his offering he had no regard."

Well, that summed up things in this house too. Because a few minutes later Mother had come downstairs in her blue negligee, cold cream on her face, with the hateful words preceding her. "Share and share alike." It was a curse really, a mask for unfairness, and the sinker had instantly stove in the back of her head. In some ways that sinker had never departed—it just retired to its cave, waiting for the next occasion with Lester. And now the same words, the same curse, were affecting her. Even Mr. Abelson, who had handled Mother's estate last year, had clucked with disapproval when he came across the phrase, quite worn around the edges now, in the homemade will. "This is not a legal term, Mrs. Burritt. It should have read 'divided in equal parts between my two children and their offspring, per stirpes.'" He shook his head. "Why did your mother write her own will when she didn't know the first thing about the law?"

She had murmured something, but she knew why Mother had done it. The phrase had turned up in the will in order to protect *him,* to shelter *him,* Mother reaching from beyond the grave to make sure. She bent her head and squeezed the bridge of her nose. No, she didn't believe that. Mother had given later proofs that she, Lenore, was equally valued. She mustn't let a few early memories run away with her so soon after Mother's death.

"I think it's clear enough," Mr. Abelson went on. "You're supposed to divide the tangible assets with your brother." He looked at her warily. "No doubt there's quite a bit of jewelry and personal valuables?"

She started to speak but he held up his hand. "Don't tell me—that will make me an accessory if the IRS asks." He permitted himself a small smile. "But I knew your mother."

Of course. Every time Mother came down from San Rafael to this office on Geary, she had worn the strand of real pearls and the starburst brooch and the watch set with tiny emeralds.

"So if you just say there were no personal possessions of value, we can let it go and you can settle privately with your brother."

"She didn't leave anything of value."

He continued to smile, even though he was aiding and abetting a tax evasion, but she had a pleasant sense of collusion. She had all Mother's things now, since she had driven up to San Rafael to clear out the house and Lester hadn't stirred from Fort Lauderdale. That gave her a certain control. Even if the hateful phrase had turned up in the will, how could they really share these things? What would Lester do with a mink coat or pearls or a lady's watch? Or, most important, an engagement ring? That sort of ring had no other purpose than to signal fidelity to a woman, a spouse, a loved one. *Legal* fidelity, which had eluded Lester all his life despite his protestations to the contrary. No, there was no reason for her to worry about Lester's claims now.

But all that was months ago, and the estate had been settled and the distributions made. It had been wonderfully amicable at first. Lester, on the phone from Florida—they seemed to have ended up as far from each other as they could get—was all agreement and sound advice. "Let's sell the house in San Rafael, keep the apartment house in Sunset, divvy up the stocks and bonds." Not a smidgen of disagreement. Sometimes, as they chatted and reminisced about Mother, she felt something close to love for her little brother. Not that he was little anymore but still. They remembered things no one else did—homes, cars, treats, trips. There had been love in that house in San Rafael. Not enough for everybody but love nevertheless. Talking to him now—just the two of them left of all that menagerie of aunts and uncles and cousins and dogs and cats—made her choke up. Only they remembered. One night, after hanging up from a particularly gentle conversation, she had turned to Jason and said, "You know, I think Lester's finally growing up."

But that was before the two letters.

The first had come from Lester about six months after the estate was settled, and its tone was not the mild one of their recent conversations. In fact, it was cool, with a familiar whine toward the end. He wrote that in fairness Mother's engagement ring should come to him, since she had kept every other piece of jewelry as well as the fur coat. "I hope we're not going to quarrel over this, Lenore. It's been wonderful feeling close to you again. Maybe it took Mother's death to bring us back together." But why should they quarrel? Aside from the implied threat—one of Lester's specialties—there was no reason to be angry. Everything was quite settled in her mind.

She wrote back, in her firm, clear hand (always praised by her penmanship teachers), that there was only one kind of marriage and only one gem that symbolized it, and Lester's idea didn't fit either one. She was glad he had found Peter, whom she really had grown fond of, and it was wonderful they had a good life, but she was saving Mother's ring for Jeffrey, who would certainly choose a wife rather soon, since he had already finished college and gone to work for the 3M Company in Minneapolis. Even as she wrote she could hear old animosities warming up in the wings, accompanied by the beat of the old phrase. *Share and share alike.* But how could they share what one woman passed to another? One mother to another? Something that symbolized the link between the generations?

She wrote tactfully, trying to placate him, keep the peace, even as she knew it wouldn't work. But that's what being a wife and mother had taught her—to keep trying, to compromise, to prevent ancient resentments from blowing families apart.

She hadn't expected to hear from Lester for a while after that, and she didn't. Not even a birthday card when the third of April arrived. He was pouting, but he'd come around once he saw the rightness of her argument. How could he insist on giving Mother's fabulous engagement ring to his . . . well, his roommate, no matter how long they'd been together? It just wasn't appropriate. Surely he wouldn't let this destroy their new closeness?

Occasionally in the weeks that followed she got intimations of a sinker. It emerged when she thought about rings and jewelry in general, but each time, she managed to push it back. Until this morning, when it had crashed through the back of her head, lured from its cave by the second letter. Not from Lester this time but from the lawyers he had hired.

The letter lay on her desk now—creamy stationery on which the black letters *Colman, Aronson & Sheehy* stood up like little insect legs. It was the jelly roll all over again, only instead of running upstairs to Mother he had driven down the interstate to Miami. She pressed her palm to the back of her head. Not that it would do any good. Nothing would do any good. It was simply the latest proof of a fate that had pursued her all her life. *Share and share alike* really meant *Lester take all*. The ring, as Mother frequently pointed out, was actually an heirloom in her own Alvarado family, a family of the most distinguished California-Spanish heritage. Once, they had owned all the land north of San Francisco, a grant from the king, and the ring was a flawless canary-yellow diamond. It was worth three or four times as much as the other jewels put together. And it was all that remained, really, of their old grandeur.

She decided to call Jason at the office. He worked in Oakland, for Blue Cross of California, and always had plenty of time. But, as she expected, Jason just laughed. "That's hot air, honey. He probably got a buddy in that law firm and he just wrote you the standard lawsuit letter. Those big guys get two hundred and fifty dollars just for dictating a letter—Lester won't lay out that kind of money."

She wasn't so sure. A few hundred dollars for the pleasure of thwarting her wasn't much. Besides, the letter strengthened his claim. Look, it said, I can go to a big law firm on Brickell Avenue, a company with a platoon of partners running down the side of the stationery, and advertise my relationship to Peter Huebsch because I'm proud of it. I'll be glad to stand up for it in court, too.

But when she pointed this out to Jason, he laughed again. "Just forget about it; he's not going to court. The IRS will take the darned ring anyway for not reporting it."

She hung up feeling slightly better but not convinced. Jason had an optimistic view of human nature—it was one of the things that brought balance to their marriage. She wondered briefly if good nature was a sealed essence, like Freon in an air conditioner. Jason never varied from his positive view of things, while she was always blowing hot and cold. But of course, he hadn't grown up with Cain and Abel in his own house. He and his sister had been close friends, and Sue brought her family from Toronto to visit them in San Carlos every year.

Suddenly she caught sight of Tom Weston outside. He was detailing her car—Jason had hired him and she'd forgotten. What a sweet, handsome lad he was, rather like Jeffrey at that age. He liked the Barlow girl who lived down the street; she'd seen them driving in Tom's VW convertible. She got up from the desk and went outside. Tom seemed delighted to see her. As they chatted she could feel the normal world reasserting itself—the world of washing cars and mowing lawns and caring about children. That was the cure for those old, dark thoughts. She had let Lester threaten her because she had forgotten her own values. Even if it came to a trial, what judge would award Mother's ring, an Alvarado diamond, to a man who wanted to give it to another man? Judges stood for something, even in the Bay Area. Also, they were sworn to uphold the Constitution, and there was nothing in that document about marriage between men, no matter how they reinterpreted it these days. She took a deep breath and offered to help Tom wipe the hubcaps. Getting up and down kept the cellulite at bay. And she enjoyed Tom's company.

She didn't care if the IRS did get wind of the ring. She'd pay extra taxes, penalties, anything, before she'd give it up. She'd even go to jail for her beliefs, like Jane Fonda, not one of her favorite people but still.

The patio never failed to please him, especially now in January, when the sky was a piece of thin blue paper and another water lily opened each day. The one-story main house, separated from the guest cottage by the patio, was glowing today. And his latest acquisition, a vargueno on a folding stand, Moorish, c. 1600, looked exactly right by the sofa. He sat by the sliding doors, where he could see both outside and in. No one, not even Peter, could understand the satisfaction that the placement of furniture, flowers, ponds, gave him. Sometimes he thought there were holes in space waiting to be filled, and when they were, correctly, he heard a slight click. Not that he was a decorator. But he understood space, the sounds that emptiness gives off, the sigh of a room in balance.

All of this had led him to real estate. When people asked him the reason for his success, he would usually reply, "Luck, mostly." But if pressed he would touch his right eye. "You have to see what wants to move in, what has its bags packed and is ready to travel." When they stared at him, and they usually did, he would switch to demographics and changing leisure habits, but they had missed the point. Deep down he was an outlander, and that had put him in touch with its opposite. "You'd think," Peter had remarked when they first met, "you'd been raised on the streets of Rio, not in some California suburb with its own private academy." "Oh, but I was," he'd replied, not bothering to explain yet. He was the fat kid at the academy—weren't all fat kids born in Rio?—and besides, he'd been a know-it-all and a pain in the ass. He used to give away candy bars to make friends, a doomed enterprise. Peter had come to understand after a while, especially seeing him at work.

They'd be driving around—Opa-Locka, Miramar, Hollywood, Dania, Hallandale, or over on the west coast, Fort Myers, Naples—and when they passed open land he would become silent, his mouth open slightly. Later Peter would make cracks about second sight, but at first he'd been impressed. Either way, it didn't matter. Lester was seeing, hearing the movement—who would surge in to buy the homes, what their families would look like, how long before the tide took them out again. When other land speculators talked about interest rates and zoning boards and environmental law, he waited for the homesickness, the ache, and then he bought. He was never wrong. He understood there was an endless supply of Americans who weren't sure where they belonged.

Peter shouldn't complain or make cracks about second sight. That's what had bought them this house and patio. Peter's earnings as a social worker would have gotten them a two-bedroom condo in Little Haiti thirty miles to the south, with a dead chicken on their doorstep every morning.

Peter, naturally, was opposed to a fuss about the ring. Said he'd never wear it anyway. He didn't like rings, least of all a diamond. "It's just some old spat left over from childhood, Lester. Why don't you forget the whole thing?"

Well, he had tried, honestly, for almost a year. Even though Lenore had kept the Spode, the pearls, the emerald watch, the brooch. He had decided to be generous. He wouldn't ask for a share, even a fair share. Good relations, love, between him and Lenore were more important. And he enjoyed their talks on the phone so much. For a while he thought Lenore would take Mother's place. He told her about his coups, his failures. About the friends he'd lost to AIDS. Even about some little squabble with Peter. He thought she understood, accepted, as his mother had come around to doing. But then, during one of their good talks, a question had come out of left field that destroyed all of it. "Tell me, Lester"— and he could still hear her tone, reasonable, judicious, maternal— "did you ever wonder why you turned out to be homosexual?" His heart had started a mad beating as the realization came to him—*She thinks I come from another planet*. And from that realization had sprung a second one—*She never offered me the ring because she thinks I don't deserve it*. He had stammered something, collected himself, then closed the conversation. Only later had the proper response come to him. "Tell me, Lenore, did you ever wonder why you turned out to be heterosexual?" But of course, he couldn't call her back and ask. Instead he had written a letter requesting the ring. It was the only way he could cope with his anger.

At first he really thought she'd agree. Hadn't she absorbed the strict codes, the compressed wisdom of their parents ("Two wrongs don't make a right." "Handsome is as handsome does")? These injunctions would rise to the top sooner or later. And thinking about it further, even if anger and revenge were behind his request, there were other motives, too. If he let her keep the ring, it would mean he was agreeing with her view of his life as something wrong, something alien. Everything he and Peter had done, everything they had bought and built—their home, furniture, boat, friends, volunteer work—would be discounted. "She really doesn't think we have any moral standards at all," he said to Peter one evening. Peter, as he expected, wasn't bothered. "That's her problem, Lester, not ours. We know what we're like." But Peter didn't have a sister whose hatred had accompanied him all his life. He was a single child, the idol of both parents.

No, he couldn't pay attention to Peter's mildness. If he let Lenore hang on to the ring, he'd be conspiring against himself. When he thought about that he saw a fat boy handing out Baby Ruths on the playing field of the academy. It wouldn't do.

After he received her letter refusing to hand over the ring, he debated for a few more weeks, then drove down to see Joe Colman. Joe, a handsome transplant from Wall Street who handled his real-estate deals, listened carefully. "She's now in possession of the ring, is that correct?" He looked at his legal pad. "Mrs. Jason Burritt, Lenore Wightman Burritt?"

"Right." Lester shifted uneasily. Now that he was here, he was having second thoughts. "Maybe if we could just scare her a little . . ."

"She doesn't sound like the type to scare easily."

"It's mostly bark and no bite. Underneath she's very . . . um, conservative. She'd never break the law."

Joe chewed his lower lip. "Withholding and sequestering property under the terms of a will can be construed as grand larceny. How much would you say this ring is worth?"

"We never had it appraised. My mother always said it was extremely valuable. Her grandmother's or before that."

"Well, if you just want to scare her, we could write one of our letters." Joe smiled. "They tend to upset people."

Lester wiped his forehead. Once Joe's letter reached Lenore, the era of good feeling between them would vanish forever. They'd revert to their old relationship, the one left over from childhood.

"Send the letter, Joe, and I'd like to get a copy."

There was the usual tangle on I-95 going north, which made him feel even worse. They were having a wrangle over the spoils, the ugliest thing possible. At one point, stalled in traffic, he beat his hand on the steering wheel. Peter was right. He had predicted they would get into a mess and they had.

He recalled the time his mother had hocked the ring. Hocked it and given the money to his father to tide him over a serious cash problem at the Kaiser agency he'd started in Santa Rosa (he should never have taken on Kaiser cars, should have stayed with one of the Big Three). He'd noticed the blank spot on her finger right off, since he always noticed everything about her hands, but she had denied it. "It's being cleaned." But somehow he knew, and later he overheard his father. "I swear to God you'll get it back"—the heavy words seeping under the bedroom door—"if I have to peddle those damned cars door to door." And he had made good. One day, the diamond, mysterious as ever, with the fire deep inside, had turned up on her finger. It had never disappeared again.

When the traffic got going, he recalled the passion in his father's voice as it flowed under the door. The diamond had been important to their marriage even though it came down from his mother's side, had replaced the tiny gem his father had first bought for her. Well, it was important to him, too. Why couldn't they understand that?

When he got home, Peter was about to leave for his afternoon stint at the Health Crisis Network. He surveyed Lester skeptically. "How did it go?"

"Joe Colman is gonna write a letter to Lenore, one of his specials."

Peter let out a whistle but Lester turned away. He didn't feel like discussing it further. It was all too complicated. But after Peter left, he experienced a sudden lightening of the load, almost a spurt of elation. Maybe this was for the best. Maybe he and Lenore could have one last fight, a real showdown, the one they'd been putting off for years. He knew exactly what it would be about too. Did Mother really approve of his life with Peter? What was her definition of fidelity? Of right and wrong? And underneath those questions lay another, more secret and shameful: Whom did she love more, really? He smiled privately. He knew the answer to the last question as surely as he knew anything in the world.

Well, the whole society was litigious, everyone knew that. Look at the doctors' fees, which went mostly to pay for malpractice insurance. But she never thought she'd be caught in a lawsuit with her own brother.

"I'd like to see a copy of the will," was almost the first thing Mr. Sakama asked her. She was in San Francisco to see him, an expert in estate matters, specially recommended. But she didn't have a copy of the will with her—and, come to think of it, she wasn't sure where it was. Lester was executor and had never bothered to send her one. Mr. Sakama, a heavyset Asian with an office on Mission Street across from the *Chronicle*—not the best address—frowned. "I'll write his attorneys." There was a framed law degree on the wall, Hastings Institute—not the best school.

"I hope they answer. I'm sure Lester told them not to cooperate."

"They have to cooperate, Mrs. Burritt."

He announced next that there would be a five-hundred-dollar retainer. "That seems like a lot," she replied, and he began explaining. She had brought her checkbook, but for some reason it didn't want to leave her bag. And she could guess why. Writing a check would be giving in to Lester. He would be forcing her hand, quite literally. She had the clear impression, sitting here above the clatter of Mission Street, that even coming this far was a mistake. She had let him choose the field, the weapons. But that wasn't the way she worked, not at all.

Suddenly she saw the jelly roll in front of her. When she heard Mother's unfair instruction to give Lester a piece, she hadn't hesitated for a second. She had scooped up the thing with both hands, broken it in half, and dumped it in the garbage. Then she had stared at them defiantly. "You can't make me!" she'd yelled, dusting off her hands.

She waited until Mr. Sakama finished one of his sentences; then she thanked him very politely and rose. She would think about his proposals and call in a few days. He must forgive her but she was very upset. A lawsuit with her own brother, after all. Her last view of him was as he sat behind his walnut-veneer desk and looked at her with wide, amazed eyes. But she couldn't help it. The time hadn't come to take out her checkbook, to let Lester have a piece of what really belonged to her.

She was a little disoriented when she hit the street. The day had been a terrible strain from the minute she got up. On impulse, she decided to take a taxi to Gump's. Gump's was her favorite store. Just walking around it soothed her, not only because of the good taste on display but because of the antiques. Antiques had an especially calming effect on her. Now, getting into a cab, she wondered if that was because they reminded her of shopping trips with Mother. An interest in American Colonial and baroque Spanish furniture was one of the things they shared. Naturally, Lester had horned in, claiming he was interested in period furniture too, but Mother hadn't really believed him. It was amazing how she and Mother had connected after she met Jason and got married, after Jeffrey was born. It was as if she, Lenore, had been born again too, into a new place in Mother's heart. Mother's old alliance with Lester had dissolved.

Of course, Lester had helped that happen, with all his shenanigans. How could Mother shoulder the guilt and responsibility he laid on her? No woman could. And so she had turned to Lenore, who was busy getting the next generation born and raised and educated. Yes, Mother had come over to her side and stayed there until the day she died.

She'd done the right thing in walking out of that lawyer's office just now. It would be ridiculous to fight Lester with accusations, depositions, witnesses, judges. It was just what he was hoping for.

And judging from the names on that letterhead, he had about a million dollars' worth of talent to draw on. Mr. Sakama, with his Hastings degree and his walnut-veneer desk, would be hopelessly outclassed.

As she got out of the cab at Union Square she began to feel a sinker oozing out of its cave. She stopped and took some chewable aspirin. The next moment the phrase popped into her head. *The necklace was paste, after all.* Where had she heard that? She had no idea. She wasn't even sure what it meant. How could you make jewelry out of paste?

She pinched the bridge of her nose and stood still for a moment, then headed into Gump's. As she expected, just entering made her feel better. She decided to start with Chinese export porcelains.

Of course, Mother hadn't entirely dismissed Lester from her thoughts. Mothers were like that—lifelong hostages. Even if Jeffrey did something terrible, she, Lenore, would forgive him. Still, it was a pity that she had to wait until she was twenty-one years old and on the verge of becoming a bride before Mother found a special, reserved place for her.

She shook her head slightly to get free of these thoughts. The diamond, the quarrel with Lester, had brought them back. She'd suspected he was trouble when she was three years old and they brought him home from the hospital, a reddish-white lump. And she'd been right. Except for those few months after Mother died, he'd been nothing but trouble—a thorn in her side, a stigma, an affliction. Even here, in Gump's, she could conjure up his thin smile of self-esteem, which always infuriated her.

She was standing in front of a Biedermeier display when the meaning of the phrase hit her. She had moved to another section of the store without noticing, while her mind was spinning. All of a sudden it was perfectly clear. Amazing.

She hardly noticed where she walked or looked after that. Her thoughts were gliding swiftly through the future, picking and choosing. Mr. Sakama would be necessary, after all. She'd have to call him before she went back to the garage to pick up her car.

She'd also have to walk over to the Jewelers Exchange on O'Farrell, which had a great many merchants under one roof, though she didn't have the ring with her.

A harsh laugh rose in her throat as she worked over her idea. She knew her brother. Stubborn, a bargainer, never conceding until he had to. Well, she'd use that against him. Lester wouldn't believe he'd won unless he could fight every inch of the way. She'd have to be as tricky as he was.

When she got home after the visit to the Jewelers Exchange, she was exhausted. It wasn't just the trip and the walking around and the traffic coming home, it was something else—something deeper, almost disgusting, that had tired her. Lester had brought out the worst in her, an old dead part she thought she was finished with. Ghosts, she thought as she went upstairs to lie down, you never get free of the ghosts of childhood. And then she recalled how awful she had felt after dumping the jelly roll, after defying everyone. She had gone to her room and cried for hours. She hated herself when she acted that way. She had outgrown it long ago. Only Lester had the power to trigger it still, Lester with his endless supply of selfishness. It was God's unfair curse on Cain, who had done nothing wrong, who had simply been pushed beyond the limits of endurance and had been punished for it through all eternity.

"Well, I can't believe it and you won't either." Lester waved the letter at Peter, who was at the counter sectioning his grapefruit. "I never saw her give up without a battle before. She seems to have settled for a little skirmish."

Peter moved his glasses to his nose. After reading the letter he shook his head. "I doubt it was the letter from your lawyers. She probably feels her relation with you is more important than the ring. She doesn't want to lose you."

"Lenore doesn't have feelings, she has moods." That sounded worse than he intended and, predictably, Peter gave him one of his looks: he set his mouth in a thin line and stared at him. Peter's hawk face and whippet leanness belied his sweetness. His welfare clients loved him even when they couldn't understand a word he said. Something was communicated. Lester looked away, a little annoyed and embarrassed. Peter still didn't understand. Maybe no one could—what could you transmit, after all? Then he remembered another kitchen, an old-fashioned one, years ago. No use telling Peter what had happened—he still wouldn't excuse or approve—but everything had a cause.

He and Lenore had been at the kitchen table while his mother stood at the stove. It was his first negotiation with his sister, who was nine—a vast age.

"You want my chocolate pudding, Lennie?" That was what he'd asked her, hope tingling through his roly-poly body. He pushed the saucer toward her.

She peered at him suspiciously. "You don't want it?"

"You can have it." He sat forward on the wooden chair. "You can have it if you promise to be nice to me."

His mother stepped closer, oohing and aahing over this evidence of goodness in a six-year-old boy. "What a wonderful thing to do—what do you say, Lenore?"

But Lenore didn't say anything, just stared at him witchily, doing her calculations. In the meantime he sat and waited, feeling all gooey and runny inside. Something wonderful was going to happen. She didn't understand how much he loved her. He was offering his dessert, his favorite dessert, because he wanted her to love him back. He wanted to walk to school with her, meet her in the playground, draw pictures with her. She wouldn't do these things now, but with this immense sacrifice she might.

She snaked out one arm, grabbed the dish, and stuck her spoon in. "What do you say, Lenore?" Mother's voice had risen a notch, a tone they both knew.

"I'll be nice to you." She licked the back of the spoon after finishing off the front.

"Forever and ever?" He leaned forward, delight streaming through him. Here it was.

"Forever and ever." She gave him a narrow smile—a smile he later came to know as an infallible sign of betrayal.

He thought again about telling the story to Peter, but it was all so childish. He should have forgotten it years ago. Everybody had losses and hurts—it was really a bad sign, arrested development or neurosis, if you let them come back. The important thing was that Lenore had conceded, was willing to give him the ring with a few strings attached. Now they could begin to be friends. Maybe —a flicker of old hope rose in him—maybe they could even find the love that had been lost.

"You know"—he picked up the letter again—"I'm not under any legal obligation to return those fees. Being executor was a lot of work. I went to New York to talk to what's his name. There were all those phone calls."

"I thought you charged the estate for those."

"Two percent of an estate isn't much for being executor. An attorney would have charged five percent or more."

Peter was looking bored and impatient. "Why don't you just send her the money, Lester, take the ring, and get it over with?"

He sent some of the impatience back. "I will, Peter, just give me a chance."

Peter got up and walked out, shaking his head. Lester sighed. Peter wasn't going to change, wasn't going to get interested in material things. His eye fell on the letter again.

Dear Mr. Wightman,

Your sister, Lenore Wightman Burritt, has asked me to inform you that she is willing to convey to you the diamond ring formerly owned by your mother. Because this gem is of substantial intrinsic value, outweighing the value of the other personal items retained by Mrs. Burritt, she believes a fair settlement would entail a reimbursement to her of the executor fees charged by you to the estate. These, according to the tax return, amounted to $9,800.

We would appreciate hearing from you promptly so this matter may be settled.

The signature was big and flashy, Charles Sakama. Some cut-rate guy Lenore had dug up, no doubt. Who ever heard of an attorney with an office on Mission Street?

Of course, Peter was right. He should just send the money and forget about it. But why hand over ten grand just to get what was rightfully his? That was Lenore all over—always wanting a little something extra.

He refilled his cup from the coffee carafe. Maybe he could offer to repay half his fee, no more. Or start the negotiations from a lower level—offer a thousand and work up from there. He sipped the coffee as other possibilities came to him. What about refusing to pay cash now but offering to provide another engagement ring for Jeff when the time came, up to a value of x dollars?

Well, this wasn't getting anywhere. He couldn't do anything Peter wouldn't approve of, and he was quite sure Peter wouldn't like any of those schemes. Peter, he reflected, had the unpleasant habit of expecting him to live up to the best that was in him. At all times. It was like a debt Peter was always threatening to collect. He sighed again and finished his last cup of coffee. He was trapped inside Peter Huebsch's absurdly positive view of the world, and though he might struggle with his own urges, he could never really act on them.

And then, in a burst of vision, the idea came to him. Why not put his executor fees into a trust fund for Jeff's future children? With interest—twenty years, say—it would double or triple. Jeff's son, if he had one, could even buy a ring for his bride. And if there was no marriage, no children—well, the arrangement would cover that, too. A wonderful idea—generous, thoughtful, forward-looking. Who could possibly object? Lenore would see that it had everything going for it. Besides, it had the advantage of not giving her exactly what she asked for, though he needn't mention that to Peter.

He went to the living room and pulled down the front flap of the vargueno. What better way to use this beautiful new acquisition than to write a letter of truce to his sister? To call for a renewal of old ties, an end to misunderstandings? He wrote quickly, excitedly, hardly noticing when Peter came in. But he did reply, when Peter asked, "I think everybody's gonna be satisfied with this, including you."

Peter, he could tell without even glancing up, was wearing a skeptical look, but that was okay. Lester was positive this was the right solution—the compromise that would make everybody happy. He really should have been a labor arbitrator or a diplomat. It was a gift he had. Lenore would do anything, agree to any proposal, that made Jeffrey's future brighter. This letter struck exactly the right note.

It was only when he was sealing the envelope that a last happy thought came to him. It wasn't Lenore's blessing that possession of the ring would confer, it was his mother's. It would be her seal of approval, her forgiveness for all the transgressions of his youth.

The coincidence was so great it took her breath away. Jeffrey had called from Minneapolis last week and said he wanted to bring someone home for the weekend. "Is it a girl you like?" she'd asked, joy shining through her. Jeff had replied, "A girl, yeah, but not that big a deal." But she knew. She knew just from the way he was playing it down. "You want us to do anything special, dear?" No, he didn't want a fuss; he was just going to show Ginny his old school, introduce her to some friends, drive around. Her name was Ginny Ventura and she worked as a teacher in Minneapolis. They had met at a social club for tall people.

When she hung up, joy surged through her again, bringing tears to her eyes. She had done the right thing. She had been vindicated. It was all worth it—the lies, the deceit, the guilt.

When Lester's letter arrived two weeks ago, she had had serious doubts. His offer of a trust fund wasn't exactly generous, even though he tried to make it sound that way. If he'd been truly generous, he wouldn't have collected those executor fees in the first place. Still, he was trying to make amends. And via Jeffrey, whom he cared about, whose future he worried about. For a few days she had considered canceling her plan. It wasn't too late to stop the jeweler, Mr. Lucena. But as she worried, turning it this way and that in her mind, trying to weigh everything—and all alone, since she hadn't discussed her decision with Jason—she wasn't able to go to the phone and cancel. And then, in the midst of all her worry and remorse, Jeffrey had phoned. It was as if a giant hand had reached down from the clouds and patted her on the back. She had a good idea whose hand it was. And here they were at the airport gate, waiting to meet Jeffrey and his fiancée.

Jason had let out a hoot when she used that word. "Better not let Jeff hear you—he won't like it."

"Well, he never brought a girl all the way from Minneapolis before."

"Doesn't matter, he won't like it."

She wouldn't say it, but she'd think it. The best part was, now she had the strength to see her plan through. There was no need to blame herself or to imagine all the things that could go wrong. Besides, hadn't Mr. Lucena told her on her second visit that she was extremely lucky because Mother's ring was exactly the same color as the substance he would use? "Canary yellow and ceezee are a perfect match," he'd said, removing the loupe from his eye and straightening up as much as his age and spine allowed. He looked like a question mark, but she had chosen him for his friendly manner. Most of the other merchants, when she walked around that first afternoon, had avoided looking at her, busied themselves with work. But Mr. Lucena, who had gray hair and remarkable blue eyes, had spoken first. "This place is very confusing; maybe I can direct you." She'd come to a halt right in front of his shop —a booth, really—and chatted. And he had responded, not in a hurry, not pressuring her. Gradually she had told him (more or less) what she wanted. He wasn't surprised. In fact, he approved. He told her that Elizabeth Taylor rarely wore the 69-carat stone

Richard Burton had given her. She wore an imitation, while the original stayed in the vault, fooling everyone, including the newspaper reporters. The story made her feel better, convinced her Mr. Lucena was the man she was looking for.

And on her second visit, with the ring, he had reassured her even more. "Ceezee," she discovered, were the initials of cubic zirconium, which, the way Mr. Lucena pronounced it, sounded a lot better than zircon. Besides, there was the color match, which was lucky in the extreme. Still, she had pressed him about the chance of discovery. "If I'm wearing the new ring," she asked lightly, "how can I be positive nobody will know? I don't want one of my friends holding it up to the light and saying it's a fake."

He handed her back her ring. "Lick it, Mrs. Burritt." She glanced at him, wondering if he was joking. She ran her tongue over the stone. It felt chilly, almost cold.

"Now try this." Using tweezers, he picked up a stone from a tray under his counter and held it in front of her. She bent forward and put her tongue to it. A pulse of warmth—heat, really—bounced back. He watched her. "One was cold, one was warm, correct?" She nodded.

"Thermal conductivity, the only way you can tell the two apart. The diamond conducts heat ten times faster, takes it away so you taste the cool stone. Not true of the other, the imitation. Not even a jeweler with a glass can tell them apart."

She waited a moment, trying to put it all together; then they began to discuss the price. Mr. Lucena was a little flexible, but not very. Before leaving, she couldn't resist asking what he thought the diamond was worth. "There are no more than a dozen diamonds of this quality and weight on the market at any time." He had refused to be more specific.

"There they are!" She caught sight of Jeffrey walking just ahead of a tall girl in a beige linen jacket and brown skirt. "Hi, honey." She glowed, embracing him. Not that he allowed it for very long. He wanted to introduce Ginny. That nervous smile on her face,

Lenore thought, will soon disappear. She would make it her project for the day. As she took Ginny's hand, then brushed her cheek, she whispered, "I'm so glad you're here." She stood back and looked at her. She was large-featured but pretty, also a little awkward. Glancing down, Lenore saw what looked like size-ten shoes. The next moment she was filled with affection and pity. She too wore size tens. Her feet had been one of the woes of her adolescence.

Driving home, Jason at the wheel, she could see how comfortable they were with each other. She could almost smell the intimacy. Whenever Ginny spoke, Jeffrey's eyes swept her own, checking his mother for approval. But that wasn't necessary. She was already won over. When they got home, she put them in separate rooms but, privately, she informed Ginny that both she and Jason were sound sleepers.

The subject of the ring didn't arise until the following morning, when Jeffrey came down in an old 49ers sweatshirt, below-the-knee cutoffs, and scuffed Adidas. It might have been a Saturday morning in his teens, she thought, except that his future wife was upstairs and he spoke more slowly, more easily. They talked about his job for a bit—he was already a product manager—and then she mentioned Lester, remarking only that he hadn't called in a while. A grin crossed Jeffrey's face. She knew it wasn't superior or even ironic. Jeffrey had no qualms about his uncle's domestic arrangements. Uncle Lester lived with Peter, who was okay too, no problem. Once, a few years ago, she had tried to explain the problem, but Jeffrey had cut her off sharply. "I know all that, Mom. I've known it since I was twelve. What's the difference?" Well, it was nice to know she hadn't raised a bigot.

Now she began to explain about Lester wanting Grandmother's ring, and his offer of a trust fund. She kept her tone neutral but, as she expected, Jeffrey started squirming. It was too soon to talk about rings and marriages and trust funds for children. She saw him looking out the window. Last night he'd said he was going to set up the old hoop over the garage doors. At last he stood up and went to the hall. "You comin' or not?" he called upstairs. It was his deep, controlled voice, the same one his father used when he was irritated.

Ginny's voice floated down. She wasn't ready. She would come when she was. Why didn't he do something else in the meantime?

Lenore couldn't help smiling. There had never been a divorce in her family. Marriages, like diamonds, were forever. In fact, Lester was the only irregularity in the family tree. Once Jeffrey and Ginny decided—and she was sure they would when they got home—that would be it. Quickly, before she could change her mind, she called Jeffrey back. "I'm having another ring made, dear, exactly like Grandmother's, to give to Lester. The original is for you."

Jeffrey stared at her. "What does Uncle Les think about that?"

She cleared her throat. "I haven't told him yet. I will eventually but not right away." She cleared her throat again. "I've thought a lot about this, and it's the only way to keep everybody happy." A new idea struck her. "I'm quite sure it's what your grandmother would have wanted."

Jeffrey looked down, around, out the window. "This trust fund Uncle Les is setting up so he can get a diamond that's a fake . . . did you tell Dad about it?"

"I'm going to tell him tonight." The words slipped out. She'd been postponing it, but the time had come. Jason wouldn't like it, but he'd come around.

Jeffrey turned and left. She knew what he was thinking. She was suddenly furious at Lester for making her act this way. She wasn't born to sneak around corners.

A few minutes later Ginny appeared in a frilly white blouse and jeans. They talked easily. Lenore had the impression Ginny enjoyed talking to older women in kitchens. Her father was a Presbyterian minister in Hibbing. They didn't mention Jeffrey, though he was a refrain under their talk, like the sound of the basketball on the paving outside. By the time Ginny left, Lenore had vanquished the last of her doubts. The Alvarado diamond belonged on this girl's finger, even though the band would have to be enlarged. Yes, what she was doing was wrong. When Lester found out—and he would sooner or later—there would be more nastiness. But she couldn't think about that now. Her duty to everyone else was clear. There could be no drawing back. A wave of relief washed through her and she straightened up. She was aware of a sinker beginning to form in the back of the cave, but even that didn't alarm her. She was ready to cope with a lifetime of sinkers if necessary.

The notice of the registered package arrived in the same mail as Lenore's letter. The letter announced Lenore's agreement to his idea for the trust fund, plus news of Jeff's engagement. Lester read it several times, full of satisfaction. They had reached an agreement. Everybody was happy—Lenore, Jeffrey, himself. There would be no more quarrels. They would be one family.

Driving to the post office, he reflected that this girl Ginny must be terrific to pass Lenore's inspection. Not that Jeff would have given her up if his mother disapproved, but there was always the bond. He recalled his own satisfaction the first time his mother had met Peter. "Oh, I like him," she'd said, her round face glowing under her blondish hair. "I'm so glad you finally found someone nice." What son didn't want that?

The registered package had Lenore's large, emphatic writing all over it. He didn't open it in the post office—you never knew who was lurking about—but on the way home he began to feel a little deflated. Slightly depressed, in fact. He had won, at last, but was it possible that he had acted badly? Peter, when he heard about the trust fund, had not been enthusiastic. It didn't quite atone for his insisting on the ring in the first place. Now, with the news of Jeff's engagement, Peter might start up again. What were they doing with a ring that Jeff could have given his bride?

As he drove into the garage his doubts coalesced into a grand gesture. "Listen, Lenore, I made my point; that's all I wanted. There are different styles of loving—the most important thing is to love somebody. Neither of us can actually wear that ring. Why don't you take it back for Jeff?"

It sounded good in his head, it would sound good on paper, but was that what he really wanted? He didn't know. So many thoughts were swimming around. Was it possible that Lenore, in her Machiavellian way, was counting on this sacrifice from him? That the whole thing was a setup to make him feel guilty? That if he gave it back, she'd have the last laugh?

He shook his head, tired of these notions. He and Lenore were wired together like rats in a maze, the brother rat and the sister rat.

He opened the package as soon as he got in the house. The ring, so wonderfully familiar, burned with the old fire. He remembered the day it had disappeared from his mother's finger, could still feel the emptiness of that afternoon. He turned the ring this way and that in the noon light, catching the reflections. Then he slipped it on his pinkie. For a few minutes he felt encircled with love, a private aurora borealis surrounding him in his own living room. What love compared to that first one?

He was due to meet Peter at Bayside that evening. They would have dinner, then go to the opening of a Frank Lloyd Wright show at the Fine Arts museum. He decided to wear the ring, imagining the complex reactions Peter would have when he saw it. A little drama right there in the restaurant. He chuckled mildly. He'd have to defend himself against criticism one more time. But now, with the ring on his finger, he felt up to it. More than that—fortified.

But, to his surprise, Peter didn't react much that evening when he saw the ring. Maybe he was tired of the subject, Lester thought, or had come to the end of that particular righteousness. At any rate, Peter merely advised him to put the ring in his pocket.

"Why?"

"Because if we walk to the museum, you'll get your finger chopped off."

Lester made a face. This was no time for jokes. But looking at Peter as he sipped his margarita, Lester realized he wasn't joking. The ring was loud and flashy. It attracted attention. It didn't even look good. With a sinking feeling he took it off and slid it on his key chain. It sat on his thigh while he ate, then bulged out as they walked, a lump against his gabardine pants. His depression of the morning returned. Maybe it had been a battle over nothing—or worse, over the wrong thing. Maybe he had laid too many meanings on the ring when it didn't really mean anything. Maybe he had just been neurotic again. He didn't enjoy the Frank Lloyd Wright exhibit at all.

They didn't talk much on the long drive home. Peter was fatigued and he himself was trying to turn off his mind. It felt as if a couple of circuits had burned out. But when they got in the house, they found a message from Jeffrey Burritt on the machine. He might have delayed calling back, but Jeff's voice sounded a little strained.

"Jeff!" His voice boomed across the line. "Your mother just wrote me!"

"Yeah, how about that?" Jeff's voice was deeper now, under control.

"I was going to call anyway. Congratulations."

"Thanks." Lester said something about passing Lenore's inspection, but Jeff didn't laugh. He was considering a mention of the trust fund, when Jeff interrupted. "I called about another deal, Uncle Les."

"Shoot."

He was prepared for trouble, every sense quickened, but as the sentences rolled across the Midwest, over the Ozarks and the Mississippi, and into his ear on the coast of Florida, he found he wasn't ready at all. Blood rushed to his face, and his hands got clammy, and he began to think about Baby Ruths. "So I'd like you to have this ring, it's really yours," Jeff wound up. "We don't want it. We got another one all picked out. Ginny doesn't want a big expensive ring like that, even if it was Grandmother's." A pause, full of buzzing in his ear. "You're not gonna be sore at Mom, are you? You're not gonna have one of your fights?"

He was never sure, later, where the words came from or how he found them, though Peter was standing right across the room. "Keep the ring, Jeff, it's yours." He had to ride over Jeff's objections, interruptions, but he kept going. "I thought I wanted it for various reasons, but they were lousy reasons and I knew it all along." He swiveled to face Peter, who nodded slightly. "Right from the beginning, Jeff."

They talked a while longer and then he said goodbye. After he hung up, he looked at Peter. "The one she sent is a fake. She had it made out of glass or something."

"Good."

He shook his head, fighting off an old despair. "I could never beat Lenore."

"Listen, Lester, you beat each other. I'm sure she feels as bad as you do."

He could feel Peter's eyes on him, pulling and demanding. They were like spotlights drawing him up from deep water. Could Peter be correct? It was hard to picture Lenore suffering—she had never let him see her in pain. And yet there had been plenty—that he knew—starting with his own hogging of Mother's attention. Then a new thought struck him. Maybe—it was a dangerous idea that he would have to explore later—maybe it was time to let Lenore have the half of Mother's affection she was entitled to. Time to stop insisting on his specialness, the primacy of his bond. If he stopped competing for something that was gone anyway, Lenore might too. Peter was still probing at him with searchlight eyes. "You're right," he said at last. "She probably feels awful too."

"Why don't you give her a ring"—Peter chuckled—"I mean a phone call—and tell her it's okay?"

Lester didn't move. "I could. But first I want to tell you a story. A story about a dish of chocolate pudding."

"Go ahead," Peter said, coming closer, putting his hand on Lester's shoulder. "I'm all ears."

She couldn't believe it. Lester had given up, given in. At first she thought there might be a catch—she scanned the mail every morning, expecting another letter from that Miami law firm, but at last she relaxed. It was over. Jeffrey had made peace between them.

They weren't going to fight about this. Maybe not about anything, though that was hoping for a lot.

Jason said he wasn't surprised, he'd been sure Lester would come around. But that was Jason's happy view of things, and it ignored her own complicity. She knew better.

As the weeks went by, though, and she heard about all the plans for the wedding in Hibbing, she began to wonder if Lester had changed in some deep way. It was hard to believe, but still. He'd been extremely nice over the phone lately, as if some old sweetness had been released. And then she wondered if all this trouble with him hadn't been based on old fears of her own. Maybe she had overreacted. But what did she, a mother and maybe soon a grandmother, have to be afraid of?

Then, one day when she was vacuuming the upstairs hall, she got her brainstorm. She had to laugh out loud. Where had it come from? She had no idea, but it was perfect.

She set aside an afternoon a few weeks before they were due to fly to Minnesota for the big weekend. She took great pains, but she'd been doing that all her life. The package had to be specially prepared—a tin box lined with heavy foil. When she was done, when the package was sealed and addressed, she drove to the post office and sent it priority mail. Of course, Lester might not grasp its significance. He might consider it a routine gift. But she'd know. She'd know exactly what it meant. After all, she'd been waiting almost forty years to let her brother taste her truly marvelous homemade jelly roll.

Silence

Sam Tindall didn't know why this was the day he started to write, but on a Saturday in May he went into the den and took out a yellow pad. The words welled up, unstoppable. He hardly had to think about what came next. He wasn't a writer, he was a doctor, though he had always admired literature—Henry James and Mark Twain, also Paul de Kruif and Berton Roueché. But his admiration had never tempted him into imitation before. He wasn't even good with words, especially the casual kind. He always felt uneasy when the conversation wasn't serious. Susan usually carried the ball for both of them, though their friends seemed to want his opinions ("Sam, what do you think about that?" "Give us the scientific view on that, Sam"). But here he was, scribbling away as if words were his natural medium. He'd often pointed out that they had so many friends in Fort Collins because of Susan, but she denied this. "Don't underrate yourself," she'd say, impatience in her voice.

From time to time Susan peered into the den. "Are you all right?" she asked around eleven, when he'd been at the mahogany desk for almost three hours.

"I'm fine." She waited for a fuller answer. "I'm writing something about Dad."

Her blue eyes widened. "What for?"

He ran his tongue over his lips lightly. "I dreamed about him last night." It was true. His father and mother had been sitting on the love seat in the old house in Connecticut, holding hands. They took turns speaking. "Sam, tell the truth," his father said, his pipe clenched between bad yellow teeth. "That's what I taught you." "Yes," his mother burst in, "you can spend your whole life hiding things."

When he woke up, aware of the tightness in his chest, a hint of tachycardia, he heard again the urgency in their voices. It was strange advice coming from them, but of course, it didn't come from them—he was the dreamer.

"When do I get to read it?" Susan's voice rose girlishly. She liked everything that was surprising, improvised. She was the one who promoted their frequent travels.

"After I get it typed up." That didn't satisfy her. She could tell he was hedging.

"I can read your writing."

"Honey, I haven't even finished it yet."

She waited a moment more before turning away. "Well, hurry up."

He began to read over the pages from the beginning. He felt surprisingly loose, free. He could imagine a malignancy dissolving, being reabsorbed into the bloodstream. Why had he waited so long? Why was today the day? He didn't have the answers to those questions. Now he wondered if he'd have to find the answers before he could let anyone read what he'd written.

His parents had married in San Francisco, but their trouble had started in New York a few years later. His father, young and impatient, with a five-year-old son, had gotten involved in a scam. A watered stock deal. And he had been caught.

When he, Sam junior, first heard the phrase "watered stock," he had imagined something in a plant store. Over the next few years that image was replaced by others just as inaccurate. It wasn't until much later, when he was twelve, that the phrase had connected to his father's two-year absence. Only then was he told the truth

—his father had gone to jail. In the years between, the years of absence and then evasion, "watered stock" came to stand for something secret and shameful. It was part of his father's departure and return, his mother's anger, his grandma's sadness, his grandpa's death. And under, or around, these changes was his own confusion. Why did people lower their voices or switch the subject when he came into a room? Why did they cluck sympathetically at him? Why did they tell him that now he had to be a little man?

Yes, through the years, "watered stock" came to stand for everything that had changed, that had made them different from other families in Brantford, and which could not be named. He'd never asked questions or even discussed the facts after he found out about them—except with one fraternity brother, his best friend, who had been sworn to secrecy. But here they were, the secrets staring up at him from the page on his desk.

When he finished rereading the account, he noticed that his pulse had quickened and there was a slight throb in his frontal vein. He hoped he wasn't getting a headache. He'd never even told Susan, not when they became engaged, not afterward when they were married. At first he didn't want her parents to find out, and later he didn't want to burden her with old family matters. But that wasn't all of it. He still didn't want to tell her.

Not until he was twelve had he been told the whole story. It had come out on an Election Day. The sixth-grade class had been studying the presidential candidates in social studies and he'd asked his father whom he was going to vote for. After a pause, he had replied, "Sammy, I'm not going to vote for anybody—the government won't let me." His father watched him carefully, then added, "I went to jail, son." As he continued explaining, Sam felt waves of ice breaking over him. His father, who was a perfect human being, had broken the law. But this must be an error. The law had made a mistake. But even as he thought this he knew it wasn't true. Jail explained everything that had been going on in his house for as long as he could remember. Even in school, or playing baseball (a born catcher, his father said), he'd felt weighed down. His image of his mother was of a tall, angry woman walking around the house with a finger to her lips. "Silence is golden," she said over and over. But he had known that the silence she wanted did not refer to his thumping or banging or dropping balls on the floor. No, the silence that was golden connected to the watered stock and to his father's long absence.

By lunchtime, after finishing the memoir, Sam was quite exhausted, as if he'd played eighteen holes of golf. He knew this was emotional fatigue, but he was aware of something else. The old tension, the weight of the years, had been transferred to paper. He had created an accomplice—the manuscript itself. It looked almost malevolent sitting there on his desk. He stifled the sudden urge to tear it up.

His mother, he thought, who had warned him in the dream to tell the truth, was no longer pleased. Her rules about silence had been broken. He could visualize her, right here in his den, with her finger to her lips.

Susan had a lot to say at lunch and didn't require much response. Sam knew she was waiting to hear about the morning's work, but she didn't ask directly. She began explaining about their son-in-law Derrick and the necessity of yet another financial bailout. Sam could hear the unasked questions piling up in her voice, but he didn't volunteer any information. He wasn't ready and he never pushed himself when he wasn't ready. It went against all his training.

As Susan continued talking about Derrick, who was failing with a used-car agency, Sam tried to think about silence itself. It was a habit, of course, that had started early and been reinforced by his medical training. But he had clung to it. He liked keeping quiet while others spoke, withholding judgment, weighing in at last with a verdict. He recalled being told in med school that a diagnosis was three-fourths complete when you had taken a thorough history. When he heard that, he'd grasped its importance at once. Every patient's life was mostly a past; what you saw and heard was only the thin veneer of the present. He had also understood that he'd be good at taking histories, listening for clues. It was his nature. Or was it the nature that had been imposed on him? Hearing Susan pause in her recital, he brought his attention back to the table. He didn't know which came first, but silence had become the medium in which he moved. Once, he'd overheard Susan telling Jill that he was highly repressed. "Your father is just so inhibited"—her words still jangled in his ear. He wasn't inhibited; he was merely silent. But he hadn't bothered to correct her.

After lunch he drove Susan downtown as requested. She was quiet in the car—irritated, no doubt. He left her outside the dress shop she favored, then drove off to watch the high-school team at baseball practice. As he pulled into the parking lot he thought about his manuscript. Maybe he should have locked it in a desk drawer. He didn't want Glen to see it. Glen had a habit of poking around.

Merrill Sayles came over at once—a burly blond man in a gray sweatshirt with a whistle on a braided chain around his neck. "Hiya, Doc Tindall." He'd asked Merrill Sayles to call him Sam many times, but that was not possible, though they were the same age—both in their early fifties. They talked about the boy now hitting fungoes. Sam listened as Coach Sayles spoke of his hopes for a regional championship. Sam kept up with the local school leagues—he knew a lot of the boys' families and some of the boys, too. He had years of medical charts in his head.

After the coach went off, Sam reflected, not for the first time, that he'd never seen Glen play on this field. Never had the chance to train him, develop his talent. His son had shown no interest or aptitude for any ball game. He was allergic to small round objects thrown toward him, Susan said. It was true. The first time Sam rolled a beach ball toward Glen, who was three at the time, he fled howling to his mother.

His daughters, Jill especially, were better athletes. But that was no surprise. Coordination came before weight or musculature. Both girls had reflexes like cats. His thoughts swung back to his own father, who had been at his side, advising, trying out, encouraging, whenever a new player was needed for their local team. It had been the main link between them. They had both been on the same quest for the perfect lineup, the perfect pitch, the perfect score. For years he'd been convinced that Glen's disinterest in sports was his own fault: he'd been too busy at the clinic, too indulgent toward the girls. Boys, after all, were more fragile. But gradually, as Glen grew into his teens, Sam saw his disinterest not as a flaw on his part but as a statement of Glen's taste and character. Glen didn't want what he had to teach him. The day Sam realized this, a new and greater distance opened between them. The closeness of Glen's early years disappeared for good.

Now, turning back toward his car, he wondered if silence had come between them. The hereditary disease in his family. They had ample opportunities to talk, now that Glen had dropped out of college in Colorado Springs and lived at home, but they rarely did. There were pockets of muteness. It was almost, he thought, as if he were gliding through his son's life, his fingers to his lips, murmuring that silence was golden.

Susan was standing outside the shop with a large box under her arm. She was smiling and waving; she'd found something she liked. He told her he'd talked with Coach Sayles about the prospects of the team. They might make it to the regional play-offs.

She hardly listened. "Can I read it when we get home?"

He pretended not to understand.

"You know, what you wrote about your father. You said you finished."

"I want to go over it again. Then it has to be typed."

"Linda can type it in the morning."

Linda was the secretary at the clinic. If she typed it, she'd tell everyone in the office—Nick and Malcolm, the other doctors, plus the rest of the staff. He had a rush of tachycardia. He had just seen a sign posted in the waiting room: *Dr. Tindall's father a convicted felon—see Linda for details.*

"Is it something you never told me?"

She wouldn't let up. He squirmed behind the wheel, pressing one hand to his precordium. "You know Dad didn't like us to talk about him."

"Oh, that was *ages* ago."

How simple it had seemed when he got up this morning. Write the story, fill up the silence. But he hadn't considered the consequences. He recalled a Rorschach test Jill had given him last time she was home—an assignment for one of her psychology courses for her Ph.D. in clinical. He'd answered all her questions honestly, telling what he saw in the blots, and at the end she had remarked, quite cruelly, "Gee, Daddy, I don't think you have any feelings at all." It had upset him, though he didn't let it show. Instead he'd complained, laughingly, that Rorschachs were notoriously open to interpretation and that everybody had feelings. Maybe his were buried, but that didn't mean he didn't have any.

Jill had apologized—she was still learning her professional manners, she said—but for the next few days he'd made a special effort to enter into the inner life of the family, listening to the talk of dates and clothes, of school triumphs and social sorrows. But gradually he had wound down, reverted. It was too much of a strain, too foreign to his habits. Now, as he pulled into the driveway of the house, he saw, very clearly, emotion as a quantifiable unit. Yes—bursts, pulsations that could be measured if you had the right instrument. He would call them emotemes—the smallest unit into which an emotion could be broken down. When you had enough emotemes, a critical mass, then love or sorrow or pity or joy was the result. The manuscript sitting on his desk had a huge number of emotemes. They went right off the chart.

They found Glen flopped on the living-room couch watching TV, though it was midafternoon. Glen was of medium height, slender, with his mother's fair coloring and sand-dune hair. His ideal position would have been shortstop or third base. He clicked off the set and sat up. "What'd you buy?"

"The most gorgeous frock. Wait'll you see."

"I thought maybe you got me something."

Susan snorted. "Get your own clothes."

"I don't need a lot of clothes." He lay down again.

It was true. Since dropping out of the premed course at Colorado, Glen had been designing jewelry. Now he went only from his workshop to the jewelry shops in Denver and the craft fairs where he sold his creations. He worked in silver mostly—twists and loops, pendants and earrings. Sam had leafed through the craft magazines he found lying around, and once, he had gone to watch Glen at his tiny smelter and mini-forge, using tweezers and pliers with the dexterity of a surgeon. He'd been impressed—Glen really made beautiful things—even as he realized he now stood farther outside his son's life than ever.

"Daddy's writing something about Grandpa." Susan had no business saying that.

Glen sat up again. "Yeah? What about?"

Sam replied through clenched jaws. "About his life as a young man. Some things he told me." They were both waiting. "He got into some trouble once. I'm writing about that."

"Grandpa got into trouble? You're kidding! Can I read it?"

When Sam didn't answer, Glen looked at his mother. She shrugged. "This is the first I heard of it. I guess it's a deep, dark secret."

Glen seemed almost elated. Sam wondered if he had a stake in bad news, apart from curiosity or his TV-trained need for thrills. Maybe he was looking for some kind of family weakness, a dereliction that would make his own situation easier. He'd had a tough break—that's how he felt. Susan had informed Sam of this many times. The problem was that he himself had been too successful—the distinctions at medical school, the rapid success of the clinic, the appointment to the governor's commission, all the rest of it. A walk around Fort Collins, she pointed out, was like a triumphal procession. It wasn't his fault, of course, but it had made things difficult for Glen. It might even be the reason, she hinted, why Glen had never had a real girlfriend.

Sam looked at his son now. His skin was glowing. If he told him that his grandfather had been a jailbird, two years in Elmira on a stock scam, and that his great-grandfather had committed suicide over the disgrace, would he be pleased?

"I'm going to take a nap." The words came out more sharply than he intended. They looked at him, but he wasn't angry. He just wanted to be alone. He headed for the stairs, then detoured to the study. He locked the yellow pages in the lower drawer, to which only he had the key. No use putting temptation in their way. Upstairs, just before closing the bedroom door, he heard tissue paper being scrunched. Susan was displaying her new frock.

Silence. The word whispered in his ear again. Why had his father never discussed the matter with him after that first exchange on Election Day when he was twelve? Why had embarrassment and evasion been the order of the day when any criminal acts came up—even the most heinous, like Bruno Hauptmann and the Lindbergh baby? Why had tax time, or even running a red light, been a cause for more fear? His father's exaggerated respect for the law had been pathological, a constant self-accusation. But it hadn't been necessary. Other men in Brantford must have gotten into scrapes. Surely there were kids in the neighborhood, boys he played ball with, whose fathers had committed minor crimes, maybe even gone to jail. But he never found out. He was locked in with his secret just as his father had been locked into Elmira. And as time went on, as he moved into adolescence, the silence had widened and deepened. It became a bog, a quicksand. He knew the danger signs—the silver points of anxiety in his father's eyes, his mother's sudden movements. After a while his reflexes got so fast, his ear so acute, he could spot a dangerous subject from way off. He had become an expert at monitoring pain long before it happened. And the quickened perceptions were still with him. Sometimes patients told him not to worry about hurting them, they could stand it.

He lay on the bed and let his mind soften into blurriness. He was really tired. Vaguely he recalled the enthusiasm that had greeted his announcement that he wanted to be a doctor. He'd been fifteen at the time, hot from reading *Microbe Hunters.* Everyone had approved. Was it possible they figured that science would keep him away from his father's error? That it would lock him into empirical fact, far away from questions of right and wrong, guilt and punishment?

His sleepiness increased, but there was one last question. Why had he gone along with the silence? He'd been a stubborn kid, hard to push around, but he had never fought back about this. The next instant his left eyebrow twitched and the skin behind it heated up. That's where his birthmark had been, a concentration of melanin that started under the brow and climbed up in an ugly brown circle. The other children had stared on his first day in school and one boy asked where he got it. He didn't know what to say, só he hit him. Sometimes he punched them when they asked, sometimes he kicked them, and once, he bit another boy on the neck. Nobody could stop him, no matter how much they punished him.

The birthmark had been excised by surgery and new skin grafted on when he was a high-school sophomore. Gradually he had forgotten about it, more or less. Like his father's prison term, the birthmark had been removed from reference. His mother had been directed to tear up all the old photos, though an odd one had turned up from time to time. But at certain moments, like now, when he was tense or confused, the skin behind his left eyebrow heated up in phantom pain. Now, just before falling asleep, he wondered if there was some connection between the scar and the silence.

Later in the afternoon he went back to the den for another look at his morning's work. He was reading, making slight changes, when Glen came in. He had the fixed, slightly embarrassed smile he usually wore around his father. Sam had done all he could to put his son at ease, to find some of their old rapport. But Glen wasn't interested in talk about sports, or about cases at the clinic, or about local doings. He considered everything his father said either irrelevant or incorrect. And Glen rarely volunteered any topics of his own.

Now Glen looked more eager than usual. He slid, unasked, into the brass-studded leather chair across from the desk. "You still working on that story about Grandpa?"

Sam sat back. "It's not a story exactly. It's a lot harder than I thought, too." He smiled briefly. "I don't know how those professional writers do it."

"They get used to it. The long hours and all. And they get carried away, just like I do."

He was talking about his jewelry. Sam nodded, hoping to encourage him. Maybe this was the break. Ten or twelve years ago, when Glen was in his midteens, he had sat at this desk hoping his son would come in, park where he was now, and ask the elaborately casual questions about sex, girls, death, contraception, that he was waiting to answer. He had asked those questions of his own father and had gotten clear, swift answers. But Glen hadn't turned up. Later Sam found out he was asking his mother the questions.

Maybe it was his fault. Maybe he had withheld something vital when Glen was growing up, though God knows they'd been close in those days. "C'mere and let Daddy doctor it." How many times had he said that after the bumps and scrapes of boyhood? And each time, Glen had trotted over for the benefaction of his father's hands, the miraculous cure. But at some point, a point he couldn't possibly locate, he had lost the power to heal his son's hurts.

Glen leaned forward. "Ummm, what kind of trouble did Grandpa get into?"

Sam picked up a pencil and tapped it on the yellow pad. It's coming, he thought. The genie is getting out of the bottle.

"Is it something he was ashamed of?" Glen's respiration was rapid and he knotted his hands together.

Again Sam wondered what his son was looking for. At the same time, something stirred at the bottom of the silence between them. Sam turned his mind away from it quickly. "It wasn't all that bad," he temporized, "though everybody . . . made a big deal of it at the time."

"Yeah? Like how?"

Sam felt the tightness in his chest again. Glen was on the edge of his chair. He had a look Sam hadn't seen in ages—sweet and open, as if all the secrets between them were ending. He had the impression that Glen was willing to give him the old power again, the power to doctor his hurts. And then he understood what was between them. He had known for years—maybe even when Glen was three and had run howling from the beach ball. The knowledge lay, glistening and shameful, inside the silence. It was the worst news a man could hear about his son—news that would keep them from being close, from sharing the things men share, from experiencing the world in the same way. To let himself hear such news was almost unbearable. "It'll have to wait till I'm through. And it's typed out."

The words had come out too harshly. He couldn't help it. Glen shrank back in the chair, then stood up. His open look had gone. The slightly embarrassed smile was back in place. "Check you later, Dad," he said in a flat voice.

After he left, Sam sat, the pages in front of him blurred and unreadable. He could hear Glen talking to Susan in the distance. They were blaming him. Susan's old verdict echoed in his mind. *Repressed. Inhibited.* What did she want from him? He'd never gotten involved with other women, never been seriously tempted. He'd married for life, fathered children for life. She'd never understood what went into his inhibitions, how they protected him.

He looked at the manuscript again, this time forcing himself to make sense of the words. The scribbles arranged themselves into thoughts. This morning he had wanted to find a way to end the silence. He had started and then stopped. But was it possible to stop?

He riffled through the pages. In writing down the story, he had released it. He had joined it to all the stories in the world. It was public property now; there was no way to keep it from being heard. He recalled the dim conversations in his childhood home, the sudden silences, the bogs and quicksand. They were here in this house too, had crept in without his being aware of it, merely by default.

Maybe silence would always win. The next moment he was aware of a new pain in his precordial area, as if all the valves were opening and closing out of sequence. Glen and Susan would always search for something he couldn't give them, for words he couldn't utter. They would always be disappointed, trapped in his silence.

His eye fell on the manuscript again. On the other hand, the story had now been told—he had taken the first, hardest step. Not letting himself think anymore, or hesitate, he picked up the pad and went to the kitchen. Susan and Glen broke off their conversation. Susan's lips were compressed in an unfamiliar movement. For a moment he had the impression she was utterly unknown to him, a stranger in the house; then he thrust the sheaf of papers at her. "Go ahead, read it."

He turned to Glen. "Your grandfather went to prison. It wasn't a catastrophe. I mean, it wasn't the end of his life or anything. But he didn't want anyone to know." He could feel his words burning the air, but their reaction was mild.

Susan was turning the pages. "It would have been better just to tell us than to write all this."

"I had to write it first."

Glen's face took on a delicate edge. "What did he go to prison for?"

"A shady stock deal."

"Like insider trading?"

"Sort of. He started a company with a friend and issued some stock. No assets, just a paper company. Really crooked. I don't know all the details."

"How come you never told us before?"

"I was ashamed. Or rather, they were ashamed, and they passed it on to me. But that was a long time ago."

Glen was staring at him now, his eyes unfocused.

"It goes back to Hoover and Roosevelt. But it was like . . . an old scar for me. Something that always made me feel different." He took a deep breath, aware of Susan's sudden gesture. "I had

trouble erasing it." He forced a laugh. "Even after it was erased."
Another thought struck him. "Maybe I had to be perfect. If your
father goes to jail, you have to be perfect."

Glen spoke softly. "Also if your father's a very big deal in town."

Sam gazed at his son. The permission was coming, the permission
to release the other story, the one he already knew. "If you think
I'd disapprove for any reason, you're wrong, Glen."

Silence.

"You really mean that?"

Sam didn't reply, just looked at his son.

"Go ahead, Glen, tell him. You can spend your whole life hiding
things." Susan's voice had an unfamiliar sound. It was almost like
his mother's.

Glen looked down and away, getting ready. Then he spoke. As
Sam listened his body ached. He realized again that all the stories
of the world were linked, and that if you could free one, you could
free the others, too. When Glen finished, Sam touched his shoulder.
"I'm glad you told me," he said. "I'm sorry it took so long."

Glen gave a tentative smile. "I've been ready for years, Dad."

"We were just waiting on you," Susan added.

Sam heard a joyful noise, almost like music, in his head. "I
appreciate that," he replied.

The Temple of Aphaia

Jeffrey knew he couldn't leave Athens without going back to Aegina, but he hadn't mentioned it to the Holabirds. He'd shared everything else with Celia and Bryan—all the restaurants, views, squares, monuments—but he'd kept Aegina to himself. Not that it was a secret. Just private.

Celia Holabird had discovered it by herself, which didn't surprise him. It was a fact that had presented itself to her. At the time, they were sitting in their favorite café just off Stadiou Street, having second breakfast and watching the early prostitutes ply their trade. "I hear there's marvelous swimming at this island right across the bay." Celia licked the flakes of *tiropitta* from her fingers. "Somebody was talking about it in the lobby this morning. It's called Aegina."

Jeffrey winced inwardly. "I was going to suggest it myself," he said, trying not to sound insincere. "It's gorgeous."

Celia fastened her round, hooded eyes on him. "You were there last time and you didn't tell us?"

"Yeah, Randy and I went a lot. It's not a bad trip and the beaches are better. Not crowded."

"Man, let's go," Bryan trumpeted unpleasantly. His horn-rims were held together with white adhesive over the nose, which gave him a wounded look. "This heat is really getting to me."

It was true. Athens in July was livid with sunlight—sunlight that glazed the buildings, thickened the air, kept the three of them sequestered behind shutters most afternoons.

Celia was still watching him, probing for something withheld. Jeffrey tried to make himself blank. The slightest niche, the merest slit of vulnerability, and Celia would nose in. "Well, it's too late today," she said. "I suggest first thing tomorrow. Thank goodness we brought bathing suits."

Jeffrey nodded. Celia liked to make plans. Although she was not pretty—blue eyes too heavy-lidded, nose too prominent, arms too fleshy—he had come to find her attractive. It was her strength and warmth. Bryan was just the opposite. Where Celia was short and sweet and roomy, Bryan was tall and spare and tight-assed. Their marriage, Jeffrey had come to believe, was kept going by Celia.

They had all met at the college in Providence where he and Bryan worked. Jeffrey taught speech and Bryan taught theater tech. Only in the last year had they gotten really friendly. This was due to Celia, who had helped with one of her husband's productions for which Jeffrey had provided some tapes. The two of them had hit it off right away. Maybe it was because she reminded him of the big, careless women of his childhood—aunts and grandmothers—who had been very free with their affection and attention. Sometimes, as he observed her, the French word for pantry popped into his mind—*garde-manger*. Celia had great storage capacity, cupboards for secrets and passions. She liked to hear, to know, though things tended to get lost. Occasionally he wondered if she was merely snooping, if she fed on other people's troubles, got fat on them—but he always dismissed that idea. Celia's natural element was emotion. And he liked to talk about himself.

He also knew that she was drawn to him because he was the opposite of Bryan. He was the antidote to all that reticence, uptightness, technology. His own life had really been one long search for the miraculous. He had brushed against it in many places, most recently with Randy Hosniak. Not long after meeting Celia he told her the whole story—about meeting Randy in Boston, the years together, the breakup. She listened passionately, licking her lips, then reciprocated with news of her life with Bryan, the constant bridging of the gaps between them, her pain over being childless at thirty-seven. She wanted, Jeffrey sometimes thought, a brush with the miraculous too.

Yes, a bond had been forged—not a deep bond, since their situations were so different, but the next best thing. They had become allies in an ongoing war, the war against the everyday. This trip to Greece was a way of strengthening that alliance, extending their phone confessionals into full days and evenings together.

Of course, three was an inconvenient number for travel. Jeffrey was sure Bryan wished he hadn't been added to the itinerary, especially when he started talking about Randy and their previous trip to Athens. At these times Bryan would look both alert and tolerant—two of his least attractive expressions—and Jeffrey would know he was biding his time. If he could, Jeffrey thought, Bryan would ban all mention of such relationships. Failing that, he would grit his teeth and endure, as his New England ancestors had endured long whaling voyages and winter gales and madness in female relatives. It was the strong man's burden.

"Well, Jeffrey, you can be tour leader to Aegina tomorrow. I'm sure you'll be better than the last one." Celia threw a sour look at her husband. Their trip to the theater at Epidavros three days ago had been his idea. They had sat on marble seats for almost five hours, too stingy to rent cushions, and it had put them out of commission the next day.

"Sure, Celia. There's a restaurant right on the beach. We can have lunch there."

He saw, quite suddenly, the green awning stretched over the terrace, the roistering Athenians, the fishermen carrying up their afternoon catch, the westering sun. He and Randy had gone there many times during their months in Greece; it had become one of their favorite spots. They'd gotten friendly with the owner, drinking ouzo with him, sharing their Kents. What was his name? He couldn't remember. It had been three years, after all.

"I hope it's better than the meals around here." Bryan snickered politely. "Hell, how much eggplant can you eat?"

As Celia and Bryan discussed the local cuisine, Jeffrey tried to restrain his joy. Aegina, finally! He could see it with wonderful vividness now, as if the Holabirds had opened a window. He inspected the brown hills and fields, the meadows of wildflowers, the vineyards and lemon groves. For a moment, very briefly, he saw the temple, too, but then banished the image. He wasn't ready for that yet.

They were going to do the Archaeological Museum this morning. As they paid their bill and headed for Omonias Square Jeffrey wondered if he should send Randy a postcard from Aegina tomorrow. A postcard of the temple, with no signature. He'd know instantly who'd sent it and why—a little shudder of delight went through him at the thought—and might even be pleased. Yes, Randy would be pleased, would call him up on his return, even suggest . . .

He shook his head, dismissing the fantasy. He was always having these little episodes, selecting some device that would lure Randy back, seduce him into a life together, keep him on the premises. It was a mania with him. He wouldn't send Randy a postcard tomorrow or any other day. That was all over.

The Archaeological Museum was huge, confusing, and deserted. Celia made her usual arrangements inside the gate. Each of them would go through the place alone; then they'd meet up again in one hour. It was an arrangement, Jeffrey thought, that symbolized Celia. Spacious, considerate, respectful. If only he and Randy had been more like that! But neither had been the sort to compromise, make room. It was amazing they'd lasted as long as they had.

He wandered along a corridor until a collection of Greek athletes caught his eye. How handsome they were, how simple and unabashed each little pointed phallus. Not for the first time he admired the attitude that had steered the ancients away from circumcision. How absurd to strip away the foreskin. It had been the first step toward the sexual guilt everybody suffered from nowadays.

He might mention that to the Holabirds at lunch. Circumcision for the sake of cleanliness had actually fostered its opposite—the association of sex with dirt. He could do a mini-rap on that subject, strictly for laughs. Celia would love it and Bryan would get his stone face. Of course, if the subject were to come up with some of Bryan's own friends, he might not have minded—might even crack one of his tight-assed jokes. But with Jeffrey, known for his peculiar tastes, there could be no laughter. Just grit and endurance. As he left the room with the athletes a sigh escaped him. Mealtimes with the Holabirds had become a drag. He would bring up a subject he thought amusing, Bryan would look uncomfortable, and Celia would use the occasion to bait her husband. There would be snappish remarks, leading to accusations. Jeffrey would have to arbitrate. He had even begun to suspect that Celia wouldn't have planned this trip at all, would have spent the summer back in Providence, unless her new friend Jeffrey had agreed to come along. Her marriage, at this point, required a referee.

The little ferry out of Piraeus was as he remembered it—a two-deck affair with one funnel, nothing like the seagoing palaces, a few piers down, that moved between the mainland and the outer Cyclades. They were the only passengers going aboard with beach paraphernalia, which Celia announced was a good sign. The crossing would take just half an hour.

After the bar below opened, they went for coffee. The bartender told them he had a brother in Xenia, Ohio. As Celia drew him out with her genuine curiosity Jeffrey looked around the room. There were the usual awful murals—Mycenae, Lindos, Sounion, and Epidavros of unhappy memory. And then, in the far corner, he spotted a temple in the Doric mode that sent a little shiver through him.

"Excuse me," he said to the bartender. "What's that?"

"Aphaia. You go there on Aegina today, very beautiful."

Celia turned to look. "Oh, yes," she said. "I read about that in the guidebook." She gazed at Jeffrey. "Why didn't you tell us it was there?"

Jeffrey laughed nervously. Celia was inspecting him. She had sensed more secrecy. She was amazing. "We can't miss it," he said. "It's on the way to the beach." She started to lick her lips, a sure sign she was going to probe deeper, but he excused himself and headed for the stairway. He wanted some time alone, away from Celia and her inexorable sharing. He was getting too near the source of his trouble to be able to explain it.

He stood amidship on the deck, watching the blue waters of the Saronic Gulf speed under him. He remembered this view of Aegina—the port with its miniature cathedral, the brown slopes among which countless chapels nested like large white seabirds. There hadn't been any new building. The twentieth century might never have happened on these islands, except for the invention of the motorcar. He could almost feel Randy standing next to him now, could almost register the wind as it ran through Randy's thinning locks of strawy gold. Time seemed to be running backward.

They had come to Greece on their way around the world—the trip of a lifetime. They'd stayed here three months, renting an apartment—a happy time without quarrels or bickering. All their troubles back home, bred of five years in close quarters, had evaporated. Greece had changed them. Jeffrey became more carefree and adventurous, less clinging. Randy gave up some of his princeliness. It was as if each had borrowed something from the other, something better or more useful.

Occasionally they would talk about this, point out the necessity of holding on to these changes, this new respect and consideration, when they got home. Yes, they swore, it would be different from then on. They would carry Greece and its freedom, its promise of improvement, with them.

Now, on the little boat cleaving the waves toward Aegina, that old vow came back to Jeffrey. What fine hopes they had had! And it was after this crossing, on a fine, clear day like this, that their promise had assumed its final form.

"What's this about a temple, Jeff? Are you holding out on us?"

Celia had come up to him at the rail, the wind ruffling her dark blond hair just as it had ruffled Randy's. She was smiling; her eyes were as blue as the water.

"Randy and I came here on our last day in Greece. Before we left for Istanbul." He waited a moment. The wind had made his eyes water. "We wanted to visit the temple one last time."

That wasn't quite true—it had been more of a whim, an impulse, and not even his own—but it would have to do.

"The temple the bartender told us about?"

He nodded. "Aphaia. That's a primitive name for Artemis. You know—Diana."

Celia knew that Artemis was Diana. She said so, then paused. He saw, in his peripheral vision, her tongue dancing lightly over her lips. "You mean it was special in some way, Jeff?"

He didn't reply. He had just become aware of a tiny pain in his chest. It expanded as he caught sight of Bryan in the bow, peering over the rail. In the next instant he realized that he didn't mind the pain in his chest at all. It was a good sign, really. The worst thing would have been to feel nothing at all.

Bryan had just seen a dolphin. He waved frantically at them to come forward. Celia shifted indecisively. She wanted to see the dolphin, but she also wanted to hear more. At last, to Jeffrey's relief, she moved off. He would have another few minutes to think.

When he and Randy landed on that last day, Randy had bounced down the gangplank and into the town square. "Let's take a taxi," he'd said when Jeffrey caught up. His eyes were blazing. "The bus sucks."

Without waiting for an answer—one of his old tricks, though this time Jeffrey didn't mind—Randy cruised down the line of cabs, all three of them, and found one driven by a handsome young man. "Aghia Marina, *pósso kostízi?*" A price was agreed on, twenty drachmas less than proposed, and they got in. The driver studied them in the mirror, always with a smile under his bushy black mustache. Jeffrey knew he was calculating their relationship. Not that the Greeks needed many clues—the sight of two men together meant one thing to them, and they were usually right.

"He's cute," Randy said, smiling into the mirror.

"I think he's rubbing his crotch," Jeffrey added.

The same thought crossed their minds. "It's our last day," Randy said. "Let's concentrate on Greece."

They had traveled in silence until they got to the temple site, a short distance above the beach. And then, to Jeffrey's surprise, Randy had tapped the driver's shoulder, motioning him to stop. "Let's say good-bye to the goddess," he'd said. "We can walk the rest of the way." Without waiting for an answer, he jumped out, leaving Jeffrey, who was in charge of the kitty, to pay.

When Jeffrey got out, feeling mildly irritated, he was almost blinded by the light. It was noon. Below him the Aegean danced away in a thousand sparkling points. Above, on the hill behind the temple, the pines showed green against the sky. On this windswept height his irritation began to disappear. He felt himself clearing, as if there were no thought, no emotion, that could not be experienced with perfect lucidity. The murk that so often clouded his life was burning away, leaving him transparent and pure. It was an exciting feeling and he wanted to tell Randy about it, but Randy had disappeared. The taxi had gone too. He was alone in front of the temple, with its tapering columns, its battered architrave, its huge floor stones. He stepped off the main road and onto the sacred way. The heat blazed up around him.

He found Randy in the center of the temple, looking slightly dazed. "It's more beautiful than ever," Randy murmured. Jeffrey thought that Randy himself might evoke the same comment but didn't say so. They weren't in the habit of paying each other compliments.

Randy moved toward the back of the temple, where the altar had been and the lustral area for sacrifices.

Jeffrey, moving with him, looked around at the half-shattered stones, then back at Randy. His eyes were bowls of blue light, his skin almost transparent. Jeffrey had the sudden notion that he could see right through him. The feeling of a moment before, that all the murk had washed away, returned, stronger than ever.

"Did you know, Jeff, that pairs of lovers used to come to temples like this before a battle? And make vows of fidelity and bravery?"

"No, I didn't."

"Can't you see it? Two guys standing here, promising to keep the faith, never disgrace each other?"

Jeffrey felt his flesh prickle even as he resisted the notion. "You make it sound like the Boy Scouts."

"It was nothing like the Boy Scouts. No manual, no knots, no church basements." Randy looked upward at the rectangle of sky. For an instant Jeffrey thought he could see Randy's thoughts flashing along the neural pathways of his brain, opening gates and closing connections. "Let's make a vow, Jeff. Right here. Our last day."

Without waiting for an answer, Randy took his hand. Jeffrey let himself be carried along. He wasn't surprised by the idea. He had seen it coming, had read it in the brilliant firings of Randy's brain.

"Right here." Randy knelt under the shadow of the back wall. Jeffrey did the same, unhooking his knapsack. They clasped hands. There was no need, Jeffrey thought in a rush of joy, to look around and see if anyone was watching.

Randy bent his head. Jeffrey observed the slender, corded nape. "I promise to be faithful and true to my friend Jeffrey Quinn as long as I live." A pause, filled with grasshopper sounds. "Your turn, Jeff."

Jeffrey repeated the words, substituting "Randolph Hosniak."

"And we will be true friends and warriors, Jeffrey and I." Another pause. "Okay, Jeff."

Jeffrey repeated the words.

"And to encourage the protection of the goddess we make this small libation." Randy reached into the knapsack and extracted the thermos. He uncorked it and poured coffee on the ground. "That's for you, Aphaia."

Jeffrey watched the coffee make a muddy stain. They had mixed Nescafé in the apartment that morning. Shouldn't it have been wine or blood? But that didn't matter. The important thing was that they were doing this. That Randy had looked into the future and seen them together, always. Jeffrey's old conviction that the dependency was mostly on his side, that he needed Randy more than Randy needed him, simply wasn't true. It was fifty-fifty. These happy months in Greece proved it.

Randy let out a whoop. "Whaddya say we hit the beach?" He got up. Jeffrey repacked the thermos, then rose, shouldering the backpack. He thought they should have sealed the ceremony with something—a hug or a kiss—but Randy had moved off. Jeffrey could see him in the field now, scanning the sky. Then Randy turned away, unbuttoning his fly. He was going to take a leak.

Jeffrey looked around one last time before joining Randy on the road to the beach. The temple was magnificent. Was it unreasonable to expect that it still housed a goddess who took an interest in friendships like theirs? Wasn't that one of the miracles his life had been dedicated to finding?

The rest of the day was the happiest he could remember. He shed all his reserve and joined everything around him—sea, sky, fellow bathers, Greece. Foreground and background, private and public, merged. As he splashed and shouted and talked to strangers he thought that this was the way it would be from now on—days full of clarity and joy. He was no longer a sojourner, a guest. He had taken possession of the earth. Watching Randy cleave the water beside him, then come up snorting for air, he wondered why he had always thought life was so complicated.

After the ferry docked, Bryan found a taxi. There was no sign of the handsome young man with the bushy mustache. This driver was old and weather-beaten, with an ancient Citroën. He spoke excellent English and refused to bargain about the price.

As they drove Celia chatted up the driver, who complained about the price of gasoline. She clucked in sympathy and would, Jeffrey knew, instruct Bryan to give a large tip. There would be an argument. There would also be an argument about the lunch tip and other matters, all of which Jeffrey would have to mediate. A gust of weariness went through him. He was really tired of the Holabirds. Maybe this whole thing had been a mistake, even the return to Aegina.

"Live in the real world, Jeff." How many times had he heard that from his father? Even from Randy. And what could be less real than to return here, secretly expecting something miraculous to happen again? Especially with this pair.

There it was. He could see the ribs of gray marble, the green powder puffs of pine. Nothing had changed. The temple was still serene, miraculous. And then, as a stinging in his ear, he heard the vow they had taken. In some awful way the vow, or his half of it, had turned out to be true. He was still faithful. Randy had moved out six months after their return, but he himself had been unable to get free. His thoughts, his dreams, still centered on Randy. Even a year with a therapist hadn't helped.

"Looks like another bombed-out temple to me." Celia's voice cut in. The car came to a halt. Bryan was first out, unstrapping his camera. Celia remained by the car, squinting against the glare. For a moment she looked as unattractive, in her heavy way, as Bryan in his slimness. It was a traitorous thought and Jeffrey put it away. But the next moment he had the strong impression that the Holabirds didn't belong here, that they were defiling the place by their presence. He moved off quickly, pacing the pathway of huge stones. The temple would shield him from these uncharitable thoughts, from the Holabirds themselves. It would give him peace. And then he had his idea. His silly and wonderful idea.

Bryan was ordering Celia around, snapping pictures. Jeffrey

moved toward the far end of the temple, trying not to hear their voices. That's where they'd knelt and made their vow, right there by the back wall. He hurried on, hoping he was unobserved. He needed a few minutes alone. He had to be alone for his idea to work.

"Jeff, where are you? Jeff-reeee!" Celia's voice broke through the chirp of the cicadas and the silence of two thousand years.

He sank to his knees. The words came easily. "Aphaia, dissolve this partnership here, now. Remove your protection. Let us each go a separate way, no longer faithful and true."

He bent his head. It was the end. He could feel it in his pounding heart, his clammy skin. He would stop thinking about Randy. Randy didn't deserve all that devotion—it was just weakness on his own part. He'd spent the better part of ten years hooked on one person. His friends slid in and out of love affairs. The objects changed, but their capacity for affection remained the same. Why couldn't he be more like that? Why was he one of those moonstruck types who kept pining for the same person, no matter how badly they were treated? There was something wrong with him, a piece missing. He was imprinted on Randy out of fear, fear of the new, the strange, the unfamiliar. But all that would change now. The goddess would see to it. He was suddenly filled with hope.

"Holy mackerel, what are you doing?"

He wobbled up, mortified, a second too late.

"Jeffrey, are you all right?" Celia was almost luminous with sympathy.

A vast irritation seized him. "Of course I'm all right." He dusted off his knees vigorously. He didn't want them to see the expression on his face.

Bryan snickered. "What the hell were you doing, praying?"

"As a matter of fact, I was."

Bryan brayed and Celia came up to him. Her perfume smelled awful amid the scent of wild thyme. "Do you want to talk about it, Jeff?"

He didn't answer, just turned and started walking toward the taxi. He wouldn't explain. It was none of their business, and it didn't make much sense anyway. He maintained his silence despite the low giggles he could hear coming from both of them. But how could he expect them to understand? What had happened to him and Randy in this place was completely beyond their experience. It might as well have happened to Martians. He didn't speak as they drove down to the beach, even though he saw he was still amusing the Holabirds, and refused to arbitrate their quarrel about the tip. But a few minutes later his good mood returned. Maybe it was the memory of his last time at this beach, or his hope of new freedom. At any rate, after plunging into the water alone he went up to the restaurant and ordered a pony of Metaxa brandy. Before drinking it he poured a little on the counter as a libation to the goddess. He'd forgotten that at the temple just now. He might as well do it correctly.

It would have been a glorious afternoon but for the fact that Celia and Bryan bickered almost constantly. Celia seemed especially aggressive and shrill. Jeffrey had never seen her like this. At one point she moved away from them and lay by herself. When the inevitable flirtations and requests for cigarettes occurred, she responded with smiles. By the time they got back to Athens they were all in a foul mood. The day, which had started out so well, had been ruined. Jeffrey made excuses to avoid having dinner with them, then slipped out of the hotel and ate at a souvlaki stand. After that, he hiked up the hill to Kolonaki, where he and Randy had rented their apartment. It was a test, he thought as he labored up the steep street, a test to see if anything had changed.

The apartment house looked exactly the same, the paint even flaking in the same spots. After examining the front he walked around back to see the balcony under the sheer drop of Mount Lykabettos. It was illuminated by moonlight. The sight brought back other moonlit evenings when he and Randy had sat there in silent bliss, not bothering to utter their thoughts until it was time to go to bed. Their lovemaking had been the best yet—slow, considerate, tidal. Another rhythm had caught them up. Now he had a clear picture of Randy nude, in that bed, and his skin prickled with lust. The next instant he was devastated. Nothing had changed. He still wanted Randy. He would always want Randy. It was a lifelong affliction, whether due to strength or weakness he didn't know. A moment later, cursing, he decided to leave Greece. He couldn't stand Athens or the Holabirds, and his memories were making him sick.

He didn't hear about the Holabirds' divorce until school started in September. They hadn't been in touch during August, after his abrupt departure from Athens—bad feelings all around. But when he heard the news, he decided to call Celia. It was time to make up. He knew exactly how she felt, after all.

He phoned her house. Bryan, she told him, had already moved out. The sound of her voice, so breathy and kind, revived his good feelings toward her. He'd missed her. Missed their talks, their revelations, their rapport. And she was delighted to hear from him. He knew right away that she had forgiven him for his rude departure, for not even telling her the real reason. It wasn't in her nature to bear grudges.

"I was sorry to hear about your divorce, Celia."

She let out a sigh. He could almost smell her mint-scented breath. "Oh, Jeff, don't be. It's such a relief, I can't tell you." She began to talk about her plans. She was going to move to the West Coast, lose weight, train as a therapist. It was what she'd always wanted; she was sure she'd be good at it. Her words exuded hope. They were both, he thought, condemned to go through life hoping. It was one of the links in their friendship.

He wasn't positive, thinking about it later, which one brought up the subject of Greece. But it was there, suddenly, between them. Celia said she and Bryan had stayed another week after Jeffrey left. Nothing went right. They had actually had a shouting match in the Plaka one night and the restaurant owner had asked them to leave.

And then the question came to him. It wasn't a question, really, but a dim certainty crawling down his spine. "Celia, when did you decide to leave Bryan? I mean, was there a precise moment?"

She paused, surprised. "What a funny question, Jeff." She laughed softly. "Only you would know to ask that." Her voice brightened. "It was right after we left that temple of yours. On the way to the beach. Something reached down and said, 'Celia darling, it's over.' " She laughed again. "Can you imagine? It was like getting out of jail."

She went on talking, her voice spreading and warming in his ear. He listened carefully. "Congratulations, Celia," he said at last. "You're going to be okay."

"You too, Jeff." She paused. "You know, you never told me what you were praying for in that temple."

He waited a moment for the jealousy and anger to drain off; then he said, "I was praying for a miracle, but it didn't happen."

"Oh? What kind of miracle?"

For an instant he thought of telling her, but decided against it. She might lose her faith. Or her new resolve might weaken. He mustn't interfere. There were only a certain number of miracles in the world, a finite amount, and it was clearly Celia's turn.

Death Writes a Story

The guy from *Writer* magazine keeps asking me how I got started. Maybe he thinks I'm not the literary type. So I decided to write it down for him—amazing how easy the words come now. The guy who said artists have to suffer had the right idea.

You see, I've always loved stories. A funny taste in a grown-up man who also loves ball games, fishing trips, family reunions, old cars, dogs. I guess I got it from my old man, who read the *Saturday Evening Post* all his life, the stories of Clarence Buddington Kelland being his favorites. When he finished one he would slam down the magazine and say, "Son, that's what I call genius." Naturally this made an impression on a growing boy.

When I was going to night school (Pace College, Manhattan, Commerce and Accounting), I took some writing courses. I could almost see my father beaming down at me when I signed up, when I started my first journal (Eugene Ebbler, *Writer's Notebook*). I think that's probably why I wound up in the printing business instead of something else—insurance or computers. I wanted ink on my fingers. With eight employees I wasn't in the pressroom much, but I still liked to hear the big webs humming, to know that words were being inked onto paper.

Of course, I always tried to make up stories of my own, even if

I didn't do too well in the writing courses. My main trouble was that I couldn't figure out what people would say and do in an imaginary situation. My mind tended to freeze up.

However, some years ago I came across the solution to this, in an article in *Writer* magazine. "Clip newspapers for fascinating story ideas, because truth is just as strange as fiction." Well, I went them one better. I clipped newspapers; also I took notes on TV shows, true-life adventures, even from great works of fiction. Once I had collected enough tips, leads, ideas, I would fit them into stories of my own.

This was easier said than done. Tying one event to another wasn't that easy. I would get a good start ("Gobi nomad finds cache of jewels left behind by Marco Polo") and maybe even a decent middle sequence ("British industrialist caught smuggling relics behind hub-caps of vintage Rolls-Royce"), and then it fizzled out. I was left with loose ends.

Sometimes, after having sat up late in my den trying to fit these pieces together, I would climb upstairs, really swacked out, and peek at my kids, Tommy and Annie. A sleeping child is one of the most beautiful sights on earth. Watching them, I would ask myself why I bothered with stories. Wasn't this enough? Wasn't this life itself? But a few nights later, after the headaches in the office, the union problems, I would start to think about my stories again. They would glow in the distance, like treasure. Maybe this evening I'd knock out the big one, the grand slam. And sure enough, after dinner Roz would get her patient look, the kids would slide off their chairs, and I'd find myself drifting toward the den. They had spotted my mood before I did. That's what happens when you have a family. Everybody got their antennas out, twitching. But no matter how long I stayed in the study, how hard I tried, I couldn't find the stitches, the seams, to my stories. Nothing came together. I had Writer's Block (also covered in the magazine mentioned above).

Roz would never ask about my work when I came to bed. In fact, she'd pretend not to wake up. She could probably tell just from the way I moved what had happened.

I remember clearly the first time I laid eyes on the person who would end my Writer's Block. It was at our liquor store, Eastbrook Wines & Spirits, on a Saturday in September. I was buying the usual, two bottles of Heublein's premixed Manhattans, which is our standard for Saturday night. A thin, crooked man with a battered face was peering at the wine display. I would put his age at just over the half-century mark. But it was his hair that made me look twice—two-toned, like a '67 Buick. The sides russet, the top burnished gold, though the colors blended together at the edges, which you don't find on a Buick. He picked out a couple of bottles of French wine and walked to the counter.

"These are rather overpriced," he said to Angelo. His voice was high and flutey and very British.

"We'll be having a sale next month, sir. Maybe you'd like to come back and stock up." Angelo was giving his number-one-customer treatment.

"Perhaps I shall." The customer didn't carry a wallet. No. On one slim hip rested a leather bag from which he took a small change purse, the type old ladies carry to the supermarket. He pulled out some crumpled bills. This took a long time. Angelo and I waited.

While Angelo was ringing up the sale the customer turned and gave me the once-over. His eyes took me in from top to bottom and bottom to top. I had a feeling he saw all of me and liked it— even the hair on my chest and the family jewels. It was the kind of look a woman would give you if she thought you wouldn't catch her at it. Then this guy smiled—not apologetic for staring. Not at all.

After he swung out the door, Angelo let out a heavy breath. "I didn't think they liked small towns."

"Times are changing, Ange." Then we talked about the league play-offs. I had the funny feeling we were fumigating the store.

You can imagine my surprise, on reaching home, to find that the person I'd seen in the liquor store was moving onto our block. That's right, a new neighbor. I saw him unloading a beat-up Mercury as I swung by. Roz, who is a member of the Welcome Wagon, had the preliminary details.

"You wouldn't believe it, Gene," she said. "His name is Storrs, he was a dancer with the Royal Ballet, and he's going to open a school right here behind the Stop 'n Shop."

"What kind of school?"

A dumb question. Roz got her patient look. "A dance school!" She paused. "Do you suppose he's got a wife?"

I thought I had the answer to that but didn't offer it. Roz likes to find things out for herself. Besides, the Welcome ladies would pay their first call tomorrow, and she'd have the whole pitch. Just then Tommy came in with two mitts and the ball. Time for our Saturday catch. Afterward we were going to Shea to see the Padres play the Mets. We are both very big Mets fans.

It was the next afternoon, Sunday about five, when Roz got back from the Welcome call. Neil Storrs—that was the guy's name— was renting the Gabler house. The ladies had intended to roll out the hospitality, but he had gone them one better. He had served tea, using a special blend, Roz said, sent over from Fortnum & Mason. "They have a file on him," she said. "It's like registering your silver pattern at Tiffany's." During this tea party he had told them about his brilliant dance career, including five command performances for royalty. When I suggested to Roz that she look this up in the library, she didn't go for it. In fact, she seemed to be more on his side than mine, for some reason. I didn't argue—it didn't seem that important. And then she dropped her bombshell.

"He's a writer, Gene. He's had several books published. Novels."

"I thought you said he was a dancer. I never heard of a dancer who writes books."

"Well, this one does. He paints, too."

"What is he, some kind of one-man band?"

She didn't answer. Instead she got up and started dipping around the room, straightening the blinds, smoothing the doilies. All signs she had something up her sleeve. I started to sweat.

"I was thinking, Gene"—she wiggled the wand for the Levolors—"since he lives so close, you and Mr. Storrs—"

I got it in a flash. "Goddammit, no!" I jumped up, suddenly wet under the collar. This is a hormonal release I can't always control.

"But there are all kinds of famous collaborations. There's . . . Gilbert and Sullivan."

"That's words and music, for God's sake."

"What about Nordhoff and Hall? What about Beaumont and Fletcher?"

"Who the hell is Beaumont and Fletcher?"

"I'm not sure—it just popped into my head."

"Well, there's also Bonnie and Clyde, and the answer is no."

I was really sore. Did Roz think I couldn't make it on my own? That I had to have assistance—and from a type like this? Had she lost faith in me?

I took out my handkerchief and started mopping. She was staring at me, feeling bad, but she didn't feel as bad as I did. If my own wife didn't believe in me, where was I? I'll tell you where—in a crowd of businessmen who ride the subways till they drop dead.

"Well, I hope you're not upset, dear. I was only trying to . . ."

She was only trying to. Half the trouble in the world comes from people who are only trying to. I decided it was time to get a little fresh air. I left her opening and closing the doors to the TV cabinet like she couldn't make up her mind how she wanted them.

I didn't intend to walk past the Gabler place, but my feet took me there. I didn't want to look in the windows either, but my eyes swung over. And there he was, dressed in a caftan, though I didn't know men wore them. Blue, with long sleeves. He was sitting in a room full of crates and cartons, reading a book. He should have been unpacking, for God's sake, but he was turning over the pages of that book like it was the most important thing in the world.

I tried to wipe out the picture, but as I walked down to the village to buy some claros it went with me. A dancer, a writer, a painter. Of course, he didn't make babies, so he made other things. This thought should have calmed me down, but it didn't. In fact, it only made me sweat more, though the afternoon was cool.

By the time I bought my cigars and had a chat with Charlie, I felt better. I had even stopped sweating. Roz meant well. There was no reason to take it personally. She had my best interests at heart.

When I got home Tommy appeared with the two mitts, but I said it was time to help Annie with her homework. By suppertime everybody was feeling good. That night I didn't go into my den. It just didn't appeal to me. Roz was extremely affectionate to me later on, although Saturday and not Sunday is our regular time. It's amazing what a woman can think up if she's in the mood. I told Roz that she was the one that ought to be writing stories. She got a big kick out of that.

My big idea came to me after a rotten day at the office a few weeks later. To be honest, I didn't make any connection at the time. It all seemed like happenstance, which shows how little we know ourselves.

First the office news. When I walked in the door, I found the big Miehle shut down because Bruno had lost the tip of his index finger through carelessness. Blood all over the rollers, the fingertip on a bench. Next my bindery calls to say one of their cutters went haywire and they ruined half the sheets we had just sent over. And last an urgent phone call from my number-one customer. His boss found out he was on the take from me, and he was being transferred out of Production.

By the time I got home that night, my shirt collar was black. Roz took one look at me and announced Manhattans, a special treat. Why not? I said, that's why National Distillers makes the stuff.

I was on my second round, beginning to unwind, Tommy giving me the rundown on the Mets' chances for the Series, when there was a tap at the door. Both kids jumped up, Roz rushed to the mirror—all par for the course—but imagine my surprise when who walks in but our fruity neighbor. I put down my drink and stood up. We hadn't really been introduced, just that stare in the liquor store, so I put out my hand.

"Gene Ebbler."

He replied with his own name, which by then I knew by heart. Tommy and Annie were introduced next. They stared, of course—you know how kids love weirdness—but he didn't seem to mind. In fact, he kind of smiled and preened, like he was onstage with the lights shining.

Roz made him come in and sit down. "We're just having a cocktail, Mr. Storrs. Can we offer you one?"

"Oh, dear." He looked around like he never heard of alcohol, but I know a taste for the sauce when I see it. "Well, perhaps a tiny one, since you're having one yourselves."

Roz went back to the kitchen. The kids sat side by side on a stool. I could see their giggles like frozen waves just under the surface.

He wasn't wearing the blue caftan. Maybe that was his house-dress. Tonight he was wearing a flowered sports shirt (orchids and ferns), tight Daks (puke pink), and white shoes, which I do not believe were white originally.

When Roz came back with the Manhattan, I noticed a maraschino cherry in his glass. She had not bothered to put one in mine. This was not a pleasant comparison.

"Well, how do you like Eastbrook, Mr. Storrs?" she asked after the guest had muttered, "Cheers," and put away half his drink in one long slurp.

"Charming, charming." He widened his eyes, which were lined with mascara. "I've always wanted to live in a small American town, and this is perfect."

The kids were getting loose again, the elbows digging back and forth. In a minute we'd have hysteria.

"Didn't your mother ask you to set the table?"

After a few groans they got up. Did Storrs's glance linger on Tommy? Or was I imagining he took an extra interest in a twelve-year-old boy?

Roz started to pump him. He had a dozen students lined up for his school; of course, he couldn't give them the real classical stuff, for that you have to start in the womb, but he'd do his best. I could see Roz enjoying this. She was using her cultural voice.

Before long we were on refills, and tongues were flapping. Especially Roz's.

"I'm dying to hear about your books, Mr. Storrs. You didn't really have a chance to tell us the other day."

She gave him her googly eyes at that, the kind she turns on the butcher sometimes. I could see her tits straining against her dress. Once or twice she strained too hard and our guest looked away, like he was embarrassed.

I was getting a little embarrassed too. Why was she bringing up the subject when she knew how I felt about it? Did she intend to spill the beans about me? Suggest we collaborate? I could feel the old brain heating up, sending juices down my neck. Pretty soon I'd be wringing wet. But don't misunderstand. I wasn't jealous—I was just trying to figure it all out.

"Well." Our guest fluttered his eyelids so the mascara showed. "I write novels. Gothics and thrillers mostly."

"Have they been published?"

"They've been published in England. I have an agent here now, who's trying to find someone to bring them out in America."

There was a slight pause. I could hear Roz's mind squeaking. She glanced at me, opened her mouth, and closed it. I guess she saw the sweat.

"How're things at the Gabler house?" The words sounded hoarse, even to me, but I had to speak up. Things were moving too fast in the wrong direction.

"I'm so glad you asked." He flapped his hand in the air. "The most ghastly thing just happened. That's really why I came over. I thought . . . someone said . . . you're very good at fixing things."

"Gene can fix anything," Roz said, not in her cultural voice.

"I'm so glad. My fridge just went out. I called the GE people, but they're closed for the night. I've got tons of food and it will spoil."

"Probably a condenser," I said, taking out my handkerchief.

"I didn't know a fridge had condensers." He flapped his hand again.

"I could probably rig up something that would last overnight."

"Oh, Mr. Ebbet, could you?"

"Ebbler. I'd be glad to." The sweating had stopped, thank God.

We got up soon after that, Roz looking a little annoyed because her Q and A had been interrupted. The kids came back to say good-bye, their faces bright with excitement, and Storrs shook hands with both—daintily with Annie and a bit longer with Tommy. We made a detour to the garage, where I keep my tools, then down the street to the Gabler house.

While I poked around the motor he kept up a babble. About being at the mercy of ruthless repair people, how kind the neighbors were, on and on. I didn't pay attention. I like to concentrate on one thing at a time. But when I finished, and the motor snapped on, he was all smiles and gratitude. He even suggested a drink, but I said I had to get back.

It was while I was heading for the can back of the kitchen, so I could wash up, that we passed the spare room. The Gablers had used it for laundry, but now I could see that a card table was set up with a portable Olivetti and a pile of typed pages. On another table I saw several shoe boxes. Something clicked in my head and I stopped.

I didn't hear him behind me. He was a creeper—the sort you can never hear coming—which had probably come in handy for his type of life.

"This is my sanctum, home of my muse!" he sang out, coming so close I stepped aside. "I dream up everything in here. Come see."

I followed him in.

"This is a new Gothic with a ballet setting, *The Ghost Dancers of Rue*—rather a good title, don't you think?" He tapped a pile of manuscript pages. Looked like he was almost finished. I started to ask him how long it took to write, but stopped myself. That kind of information doesn't help anyone with Writer's Block.

"And these are my story ideas." He went to one of the shoe boxes and lifted the lid. It was jammed with three-by-five cards. "These are books I will probably never write. Don't have time. I'm too busy with the wretched business of earning a living." He fluttered his eyelids and smiled for the fiftieth time.

I looked harder at the box. It was about the same length as the one I used in the office for ink suppliers, of whom I have a great many. "You mean all those are story ideas?"

"Every one of them would make a marvelous book." He flashed his eyes again. "I have this penchant"—he gave the word a French twist—"for plots. I dream up one a day. If I could afford a secretary, I could dictate a book in an afternoon, like Barbara Cartland." He let out a little screech.

I shook my head slowly. What I'd been working on for years—all my life, really—this guy could do in an afternoon. A fucking afternoon. No wonder Roz had given up on me. The kids, too. I could feel the old body heat starting to rise. And then, moving toward the back, I caught sight of something I had missed at first—don't ask me how. A painting on the wall. A young boy about Tommy's age, sitting by a window, a vase of lilies on the table next to him. Storrs followed my glance. "Beautiful, isn't he?"

I don't know what I said. Between the sourness in my gut from the Manhattans, the troubles at the office, the confusion over Roz and the kids, the sweat old and new, I was too confused to say much. I don't even recall how I made it to the can and out the front door, finding a passage through all the crates and cartons. But on my way home the painting stayed with me. A kid about Tommy's age. *Beautiful,* he said. Some other details of the evening came back to me. How he'd stared at Tommy. Held his hand a little too long.

And then, walking up the front steps of my house—the house I had bought for my bride, Rosalind DeMarco, fifteen years ago—I had my bright idea. Funny how one second can change your life. I had concocted, without even trying, the greatest story in the history of the world.

The family noticed the change right away.

"It comes from being a good neighbor," Roz said a day or two later. Then she went on about virtue being its own reward, a statement I have never had occasion to agree with. The kids, who are like walking pieces of litmus paper, turned blue and pink with bright ideas. Annie was planning a big Halloween costume. Tommy had a scheme to sneak into Shea for the last game of the season. All because the old man was full of jokes and cheer.

What they didn't know, of course, was that I had already made my first move. Called up my friend Little Richie Lubanski, who had once helped me clear up some Teamster problems, and set up a meeting the next day at the town dump, a terrific spot for an opening scene. At that meeting Richie agreed to talk to some of his people. He would get back to me on the weekend.

Next evening I went in the den and took out a clean sheet of paper. The time had come to line out the big one, the home run. A few lines for the opening scene went right down:

> The gulls wheeling over the mountains of garbage in the town dump did not, for all the keenness of their vision, notice the two men talking alongside a green Lincoln Continental. One, in his midthirties, tall and dark blond, with the build of a natural athlete, appeared to be giving instructions to his companion—a small man with black hair and shifty eyes.

Came out just like that, no problem. Next I would have a little conversation. Dialogue opens up the page and is easy on the eye. But believe it or not, I couldn't get a handle on it. Even though I remembered every word Little Richie and I spoke, down to the five-grand part payment he wanted in advance and my instructions for delivering the shoe boxes. I wrestled with the sentences, the spacing, even the punctuation, but no go. Something was stopped up.

Then I remembered a piece of advice from the experts—Make an Outline. I'd never been a star at this, ever since Miss Osborne in the eighth grade spent an afternoon telling us about *I* and *A* and *1* and *a*. Looked like a lot of hard work for nothing—I mean, whose hand can fit around something like that? It's like trying to make a shortstop wear a catcher's glove. Still, I decided to give it a try.

I was still working when Tommy turned up. I hadn't even heard him open the door, I was that wrapped up. He was dropping the ball into his mitt, right hand, left hand.

"Would you like to play catch, Dad?"

His eyes, big and sweet, searched mine. It was all I could do not to rub my knuckles over his skin, smooth as coated stock.

"I'm working, son."

He looked at the page with the few lines written. Had Dad finally made the breakthrough? Was he about to pole the big one? I couldn't resist telling him. "I think I'm onto something exciting, Tommy."

In his smile, his love, I saw what I'd been waiting for, coming my way at last.

The next minute the doubts I'd had about the whole operation disappeared. My first responsibility was to my boy, wasn't it? Maybe Roz and the Welcome ladies had been taken in by the tea from Fortnum and the command performances and the rest of it, but not me. I could add faster than any of them. Besides, they hadn't seen the painting, heard it described. I looked at Tommy, at the hope and trust and newness of him, and thought, *Yes, he's beautiful, but not in the way that guy thinks*. And so my conscience eased. Any father on the block would go along, even if he didn't have the guts to take the responsibility.

As agreed, Richie Lubanski called Saturday afternoon.

"Hey, Gino." I don't know why he called me Gino instead of Gene—maybe he saw *The Godfather* too many times. "It's all set. One night next week. We have to make that little transfer we talked about."

The phone is in the hall, and the door to the kitchen was open. Roz was in there making spaghetti gravy.

"Uh, yeah, I'll meet you at the same place. Monday night about seven."

"The town dump is closed Mondays, Gino."

Why hadn't I thought of that? It's the details that matter in writing, like everything else. "What about meeting me at the railroad station?"

"Good idea. Tell ya what, I'll park at the end of the lot. Seven o'clock. Then we'll wheel over to your block and view the premises."

I hung up to find Roz standing in the doorway. She likes to monitor phone conversations. "Who was that?"

"Ed Milligan from the office."

"He's going to meet you at the station Monday night?"

"Yeah, so I can check some color proofs, then go right back to the city."

I'm not sure she believed that, but finally decided it didn't matter. I waited a minute, then went into the den.

The following Monday evening, the men who had met at the town dump made their second contact, this time at the railroad station. The bigger and huskier of the two, whose name was . . .

What the hell was his name? Stumped again. I cast around. Ted, Lennie, Frank, Bill. For some reason I couldn't make up my mind. Why was that?

All of a sudden Tommy was there. The Mets had gone two innings already. I'd been racking my brain for almost an hour.

We were in the fifth, a 3-2 pitch coming up, when Roz walked in and dropped her bomb. "I've invited Mr. Storrs for dinner. I thought he might be lonely on Saturday night. What's the matter?"

"Nothing's the matter. You made me miss the pitch."

"Oh, the pitch!" She made a face and flung out. Sometimes I wonder if she resents the closeness Tommy and I have developed over sporting events. My mind started working fast. Did this visit mean an extra scene for the story? Was there a chance for dramatic irony? I read an article about that once. It is something much appreciated by editors.

I went in the kitchen for a beer. Roz was nowhere around. Neither was Annie. Probably gone to the Stop 'n Shop for some fancy food. But when the game was finished (Mets lost), they weren't back. I went upstairs for a nap while Tommy went visiting. I was tired from all the excitement.

I didn't find out where the distaff side had gone until we were sitting around with our Heubleins before dinner. Roz had painted her fingernails, all ten of them, silver. This is the sign of a big event, though why she would consider a visit from Storrs special, I don't know. Maybe she was looking forward to a conversation about the decline of the novel.

"I'm going to study dancing with Mr. Storrs, Daddy."

I guess I wasn't paying attention because Annie repeated it, her voice looping higher.

"I haven't told my husband, yet," Roz confided to our guest.

"He won't mind, I hope," Storrs replied.

I had the sudden impression I was not in the room.

"Well, I'm not sure." Roz let out a little fake laugh.

It was time to speak up. "How much is it gonna cost me?"

"Oh, let's not talk about that, Gene." Roz shrieked gaily at the idea of discussing money.

"Oh, Daddy!" Annie was adenoidal with embarrassment.

I hitched around in the wing chair. No point in making a big deal out of it. There'd be no payment of any dance bill around here.

"While you and Tommy were glued to the TV this afternoon

Annie and I went to Mr. Storrs's studio." Roz flashed her silver fingers. "He thinks Annie is just loaded with talent."

"Yes, quite. Definitely." Storrs, who was wearing a leatherette outfit this evening, vest and little tie of vinyl with matching pants, gave his eye flash.

Well, why not? I thought. "I think that's a great idea."

I was rewarded by a hug and a kiss from my little girl, the sweetest sugar in the world.

"I knew he'd go along," Roz was confiding to our guest again, who flashed his eyes and flapped his hands. Then they started discussing classes for adults—a project Roz had dreamed up. Seems like all the ladies on the Welcome committee were dying to cram their butts into leotards and prance around. *That's a bill that won't come due either,* I thought, aware that I was beginning to drip a little. I got up and opened a window, then went to the hall to mop up. Funny, I was self-conscious about my body fluids with this guy around, even in my own home.

Dinner was okay, though we took sides at first—me and Tommy against them. I wasn't surprised to find that the spaghetti and gravy had been replaced by lobster Newburg. Conversation wasn't too difficult because the guest did all the talking. He told us about his season in Monte Carlo and his adaptation of Maori hunting dances and his invitation to learn Kabuki in Tokyo and God knows what else. The kids, even Tommy, kept asking, "What happened then?" which upset me a little. But of course, remembering his shoe boxes and his three-by-five cards, I wasn't surprised he could spin a story. In a week or two I'll have my own story, I thought. Just hang on. That made me feel better.

It was when I came back downstairs, after seeing the kids to bed, that I got my big shock, though. They were both sneaking out of my den! That's right—Roz and Storrs, guilt plastered all over their faces, were in the act of stepping over my private threshold!

When Roz saw my face, she gave her fake laugh, now crossed with a sputter. A minute later she lost her poise, which is her favorite possession next to the kids and the house. She stammered, looked around, and took out her hankie. The guest, who, to give him his due, picked up signals fast, decided it was time to split. Which he did very gracefully, with a remark about the pleasure of having Annie as a pupil. At the door I thought he was going to give us a curtsy, but he did his seal-flipper movement and departed.

Roz was quiet, cleaning up. I went to the TV. A *Love Boat* rerun is not my favorite show but it didn't matter. I didn't trust my mouth at that point. Every so often Roz came in for a checkup but I didn't turn around.

She was already in bed, very innocent, when I finally went up. I gave her a hard look. "Why did you take that guy in the den?"

She wriggled under the covers. "He asked to see the house."

"It's private in there."

"What's private about a desk and a bookcase?"

You can never tell with Roz, or any woman for that matter. Lies come natural to them. "Did you show him any of my papers?"

"Oh, Gene, you know I wouldn't do that."

She was either telling the truth or giving an Academy Award performance. Probably the latter. "You didn't say anything about us collaborating?"

She widened her eyes, probably having learned that from our friend. "You said not to."

"That's right, I said not to."

As I mentioned earlier, Saturday night is main-event time in our house, but tonight I wasn't in the mood. Even though Roz reached over and turned on our special light—red, inside an abalone shell, which we bought in Bermuda. When I made it clear how I felt, she flipped on her eye mask and said no more.

One of the advantages of having your own business is the freedom of movement it gives you, cashwise. There was no problem making out ten checks to petty cash for five hundred each and backdating them. This might trigger an IRS audit, but Roz would never find out I needed five grand in a hurry.

Just before seven on Monday night I drove to the station. Little Richie turned up in his Continental, which he parked alongside me. I switched off my motor. When he released his passenger door, I slid in. The money was in a number-ten window envelope, no return address. He put it in his jacket pocket without counting. A nice detail, I thought, something to remember.

"Let's go, Richie," I said, thinking this was not a good line of dialogue. Just as we pulled out, the 7:02 from the city arrived and the usual wrong-way housewives, meeting their husbands, gummed up the lanes.

"There's number 134." We pulled up in front of the Gabler place. It was dark tonight—no lights at all.

"What's the setup?" Richie asked.

I laid out the ground floor to him, including the back door. Then I warned him about noise. "This street is one big radar trap, Richie. The Elm Street Ear. Your man has to be careful."

"No problem." Richie looked easy. To tell the truth, now that we were getting close, I was sweating around the clock. Richie studied me. "This is a piece of cake, Gino. Relax. We got quite a bit of experience."

"Maybe you do. I don't."

"You'd feel better if you knew the plan, but . . ." He trailed off. "Tomorrow's the night."

"Tomorrow," I said, mostly to myself, taking out my handkerchief.

After I got home—Richie had driven me back to the station to pick up my own car—I stood in the yard a long time, not ready to go inside. Roz was still in a mood, the kids were always fretful on Monday night, and I was not in top shape myself. Still, there was no place else to go. Only as I turned to move did I check out the Gabler place again. The lights were on in the back now. Probably in the study, I thought, writing up new three-by-five cards.

The next day was the worst in my life—or should I say the next to worst? My ex-secretary, Sabrina, needed more money. I'd already paid for the goddam operation, even though she'd probably been banging half the guys in the pressroom. Also, her kid sister Norma had been blabbing, so now there were some very nasty statements coming over the phone.

"Okay, Gene." Sabrina's voice sounded just like a man's—women get this hormonal change sometimes, don't ask me why. "I want another grand by Federal Express tomorrow or Norma goes to the DA."

Now why should that make me feel guilty? In ancient times fourteen-year-old girls were practically grandmothers. Still, listening to Sabrina talk about some of the cases now getting publicity, I decided not to argue. What's another grand?

But this wasn't all. Right after lunch we had a press breakdown, followed by an accident with a messenger on a bike. All this was in addition to my little problem on Elm Street.

But everybody was happy when I got home, not even noticing Daddy's discomfort. Annie had had her first dance class, Tommy had just got a photo of the whole Mets team, and Roz's mother was coming for a visit. I wondered if this was more dramatic irony coming down on me.

Once or twice during the evening I went to the front window, craning my neck to look at the Gabler place. I was having my doubts again. And then the worm really began to gnaw. Was I doing this because I was jealous? Because God had given this creep the talent I deserved? My forehead started raining, and then I was saved by a good thought, the way a great catch can save an inning. I was doing this for Tommy! I pictured him being invited into the house, offered some Perugina chocolates (only the best), lured upstairs. I pictured all that innocence being corrupted. And then I knew I was doing the right thing, not just for Tommy but for all the kids on the block.

I lay awake most of the night. I guess I was expecting a phone call. Or a police siren. Or maybe a scream. But it was silent as the grave. I tried to pass the time by picking a title for my story. I decided it should have *death* in it. Death sells books. I finally decided on *Death of an Artiste*. The little *e* at the end was dramatic irony, in case you didn't recognize it.

Then I thought about my Writer's Block. I still had it. All of a sudden the cause came to me—I didn't know the details of the ending! How could I write the story before I knew the most important thing? For example, would Richie's friends use a silencer on a Duromatic .22 target pistol, the kind the mobsters used on Sam Giancana? Would it be a garotte—the old Sicilian method? How about something more American, like an ax? Flopping over for the hundredth time, listening to Roz complain in her sleep, I realized the story would pour out like syrup once the ending was set. There was nothing to worry about.

Next morning was like nothing ever happened, everybody going about their business, kids spilling milk, Roz making an appointment at the beauty parlor. I hung around, not going for the 7:42, even though I had plenty of time. I went out back and straightened my tools, putting a little oil on the blades. Roz looked out the kitchen window but asked no questions. Antennas waving all over the place. When I missed the 8:13, she came to the back porch. But by that time it didn't matter. I had just seen the patrol car.

I got out the power mower and moved it to the front. A good way to listen and watch, hunkering down, tinkering. I didn't know the guy who got out of the car—a rookie, probably. I watched him knock, then go into the Gabler house.

Like I said, I'm slow. It took me a few minutes to realize. There was only one person who could have let that rookie into the house, and that person should have been on his back with his legs sticking straight up. Talk about sweat! In thirty seconds every article of clothing was stuck to my skin. I would have to change before I went into the city—that is, if I ever went in.

When the rookie came out ten minutes later, he made a U-turn and drove my way. I flagged him down.

"Any trouble, officer?"

"Not serious, sir. A break-in last night, nothing taken. We'll check it out."

He nodded and pumped the gas. The car shot off—those babies have extra horses inside. For the first time in twenty-four hours I began to relax.

"Gene!" It was Roz on the front porch. "What's the matter?"

"A little trouble over at the neighbor's, honey."

She came out fast. "You mean Mr. Storrs? Is he all right?"

"A break-in. No damage."

In two seconds Roz was on her way across the street. I just had time to call Richie Lubanski.

Richie's voice was low and fast. "They muffed it, Gino, what can I tell you?"

"Tell me anyway."

"He wasn't there, that's what. We didn't figure he'd be sleeping out. Maybe he got a girlfriend."

"Believe me, there's no girlfriend."

"Well, we gotta lay off for a while. I'll be in touch."

Richie hung up and I went upstairs to change. My head was clearing. I'd been given a second chance. But to do what?

I caught the 9:08, and believe it or not, everything was good at the office. Barney, our messenger, was off critical and doing well. Even Sabrina called to say Federal Express had come through and she wouldn't bother me anymore. By the time I got back to Eastbrook, I'd more or less made up my mind. I couldn't take another night like the last one. Even a great story wasn't worth all the hassle.

Once again I was too slow. Way too slow.

The doorbell rang at seven that night, just as we were settling down for the league play-offs. It was Storrs, dressed to the eyeballs in fur. You heard me—a mink coat. I thought only Joe Namath could get away with that, but I was wrong.

Roz was all girlish glee when she saw him, invited him in, doling out the "oohs" and "aahs" like a massage. I didn't say much, just nodded to keep it polite and stayed with the game. But at last I heard something that broke my concentration.

"It's my what-if technique," he was saying. "I always use it when I'm plotting a new book."

I heard Roz egging him on, like he was some kind of wizard.

"What if someone wanted to steal a writer's story file, which is really his capital?" His voice rose slightly. "What if, just to take it one step farther, that someone planned a murder to cover up the theft?" I turned and looked at him. His eyes—lots of mascara tonight—were focused on me. I could read hate and arrogance in them, a one-two punch.

"Now what if the assassin's wife, trying to be helpful, shows the victim a plan of the crime, outlined rather stiffly as a schoolboy might do it? And the victim, now warned, attends a rendezvous at the local railroad station and follows a green Continental to his own home?"

All of a sudden my body hormones were going crazy. Tommy came over and stood next to me.

"But, and here's the interesting twist, what if the intended victim, with the help of the local constabulary, sets up his house with some discreetly placed camcorders—high resolution and autofocus in a low light? That would rather put a crimp in things, wouldn't it? Especially when it is learned that the driver of the Continental is not only a mobster but a coward, eager to shift the blame to the person who hired him?"

He paused. Nothing could be heard but a baseball bat connecting and my pores opening and closing like slats on a venetian blind.

"Yes. If all those what-ifs were put into place, I think we'd have a plot for a mystery, don't you?"

Nobody answered, but Roz's eyes moved from Storrs to me. I started to speak, but Storrs raised his hand.

"Of course, one must have a title. I have decided to call it *Death Writes a Story*. It's always good to have *death* in the title of a detective novel. And the cover has been selected too—a painting of myself as a very young boy. A very beautiful young boy almost forty years ago. That, too, will figure in the plot, in ways I am not at liberty to divulge at present."

He stood quietly. Nobody else moved until Roz went to the TV and switched it off. Then I heard a fender scraping paint against the curb out front, followed by a slamming door. I had a good idea who it was, but Storrs filled me in anyway.

"Detective Marceau is a perfectly charming man," he said, buttoning up his mink coat. "His only shortcoming is that he never reads mystery novels. He thinks they clutter up his mind. Rather a pity, don't you think?"

He held the door open for the new arrival, a big man with a tough face, then swept out with a last wave to Roz and the kids. After that the visitor took out a pad and pencil and started asking me questions. Mostly out of curiosity, of course, since he already knew the answers.

I will skip what happened next because by now you must have a pretty good idea. But let me say that one good thing came out of all my troubles. I overcame Writer's Block. I'm on my third book now, which is based on the true-life experience of an inmate who was scalded to death in the kitchen. I'm calling it *Death by Degrees* and it's coming out in big chunks every day. I'm such a success, believe it or not, that *Writer* magazine is doing a profile on me. They say my life could become an inspiration to others.

Of course, I have pointed out that nobody can become an artist without suffering a lot. I thought I used to suffer, what with Roz and the kids and Sabrina and her baby sister—to say nothing of that creep down the street. But that agony was nothing compared to this. Believe me, in here it's the real thing.

The Cannibals

George Maldonado saw the first Caribe Indian while he was helping an elderly lady locate a book on crewelwork. This was in the library on Columbus Avenue, where he was in charge of returns. As he took down the book he saw a big woman with coppery skin, rounded breasts, and heavy thighs. She was wearing tight cotton bands around her ankles, and her Oriental face was full of slyness and cunning.

George muttered "*Ay bendito*" to himself, then handed the book to the library patron. The next instant he saw a powerfully built Caribe warrior, wearing only a little apron of woven bark over his groin. His chest was marked with intricate red stains and he had a flat wooden mace in one hand.

George shook his head, trying to get rid of these images as he made his way back to the returns desk, his fortress by the door. It was crazy. He wasn't the hallucinating type. He never used drugs, never went to horror movies, and didn't read science fiction. Most evenings at home he spent listening to classical music or watching talk shows. But here he was, staring at stills out of a nightmare. He knew about the Caribe Indians. He'd studied them in Puerto Rico before he moved to New York. They were cannibals who had been wiped out by the Spaniards, except for a handful now living under government protection on one of the islands. But today, inexplicably, they were loose in Manhattan, in the heart of the Dewey decimal system, on an afternoon in October when he wasn't feeling well.

The fever was intermittent—some days he felt okay—but this morning, as soon as he got up, he knew it was going to be a bad one. His legs ached and he felt light-headed. He hadn't bothered with the thermometer—he knew he would be weak and sweaty but not sick enough to stay home. He'd used up all his sick days anyway.

He kept busy, taking his Tylenol every few hours, but around three o'clock he saw the Caribe woman again. This time she was holding a gourd and smearing a young boy with grease from it. George knew the grease had been cooked down from human flesh. A few minutes later he saw the warrior lying in a hammock, then getting up to start burning out a huge log. He was going to make a canoe.

George desperately wanted to go home, but he couldn't leave early. Miss Quigley, who was at her reference desk in the center of the room, had already warned him about that. Next time he'd be docked the whole day's pay.

A familiar despair came over him. He had talked his mother into moving to New York a dozen years ago, right after he graduated from the university in Río Piedras. He'd persuaded her to pull up stakes on the island, give him a chance at a career, let Sarita become a real American. And now he was sick. He never said the word aloud—it was unpronounceable on his tongue. His people didn't have a good attitude about it. His mother was always harsh in her condemnation, and their friends and neighbors were worse. The stories that filtered up from the island confirmed his fears. The clinics—the big one on Fernández Juncos, even the one at the UPR Medical where they trained doctors—made those patients wait all day. Yes, wait while the mothers and babies were treated; also the old men with the cough and the young men with the clap. And only when everybody had left did they call *them* in, the sad young people, doctor and patient ashamed to look each other in the eye, as if they were criminals. And there was no cure anyway. The hospitals, too—he'd heard about them, Auxilio Mutuo and Perpetuo Socorro, where no one visited because the families were ashamed. And when they died, the sickness was given another name.

The despair crept upward, giving him a headache. He got up from the returns desk and went to the employee washroom, aware that Miss Quigley was observing him. He'd splash some water on his face, maybe take another Tylenol, even though too many upset his stomach. But the trip to the washroom didn't help—the Caribe couple was waiting behind the mirror. In back of his own round, dark face he saw them standing under a big tree loaded with avocados. What were they waiting for? Why were they here? He passed his hand over his eyes and darted out.

But he had a stroke of luck an hour later. Miss Quigley had to go to a staff meeting downtown. He went right to the travel section (910–919) and pulled some books. He had to learn more about the Caribe Indians. Much of what he read now was familiar, but he'd forgotten the details. He also found a recent travel book which he took home.

When George got home that night, he went right to his room. He told his mother he didn't want any dinner, though that wouldn't stop her. He could hear the TV going; Sarita kept it on while she did her homework. "*No puedo más,*" he whispered to himself. "No more." He read the travel book for a while, an account of a trip to the island of Dominica, until his eyes got tired. Then he lay down.

He had persuaded his mother to come here for better schools and jobs, but those hadn't been the real reason. He had no privacy on the island, no life of his own. On their street in Guaynabo people got suspicious if you kept your front door closed. "*Abre, abre,*" they called across the street, from the other porches, and you opened it so they wouldn't think you had secret vices. How could he have a life of his own? Of course, there was Jaime, who worked in Río Piedras, whom he'd met in the plaza. Sometimes he and Jaime had a quickie in the back of the shoe store where Jaime worked, but that was all. They had never even discussed spending a weekend together. Jaime lived in the *urbanización* in Carolina, one of those concrete ant colonies, and he himself was in the house in Guaynabo. How could they get away unless they rented a car and went out on the island? But that was expensive and it would look suspicious, two men in the same room. He and Jaime might spend the next thirty years meeting in the back of the shoe store and nothing else.

He'd also met various gringos on the Condado Beach in front of the Sands Hotel, but that just meant a visit to a room and a promise to write. After a while the blond tourists had stopped appealing to him—he didn't like the way their interest, even their politeness, disappeared as soon as the sexual act was over. One day, not long after he graduated, he'd been sitting on the seawall on the Paseo de Don Juan watching an elderly man stare at the young Americans. This man was Puerto Rican, but he was dressed in a two-toned denim shirt, faded jeans, a silver belt buckle with a jade centerpiece, and boots sculptured with the word *Phoenix*. In the next instant George—or Jorge, as he was then called—saw his future. He would become a fake Puerto Rican cruising the beach for the rest of his life. He would never find a companion, never have a private life, and would be caught between two cultures forever. An intense longing seized him. He had to go north and establish his identity. Luckily, his mother's favorite sister lived in the Bronx.

But the United States, so attractive from the island, took on a different appearance up close. He had to live in the apartment they found on West 104th Street, work at two jobs for a while, then go to school at night to get his degree in library science. There hadn't been time for much more. But even after he passed the exam and got his job, established his right to independence, he hadn't found what he wanted. In a city where other young men had good jobs and their own apartments, he had been baffled in his search.

He had to continue living at home with his family. Still, he'd made checklists, in his careful way, of bars uptown and downtown, East Side and West, where he might meet someone. But it hadn't worked out. There was the usual scattering of people who disliked Puerto Ricans. There were also the ones who adored Hispanics. His friend Papo called these "rice-and-bean queens" and told him to stay away; they were just like the tourists on the Condado Beach. There were also blacks, some of them quite handsome, who were not terribly friendly either. Sometimes George thought the Puerto Ricans and the blacks were fighting each other for next-to-last place, though he never mentioned this to anyone. Only once or twice had he connected with someone, but it had never lasted. Complications popped up, or the passion died down. Or the other person wasn't "ready." That had become the phrase he waited to hear whenever he made a second date with a new friend. "I'm not ready, George." It ran through his head in a kind of song.

Gradually he had lost heart. Instead of straightening out his life, New York had made it more difficult. He had become more confused. He had been deposited in the wrong nest.

Around 1982, after half a dozen years in New York, he began to think about going back to the island, even though he knew he'd have to go alone. He started to read books about the act of returning home. He capitalized it in his mind as *El Regreso*. There were thousands of such returns—to Israel, Africa, Warsaw, Mexico. Reading about these Poles and Jews and grandsons of slaves sometimes brought tears to his eyes. They had been deposited in the wrong nest too.

He thought more about going home. Maybe he had given up too soon. Maybe he had scorned the island wrongly because jobs were scarce and there were Coca-Cola cans in the lagoons and rats in the palm trees and fake cowboys cruising the beach. There might be another island under that polluted one—a place of clear skies and pure waters. He just had to find it, maybe in Aguadilla or Isabela or Boquerón. But even as he told himself this he knew he was pretending. There was no homeland, not even an original language. All that had been destroyed by the Europeans, starting with Columbus, who was an invader, not a discoverer. The Spanish and English and French and Dutch, followed by the Americans, had erased Boriquén, the lovely island of the Taino Indians. The place had been rebaptized with a name from the calendar of saints. It was as much a hybrid as New York City.

And so the years had gone by, another half-dozen, and then he'd gotten sick. Not sick to the point of madness like Papo, who had died in St. Clare's, but just a warning flick of God's hand. Still, it was enough to change everything. And he couldn't even go to Dr. Oquendo, who would stare at him and make terrible marks on his pad when he realized the truth.

His mother's voice broke in. "*Ya, Junior,*" she called from the kitchen. His usual irritation returned. He was Jorge Maldonado, *hijo*—not Junior. The word *junior* was American. It certainly didn't appear in the dictionary of the Academia Real published in Madrid. It was another bit of mongrelizing. He sighed and pushed himself slowly out of bed. Puerto Rico was full of young men called Junior.

At the table his mother put the usual in front of him—Campbell's soup, followed by hamburger and a frozen vegetable. She had given up on the old foods—*ñame, chayote, plátanos, yuca*—even though they were available at the bodegas in the neighborhood. She said Sarita preferred this food and it was more convenient. The old roots and tubers required a lot of time to boil and mash; they had to be specially seasoned. His mother didn't have time—she worked in a purse factory on Delancey Street all day, and most nights she went to services at the mission. He glanced at her as she moved around the table. She looked a little like the Caribe woman he'd seen today—the same smooth, slightly Oriental face, tight mouth—but of course, she wore glasses, a crucifix, and a digital wristwatch.

He pushed his food around on the plate and, when his mother was at the sink, gave Sarita his hamburger. His mother began talking about the meeting tonight. A new *evangelista*, visiting from the island. It would be an inspiration—why didn't he come with her? But he shook his head. He didn't want to sit on one of those folding chairs, listening to a young man in a necktie quote from the Bible. Nowadays they talked about disease a lot, disease and the wages of sin. And they always ended up the same way—"*Sólo en Cristo hay esperanza.*" He didn't want to hear it.

He recalled his visions at the library today. The Caribes had no gods, no religion. Was this because they were without fear? Because their world was based not on punishment and sacrifice but on courage? He knew they trained their boys with fasting and torture, taught them to endure pain. Now, listening to his mother talk about Don Ismael, the visiting speaker, he wondered if the Christian religion wasn't a form of corruption too, like the rats in the palm trees and the fake cowboys.

Finally, to stop her, he said he didn't feel well enough to go out tonight. "Ah!" She waved her hand. She didn't believe he was sick. He was too old to be sick and he was a man. His father had never admitted to any sickness until he fell over dead at the age of forty-three. He suggested that Sarita go with her.

Sarita let out a yell. She didn't like the services and she had homework. But he knew she wanted to sneak out and meet her friends at the moon fountain in front of St. John's. He put down his fork. "*No puedo más.*" The phrase came back. His fever was soaring; he was drenched in sweat.

He got up and went to his bedroom. He'd had numbness in his legs for the last few weeks, but now they felt worse. He imagined the sickness climbing through him like a poisonous snake. He closed his eyes. In the distance he heard the shots and screams on the TV. And then he began to think about the island again. It had been a paradise once, the hills covered with giant ferns and frangipani and unmoving ceiba trees. Some authors had described it as the original Garden of Eden. Above all, it had been natural. Even the Caribe Indians, who raided other, peace-loving tribes like the Arawaks and the Tainos, had been natural in their way. He smiled, not opening his eyes. Yes, the Caribes, with their cannibalism and their taste for sodomy—the Spanish priests had been especially shocked by that—were natural. No one had to live in two cultures at the same time. There had been disease and sickness, but none that the *evangelistas* and priests could pretend to cure with miracles.

His mother appeared in the doorway holding the hat she wore to the mission. *"Bueno."* She waved her hand. *"Si no regreso antes de las nueve, lláma a la policía."* She always said that, but there was no danger; the two blocks she walked were full of people. Still, he felt a little guilty. A few minutes later he heard the front door close quietly. Sarita had slipped out too.

He felt the side of his neck, under his ear. Something hard was forming there. At first, when the fevers started, he thought he had the flu, *la monga.* He had treated himself the usual way, with orange juice and aspirin. But underneath he had known the truth—even before going to the Department of Health to be tested. That had only confirmed it.

He had to tell his mother. He thought about that now, the words coming to mind—words that would explain, exonerate. But it was impossible. He hadn't even discussed Papo's illness with her. He had gone to St. Clare's Hospital several times to visit Papo, but he remembered the last time best. Papo was blind by then and covered with sores. George stood at the foot of the bed for a long time, then moved around to the side and took Papo's hand. The words came out of him like music. "You're going to feel better, Papo, because tomorrow we're going back to the island. The island will make you strong. You'll take the fresh air, look at the sea, smell the frangipani flowers, eat mango and oranges and coco."

He said this very low, in Spanish, but he wasn't sure Papo heard. He couldn't tell what was going on behind those gummed eyes and the brown spots that looked like the eyes he'd lost. Papo's hand didn't move in his. He started again, the words still humming out of his mouth, giving the names of all the fruit they would eat together—*guanábana* and *tamarindo* and *guayaba* and *papaya*— and just when he ran out of names, he felt a squeeze. Papo had heard. To make sure, George whispered, *"Oíste, oíste?"* and Papo squeezed again. A line of tears like crystal ants ran from one gummed eye.

Next day, when Papo died, George didn't feel so bad. He was sure Papo was back on the island. But when he told his mother the news, she crossed herself and whispered that God had punished him.

Suddenly he recalled something else he'd read about the Caribes today—they had refused to become slaves. They preferred dying. It came to him in a burst of clarity—dying was natural for them. They weren't afraid of that either.

He called in sick the following day, which made Miss Quigley angry. She said they would be shorthanded on Wednesday—their busiest day, when they stayed open till ten—but he couldn't help it. He'd sweated all night and now his eyes wouldn't focus. Even his mother had become alarmed for the first time. He promised Miss Quigley he'd come in tomorrow for sure.

But that afternoon his fever went up to 104. At first his mother didn't believe the thermometer, shaking it and giving it to him again, but he knew it was true. His forehead had the icy heat that certain chemicals give, and his joints felt as if they were being pounded with sledgehammers. He heard his mother on the phone in the other room talking to his aunt Awilda. Later he heard the *wow-wow-wow* of a siren, penetrating his dreams.

As he waited for the plane to take off he listened to selections from *Kiss Me, Kate* on the stereo headphones. You'd think the airline would offer something else on this route, a salsa or merengue, but no, it was musical comedy or jazz from New Orleans. He closed his eyes and reclined the seat, even though the stewardess would soon ask him to bring it to an upright position. Not that he was weak or tired. He actually felt better than he had in a long time.

It hadn't been easy to get this far. Miss Quigley had refused his request for a leave of absence, pointing out that they had a long waiting list for his job. But he hadn't let her intimidate him, not even when she heaved her bulk in the swivel chair and snapped her mouth shut like a letter box.

He didn't tell his mother about resigning, of course. She believed he was going to the island because the library was closed for inventory. There was no point in upsetting her.

Soon after the plane took off, he fell asleep. It was a sweet, dreamless rest. He knew why—his mind was smoothing away, his worries forgotten, because he was going home.

His first sight of the island was a green blur to the left. Soon they would bank over the harbor and he would have a good view of El Morro and the old city. After that he strained for a glimpse of Guaynabo to the south. He liked to pick out the old neighborhood from the air.

And then, as the plane banked over the beach, with its strip of fluttering coco palms, he had the strangest vision of all. He saw hundreds of war canoes landing on the shore, right in front of the wall of condominiums. In each canoe were forty or fifty Caribes, painted red and holding war clubs. He leaned against the window, trying to make out the details. There was something else, something he couldn't make out yet. And then he did. Kneeling in the prow of the lead canoe was a young man with a round, dark head. His chest was marked with an intricate red design. And then he almost stopped breathing because he saw that the young man with the tattooed chest was none other than himself, Jorge/George Maldonado.

His cousin Chucho, who was an officer of Citibank de Puerto Rico, was waiting at the gate, along with other members of the family. As he walked up to them he felt even stronger than on the plane. The nap had refreshed him, but it was more than that—it was also the sight of the canoes and arriving home and knowing that he wouldn't have to leave right away. After all, he no longer had a job to go back to.

Everyone was bursting with excitement and happiness, his grandmother especially, who seemed smaller and frailer than two years ago. Their cries, the press of their arms and bodies, strengthened him even more, as if they were passing on some vital powers of their own.

At the little house on Calle Calma he distributed the gifts. He'd had an argument with his mother about these—he'd said he wasn't going to carry a load of electronic junk—but now he was glad he'd agreed. The Walkman was the biggest hit, though his grandmother liked the miniature fan that ran on batteries. She would use it when she sat in the yard.

After the first drink—rum always tasted better here—he stepped outside for a look around. The oleander bushes were huge, and the Reina María tree was raining purple flowers. He breathed deeply, inhaling the soft air, then looked eastward for a glimpse of El Yunque. He recalled the early definition of Boriquén as the original Garden of Eden and wondered if he'd gotten sick so he could return here for good. Then he dismissed that idea. He hadn't returned here for good; it was only the first leg of his journey.

He spent the next few days wandering around the metropolitan area, revisiting his favorite spots. As he expected, he continued to feel good. His fever didn't return and the hard place under his jawbone became softer and less sensitive. He went to Río Piedras and walked around the campus, saluting some of his old teachers and observing the current crop of students. They looked very young. He also went to the university library to greet Don Emilio, who treated him with respect as a colleague—totally unlike Miss Quigley in New York. Afterward he strolled to the town plaza, where he had met Jaime Vélez so many years ago. In New York you could always tell which people had nothing to do by the way they walked. Here everyone walked that way, not by clock time but by an older rhythm. Eyeing the old men in the plaza, the endless games of dominoes, the piragua carts, the schoolchildren in their academy uniforms, he realized he should never have left. He should have been content with meeting Jaime in the back of the shoe store and a lifetime of nights alone. It was a mistake to demand more. But of course, it was too late to change any of that.

After Río Piedras he traveled in the opposite direction to Old San Juan. He counted six cruise ships at anchor, all of them gleaming white like their passengers. There were many new shops and cafés and galleries, especially on Calle Cristo.

These outings boosted his spirits even more. He could feel good health fanning through him. One evening, when Chucho took down his guitar and offered him the courtesy of playing first, he struck up one of his favorite tunes, "*Campanas de cristal.*" He sang with a level breath that would have been impossible just a week ago. And when he went into the "*Lamento borincano,*" he sang it so beautifully his grandmother wiped her eyes. After things quieted down, he made his announcement. He would have to leave soon. He was taking another trip, this time to the island of Dominica. Some of them didn't know where that was, so he told them it lay between Guadeloupe and Martinique, almost at the end of the island chain. His grandmother pressed her hands together—why was he leaving so soon?—but he promised her he'd be back. He didn't tell them his real reason for going. That would have required too much explanation, and he wasn't sure he understood it himself. He merely said he'd always wanted to see for himself the preserve where the remnants of the Caribe nation still lived.

That night as he lay in bed listening to the planes overhead—the commuter lines that had made an American suburb out of San Juan—he recalled his bedtime reveries in New York. How useless they had been. He had tossed and turned, thinking about someone to love, someone to share his life, then about Papo's sickness and finally his own. Why had it taken him so long to realize that no comfort could be found there? New York was a trick, a deception, a stony mirage.

A few days later his cousin drove him to the Isla Grande airport. He had never flown LIAT before and was surprised to see how small the plane was. It looked like a toy. Settling into the little seat by the window, he felt excitement mixed with fear. So many things could go wrong, including the engine of this aircraft. He had no idea what to expect when he reached Dominica—whether he'd be welcomed or treated as an outsider. He buckled his seat belt and sat back. It was no good to worry. And he had his health again— that was the most important thing. As the plane wobbled down the runway he couldn't help smiling. He was Christopher Columbus in reverse.

He found that the plane was knocked around a lot. The first time it shook and fell—they were over Tortola—he grabbed his seat in panic. But seeing that the other passengers were calm, he relaxed. He wouldn't come to harm until his journey was complete.

The plane landed at St. Martin, St. Kitts, Antigua, and Guadeloupe. At each island he got out, inspected the white tourists and dark natives, and decided this place had nothing to offer him. Coming in at last to Dominica was a hair-raising experience. The tourist folder said the airport occupied the most level land on the island, but from the air he saw only peaks and cliffs. Just when he was most nervous the water under the wings changed to palm fronds, and a moment later they were bouncing onto a field. He could see black people everywhere. They looked thin and undernourished. At last, with a buzzing head, he left the plane. The local patois sounded French. He was relieved when the passport people addressed him in the lilting English of the British islands.

The taxi that drove him from the airport to Roseau was an antique. The road wound around lianas, tree ferns, waterfalls, and over ravines. At one point they passed through a luminous mist that turned the air to mother-of-pearl. The driver, whose name was Waddy, told George this was the island's famous liquid sunshine. When George asked about the Caribe preserve, the driver motioned to the east. "I take you tomorrow if you want. We leave at nine o'clock sharp." George agreed, even though he had wanted to explore Roseau first. Now that he was here, there was no big rush. In fact, his nervousness on the plane had turned to another kind of unease. Suppose he was making a terrible mistake? Suppose this whole thing was just a bit of wishful thinking? His finger went to his neck. The swelling there had completely disappeared. The skin was smooth and soft. He smiled, reassured. What further proof did he need?

The taxi deposited him at a hotel on the main street of Roseau. It was a two-story wooden building with a corrugated tin roof. A sign over the door read: *Strawberry Lodge, Reasonable by the Month*. The woman at the counter said they had plenty of room and told Waddy, standing nearby, to bring in the luggage. As he followed a boy upstairs he noticed that the other residents were elderly blacks, sitting on rocking chairs in rooms that were topless cubicles. His own room had a picture of John F. Kennedy on one wall and Queen Elizabeth II on another. This idolizing of white colonial rulers seemed wrong, so he took down the photos and faced them against the wall.

He had dinner in the little dining room off the front lobby and afterward went for a stroll toward the waterfront. Most of the people were going in the opposite direction, so he turned and followed them. They were heading into a big white building. A sign in front announced "Cactus Killer" starring Lorne Greene. George thought of all the movies that might have been made about these islands—romances, war stories, heroic legends—but instead there was an old episode of *Bonanza*. He recalled the elderly man dressed as an American cowboy on the Condado Beach. There was no escape. His finger went involuntarily to the smooth spot under his jawbone. He really wanted to reach his destination as soon as possible.

Next morning, when he was having breakfast, the woman who had checked him in came to tell him Waddy Riviere was outside with his car. "You will be needing lunch if you go the preserve," she added. When he didn't reply she remarked, "They live on canned goods and dried fish which the trucks take once a week from Roseau." She pronounced it "Rosy." He didn't want to take a picnic and said so. She looked distressed. "You will be starving when you come home tonight," she said, turning away.

George went outside. When he saw him, Waddy tossed an empty Coke can in the gutter and opened the back door. In the hard morning light the city looked poor and its people shabby. George didn't understand the Creole dialect, he didn't like the general air of decayed Britishness, he didn't like the near accidents at every intersection. Again it seemed important to reach his destination as soon as possible.

"Are you here to study the purebloods?" Waddy asked as they left town and ascended a series of turns into the hills.

George tried to relax. The landscape was changing, back to the tree ferns and ravines. In a few minutes they might be in the liquid sunshine. "To tell you the truth, I had a dream about them—that's why I'm here."

Waddy studied him in the mirror. He seemed pleased with this idea. "If you are offered something in a dream, you must take it right away, otherwise you will never get it."

George nodded. It was good to hear his actions approved. It hadn't been easy to get this far, and there was no telling what lay ahead. But here in the middle of the Caribbean his motives made sense. He was overcome with the desire to tell this intelligent young man the whole story. He leaned forward and began to speak slowly, in his best English. He told Waddy about his job in the library and the appearances of the Caribe man and woman. He told him about his mother and her crazy interest in evangelists. He told him that he hadn't been feeling well but now he felt fine. He tried to stay calm, to sound logical and scientific, but his excitement grew. When he got to the part about the war canoes landing in front of the condos and hotels in Puerto Rico, he was shouting and laughing. At last he sat back, feeling good. He had finally told someone. Not even his relatives in Puerto Rico had heard it all.

Waddy adjusted the mirror before speaking. Then a little smile played under his pencil mustache. "Sound like the obeah man got you."

George felt a rush of disappointment. Waddy hadn't understood.

This wasn't obeah or voodoo. It had nothing to do with slavery or black people, with Europeans, or with white people. *It had all happened before they came.* He started to explain this, to point out the driver's mistake, then checked himself. Waddy wouldn't understand that either. He didn't have enough history or experience to grasp it. George sat back and they drove on. He was alone. He had always been alone. No society had ever smiled on him. Why should it be any different now?

About half an hour later they came to a four-way crossroads. The signs pointed to Roseau, to Portsmouth, and to the airport. The fourth arm pointed to something called the Emerald Pool.

"What's that?" he asked.

"It's just here, mon." Waddy swerved left. They drove a few yards and stopped. A path ran from the road through a lush undergrowth. "Come on," Waddy said. George followed him eagerly through a profusion of leaves and vines and flowering trees. At last they came to a circular pond of jade water. The surface was still and untouched. It looked, George thought, like the eye of a jaguar. He glanced at Waddy, who nodded. "It is all right to swim."

He slipped out of his clothes and into the cool, light-strewn waters. His ancestors had bathed here too, he was sure. It had been a sacred spot. He swam back and forth, aware that his legs were thickening with new muscle, his torso gaining in suppleness, his breath coming deep and sure. Afterward, as he sat drying in the sun, he thought of all the medicines Papo had taken, capsules and pills and intravenous drips and a tube that went directly into his chest. None of those had been as powerful as this life-giving pool.

When they started off again toward the preserve, he was overcome with optimism. How could anyone be sick in the Garden of Eden?

There was no border separating the preserve from the rest of the island. But after driving for an hour on a road that had changed from blacktop to dirt, George noticed a young woman walking along the road. She was wearing yellow pedal pushers and a pink halter. Long black hair flowed down her back. Her skin was olive-yellow, her eyes were narrow, and her face had the flat, impassive look of the woman in his vision. "She's a Caribe!" he yelled.

Waddy let out a chuckle. "They are a mad people but they have verree fine hair."

They drove past various houses. Some were of wood—slatted boards on top of one another, with unscreened openings for windows—and others made of palm thatch only. Waddy called these "trash houses." "They are too lazy to cut the wood, I think, though it is all around them." He said there were no beds or chairs inside the trash houses. Everyone slept in hammocks.

They passed a man weaving a basket of vines, another painting a dried gourd. It looked just like the one George had seen in his vision. His excitement increased and he had a powerful sense of homecoming.

At last Waddy stopped the car. They had reached a clearing in front of a large wooden building with a thatched roof. In the distance George could glimpse the sea and, nearer, a series of escarpments going down in giant steps. Waddy pointed to it. "That is where they say they stepped out of the water and became human, oh, a long time ago."

George inhaled sharply, unable to speak.

The large building consisted of just one room. It contained no furniture, just some gourds on the floor and several flat maces in a corner. George recognized them as the type the warrior in the library had been carrying. They were samples of the war club with which the Caribes smashed their victims.

He was wondering what to do next, when a boy came in. He saw George and ran out through a rear door, but not before George had gotten a good look at him. The boy resembled him as he had looked at thirteen or fourteen. The same round head, heavy-lidded eyes, short, beaky nose. Also the same pudginess. Surprised and amused, he also went out the back door. He found himself on a path. He was headed toward the sea, toward the legendary steps from which his ancestors had emerged.

He walked several dozen yards down the path, around a bend

and into a clearing. Waddy stayed behind with the car. In the clearing he saw five men sitting on the ground. He realized at once this was the Caribe council—a chief and four elders who decided disputes about boundaries and other matters. One of the elders, whose eyes were almond-shaped in a face the color of putty, and whose hair hung down his back in greasy curls, had to be the chief, George decided. He inclined his head toward him, trying to stifle the nervousness that had erupted again. "I think I'm related to you . . ." he began, aware that his voice sounded thin and unsure in the open space.

One of the men laughed. "This is a private meeting."

George stepped back. This was what he'd been afraid of. They wouldn't accept him. He had lost the right to speak in their debates. In a rush of disappointment he felt his illness coming back. His forehead began to burn and his breath came short. The numbness in his legs began creeping upward.

He closed his eyes for a moment. He had to convince them and he didn't have much time. "I'm related to you," he said again, steadying his voice, "but my people didn't keep their blood pure." He stared at each man, but no one met his eyes.

And then he understood how to win them over. He would tell them about his plan to recapture the islands. He would describe the war canoes and the landing on the Condado Beach. He would picture their victory and the great feast to follow. He started to do this, speaking slowly, his voice gaining power and authority. They kept their eyes on the ground, but he could see they were impressed. And why not? He was offering something they hadn't heard in hundreds of years.

When he finished, the chief looked at him for the first time. "Who are you?" he asked.

"I am Yaureybo, the brother of Cacimar," George replied.

They all turned to stare at him and a fierce jab of authenticity went through him. He had been Yaureybo all along but nobody had known it, not even himself. He had to come here to find out.

The five members of the council stood up. They were all talking at once. They wanted him to come along. There would be a war meeting. They would plan the raid. They would discuss weapons and captives and terrorizing the world. He followed as they moved off in single file.

When Jorge/George Maldonado died in St. Clare's Hospital two weeks after the ambulance picked him up at home, the night nurse noticed an odd pattern to the rash on his chest. She called another nurse, who whispered that AIDS patients often had rashes, and they mustn't disturb the young man's mother. This lady was kneeling by the bed weeping while the clergyman she had brought along offered up prayers for the soul of the deceased.

A Faustian Bargain

It was that moment, the worst, when he wondered why he was here. The worst possible kind of thought five minutes before the concert was due to begin, five minutes before he had to stride onstage, tails flying, looking as if he knew everything there was to know about Scarlatti and Schumann and Beethoven.

He could hear the audience from where he stood. Rustling, coughing, shifting, stamping snow from their feet. Getting ready for the tones that would stir them up, amaze them, transport them. The only trouble was that he, David Lichtenstein, third guest performer in the Young Artists Series, was in no condition to stir or amaze or even hold their attention. He was dead.

Well, that was a slight exaggeration. He held up his fingers, then wiggled them. He'd just had a good warm-up on the piano upstairs. His fingers seemed to have a life of their own. He wiggled them again. They would go on poking, spinning, sliding, no matter what else was happening. Unfortunately, that wasn't enough to make music. You needed other things—heart and mind and history—and they could not be counted on tonight.

The house manager was at the lightboard reading a paperback. Virginia Woolf. What would you expect at a concert hall in Bloomington? David envied her. To sit at a panel and push a few buttons and read *Orlando* seemed like a wonderful life. Maybe he had been meant for a life like that—mild and unexciting. No need to practice, no tyranny of scales and arpeggios, no fear of losing dexterity or forgetting. But he'd taken a wrong turning somewhere, gotten lost on the obstacle course to fame, and now it was too late. If he turned back, tried to retrace his steps, he would lose his place. He wouldn't know who he was. He was suffering, he thought grimly as the house manager looked his way, from a paucity of options. He was this or nothing. He nodded and the house manager put down *Orlando*. She looked wonderfully alert and competent.

David watched her fingers punching the buttons, heard the audience grow quiet. He felt as he had at summer camp when he was at the end of the high-diving platform and there was no place to go but up and out. Now he had no time to worry about being dead. There was only the leap, the falling, and remembering to keep his toes pointed.

The audience applauded with the exact amount of enthusiasm he had come to expect. Part politeness, part hope, part skepticism. We might like you, but you'll have to convince us. In the meantime we know our manners. Certainly not the way they used to greet Horowitz or Richter, but then, he was David Lichtenstein, one of the Young Artists, and half the people in the hall had hopes of being Young Artists themselves in a few years.

And then he forgot all that. The keyboard, its white fangs bared, was directly in front of him. It was time to begin.

David called his wife when he got back to his room—not the usual hotel room but a suite the university reserved for visiting performers. This was the third time he'd used it. Unfortunately, there was still no television, his favorite method of unwinding after a concert.

"How did it go?" Frieda sounded sleepy. She'd probably been dozing by the phone in New York.

"Not bad."

"Did you do all the encores?"

"Yeah." As a matter of fact, he'd done only two, and that had been milking the applause a bit. But they had gotten the best hand of the evening. "How're the kids?"

As Frieda gave him a rundown on teeth, food, and amazing remarks, he felt the tension begin to ease. He kept her going with extra questions. As she went on, no doubt sensing his desire not to talk about the concert, David pictured her. She would be in the woolen bathrobe he hated, the one she wore only when he was away. Her blue eyes, without her glasses, would be bulging slightly, and her small, capable hands would shift the receiver from ear to ear. After a while she paused, waiting for another cue from him. But he didn't want to tell her about his problems, about the dead feeling that had come to him before each concert on this tour. It was too complicated. Besides, it would upset her.

"I'll be home next week."

"Next week," she murmured. She really sounded half asleep.

"Kiss the kids for me."

"I will."

"You too."

After hanging up he poured himself a slug of Scotch from the leather decanter in his suitcase, then took out a paperback, a detective story. But it was impossible to read. The words didn't connect. His mind was still on the concert. The Schumann had been especially disappointing. That used to be a surefire number for him. But tonight the lights and darks so dear to the German soul had eluded him. He hadn't been able to release the rapture. The Fantasy had been as cold and unconnected as the words in this silly mystery. A sudden chill went through him. Where had it all gone?

He forced himself to read a little. Words always worked at times like this; it was just a matter of getting started. And then, as his eyes skidded down the page, the image, the unavoidable image, presented itself. Tonight it was the young man with corn-silk hair and sleepy gaze who had sat in the front row, stretching his long legs not ten feet from where David sat pounding and trilling and sweating. He had noticed the young man when he took his opening bow, spotted the lankiness, the casual grace, the arrogance. Then he had blocked out the sight. Simply willed it out of existence to make room for the music. The two could not coexist in his mind.

He wiped his forehead; a cold dew lay on it. There had been other images recently, too many of them, in fact. This tour, all six weeks of it, had been full of such things. Then a new thought struck him. Robert Schumann had been in touch with his fantasies—had written them down, harmonized them, dramatized them. Was it possible that the young man in the front row, like those before him, had been David's C Major Fantasy and that in banning it he had also banned Schumann's? It was a miserable thought and he quelled it. Music was music, and this other was . . . well, something else. If he didn't keep them separate he might end up blocked and paralyzed like his friend Jim Levitsky, who now sold sheet music at Patelson's because he believed his fingers were made out of glass.

He returned to the mystery story. A perfectly sterile but intricate plot was waiting for him. But he knew the symptoms by now. Nothing would work. Not the mystery or another slug of Scotch or the thought of his children. Sleep would only come if he allowed the forbidden image into his mind. It was getting to be a habit. A nasty and depressing habit with predictable results.

Ten minutes later, after cleaning up, he was fast asleep.

Frieda had brought the girls to the airport, a special treat. Perhaps, David thought, catching sight of them, she had heard something in his voice in the last few weeks. After five years of marriage Frieda was in tune with all his moods—not the least of her burdens.

When Frieda saw him, she scooped up Bunny and waved her arm for her. David felt a surge of delight. The kids looked like Christmas ornaments in their snowsuits, and Frieda looked like an older sister. It was a wonder they had popped out of that miniature frame.

He kissed Frieda, noting with mingled guilt and pleasure how completely she yielded to him—her firm little body pressed spinelessly into his—and then he took Bunny.

"Did you miss Daddy?" He squeezed her bulbous behind, which she didn't like. She beat at his lapels with her fists. David lowered her to the floor and hugged Sandra.

Sandra looked away. She was suddenly embarrassed. Sometimes children had the shyness of wild animals. "Did you miss Daddy?"

"No."

"Why, Sandy, you never stopped asking when Daddy would be back."

"No, I didn't."

David laughed, then stood up. Both children clung to him. They made a splendid homecoming frieze. Several elderly ladies were looking and smiling. He had the sudden sense that they were at the very center of the universe, which radiated outward from them in spokes of light.

"We're going to have a marvelous dinner," Frieda said as they headed for the luggage area.

"Chocolate cake!" Sandy said, suddenly unembarrassed.

"Chocolate cake?" David echoed.

"Yes." She was looking at him reproachfully for some reason. "I helped."

"She sure did." Frieda laughed, her sarcasm audible only to David. Again the sense that they were the very rock and core of life on the planet came to him. In the next instant all his troubles of the last few weeks dissolved. They were minor, imaginary products of performing stress. Only this moment, these children, the time they would have together, seemed real.

They took a taxi to the city. The girls took turns sitting on his lap. They couldn't get enough of Daddy, now that he was really here.

David stayed away from the piano for a week. He always did that after a long tour. He spent as much time as possible with the children, taking them to Riverside Park, to the Museum of Natural History, playing the games they liked, helping Sandy with a huge puzzle her grandmother had given her. During this week he slept extremely well, without tension or insomnia. Sometimes he wondered if Frieda, next to him, kept the old demons at bay. Her calmness, her penchant for order, permitted no untidy images in the apartment.

Of course, he had occasional lapses when he was on the street. His glance seemed to have a will of its own, pulling powerfully and automatically toward undesirable sights. At such times he had to fight the urge to hurry home, lock the door, and embrace Frieda. But in spite of this, it was a happy week.

Nor did he fail in his conjugal duties. Actually, Frieda wouldn't let him. When she was in the mood she made him strip, arranged the lighting, put on her favorite tape, and assisted him with her slim, strong hands until they both got what they wanted. She was never self-conscious afterward, perhaps owing to the frankness about sex in her own family. Orgasm was on her menu of delights, like chocolate cake, and there was no reason to diet. False shame was not in her. She insisted that both children take showers with Daddy. She said she wanted them to feel comfortable around the male body, right from the beginning.

It was Frieda or no one, he often thought, but she had not been his own choice. It had been arranged, more or less, by his grandmother. Nana had met Frieda at a Succoth party—she was the niece of one of her friends—and had invited her home to hear David play. He was always being produced, a genie out of a bottle, and expected to perform miracles at the keyboard. But he didn't mind. He'd play for anybody in those days. So he'd trotted out some of his showpieces for this slim, agreeable girl of eighteen, who seemed to be instantly at home in Nana's big apartment on Riverside Drive. After that Frieda kept turning up—at Nana's, at his own house in the suburbs, making friends with everybody in the family, even joining them for the high holidays and helping out with the food.

He'd gotten used to her little by little, inviting her to functions at Juilliard, to concerts, to parties, to Jones Beach. When he played his graduation exam—he was then twenty-two—he'd known Frieda Zimmerman for two years. In that time he had rarely been alone with her. He certainly hadn't thought about marriage, despite the hints and sighs and suggestions dropped by almost everybody. It had taken a last shove, a final bit of manipulation by Nana, to bring that to pass.

At the end of his vacation week David went to the piano at nine in the morning. He had decided to learn the Diabelli Variations. It had occurred to him, during his week of rest, that he might be getting too old for the big Romantic repertory. He was thirty, after all. Maybe he'd been having trouble with Schumann because all that yearning and burning, that Sturm und Drang, no longer suited his temperament. Maybe this was a sign of growth, maturity. The structural solemnities of late Beethoven might suit him better. He might even turn into a Beethoven specialist.

Even while he told himself these things, however, he had the unpleasant feeling that he was really kidding himself. You never outgrew the great composers. Still, he convinced himself that he ought to give it a try. There was the plateau theory to back him up. He had discussed this with Frieda just last night—artists reach a certain level, then have to wait around, go through a crisis, before they can ascend to the next plateau. This had appealed strongly to Frieda's sense of order, as well as confirming what she knew about her father's business. Jack Zimmerman, who was a dress manufacturer, had seasonal slowdowns. If David was stalled, it was like being caught between the spring and winter lines.

David spent all morning on the first three variations, then took a break around noon. He was alone. The mail had arrived, slotted through the door. He picked up the envelopes and went into the kitchen. Frieda had left some lentil soup on the stove. As he heated it up he looked at the letters. The usual, except for one from an upstate college. The Office of the President. He opened it first.

The letter, on creamy stationery with a seal embossed at the top, contained an inquiry. Would he be interested in applying for the post of musician-in-residence at Benson College? He had been recommended by several musicians and professors, and the president felt confident that his application would be viewed favorably, etc., etc.

David read the letter several times during lunch. It contained references to his growing reputation, his successful tours, his youth, and his potential as an inspiration for students. It was all very flattering. But even as he basked in the praise a note of caution sounded in his ear. Two years off the circuit would set him back. He was on the cusp now—not quite out of the Young Artists category and not quite into the next, whatever that was. A couple of years away might keep him from an essential progression. Agents, critics, recording companies, the public—they'd forget him. Even worse, he might end up as a music professor. He knew several of them: mild, embittered types condemned to play in school auditoriums forever.

He left the letter propped up on the table for Frieda. As he washed his dish he wondered about her reaction. A few years in the country would be marvelous for the kids. A yard, a garden, a bicycle for Sandy, new friends for Frieda . . . wasn't all that just as important as his career, his eternal career?

Feeling mildly depressed, he went back to the piano. It seemed that an important decision had to be made, but he couldn't find all the elements that would have to go into it. Even Frieda's bright practicality, which so often brought him back from his own confusion, wouldn't uncover what he needed. The roots went back and back, down and down.

Down, he thought, starting Diabelli's silly little waltz on which Beethoven had reared a scaffolding that grazed heaven, to his late-night fantasies in hotel rooms across America. Yes, they were part of the decision too. And then he was able to put the problem out of his mind as he dug into the Beethoven. It was only later, when his family was seated around the dinner table, that he looked at their glowing faces and wondered again how he could ever locate all the truths needed to make the right decision.

A few weeks later he was ready to play the Diabelli for Frieda and for Maria Boleslav, his teacher. She wasn't his teacher anymore, of course, but a colleague, a friend. Still, he liked to try out new repertory on her. She would come for dinner Tuesday night; afterward he would play.

During this period he and Frieda discussed the Benson offer several times. He could tell from the sparkle in her eyes, the animation of her manner, that she wanted to go. He even overheard her, once or twice, telling the kids about the birds and animals they could meet in the country. But it wasn't her nature to prod or manipulate him. She would, he knew, accept whatever decision he made—a decision based on the requirements of his career. She was in the habit of putting that first. Her mother, married to an entrepreneur, had been the same way. But every time he opened his mouth with the intention of announcing his decision—yes or no, country or city, teaching or touring—he stopped. The words wouldn't come. The knowledge that would produce the words was still unavailable.

On the afternoon of Maria's visit he played the Diabelli straight through twice. It wasn't up to performance level, but there were some nice things in it. He knew more or less what Maria would say—eight years as her pupil had taught him that—but he looked forward to hearing her. They would have a discussion. Discussions with Maria were fun now. It was hard to believe he had once been terrified of her opinion.

Maria arrived with stuffed animals for both the children. She had, some years ago, appointed herself honorary grandmother, and insisted on putting them to bed to the sound of Polish lullabies when she came to visit. Tonight this seemed to take longer than usual. David and Frieda waited in the living room, Frieda with her crocheting in her lap, amused, and David diddling at the keyboard, fretful. Now that the time was actually here, he was having serious doubts. Maria had a hopelessly reverential attitude toward Beethoven. She even placed him above Mozart, which was absurd. Once, when he was a teenager and mangling the Appassionata, she had advised him to avoid any impure thought or action while preparing the piece. And he had done it—approached the sonata like a novice in a nunnery. What nonsense! Beethoven's music was about sex as much as anything else. And tonight she'd probably start handing out the same kind of gobbledegook. Irritation spurted through him. Maybe this wasn't going to be as much fun as he'd thought.

Maria came out of Sandy's bedroom at last, looking guilty. She had her purse with her, which meant that she had been slipping the children chocolate drops, against orders, but neither of them said anything. She lowered herself swiftly to the couch; although she was past seventy, she was decisive in her movements. In her opinions, too, David thought, watching her. You never had to wait long to find out what Maria thought. Her square glasses, rimless, sparkled in the lamplight like windows at sunset.

"The piece is just beautiful, Maria. He's been working so hard." Frieda was making obligatory sounds, which increased David's irritation. There were so many rituals in his life, so many things that had to be said. None of them had anything to do with his music, which depended on impulse, spontaneity. And on other things that now, in this living room, seemed hopelessly remote.

"Ah, good, good." Maria pursed her lips, and a humming sound emerged—the Slavic schwa. She nodded rapidly. "The Diabelli . . ." She moved her slender hands through the air. David tensed. Something reverential was coming. It was hard to believe, in Maria's presence, that Beethoven had ever picked his nose or gone to the bathroom. "The Diabelli is one of the mountain peaks, like *King Lear*." She stopped there, thank goodness. "You are taking the repeats, of course." He hadn't intended to, but he found himself nodding. Why was Maria always so sure? Why didn't she have any doubts? Maybe it had something to do with being Catholic and Polish.

And then, as Frieda poured Maria some coffee from the service in front of them, his irritation disappeared, and he wondered if he should discuss his dilemma with Maria. Not the offer of the job upstate—they'd already gone over that at dinner, and Maria had been vehemently opposed—but his confusions about it. Perhaps even the images that had plagued him during his recent tours. It wouldn't be the first time, after all.

He looked at the two women. Maria was examining the crocheting, a sweater for Sandy, and making suggestions. She was an expert at handicrafts, too.

It had been one of his bad days, when he was nineteen. Maria had asked him to stay for tea after his lesson. She did that once in a while, when she sensed personal problems, heard trouble in his playing. He had never liked to confide in her—she wasn't the motherly type, and most of her private attentions went to her husband, a dim man with several fingers missing (frostbite in a Soviet labor camp), now dead—but this time he had taken the plunge. He told her about some escapade involving a subway john where he had been spotted by police and sent home with a warning. She listened quietly, nodding rapidly from time to time as if she wanted to get it over with as quickly as possible, and when he finished, she hissed out her reaction like steam from a radiator. "David, you must fight against this. You must not hurt your great talent because of some little-boy desires, some few minutes of excitement. You will regret it all your life."

He had started to argue, to bring in Tchaikovsky and Mussorgsky and Saint-Saëns and Gershwin, but she cut him off. There was nothing more to be said. He had to be strong and that was all.

And, miraculously, her words, harsh as they were, had helped. Sent him back to the piano with new determination, at least for a while. Was it possible that now, more than ten years later, she would infuse him with strength once again?

Maria consulted the watch on her lapel, which had an upside-down dial. She never left home without it. "All right, it is late. We begin now, please." The old command—how many thousands of times had he heard it? He smiled. Some things never changed. And Maria would help him with his trouble, pass on some of her sureness, her simplicity. He reached out and touched the plaster cast of Paderewski's hands on the little table to his left. It had been a wedding gift from Maria, one of her precious possessions. She said it would be a talisman for him, a source of strength. She was right, as usual. Before she left tonight, he would ask if he could come to see her in the old apartment on 110th Street.

They were ready. He faced the keyboard, gathering his forces. For an instant he was baffled by the knowledge that there were too many ways to play this music. Then his eyes closed in the powerful perception that there was only one way to play it, and it was his, David Lichtenstein's, way on this particular evening on West Seventy-fourth Street in New York City, and it was up to him to convince his hearers that this was the right, the inevitable, way.

He dropped his hands and began. By the time he was into the sixth variation, the first real stinker, he realized that the important things were eluding him. The bass trills in the tenth variation weren't rumblings over the void, and the rests in the thirteenth didn't hold their tension. The twentieth variation, the andante, didn't move behind the stillness, and the fugue lacked surprise. He kept trying harder, going for sharper rhythms, more rubato, dynamic reversals, but the center of the music didn't hold. Beethoven's intellectual passion, his honesty, his recklessness, everything that should have been natural, was forced. He couldn't find the secret entrance to the music. It was as if his special voice, his private line to the piano, had broken. When he lifted the pedal for the last time, staring dully at the keyboard, he felt naked and ashamed. The deadness had come back. Right to his own living room, his own Steinway.

"I thought it was beautiful, dear." Frieda, tuned in to the tension, was being helpful.

He took out his handkerchief and wiped his forehead. He was

sweating like a pig. He didn't turn to look at Maria. He could almost hear her mind snapping.

"Why don't you have some coffee, dear?"

"Oh, God!" He turned his face away. Now everything was worse. He was acting like a child.

"David." Maria's voice cut like a razor blade. "You must not be too hard on yourself. You have made a good beginning."

He looked at the two women side by side on the couch. Boxes, he thought, they live in little boxes, and they have no idea what it's like outside. The next moment a terrible thought took possession of him. Was it possible that they were secretly pleased? Pleased because his failure at the keyboard gave them power over him? If he had played well, there would be nothing for them to do. But he hadn't played well, and now it was up to them to correct, advise, comfort. His performance had made him their captive.

He stood up. They stared at him. What was he doing? He hadn't acted like this in years. He walked out of the room, wondering if they would forgive him. Beethoven, who should have made sense of the world, had confused everything.

In the kitchen he poured himself some Scotch. He could hear muted voices—not hard to imagine what they were saying. "He's always irritable with a new piece." "I've known many musicians, dear, such difficult men." He doubled the amount of liquor in the glass, added tap water, and drank off half. As he did so he heard laughter, low, discreet. They were amused! His rotten playing, his tantrum, struck them as funny. But of course. People were always delighted to find they had power over others. The next moment, in his rage, he saw Nana. Nana on her deathbed, at the very instant she had said the things that led to this madness in his kitchen, the Diabelli in ruins around him, the two women he loved most discreetly celebrating his failure. She had had power over him, the most of all, as it turned out.

She'd been lying in her bed, the mahogany four-poster that had been her marriage bed, looking thin and jaundiced. She was dying of liver failure. Still, she managed to give him a fierce hug when he approached. Her David, her precious grandson. When he pulled away, almost losing his balance, she hung onto his hand, searching his face as if looking for the least scrap of information he might selfishly wish to withhold. *Tell me,* she cried silently, *tell me everything you think, feel, know, imagine. Keep nothing back.* Even now, standing next to his daughter's high chair, which had a bear in a gingham apron stenciled on the back, he could feel the violence of his grandmother's gaze.

After he'd gotten loose from her grip, he had begun to humor her, tell her she was looking better. But she would have none of it. "Don't be a fool," she said quite furiously, lying back. She had become even more tyrannical in her last illness. Perhaps the sickroom had its consolations too—total control over everyone who entered.

"I'm leaving you something in my will, David," she had said a few minutes later. "I want you to use it for your music."

Tears had welled up in his eyes. Tears of gratitude, love, guilt, responsibility. A regular mishmash of conflict and confusion. But he had cried too soon. Nana was watching him, her yellow tiger eyes ringed as usual with too much mascara. She was making her calculations.

"You'll get the money when you marry, David." And then, as he said nothing, too surprised and puzzled to sort out his speech, she had added, "I want you to marry. It will be good for you."

He had stared back at her, his tears drying, his throat constricted. Had she guessed something, looked into his private passions without permission? Was this her last bit of meddling in a lifetime of meddling? There was a lot of money, he knew. From her father, born in Germany, who had wound up the only doctor in a small Ohio town. From Grandpa, who had made a fortune supplying buttons to the military. For a moment he thought she was going to mention Frieda—after all, she'd been the one who met Frieda, invited her home to hear him play—but she didn't. She didn't need to. With that yellow stare of hers, with that bottomless probing of his shadows, she had seen it all. Seen, and acted accordingly. It had been the final, overwhelming expression of her love and an act of fierce posthumous control.

He could hear footsteps coming toward the kitchen. Frieda would be here in a minute, ending both his tantrum and his reverie. He polished off the Scotch. There was one last thought, mixed up with all the rest. He'd sensed it, glimpsed it, several times in recent months, but hadn't gotten it free. Now he would, quickly, before Frieda walked in.

Money plus marriage. That was the bargain he had struck with Nana, and it had given him an edge at the start of his career. He'd been able to finance his early tours, send recordings to critics, hire a publicity agent, avoid the contest trap, even buy this co-op. By the time he'd been out of Juilliard for three years, he was ahead of the pack and had stayed there, at least until recently.

"David, what's the matter?" Frieda was almost bloodless with exasperation. Her small face was clenched like a fist. A shudder went through him. Frieda was part of the bargain, part of Nana's legacy. Was it possible that he had never really examined the cost? That, in fact, its two halves—money and marriage—had simply canceled each other out? That his career was failing precisely because of his marriage? Another shudder went through him. Who was he? And who was this small woman glaring at him in the blue fluorescent light of a kitchen whose appliances looked like the accoutrements of a morgue?

He shook his head, coming back. "Nothing's the matter, Frieda."

"Maria is very upset."

"I know she is."

"You were the one who invited her."

"I know. I know." He twisted away. "Gimme one more minute and I'll go talk to her."

Frieda exhaled sharply. "I hope you say the right thing when you get there."

She wheeled out, heading for the children's rooms. He had transgressed. Frieda would tolerate a fair amount of temperament on her own account but none toward friends or guests. He fought back the sense of dislocation and returned to the living room.

Maria sat on the couch, a ramrod. Her glasses glittered coldly. What could he say to thaw her out? An absurd sentence took shape in his mind. *Listen, Maria, at night I have these thoughts, these pictures, in my head, and I know you think they're a sign of weakness, that I can get rid of them whenever I want, but it doesn't work that way . . .*

He took a deep breath. It was time for honesty, or at least an imitation of it. "Something's been wrong lately." He sat on a side chair.

"I can tell."

"I don't know what's causing it." He drummed his fingers on his thigh. "I've been playing badly all winter."

"I heard that."

Of course. She had connections everywhere—Bloomington, Pittsburgh, Chicago, Denver. The jungle telegraph had throbbed with the news: *David Lichtenstein has lost it.* He scanned her face, trying to read it. Impossible, as usual. She didn't betray her emotions easily. He used to think the nuns had caused this iciness, but now he wondered if disappointment might be the reason. She had given up her own concert career to tend to her husband, that dim man in gray clothing who was missing two fingers.

"Perhaps you'd like to come tomorrow. We will have tea."

The old summons—confessional tea amid the busts and portraits and posters. But now he didn't want to. He could see too clearly what the result would be. Another injunction, a greater exhortation to restrain himself, be strong.

She heard, or sensed, his reluctance. "I would like to play the Lhévinne recording of the Diabelli. I think you would get something out of it."

She had sugarcoated the pill, but still he didn't want to. He could see Frieda's shadow just outside the living room, wavering against the wall. She was eavesdropping. A sudden impulse to get up, walk out, run away, came over him.

"Yes, why don't you go, David?" Frieda hurtled in, a small, intense presence. "You haven't been up to Maria's in ages." He had the impression that a trap was closing, one of those pincers movements in tank warfare. "I'm taking Sandy to the doctor anyway and I'll take Bunny, too."

Yes, a closing trap, and the crazy thing was that he had set it up himself, given the women in his life, going back to Nana, the power to run things, make his decisions.

"Good." Maria was still examining him with steely eyes. "Three o'clock, how is that?"

"No."

Whose voice was that? Could it have been his? It certainly didn't sound like his. Too deep, too hoarse. As if somebody else had popped out of his larynx.

"David!" Frieda was deeply angry. Fans of color ascended each cheek, and her lips disappeared. He had seen her like this only once before, when a babysitter had been careless in her duties toward the children, endangering them.

"I'm sorry," he began, then stopped. Why was he apologizing? He didn't want to go, that's all. They wouldn't understand. He had a sudden vision of Maria at home tonight. What would she do? Weep? Laugh? Sit down and unwind her hair and think about Paderewski? He didn't really know any more about her than she knew about him. And what, for that matter, did he know about Frieda, this small, positive woman whose life was tied to his own? Was it possible that his relationship with these women was unraveling because it had been a masquerade from the very beginning?

He stood up. He had just seen what he had to do. It was too bad it came to him only now, when it would cause the maximum amount of pain and upheaval, but there was no help for it. He'd waited too long. To postpone it further would be obscene. He suddenly recalled the young man in the front row at Bloomington, the one with the long legs and sleepy blue eyes. The man had been in the receiving line after the concert. He'd actually shaken David's hand and looked at him curiously, invitation in his glance, ready to respond to the slightest hint. But David had averted his eyes, passed on quickly to the next well-wisher, then forgotten the whole thing after returning home. Forgotten it until tonight, when it had returned with dreadful vividness as Maria and Frieda stared at him. But of course, its return now was a signal, a confirmation.

Aware that nothing would ever be exactly the same, he went to the hall closet and got his coat. The apartment was silent around him. It was silent when he opened the front door and when he closed it. He thought of faces frozen in a photograph as he waited for the elevator; then he refused to imagine anything else.

He had passed the bar often in his strolls around the neighborhood, noted the men going in and out, glimpsed the interior. It had always seemed quite out of reach, as if it were on the moon or Mars instead of the corner of Amsterdam and Seventy-sixth. Now, walking in, he marveled at the simplicity of the act. He was like a homing pigeon that had lost its way for years.

He asked for a beer. The bartender was wearing a metal gauntlet; he opened the can by hooking the tab with a little ring on the pinkie. Then he rapped the bar twice and said, "Enjoy."

David moved to a corner and looked around. His excitement and anger had given way to light-headedness. He really felt quite dizzy. He leaned back, closing his eyes, but reopened them quickly. Frieda and Maria were waiting just under his eyelids.

The men around him seemed to be having a good time. He had never participated in this world, even while he was a student. He'd been too busy, too scared, too involved with music, family, career. He hadn't learned its ways, its code and signals. He would have to do that now. A slight confusion seized him. If he learned how to operate in this world, would he forget the other? Would he lose his knack of talking to other parents, playing with Sandy and Bunny? He shook his head. There was no need to think about all that yet.

A young couple entered the bar, two handsome men, both dressed in loose white jeans, white blouses, and sneakers. A gem sparkled in one ear of each. As David watched them greet friends, hug and kiss, his dizziness returned, but this time with a thrill of recognition. This was what he had in mind. He had a vision of intense conversations, shared wardrobes, and seasons by the sea. Beyond that, he glimpsed the happiness that would open up the music of his youth again, the fantasies and variations and sonatas, just as the great composers—passionate men all—had meant them.

"This your first time here?" A man his own age had appeared alongside him. He had dark blond hair, a square face with a thin nose, cloudy blue eyes. David nodded. "I thought so. Haven't seen you around. You live downtown?"

David studied his beer. Now that the moment had arrived, he didn't know what to say. "No," he managed at last. "I live right around the corner."

This seemed to please the stranger. "So do I." He put out his hand. "Merrill."

"David Lichtenstein."

The man blinked rapidly, appearing to flinch. Then his blue eyes lightened a bit and he said, "My last name is Stark. Merrill Stark." This was followed by a smile and an appraising stare. David had the impression he had broken a rule of some kind, but he didn't know which one. "Can I get you another beer, David Lichtenstein?" The man was teasing him, but David laughed and said yes. Everything seemed very dangerous and very easy at the same time.

Watching Merrill return with the beers, David felt that things had been decided too quickly. That they hadn't had a chance to talk, to get acquainted. Then he wondered if this wasn't one of the rituals here too—the slightest gesture, the least acquiescence, was charged with meaning. Again his confusion returned. Yes, he would have to learn a whole new language.

"Here ya go." Merrill's hand was large and square and covered with curling caramel hairs. David couldn't help comparing it to Frieda's tiny, dexterous paw. His life would be very different if hands like these were sharing and shaping it. He lifted the beer to his lips.

"I work right around here too." Merrill spoke cheerfully, quickly. He was a partner in a video store on Broadway. Business was good. They were thinking of opening a second store farther uptown. His open, easy manner, David thought, came from speaking to strangers all day. Maybe he was at his best in situations like this.

Merrill changed the subject to health. His chief fear was disease. He peered at David as he said this, as if trying to see into his bloodstream. David murmured that he had the same fear himself.

"Of course, safe sex is just as much fun as any other kind," Merrill said.

"That's the only kind to have," David replied, wondering where all this glibness came from. "You can't be too careful."

His answer seemed to reassure Merrill. "What d'ya say we get out of here, David?" He obviously expected no resistance because he put down his beer, then went to the door and stopped. Again David marveled at the speed and efficiency with which he had compromised himself, though he didn't really care. Merrill Stark was more or less what he'd had in mind when he walked out of his apartment tonight, crossing a space wider than that which separated the moon from earth. He put down his beer and followed Merrill outside.

Merrill lived on Eightieth Street between Broadway and West End. As they walked, Merrill chatting easily, David thought he might have passed his new friend on the street many times. Merrill might even have been one of those young men whose glance he had always avoided, whose appearance made him hold his children's hands more tightly or sent him scurrying back to Frieda. Well, that was behind him now, thank God.

As they crossed Broadway David suddenly had a clear picture of Frieda. She would be in bed by now with her pink curler, the only one she used, hanging over her forehead. He glanced sideways at Merrill. With his height and good shoulders and square hands and easy manner, he was about as far from Frieda as could be.

Then an exciting notion struck him. He was now on a new life, parallel to the old one. Why couldn't he maintain the two tracks forever? Frieda and the children on one line, Merrill and his music on another? The two would never have to intersect—just go on and on, as far as the horizon. It would be easy in New York, where you could live for years and never even speak to your neighbors.

By the time they got to Merrill's apartment house, one of those slightly decayed, doormanless structures from the 1920s, David was filled with euphoria. Hadn't he solved his problem? Tonight and with a minimum of fuss? Solved it with a logic and daring that were completely beyond Maria's limited experience? Why had he ever thought of turning to her for advice?

Merrill's apartment consisted of two large rooms, separated by sliding doors of small glass panels, plus a kitchen. David could see it had been carved out of a larger apartment. He remembered these spacious flats from his childhood, their rooms often bounded by tuck-in glass doors like these. Nana, in fact, had resided at 210 Riverside, a huge place of many rooms overlooking the Hudson, not far from here.

But the resemblance stopped there. Where Nana's apartment, like his own, was full of heavy, Middle European furniture, this one was hardly furnished at all. By the light of the one lamp Merrill had turned on, David could see two futons, a low bookcase, a wall devoted to audio and video equipment, and dozens of wicker baskets. In fact, there were baskets everywhere—hanging, sitting, dangling. They were all empty.

"What did you do, inherit a basket factory?"

Merrill laughed. "Don't worry, they'll be gone this time next year. I like to keep changing things around."

David sat on a futon covered in a bold geometric pattern while Merrill got some beers. Again he marveled at the suddenness of the change. He might have fallen through a hole in the sky. From the nineteenth century into the last of the twentieth.

Merrill sat next to him on the futon. They had to lean their backs against a radiator, which was quite uncomfortable. After they opened their beers, Merrill turned toward David, whose heart began to beat rapidly.

Merrill's lips were rubbery, probing, aggressive. His tongue darted quickly into David's mouth. The sensation was not pleasant. David broke away. Kissing Frieda was very different.

"You're not supposed to kiss anyway," Merrill said.

"You're not?"

Merrill eyed him skeptically. "You didn't know that?"

"Oh, yeah, I guess I forgot."

Merrill examined him for a while, then got up. "Let's go in the other room."

David followed him and stood around indecisively as Merrill unrolled a large red pad. It reminded David of a gym mat. When it was flat, Merrill began to undress. Apparently they weren't going to use any sheets. "What're you waiting for?" Merrill asked. His voice was brisk, authoritative. As in the bar, David had the feeling that everything was scheduled from here on, with no detours or hesitations permitted. Again he thought of Frieda. Once she got them started, she never tried to control things. She left that up to him.

Merrill was nude. He was terribly handsome—wings of caramel hair flying upward on his chest, his stomach flat, his thighs powerful, his sex lengthening into a massive club. David didn't take his eyes off him as he undressed, hoping Merrill would find him equally attractive, even though his stomach was flabby, he had a bit of a rubber tire, and his posture was poor. Still, he had a naturally good physique, shoulders and hips in good proportion, nice legs, smooth ass. He had nothing to be ashamed of, really. Besides, Merrill had already reached out to grab him. "Nice," he said, yanking David down so that it hurt.

"Be careful!" he yelped. But Merrill was on top of him, grinding him into the mat, squashing him. David managed to wriggle free. They lay side by side. Merrill's body now felt wonderful, its hills and valleys fitting perfectly into his own. He stretched his legs against Merrill's, pointing his feet in ecstasy. He wanted to make contact with every square inch of skin, every nerve and tissue. He began to kiss Merrill lightly, just grazing. It was tremendously exciting.

"That's a no-no," Merrill said between breaths.

"A no-no," David mocked. He felt that a door had finally opened—a door behind which waited thousands of sensations as exquisite as the ones he was now experiencing—and that he would be able to pass through the door any time he wanted for the rest of his life.

In the next few minutes he was gently prevented from doing half the things he wanted. Merrill would whisper or shake his head and raise David to another position. As they battled their way toward orgasm David had the feeling he was making love only to the surface of Merrill's body, to its contours instead of to its entrances and exits, but that was okay. His climax, the result of minimal friction, was satisfactory, and judging from Merrill's noises, his was too.

A towel appeared and Merrill mopped up. Then he lay down beside David. It was cold without a cover, but David didn't complain. It was so good to feel Merrill next to him, as if they had undergone some trial and could rest now because they had come out equally successful. Best of all, he didn't feel alone. He often did after sex with Frieda; the bridge between them seemed to vanish. But this time he had shared everything with his partner, not only the beginning and end but the instrumentalities along the way. It was an entirely new sensation and would, he thought, last as long as they lay here.

But Merrill, after no more than five minutes, sat up. "It's getting late," he said. He looked down at David. "Do you want to sleep? I'll get some covers."

David struggled up. He couldn't spend the night. That was out of the question. He pictured his apartment with its sleeping forms. They seemed to exist on the other side of a vast divide.

Merrill was waiting for an answer.

"I . . . I can't stay."

"No?" He looked amused.

"No."

"Somebody waiting for you in bed at home?"

Several lies passed through David's mind, but he dismissed them. If his plan was going to take effect, if he was going to run his life on two tracks simultaneously, he'd have to start with the truth. "I'm married," he said.

Merrill didn't reply at first, just stared at him in the dimness. "That explains it," he said at last.

"Explains what?"

"There were some things you should've known. You didn't."

David thought back. He had been stupid, given himself away. But did it really matter? Did anything matter except his desire to see Merrill again, to repeat tonight's experience? "We've . . . kind of come to a dead end. My wife and I." That wasn't strictly true, but it would do for now. Later, maybe next time, he could talk to Merrill about his music, about the Schumann Fantasy and the Diabelli Variations and all the rest of it.

"Yeah? A dead end?" Merrill's voice had gotten neutral. It was as if somebody had opened a little trapdoor under the syllables and all the affect had fallen through.

"I'm not getting everything I need." Stated that way, it sounded quite selfish. Childish almost.

He sensed rather than heard Merrill snicker. "You and everybody else." He turned slightly away. "I don't think I can help you, David."

"I'd just . . . just like to see you again." He tried to keep the urgency out of his voice.

"When? When you get tired of fucking your wife?"

"No!" He reached out and touched Merrill's back, which now felt cold and slablike. "I'd like to see you all the time." He paused. That wasn't what he had in mind. "Regularly," he amended, which didn't sound as good.

"You got kids?"

"Yes."

"Then it's all bullshit, David." Merrill lurched upward and disappeared into the gloom. A light went on in the bathroom. The toilet flushed.

David began to shiver. It was really freezing in this room. He got up and started putting on his clothes. He felt quite disoriented, though that was probably due to the cold and the lateness of the hour and his general exhaustion. He tried to marshal his thoughts, to find the words that would explain his needs to Merrill. It struck him that if he couldn't find the words, couldn't convince him now, his own future would consist of brief engagements like this— hundreds of Merrills standing in line behind the magic door, each a little more aloof, a little less interested, a little more impatient.

Merrill reappeared, wrapped in a robe. David thought of a model in a Macy's ad. Merrill had the same rugged, tender look. A slight terror darted through him. Would he ever meet anyone like this again?

"There's no reason we can't go on seeing each other." His voice was calmer now, no trace of terror.

Merrill didn't reply. He was waiting for David to finish dressing and leave.

"I could arrange it any time you want. Almost any time," he added, thinking of his tours. "My wife wouldn't object."

Merrill's eyes flickered. "You mean she knows about this sort of thing?"

David twisted away. "No. Not exactly." As Merrill became stony-faced again, he said, "Not yet anyway."

Merrill took a few steps. "You ready?"

David felt himself flush. Merrill was practically shoving him out the door. It was really quite rude considering what had gone on here just a few minutes ago. "Yes, I'm ready," he replied with equal coldness.

But in the hallway, waiting for the elevator, Merrill standing tall and empty-eyed at his door, his iciness gave way. "Give me another chance, Merrill." He cited his address. "I'm in the phone book. My wife's name is Frieda. You might even get to like her."

A slight smile appeared on Merrill's handsome face. "No way," he said, and then the elevator arrived and David stepped into it.

He leaned his head against the inlaid paneling and closed his eyes. Merrill had turned nasty out of jealousy, selfishness, fear. Why wasn't there room for more than one partner in a life? Why was everyone so exclusive about love and sex? Why did they parcel them out so stingily? It was the curse of the human race. Or—a new thought—maybe it was a feature of men living lives like Merrill's. Maybe they suffered from extra insecurity, possessiveness. They hadn't been tempered by marriage, by children, hadn't really learned to share.

But as he stepped out into the street, deserted at this hour, that thought collapsed. Merrill was right. He had realized at once that a life couldn't be split in half, couldn't run on two tracks, not even in New York, a city of countless nooks and crannies. The price of Merrill's companionship, he saw now, was divorce. But that was impossible. He'd never considered divorce—not when he walked out on Frieda and Maria tonight, not when he stepped into the bar, not when he walked home with Merrill, both of them choking with lust. He would never leave his children, never deprive himself of their growing up, even at the price of a career that had gone cold and dead. The children, he thought, stopping in the street, meant more to him than his music. The children and Frieda and, yes, the apartment with its awful Middle European furniture and maybe even Maria's frozen reverence for Beethoven. It was too late to abandon any of that. They had become part of him. They were who he was.

A brief pain darted through him and he wondered if he had been unequal to his destiny, the destiny he had glimpsed from various keyboards and platforms as a teenager, as a young man, when he thought all the world's music lay under the curl of his ten fingers.

And then the pain passed, and he was left with only a faint bitterness and the taste of Merrill's cologne on his tongue.

The next instant he had a clear vision of Nana. She had materialized at the corner of Broadway and Seventy-fifth and was staring at him with tiger eyes now alight with triumph. His flesh chilled and he hated her. "You won," he said to the vision. "You won." Then she moved, and he saw that she was trying to reach him in a gesture of love and apology, but it was too late. He shook his head and marched on.

Frieda woke up when he got into bed. She turned on the light and reached for her glasses, but he refused to answer her questions. "Go to sleep," he said. "I'll tell you in the morning." She studied him, then threw herself down, her back to him, keeping as far away as possible. He tried not to touch her, even by accident, during the night.

The house was really very nice—yellow brick, Federal, with Doric columns on either side of the front door. This afternoon, a time of bright sunshine in upstate New York, Sandy and Bunny wanted to bring their box turtle inside.

"You can't," David said. "It doesn't like the house; it likes the outdoors." To divert the children, he invited them inside to play "Chopsticks." As he sat Bunny on his lap and positioned Sandy alongside, it occurred to him that although he had sold his soul to his grandmother, he had gotten two souls in return—two brand-new ones, in fact.

"We have to play softly. Mommy's taking a nap," he whispered.

"Softly," Sandy shrieked, banging her fists on the keys.

"Softwy," cried Bunny, imitating her sister as usual.

Yes, two brand-new souls; and if that was so, couldn't it be argued that he had gotten the better of the bargain after all? Perhaps, he thought, removing the children from the piano. It all depended on your point of view or, as the students at Benson were fond of saying, where you were coming from. Besides, his recital last week had gone quite well. He had even managed to get through the Schumann. Of course, the people around here hadn't heard him in the old days. But those days were fading even for him, except at certain times when he was alone in the woods or face-to-face with a particularly dazzling undergraduate. At such moments he would hear a distant harmony, a faint echo of the old forbidden fantasies. But the next instant these tempting sounds were gone, thank heavens, and he was himself again.

The Language Animal

They wake me every morning—Hassan beside me, murmuring sleepily in Arabic, then reaching for a cigarette and twisting impatiently until I stir. He squirms some more, and we cuddle for a while, his one eye blank and unreadable. We can hear Laurent making morning noises in the bathroom and kitchen. It's time. I have to get up and put our lives together. And they know the difficulty as well as I do. I've almost run out of candlepower, hope, glue—whatever worked so long and kept us together. They also know I'll get up anyway.

Hassan watches as I dress, his face a study in false simplicity. The blank socket, squeezed shut (he refuses to wear an eye patch), contributes to the faux naïveté. He lost it in an explosion in a metallurgical factory outside Marseilles. He used the payment to buy a house for his parents in Larache, halfway between Tangier and Rabat. His favorite statement is "*Pourquoi mentir?*" followed by a shrug. Why lie, indeed?

I juice myself with Laurent's fixin's—strong coffee, some brioches bought in the village, and a few less benign compounds that will get me started. When delay is no longer possible, when we have discussed the weather, the condition of the Citroën, if Laurent will work on a canvas today, and impending guests—when all that has been chewed over, I begin the climb, three flights to the torture chamber. Somerset Maugham, at the top of his villa at Cap Ferrat, kept his back to the view, but I don't. I love the hills running to the azure border in the distance. Cézanne loved it around here too.

I tap the keys for a while, until I hear the sounds below fade away. They're reassured for now, and I can stop. I look at the keys, each letter an accusation, and think about the hours ahead. The dismal profession.

The words have stopped. I'm chilled out. Laurent believes that writing is just a matter of proper placement—nouns and verbs and adjectives holding hands like the cygnets in *Swan Lake*. But I know better. Self-control is fine up to a point, but then it becomes just another bad habit.

Neither of them downstairs realizes that I'm imprisoned in their needs, their fiction of Jelson Raines. I write for them; they write me—a reciprocal deception. We all pretend not to notice. We are trapped in a social contract without an escape clause.

Later, returning to the kitchen for a second cup of coffee, I say the right things. Ideas are poppin', just you wait. Hassan grins; Laurent pretends not to hear, believing that severity is more productive than approval—something to do with being taught in French schools. But this morning in bed, when Hassan hugged me, he transmitted his true feeling: fear. *Keep us going, Jelly, write us into the story.* For a moment I saw death at the foot of the bed, but maybe I'm wrong. Maybe there are a few fucks and a few books left in me. I lay there quietly, hearing the whine of the Renaults and Saabs on the autoroute below, trying to go back to sleep, but with no luck. Everybody has his own brand of self-betrayal—it comes with your initials on it—and I had chosen mine years ago.

Words. Yes, words. Growing in me, reverberating, struggling to get out. I was basically a boom box for vocabulary. Big-eyed and brown-skinned, reedy as an ailanthus, I fought against the sounds. Fought hard, hating the noise in my head, the long strings of letters, the sentences extruding like taffy candy. Why shouldn't I fight them? I knew about the penalties, the sneers and beatings piled up in the vacant lots. *Where you learn them fancy words, ass-wipe? Them words bigger'n you, jerk-off. How you like to suck them words off my dick, faggot?*

But what could I do? The words came looking for me. They stuck to the roof of my mind like gumdrops, yellow and blue and pink. The English teachers, white and enthusiastic, doted on me— walking, talking proof that the Darwinists were wrong about the inferiority of my race, that a new egalitarian genetics could get a headstart in East Orange, New Jersey. It was a kind of doom, really. Nobody understood that I wanted free of the words. I wanted to hit, throw, slide, catch, feel up the girls like everybody else. Vocabulary was ruining my life. When I tried to explain this to Miss Edelstein, who had told the school librarian I might take home extra books, she told me to hush up. "You're a gifted child, Jelson. You mustn't be ashamed of it." She didn't know she'd put an extra curse on me, but the other kids knew—and proved it was true.

My mother knew too. She warned me. "You feel the urge to utter and imprecate, son, just close your mouth tight." I closed, but next minute the words popped out again, like the star that got loose from the closet in *East of the Sun and West of the Moon.* One minute it was locked up, next minute it was dancing around the sky. My mama didn't even know how much I inherited from her. "Utter and imprecate," she said. The other ladies would have said, "Stop shootin' off your mouth."

What could I do? The sentences got longer. Maybe the voices in my head were older than me, leftovers from the jokes and sorrows that people hadn't been able to express while they were alive. Maybe they went back to the forest and imitating the birds and sassing the monkeys and calling out your secret name to the snakes. The words had taken charge before I even knew what they meant. By the time I was in eighth grade, Miss Edelstein had driven me all the way to Trenton for the All-Jersey Debating Finals and I was officially a credit to my race. The subject was "Resolved, The United States Is the Freest Country on Earth." I spoke con and had them cheering when I finished, though what I said was swiped or mis-remembered from two dozen books. As I say, a kind of doom. My father thought I was giving him backtalk when I asked him to pass the peas. My sister, Elvira, said, "Don't enunciate so much, Jell, people gonna think you some kinda freak."

Just in case I haven't made it clear—I didn't think about the English language, it thought about me. I could have cut my throat but the words would have poured out, making bloody sentences on the kitchen floor. I stood still for kicks, fists, sticks and—worst of all—the giggles of the girls. I learned that hatred doesn't have to have a reason, it comes natural, and that contempt cuts deeper. I waited for someone bigger to offer protection, but it never happened.

Sometimes I wondered what life would be like with quiet in my head. Not wordlessness—everyone, including my tormentors, knew plenty of words—but simple tones, words without song. But I never wondered for long. I had no choice, after all. Those books the librarian gave me swam right into my bloodstream.

And then things improved a little. A scholarship to Amherst for starters, a college geared for more than a century to welcome a few handpicked darkies. I packed in a frenzy. Things couldn't get worse. At Amherst, meeting pink-and-white boys who had come from places like Andover and Hackley and The Hill, I began to relax a little. Some of them liked to talk fancy. They checked out library books when it wasn't required. They thought I was exotic and could help them in their battles with parents. I was a living, breathing taboo. Gradually I concluded I had been born to consort with these Tylers and Joshuas and Grants. There was a solid, un-natural bond.

I didn't worry about a split identity—hell, I'd never had a whole one anyway. I was so glad to get the words out, to lay them down without hearing threats, that I expanded, I flowered. Miltonian periods, Shandyan melismas, Joycean streams, poured from me. In fact, my identity was buried so deep in all this fancy talk that I lost it completely.

I became a track star, too. Even though I had an aversion to balls of any shape—round, oval, rhomboid, conic, or iconic—I knew how to run. Christ, could I run. That must have been genetic too, though at least one ancestor had failed the course. In my last two years I took most track-and-field events in the league. The local press called me the Brown Streak and labeled my javelin an assegai, but I didn't mind. Pretty word, *assegai*.

In my junior year my adviser, Mr. Moon, started talking about medical school. He knew more about survival than I did, but I didn't pay him much mind. Medicine wasn't for me. It wouldn't begin to use all the new words I'd learned. And I'd made another discovery. Words came packaged in seductive ideas. I could use individual tiles for larger constructions. Why hadn't anybody told me about Socrates and Marx? About the world as an act of will? About the structure imposed by the mind on its surroundings? That the state was arbitrary, justice impossible, life brutish and short, observable reality a convention we were all dreaming? I played with the coins of major abstraction, positive I could add them up to a fixed sum. I loved every minute of it.

I was also discovering sex, first with a girl from Mount Holyoke who was visiting her brother in my dorm. I took off my clothes for Meredith on a Sunday afternoon. She was expecting a cinnamon dick, like my skin, but found something much darker, a concentration of melanin, an imp of darkness that thrilled her half to death. I didn't let her enjoy her terror too long. I pointed out it was the same color as her brother's once I put the Trojan on.

When she got back to Mount Holyoke, she published a story in the college mag about a girl who "saves" a Harlem boy from a life of drugs and crime. It was my first view of upper-class liberalism as a therapeutic art form. After reading the story I refused to give her any more of my spunk for a sequel. I wanted to save my salvationist fantasies for myself.

Maybe I got too much attention at Amherst and that's how error started. Instead of being shunned for being different, I was admired for it. It was the mirror image of East Orange and proves that corruption comes in the most subtle forms. There was still no way to be me, plain old Jelly Raines, who beat off most every night to shadows in his mind, who wondered why he never said ten true words to anybody, who didn't much care that his father had a heart attack in his garage and that his sister, Elvira, had to get rid of a baby. I began to wonder if Jelly Raines existed at all. Maybe I was a cubist painting—a grid of abstract shapes with only a few clues to the figure inside. A shoulder, a forearm, a pipe. And of course, numbers, menus, phrases, newspaper clips, pasted on.

In my last year at Amherst everything got easier, except the figure in the grid became more elusive. I began to doubt he was even in there. The grandees took me up. I went from house nigger to party nigger. Tea at the Athenaeum, lunch at the Signet Club, once a Waltz Evening at the Copley with white gloves on my hands ("Why are the gloves white, Mrs. Endicott Peabody?"). I got so polite I didn't recognize my own voice. The waiters at these functions wouldn't look me in the face—they wore white gloves too. I eyed them in horrified embarrassment. How did we get on opposite sides of the punch bowl?

It sounds crazy, but I was also happy in my illusions. I was breaking the mold, the latest in a long line to prove that good diction could change the world. Yes, the Eliza Doolittle of Back Bay. If I felt I didn't belong, if doubt visited me, I just decided to try harder. Harder with J. S. Mill and T. B. Macaulay and all the Huxleys. What was there to worry about? I was creating new histories, new narratives. One night at a dinner party in Louisburg Square, as we sat around a coffee service that had come over on the *Mayflower,* I had the impression that I was *Webster's Unabridged* come to life, and all these gentle, nasal folk were waiting for me to redefine their existence. And why shouldn't I be confident? They'd been sheltering runaway slaves for more than a century. All I had to do was watch my manners. They'd gotten me into the drawing room and might even get me into the bedroom.

Yes. What did I know at twenty-one except that I had to use the weapons I had—my sparkly teeth, my blade profile, my runner's build, my trusting smile, and a random retrieval system that brought up the words before anybody knew they were needed. Elvira, when I visited her back home, said I was turning into a miscegenated man, but I paid no mind. I was gettin' over. I was movin' on. How could it stop with Waltz Evenings and dinner parties on Beacon Hill? My old friend vocabulary, now wedded to charm, was going to take me even farther.

All the way to New York City, in fact, which is downtown America. After graduation I went to work at Gimbel's with the famous Bernice Fitzgibbon, who was doing something new in the ad business. She told me I'd soon be ready to create my own cute little ads with curlicue line drawings, but first I had to type for a while. When I got tired of that, I was hired at an office on Pearl Street, writing catalog copy for a Syrian importer of maritime delicacies. Then on to a job at a little magazine called *Parthenon*, bankrolled by a Greek pederast, where I spent most of my office time working on a novel.

Yes, writing was the beast lying in wait for me. I only had to set down the words with the same grace I spoke them. My fellow Americans wanted me to be spontaneous, cool, and a little bit streety. To these I would add a plot line. It took me a while to master all this, but I did. Another kind of doom, really, though I didn't know it at the time. The words hadn't let go; they were just assuming permanent form, where my critics and enemies could get at them. Not that this first novel was worth shit. Too much crying and carrying on. I snuck out one night and dropped it in a trash can, recalling some story by Fannie Hurst where the heroine does the same with her aborted fetus.

When I was low, the word *success* dropped into my mind like a drug. I knew this was obsessive. I understood overcompensation, the sterility of public approval, but that didn't stop me. I still believed success could buy off the bullies, protect me from hatred, earn me an existence. No amount of logic could clear my mind of these notions. Maybe they were atavistic, related to power or territory. Maybe I was improving on your basic American guarantee—the pursuit of happiness means you got the right to overtake it. In any case, when I was blue, when I lost what little sense of myself I had, I would give myself over to the lust for success. Fumes would clog my brain. I would peer into the future as a teenager would check out the jewels in Tiffany's window.

New York wasn't legally Jim Crow in those days, but service was slow. Slow at the lunch counters, in the bars, in doorways to apartment houses, in taxis. The bartenders never smiled at me, no matter how familiar my face, or how much I paid for their poisons. Women wouldn't step alone with me into an elevator, not even in the Empire State Building. My secret promises to myself helped with some, but not all, of that. Darkness is just light that's holding its breath, I reminded myself. Why didn't they know that? I walked around the city waiting for the insult, the punch, the shove. It didn't come. I figure they knew a runner when they saw one.

In the meantime I had a little apartment on Fifty-eighth Street, four flights up, where I could see my favorite Erector set bridge across the East River, and a growing pile of pages for my second novel. This one was different. I was tellin' the truth. The truth starts in your toes and rises up back of your eyes. I told about Mama and the bullies in school and trying reefer and going down on my older tormentors. I wrote about my father's truck-repair business and how a good man can be hollowed out till he's nothing but a shell. I wrote about playing robber casino by candlelight and grasping instantly that it was this game, not Monopoly, that summed up America. I mean, if you can steal your neighbor's worldly goods that easily, because your card matches his, you know you're onto something. I wrote about private colleges and New England liberals and seducing debutantes. The book was a long, slow implosion, an orgasm withheld for two hundred pages. I also discovered I had general things to say about America—well-formed statements that would rear back and give me a shape too. My themes surfaced— race, innocence, hypocrisy, escape. Not that *Years of Banishment* developed these very well, but they were there, under the surface.

"The Negro Flaubert," the *Times* called me. "A naturally aristocratic style," wrote Irita Van Doren in the *Trib*. And *Time* magazine promoted me from a credit to my race to an ornament. I pictured myself hanging on the National Christmas Tree in Washington.

I got so much attention I caught clearer glimpses of the figure in the cubist grid. He was steppin' out in a jacket from Brooks Brothers (natural shoulders) and a black knit tie. He was important, Lawd a'mighty, he was important. He could pronounce on any subject, including the swimming pool in East Orange that was drained and refilled every Wednesday. A purification ritual, I pointed out, allowing the black people to use it half the time without infecting the whites who used it the rest of the week. But this bizarre ritual didn't change my behavior. I mean, I never went back home and jackknifed from the tower on *their* day, with the press looking on. The words, the words were enough, wrapping me in betrayal, a Judas embrace. I wasn't W.E.B. Dubois or Richard Wright or Jimmy Baldwin, full of anger and action. I was only me, Jelly Raines, with my ancient conviction that I could beautify the world, revise reality with the right words, slipping along the downward slope from major truth to minor solipsism.

After *Years of Banishment* came out, there was no more poverty for this jive-ass Flaubert, no more waiting on Miss Fitzgibbon or Mr. Angelikos to give me a chance. I still had trouble with doormen and waiters and taxis, but in better parts of town. I began to run with the young writers. A natural fit. We were all broken in different ways, but we shared one illusion—the Allies had saved democracy so we could say what was wrong with it. Of course, we had bad times, when we helped each other. We fixed what needed fixing— landlords, lovers, writing blocks, vermin in the kitchen. I learned there were people, mostly women, who had no limit on their capacity for love, who could be trusted all the way.

A published novel is an aphrodisiac, in case you didn't know. I put a copy of *Years* under my mattress and showed it to the ones who interested me, peeling back the bed, making the joke. Never failed, not with either sex. They thought it was voodoo, and it robbed them of their will to resist. We had some good times in that bed and no one was hurt.

I remember one night at Small's, where we had gone to see and hear Miles—all of us friends now, me linked up with Nancy Jamison, a blond schoolteacher from New Jersey who had written me a letter. Just across from us was Ron van Over, a fine poet doing too many drugs already. The camaraderie was complete. We were making a new world in the heart of Harlem. Now the doors would stay open, the ghettos melt away, a shining brotherhood arise. I could feel the New Jerusalem taking shape around us. I jumped up on the table in my Bass Weejuns and my chinos and jacket from J. Press and lifted my glass. "Time starts now!" I roared. The others pounded on me. I was the living proof that doors could open, arms embrace. Hadn't I been welcomed in Back Bay and Sutton Place? Hadn't I sat on Eames chairs and Louis Quinze fauteuils and chesterfield sofas? Hadn't I left the past behind me?

Today's ballplayers would say I was in the zone. Others would say I had decided to live somebody else's life—not my own—and was succeeding at it. In this I was abetted by the American passion for surrogacy, which is as much a national habit as Coca-Cola. *My life is unsatisfactory, so I'll live yours.* My readers were doing it to me and I was doing it to myself. I was ascending the throne of otherness. Around this time, when Elvira came to town with a new baby she decided to keep, she looked at me real hard and said, "Who are you, Jell? I think you're renting out space to five or six people in your head." She laughed. "I hope you chargin' them rent."

We had one of our arguments after that, not one of the good ones but mean and spiteful. I was still hiding, you see, even while exposing myself. As I said before, everyone has his brand of betrayal—it comes with your initials on it. Still, in my rare moments I wondered if my doubleness, my tripleness, might not turn into an asset some day. "Use it, baby," I whispered to myself on these occasions, wondering if I heard right.

It's unfair to talk about the burdens of praise and publication when all around you thousands are perishing to assume those burdens, but things started to change even more after my next book. *Love in a Minor Key* was the story of an interracial marriage—a black man and a white woman, a dangerous combination for those days. The national psyche was touched, the knowledge that black men, in their darkness, have something white women want. The book was banned in Boston and quickly rose in the charts. *Strange Fruit* had done it a decade before; now it was my turn. I became Jelson Raines, spokesman for mongrelizing the races. Hate mail started turning up, tut-tuts in the "responsible" press, vituperation in the southern reviews. What was I trying to prove? What morality could be served by marriage between Negro and Caucasian? And underneath, the more fearful message: What does this character, Malvern Bothwaite, possess? Fascination with the primitive is a disease of an anemic culture.

Why did I write it? That's a question I ask myself now, in this room on the coast of France, where I don't write anything. Where did the guts, the carelessness, the sureness, come from?

The explanation reflects no credit on me. I had simply invented a new self to go with the new words—the figure had still only partly emerged from the cubist grid. The words were the entire and essential me.

After *Love in a Minor Key* the last barriers came down. Upper Bohemia flung open its doors. I won prizes, I was called by radical periodicals for comment, I sat on platforms and looked modest. I was confirmed in my ancient hypothesis—words would make me free. I became a mighty self-satisfied young man. My enunciation improved so much you could hear me across town. *Life* ran my photo, Earl Wilson noted my presence in the clubs, and I appeared on *Author Meets the Critics*.

It was about this time Elvira called up to say, "Jell, I passed you on the street and I didn't even recognize you. Honey, you done turned white." I told her to mind her own business, I was through with that self-hating shit.

We're going to the Poisson Rouge for lunch. Laurent and Hassan have just announced it. A reward of sorts. I've been upstairs typing for hours—what you've just read, not the work I've been paid to do. They troop upstairs, uninvited, and see the pile of pages. Jelly's on a roll, they think, not knowing I'm writing this long slave narrative, this tale of someone caught in the Middle Passage, for which no one will pay me a dime.

It's a tricky drive to the restaurant but Hassan loves it, loves the theater of the road, having to twist his face so the one eye registers. He's not allowed a license, of course, but that only makes it more exciting. I'm alongside, Laurent squashed sideways in the back. I take in the odor of the pines, the hints of rosemary, the palms like inverted feather dusters, the cruise ships on the horizon.

Étienne, the owner, welcomes our little group, conducting us across the terrace to a table by the stone parapet with a dozen pots of *rosiers* on it. A V of Mediterranean below, above us the hills, around us the customers, smiling and pointing. I nod, dip my head, experience a moment's pride, phantom pleasure. But then the pain comes back and I'm face-to-face again with the fraud. It doesn't keep me from giving another little wave. Étienne brings us a bottle of Montrachet, which he opens with his jackknife corkscrew and pours without airs or graces.

Laurent and Hassan are preening now, showing off too. We exist, after all. I've known Laurent since I started making my trips to Europe, meeting him first in a bistro, part of *le milieu,* as I made my first sorties and forays into Paris. He was slender and handsome then, full of the usual plans, and I was able to lose my head over a man, in Paris, for the first time.

"There's Madame Thrill," Laurent mutters, nodding at a middle-aged American lady in harlequin glasses. She's been trying to catch my eye. Now she lifts her glass. I do the same.

"That's her, all right." The wine is smooth. "If I smile too long, she's going to come over and tell me her life would make a great novel."

We continue joking, displaying animation for the fans. I wonder briefly why I feel compelled to help the putative Mrs. Thrill. What psychic necessities, what laws of supply and demand, have turned me into a fabricator of fantasy for ladies who turn pages hoping for a ghetto rape or lustful murder or desperation beyond their own capacity? Narrative may be the only life they have, but then it's the only one I have. Actually, we need each other.

And then I see a familiar face on the far side of the terrace. Polly Laderman. Memory rushes through me, but no, it couldn't be. Polly is older than that now, might even be dead. I look again, noting the hawk profile, the greedy eyes, the soft freckled skin. Not Polly, but close.

She was fifteen years older than me, in her midforties when I met her, not long after *Love in a Minor Key* appeared. She sat next to me on the platform for the Negro College Fund banquet. She was wearing a turban and worked for the company that had staged this thing. There are some women who try to make themselves small—lacing their hands, tucking in their feet—but not Polly. She occupied space. Not just her flesh but her spirit. When I came back after my little speech about Opportunity and Nurturing Talent, she leaned over and remarked hoarsely, "You can do better than that, Mr. Raines, a lot better."

She was baiting me, setting the widow's trap, and I fell in. "Who asked you?"

She gave a little pleased smile: *I cared.* "I read both your novels," she went on. "Why don't you tell them what you really think?"

"Which is?"

"Education won't cure what's wrong with race relations in America."

We went on like that for a while. I told her about my debating victory in junior high school. She liked that—it proved I was historically committed. I didn't know it yet, but she was a Jewish

Hedda Gabler and she wanted vine leaves in my hair. At parting she invited me for dinner. I accepted all invitations in those days; I hadn't spent those evenings on Beacon Hill for nothing.

Polly took charge pretty quick. The first night, she plopped next to me on the couch and let me look down her décolletage. She gave off a winy odor, like fall leaves or newly turned earth. I followed her invitation and we wound up on her brass bed with the green taffeta cover, which she didn't bother to remove. She had an amazing lack of inhibition, proving again that a woman out of her clothes is another being.

But when we finished—an encounter that wasn't all that different from my first one with Meredith Trainor of Mount Holyoke, although the details varied—I felt the old resentment. It wasn't me Polly wanted; it was my black ass or my funky smell or my extra two inches. Or maybe something else, something between Jews and blacks that I hadn't figured out yet. All I could do then was smell it.

Lying there, resting, I recalled a train trip to Westchester a few days before. I sat just down the aisle from a woman who boarded at 125th Street. She wore an apologetic smile, permanently in place. Something about her was familiar. I studied the broad face, the coppery skin, the haunted eyes. Then, in a freezing flash, I realized I was two seats away from Miss Marian Anderson. When the conductor came along, clicking and snapping, she handed over her ticket timidly, as if she had no right to be there, as if she had to excuse her intrusion on the earth. My first reaction was irritation, followed by anger. Why was this woman cringing like that?

I got up—I was on automatic pilot now—and went toward her, calling her name. She looked up, scared. She wanted to be invisible. Everybody was staring. I watched her shrink under me, studying her hands. I congratulated her, told her how much she meant to me, to all of us. She said nothing, just kept smiling like she wanted to keep it a secret. At last I shut up and moved back. I was all mixed up—angry, embarrassed, self-righteous—while the blue-eyed devils around us clucked and whispered. Miss Anderson never looked at me again until she got off at White Plains. Then she gave me the tiniest nod.

I couldn't help comparing this little episode to Polly beside me, sprawled on the green taffeta bedspread. She considered herself royalty, even though she'd never sung at the Lincoln Memorial, never been invited to the White House, never turned up on a postage stamp. That opinion was engraved in her skin, her parentage, her past. She was a lioness of Judah.

But when we started up again, I was ready. I fucked her as if my cock were a knife and I could undo every humiliation Marian Anderson had ever suffered. A little smile tugged at the corners of her full, smeared mouth as I prodded and stabbed. She didn't mind. It proved something again—*I cared*. She could encompass that, too. When I finished off, finally, I wondered if I'd have to do this to every white woman in the world just to keep from going crazy.

She didn't say much afterward, cleaning up, but I could tell. The ghetto boy had enslaved himself with anger. Now she could shape him to her satisfaction. I was her raw material, and she'd messed with all kinds—clay, oils, stone, flesh, dreams. But black confusion was her hands-down favorite.

I fell for it. Maybe I was still hooked on teachers. Maybe I hadn't done with the subtle eviscerations of patronage. So I accepted Polly's invitation, held her hand at parties, spoke up at the dinners with her friends from *PM* and the *Reporter* and the *New Leader*. I joined in late debates at the Ethical Culture Society and provided useful fodder on which to base their theories of the coming equality of the races. Max Lerner especially liked me—he recognized another meshugganer when he saw one. The ghost of Ayn Rand stalked all our discussions, though she never appeared in person.

My ascension from East Orange to Amherst to New York was clear and palpable to these analysts. Inevitable, like the Rise of the Bourgeoisie or the Triumph of Free Verse or the Opening of the West. My arc was precise, graspable. I was the secret antidote to their own fear. These outsiders could belong too, and maybe a little closer in than me.

Watching their faces, their smiles, as they stabbed out cigarettes, I gradually realized that they didn't give a rat's ass for old Jelly Raines; I was simply the metaphor they needed. I thought back to Meredith Trainor at Mount Holyoke. Maybe that had set the pattern, and nothing could change except in details.

In the meantime my nights were spent in Polly's bed (we finally got around to removing the taffeta cover) and in various other beds around town.

As I say, the realization was gradual. For months I wavered, approaching and drawing back from the thin line in my mind. On one side lay my old faith, the desire to believe, my trust in improvement. On the other side lay my private emptiness, Elvira's skepticism, the little signs—despite my new success—that I was not the cultural totem, the bridge, I liked to think I was. Faith and doubt, fire and ice, Jesus and Judas—all the contraries fought in my gut. Whom should I believe, Polly and her progressive friends or that part of myself to which, in spite of all attempts, I could never tell lies?

And then one night, in Polly's brass bed, where our fucking had become less sadistic and more baby-at-the-breast, everything fell into place. Lying next to her, oak leaf against pearl, nappy head against chemical blond, I understood her. White supremacy needs us to maintain its balance. True equality, true respect, was no more possible here than on a plantation in Alabama. She wouldn't stop feeling secretly superior if I had written the collected works of William Shakespeare. It was in our separate blood, our histories, our religions, the way we came to America. I would never be exceptional enough for Polly to admit me to her club.

I was trembling when I got up and put on my clothes. She kept asking what was wrong, but I didn't answer. I was tired of being her reassurance that things could still get worse. It had taken me a while to understand, that's all. My days as an antidote were done.

A few months later, after giving away the furnishings in the flat on Fifty-eighth Street, keeping a few books, some clothes, my manuscripts, and the Remington, I set sail on the *Flounder*. A cold crossing we had of it, but I didn't mind. I played hearts in the tourist lounge until noon, when they opened the bar. After that things took care of themselves. I was nervous, but being afloat in the middle of the Atlantic helped. I liked being neither here nor there. Wasn't that where I'd spent my life till now? I started making notes for my next novel. The rest of the time I screwed around with American college boys—an old specialty. I was still struggling with my innocence, the helplessness that had descended when I opened my first book in grade school, heard the first marvelous words lofted into the air. I had lots of people to thank—not least Polly Laderman. And yet I couldn't forgive her, finally, for not knowing what she was doing. Our vulnerabilities should have meshed; instead hers were kept to manageable size by insisting on mine.

Paris was a poor place in the fifties—coal and kerosene in short supply, everybody scrimping, wearing gloves and scarves in the cafés, the arts just starting to blink and open their eyes after the darkness of Vichy. Only a few, like Raymond Duncan, were left over from the old days. He was still doing his flock of sheep on tiny Left Bank stages, untouched, in his mad way, by the plague that had contaminated Europe.

Laurent, whom I met soon after landing, introduced me to his friends. "Jellichat," some of them called me, a harbinger of a famous poem to come, or just plain "Jel-*sohn*," which I preferred. In any case, they found a place for me, not because they had read my books (untranslated) but because they had an open space for *les noirs*. Not coterminous with the space vacated by Polly Laderman and her friends. No, this was different, without competition, without the need to get over or prove something. We were, above all, *interesting*. If the French find you interesting, most all your social battles are won.

I settled down with Laurent in a flat and started on a third book, a homosex love story, that I knew would undo the literary success I'd had. But I couldn't stop. Maybe I was still in the grip of the old innocence and was now preparing to create a better world for another minority, with my traditional weapons. Maybe my discovery of Laurent, who had introduced me around, held my hand in public, and taken me to meet Cocteau, was another reason I persevered. But the subject didn't seem so toxic in Paris, a place where every foreigner loses his head at least once. Now, when I go up to Paris for a few days to give a talk or pick up a guest at Charles de Gaulle, the city seems the seediest stage set imaginable. How could anyone fall for those saggy buildings, that stagy light, the false romance of it all? Picturesque is just another word for overpriced. But back then I was still caught in my old dream, my need to recast reality—and it seemed more manageable, more attainable than ever.

I'd never have found Laurent, or that part of myself he presided over, in New York—not in a bar on the Bird Circuit, where everyone, even when lifting a voice in imitation of Carol Channing, was too mistrustful for a shared life. I wouldn't have found him or *A Touch of Strawberries* or the wide, wide world.

You mustn't think the pale, overweight man with whom I share my home now is anything like the old Laurent. He was painting a new kind of light then, something never seen on land or sea, and wasn't afraid, at least not in the ways a foreigner, an American, could easily tell. But of course, you can see only those terrors you have already glimpsed yourself. I knew all about outsiderness, liberal overcompensation, the worm of race—but very little about the pain of belonging and the obligations it imposes. Laurent's family, the Denoyers, had been established in Dijon since before the first barracoon went up on the Slave Coast. He had failed—was failing—them. There was no way he would budge, no way they'd forgive him. And then I came along. It took years before his own doom caught up with him.

In the meantime we were busy. *A Touch of Strawberries* made a terrible stink when it appeared. This was pathology, unforgivable, and I was demoted from spokesman for my race to denizen of a swamp. I had good company there—Tennessee Williams came through Paris regularly, and we invented a drink called Swamp-water Punch: two parts brandy, one part Cointreau, and a jigger of green crème de menthe for the algae. The recipe appeared in the Paris *Trib*.

But there were other, less happy repercussions. Bernard De Voto condemned me in the *Atlantic*, saying I had lost my franchise as a "serious writer." John Fischer devoted his whole column in *Harper's* to my dereliction, pointing out that I had joined the "magnolia and moonlight" crowd he detested. Mary McCarthy, in the *Partisan Review*, opined that my creative powers had declined along with my choice of subject, for which, she confessed, she had always felt "a slight distaste." Polly Laderman wrote me a long, forgiving letter, saying she understood my need. That was probably the worst review of all.

What no one understood—perhaps I didn't see it all that clearly myself—was that I was still trying to shape the world into a pattern made of words. The linguistic fallacy. The book sold poorly, of course, though its reissue last year, twenty years later, was a big success.

Étienne is hovering again, taking orders. Laurent and Hassan will have *civet de lapin*. I'll settle for a *salade niçoise*. Inside, we hear a piano playing. Laurent tells us it's an old Marguerite Long recording, Ravel, and I glimpse, for the thousandth time, the cultural gap that separates us, over which we have thrown bridges of love and habit.

I survived the bad reviews. Things changed in Europe. More heat in the cafés, new uniforms on the gendarmes, the first backpackers from England and Germany. St.-Germain began to look a bit like Sproul Plaza, and my French improved. I made existential jokes in the fashion of the times. "At the end of the world," I would say at a certain point in the evening's drinking, "there are three signs. The first says 'No Parking.' The second says, '*È vietato fumare.*' The third says, '*Au delà de cette limite les billets ne sont plus valables.*' And beyond that everything is blocked off with screens made out of old newspapers." I pretended to an absurdity I didn't always feel; inside gnawed the old conviction—*You can do it, Jelly, you can be the first.* America forever.

We began to look around for a house in the south, perhaps near Hyères, where we had spent a happy fortnight. I liked to think the Mediterranean had something special to offer. The waters laved Europe and Africa, after all. Laurent went along, glad to get out of Paris, out of *le milieu,* away from the galleries and critics, searching for a place where he could polish his vision to the fine transparency he saw when he closed his eyes. And so when the village house in Roquebrune was offered, we closed on it quickly—which in the Alpes-Maritimes means six months. It takes them that long to smile, which means they have outwitted you in the sale.

It was a cold, brilliant March day when we took possession. The front-door key was as big as a crucifix, and the lock wouldn't keep out the neighborhood dogs. But we ran through the rooms hallooing our names, visualizing furniture, visits, parties. It was to be a place where our lives could stop leaking away. I remembered when my mama stamped through the house on Prospect Street, bought with my daddy's first earnings from his garage. "We gonna be happy here," she announced, watching Elvira and me skip around. "We gonna be a family." Well, now Laurent and I were going to be a family. And when we met Hassan in Tangier, on one of our regular visits, and he shrugged for the fiftieth time, fixed us with his implacable eye, and mumbled, *"Pourquoi mentir?"* we knew that he'd be part of our family too. There never was a minute's doubt over Hassan; he took to us both and had a girlfriend in Nice for his evenings out.

And then, to everyone's surprise but my own, my early predictions came true. The ghettos began to stir. The city boys in Detroit, Watts, Chicago, started making trouble. Where Father Divine used to keep the peace by riding around in his white Rolls-Royce and waving his hand, Malcolm and Rap and others acted differently. And of course, there was Selma and Dr. King.

I crossed the ocean several times, to march and sing and sermonize with my people. I began to feel a buried self emerge. I was Jelson Raines, not a credit or a spokesman or a disappointment but a Black Man. The students understood right off. They came to hear and meet me. They'd read my books and didn't disapprove. Coming home to them was like a triumph long delayed. Maybe I'd left America for this, so I could come back and speak. I hadn't been betrayed by aphorism, after all. Wasn't I here, shouting, holding hands, prophesying? Maybe the words had turned into action at last.

When I got home after these expeditions into what Laurent called *la fantasmagorie américaine,* I was fired up for weeks. I was over fifty, I had been everything, but now I was myself. The identities had blended. The words had created me in their image, in balance at last.

Yes, the late sixties and early seventies were my best years. I wasn't writing anymore, just talking—the original gift. They loved me on the talk shows, the phone-ins, the platforms. America, in my absence, had become even more expert-haunted. There was a huge industry dedicated just to filling the blanks in people's heads.

My costumes changed too. I took to loose garments, amulets and charms and beads. You could hear me coming a block away. If I was going to speak like a prophet, I'd look like one. A radio host in Denver called me the black Lawrence of Arabia, Jelly O'Toole. Everybody loved that. From the moment I hit any airport lounge, strobe-lit, cameras at the ready, little herds of newsmen gathered, I was onstage. This was jubilee. I had my prescriptions, my salvations. I was still on the word machine, but it had lifted off the page and was moving through the heavens. I had found the place where all meanings overlap, become supermeaning. Maybe I was stoned or hallucinated, but I imagined I had finally gotten over all of them—the bullies on the playground, the preppies who had patronized me, the hostesses who had put white gloves on me, Polly Laderman and her condescension, even France with its fondness for *les noirs.*

But after a few years, flight and return, flight and return, I realized something had changed. The struggle was going stale. Small improvements had come, but the white guards who kept watch in the towers, guns across their knees, were still there. We had lost the main battle and were settling for bits of this and that. An office job here, a tenured professorship there, a black studies department or a foremanship at General Motors. It came to me one night in a cabaret in San Francisco, where I was introduced after a stand-up comic had done his turn. Adjusting the mike with a practiced hand, looking at the audience for whom I was the big draw, I noticed there was only one couple of my race in the house. It struck me that now I was on *60 Minutes* or the six o'clock news—I was an injustice you could switch channels on. They could go home afterward feeling endangered and virtuous. They had come to the Cutting Edge to hear Jelson Raines beaming in signals from outer space.

I got a little mean that night. The meaner I got, the more they loved me. They traded looks—this was the real shit comin' down. I figured every couple in the place would go home for a far-out, loosened-up fuck. Nothing had changed in America; it never would.

After the show (a standing ovation) I put in a call overseas to Laurent. I told him the American episode was over. This prophet was coming home. As I spoke I sensed checkerboards of shadow and light playing over me, an abstract grid that reminded me of my old cubist fantasies. What was I—black or white, European or American, homo or hetero? I felt borders, edges, alternations. I felt my solids turning to liquids and back again. I had come all this way, to the edge of the continent, to the edge of my life, and I was still split by the old divisions. I had never gathered into one person.

When I got back to France, I found myself alone with my reams of printed matter. There was nothing else left. And that's when the uselessness hit, a uselessness so profound that some days I couldn't get out of bed. I had finally split apart. On one side was the boom box, on the other side was everything else. I just couldn't consolidate. Hassan and Laurent helped, talked, covered for me, predicted recovery. We made a few trips—the Citroën was new then—to

Berlin, Vienna, even took the car across the Straits from Algeciras. Upwards of a year went by, and finally a series of words started piling up like thunderheads. I was back in business, sort of.

Two more novels got written. *When Summer Comes. The Dark Tower.* Neither made any difference. Nobody paid attention. I rehashed New York; I appropriated chunks of Elvira's life to grind into fiction, ignoring her right to privacy. I took an imaginary trip down south and wrote about Reconstruction. Every critic, and most readers, recognized what was missing—I didn't really *need* to write these books. I was no longer consonant with my times; its passions were no longer my own. The fizz was missing.

Lunch is over. We were each served a *ballon,* a salute from Étienne, and Hassan and Laurent are pleased. They have been reassured that I'm okay, the good times are still here. Me, I'm simply tired. I think about perpetual banishment, and whether the existentialists weren't right—the world is always over there, out of sight. The screens of old newspapers are still blocking the view.

There are errands on the way home. Driving around, we see the fall tourists, backpackers from the north, enjoying the crispness, the early wine, the reduced rates. I spot a sad young man drooping in front of our favorite charcuterie. I ask Hassan to stop. He's American, his eyes so pinned it's doubtful he can see me. I give him some money and feel a meretricious glow as I climb back in the car. It was a brief visit to my young, immigrant self. I tell an anecdote about another young man I met in San Francisco once. His name was Brian and he was a Polk Street hustler. I took him to the New York Deli for some soup, and when he heard I was a writer, he asked me to teach him some words. When I hesitated, he said, "Man, you got more than you need, you got *thousands.*" I tell the story in English. I'm not sure they understand, but they laugh anyway.

My thoughts go back to Mrs. Thrill at the café, who had stopped by our table on her way out. "Mr. Raines," she said in a voice as thrilled as her imaginary name, "I just want to tell you . . ." I listened to the compliments, feeling even more fraudulent. The Jelson Raines she was talking about is a construct. I might have met him at certain times, but he has disappeared now, for good.

And then, just before Hassan makes the steep turn to our driveway, his hand moves toward my thigh. The next moment Laurent, in back, pats my shoulder. Maybe they want to reassure me. Maybe it's the need to prove we exist in the flesh. I respond with squeezes. It occurs to me that a partner defines your limits, your emotional range, and I have two of them. My boundaries have always been more complicated.

We've reached home. Hassan, after backing into the shed, steps out of the car, peeling off the racing gloves, a gift from Laurent. His implacable eye rakes me. Hassan, with a single orb, is free of double vision—or is that due to his family, his country, his culture? He is Muslim. He is from Larache. He sleeps with whomever he likes. We are his friends and he depends on us for now. One day he will make a different decision. He doesn't worry about the future.

He smiles when he notices me staring. *"Ça va?"* The all-purpose inquiry. I reassure him, glad that I needn't express my thoughts. As we climb the steps to the house he slips his hand into mine.

After my last book came out, to keep my publisher from dropping me altogether I agreed to go back for a book tour. I made my way finally to East Orange to see my mama, more or less content now with her clubs and church, and also to see Elvira and her brood. In the back of my mind was the thought that I might find something. This was where it had started, after all.

One afternoon, after eating too much, I walked over to the parade ground where the cannonballs from the Union Army lay half buried in the dirt. My feet took me toward them, and in a minute I was slipping and sliding over the rounded tops, laughing and trying to keep my balance, fifty years reversed by the sensations under my soles. The next moment, still poised on the cannonballs, I felt the rebukes of Elvira and Meredith and others coalesce into a wave of heat against my face. I wanted to be white, they said; that was the source of my trouble.

Was it true? Had it been true all along, from the first sizzle of the boom box, from the logorrhea of grade school, from the endless rap that led to my first books? Had I yearned through all that for another skin? Had I broken the backs of words so I could be somebody else?

I can feel a faint heat, an echo of that other wave, stinging me now in the kitchen. Then I hear an old instruction to myself—it comes back as an auditory hallucination. *Use it, baby*. I hadn't paid much attention when I heard it, but now I understand. I've followed that advice without knowing it. I wasn't white or black or queer or straight. I wasn't American or European or African. I was all these things. I had absorbed apartheid and community, had loved women and men, had pitched my tent in two cultures. Yes, I had wanted to be white, but I had also wanted to be black and everything in between. Maybe that was America's greatest gift to me—perpetual oscillation.

I listen to Laurent and Hassan gossip in French. Laurent with flashes of his old brilliance, Hassan of the single aspect, and me, Jelly Raines. They are my boundaries and I am theirs. We understand each other—an entente cordiale.

I stretch out my arms. They glide in and we lock together, a round-robin of grace and approval. We hold it for a moment, then break away. Time to move on.

I head upstairs to where the blank pages, the still-unwritten portions of myself, are waiting. If the words put me on another road, who is to say which road is the real one, which the imaginary? Maybe the two parts blend and overlap in ways too subtle for me to understand. Besides, there was never any other way.

Manhattan Transfer

After Davey died of AIDS, Martin made a wide circle and ended back where he'd started, more or less. It was like a discharge from a cannon that propelled him around the country and then gave out.

In fact, after Davey's death Martin found it impossible to stay put. Everyone advised against leaving New York. After all, he was over fifty and had reached the standoff with the city that is known as adjusting to it. There was also the rent-stabilized apartment he had shared with Davey.

Martin didn't listen. It was no longer possible to live here, that's all. Every movie house, restaurant, grocery, in their neighborhood sent a dagger of pain through him. That Chinese restaurant was the site of their last dining out; that bar was where they'd had their last drink; that deli was where he'd filled Davey's last request, from his hospital bed, for a Virginia ham on rye. The area was saturated with time and death. If he didn't leave he'd carry the space, bent to the shape of their lives, around with him forever.

His friend of many years, Lewis Meecham, who dated back to undergraduate days at Cornell, was especially dire in his predictions. "You're just going on a geographical, Martin. Why can't you see it?"

Well, he did see it, and Lewis might be right—most of those AA people were wise in the ways of crisis—but that couldn't stop him either. His bond with Davey wasn't like the connections Lewis made, with his mini-affairs, his casual encounters, his faith that someone equally nice was waiting around the corner. Davey and he had been glued together. There had been a permeable membrane between them, a screen so porous that it transmitted every nuance of feeling—love and irritation, selfishness and anger, jealousy and self-sacrifice. No one else understood this kind of merger, or if they did, they disapproved strongly. Warnings were issued about fusing, codependency, lack of self-esteem. These remarks didn't interest Martin either—then or now. He had to get away, and that was that.

He put his furniture in storage and took the bus to Florida. He had heard good things about Orlando, also about North Miami, but when he got there these places didn't appeal to him. Too suburban or too hot or filled with alien people. He headed west to California, moving up the coast until he reached the Bay Area. This was every faggot's second home, after all. He decided on Potrero Hill, renting a small apartment with a view of the bay, and sent for his furniture. He found a job proofreading at a law firm, which paid amazingly well if he worked from midnight to eight A.M. He also joined a grief group, a hospital volunteer group, and Sexaholics Anonymous. He'd been filling his spare time with cautious but compulsive sex, and he figured the combination of his job, with its graveyard hours, and these three programs would keep him out of trouble. They would also keep him from obsessing about Davey.

It didn't work out that way. He'd never been really good at making new friends—he used to tell Davey it took five years to cement a friendship—and now it was even harder. Without Davey he was an incomplete social unit. He recalled his mother's complaints about having to invite widows and divorcées to her dinners and bridge parties. "They're always a problem, don't you see, because they're an odd number." That was hardly applicable to the Castro scene in San Francisco, but the stricture echoed in Martin's mind. Without Davey he was an odd number.

At first he liked the grief group, which met once a week at an elementary school on Dolores, in a room filled with tiny desks, fuzzy animals, and large painted cubes. They sat on folding chairs, ten or twelve dazzling men in their twenties and thirties—he was usually the oldest—who spoke about their ordeals with a good humor that occasionally vanished, like a theater scrim when the lighting changes, to reveal landscapes of devastation and despair. Martin told his story several times, explaining how he had come out here to start over and was feeling better now. This wasn't strictly true, but it seemed to be the prevailing ideology, endorsed by the different group leaders, who nodded and smiled whenever he said he was definitely getting his life together. But when the group broke up each Thursday, and the men went down the steps of the school chatting about everyday things, Martin felt betrayed. He hadn't told them how he really felt, hadn't confronted the real emptiness in his life. He began to dislike the group and San Francisco itself. He began to see it as a stage set rather than a place to live his life. He also knew this was his own fault—there was nothing really wrong with San Francisco.

He stuck it out for a full year, heeding the advice that came his way about time and roots. But the truth appeared, sharp and clear, well before the year was up—he wasn't going to make it without Davey here either. It wasn't New York that was intolerable, it was life without his friend. He might as well go back—he realized, with a feeling of defeat, that New York was still home. He waited a few more months, and then one night Lewis Meecham called. They talked every few weeks, but this time Lewis's voice was different.

"How you doing?"

"About the usual," Martin replied. "Hanging on."

"Well, last time we talked, you mentioned coming back to New York. You still thinking about that?"

Martin blinked, concentrating. Lewis wanted something. It was his hidden-agenda voice. "Why?"

"Well, Hilary and her girlfriend are moving out. Before I start looking for someone else to share the space, I thought I'd ask you."

Martin's palms started to sweat and his heart rate speeded up. "You mean live in the loft?"

"Well, I think we could get along. It's not as if we haven't lived together before."

The answer was spoken before he even had time to think. "Save it for me—I'll be there as soon as I can."

After hanging up he was swept with exhilaration. His geographical, which was a form of penance, was over. He could go back where he belonged. But best of all—it was a thought that rang jubilantly in his head for hours—he would be living with Lewis. Lewis, his oldest friend, whom he loved in a way.

They'd made friends at Cornell, headed for New York together, taken a converted cold-water flat in Yorkville for a while, kept in touch through all the jobs and phases and moves and traumas. They'd gone to shrinks at the same time, lost their parents over the years, helped each other through career upheavals and returns for graduate degrees, shared victories and craziness and trouble. Lewis had gotten his Ph.D. at the Yale School of Drama and now taught at Rutgers, while Martin had vaguely set his mind on a Ph.D. in English but had dropped away and been stuck in editing jobs, or worse, all his life. Lewis was brilliant, an expert on Romantic drama, Schiller and Hugo and Goethe, his lectures bound into books, copies of which he always gave to Martin with a smile that was truly modest. But Lewis also had a darker side, a nighttime self, and a few lost years before he wound up in AA and at Rutgers. And he had never had the domestic stability that Martin did.

Looking back over the years as he began to make plans to move, Martin thought that he and Lewis took turns at prosperity. When one was up the other was down. Right now Lewis was at the top of his cycle—not only the owner of a large loft in Tribeca but tenured at Rutgers and contributing articles to important periodicals. Last fall, Lewis told him over the phone, he'd appeared on a local cable show to discuss a revival of *La vida es sueño*—not his period, but he had lots to say. By contrast, Martin was definitely in a downswing. Briefly he wondered if their lives would continue cycling or re-cycling right up to the end. On the other hand, things might continue as now—Lewis ascending to more satisfaction and success, he himself . . . He didn't finish that thought. It didn't do justice to their long friendship, their concern for each other. For the first time since Davey's death, Martin felt a surge of optimism. Everything was going to be all right. He was going to snap out of it. Lewis would help him. That was why he had called, after all.

Martin found the loft rather different from a year ago. He followed Lewis around, making noises of pleasure and surprise at the new washer/dryer, the new pot-and-pan rack, the upright piano, the glassed-in greenhouse (formerly part of an elevator shaft), the new furnishings in the living area. "I thought you could sleep in here." Lewis pulled back some drapes that curtained off a little niche next to the living area. Unfortunately, he said, he'd run out of money before he could redo this roomette, which would one day include a permanent, soundproof partition. "But," he went on, "this is just for sleeping in. I want you to use the whole loft, including my bedroom across the way. We'll just flow depending on what we're doing."

Martin poked his head into the cubicle. It was interior, without light, and contained a rollaway bed, a standing lamp, a peeling bureau, and a rack on wheels for his clothes. He didn't like the look of it. He wouldn't have any privacy right next to the living area, and there wasn't an ounce of coziness. Still, he might go to the warehouse where he'd stored his stuff for the second time and fetch some pictures and decorative objects. He might even put up some shelves.

"This is strictly temporary," Lewis continued. "I'm really going to fix it up. Your rent will go into that."

Martin expressed the desire to add some of his own gewgaws, to which Lewis agreed instantly. "I know you like to be cozy," he said.

Martin smiled, warmed at the thought. Lewis really wanted to integrate him into these quarters. He'd had a strong sense of homecoming from the moment he arrived this morning, after the midnight flight from the Coast, two suitcases in tow. He was in a place he belonged, with someone who had known him for years and years. The little bedroom cubicle didn't matter, nor the absence of decent furniture. The main thing was that he was here. "This'll be fine," he said, giving the wheeled clothes rack a push. Why hadn't Lewis built in a closet when he was redoing the loft? "I'm not fussy."

Lewis let out a whoop. "You're not fussy? Tell me another one."

"Well, I intend to get over it."

He meant it too. It was time to overcome his obsessiveness about comfort, homemaking. What was it but the desire to control? He knew the cause—they had moved every few years when he was a kid. The petroleum company his father worked for had transferred him all over the middle states—Ohio, Kentucky, Pennsylvania, Tennessee. Each uprooting had been harder than the one before.

"Well, dear, don't make any promises you can't keep."

After Lewis went off to the kitchen, which was an extension of the living area, Martin began to unpack. New York, on the bus ride from the airport, had looked marvelously welcoming, like an old friend—like Lewis, in fact. The cabbie, on the ride from Forty-second Street, had been a handsome young Romanian who, Martin sensed, would not have been averse to accepting a phone number or a business card. The streets, the air, the buildings old and new, were full of promise. This was where his life had been lived and would be lived again.

When Lewis called that lunch was ready, Martin stopped unpacking. Sitting down at the table that acted as a divider between kitchen and living areas, he gave his old friend a special smile. It was the kind of smile he used to signal total trust. In fact, as he watched Lewis dish out the stir-fried chicken, cashews, and broccoli, he had a momentary sense that he was drifting back, warping through time, to some old, safe childhood place.

"If this is too salty, let me know. I usually go heavy on the soy sauce."

"Tastes just fine."

"We might as well adjust to each other's tastes. I know you can't tolerate fats."

More happiness. Martin's mother, and then Davey, used to cater to his whims and tastes. Hepatitis and bouts of amebiasis had damaged his liver; it was nice that Lewis remembered. Martin glanced at him. Lewis was graying, chunky, but still handsome. He had been a great beauty in his youth and people were still drawn to him, though that might be due to his remarkable charm. Put Lewis in a room with anyone, Martin thought, anyone at all, and within ten minutes they'll adore him.

After a while Lewis began to tell him about Drew. Martin knew about Drew from their transcontinental phone conversations. Lewis had met him a few months ago. Drew was around thirty and worked for a genetic engineering lab in Pearl River. Believe it or not, he had recognized Lewis from that talk show on Lope de Vega and approached him in the lobby of the Cocteau Rep. One thing had led to another. Now he came in almost every weekend.

Martin listened with mixed feelings. Another resident was rather an inconvenience. It might create tension. Still, he'd gone through many of these affairettes with Lewis over the years. They were intense but not long-lasting. Lewis's work—his lectures, play productions, writing—tended to separate him from the trick of the moment. They always parted friends—no one ever seemed to blame Lewis for breaking things off—but he had never made a total commitment to a shared life, as Martin had done. He said a live-in lover was like an extra job. Too much work. Not that he was to be blamed for this. It was simply a choice.

After Lewis finished, Martin nodded. "I'm sure we'll get along just fine. I'll be running around on weekends anyway."

Lewis heaved up from the table. Lunch was over.

After stacking the dishes in the dishwasher, Martin finished unpacking, then lay down for a nap. The bed had a disconcerting way of rolling whenever he turned, but he managed to fall asleep anyway.

When he woke up, Lewis was gone. Martin wandered around the loft, noting little things, absorbing himself into the space and vice versa. It was wonderfully quiet here—so quiet you could hear a Chinese menu being slipped under the door. Walking around and looking helped his spirits even more. He began to feel proprietary, to fill up the space with his own future activities, to imagine dinner parties they would give. Sometimes, when he and Davey had given a dinner that went especially well, he had had the sense that the group and the apartment were unmooring themselves from the city. He would imagine that the table and chairs were levitating, carrying them all to a new existence, freer and more intense. That would happen again here in the loft with Lewis, he was sure.

Drew Kuhnwalt arrived the following Friday evening. Martin noted that Lewis was knocking himself out in the kitchen. None of his stir-fried shit tonight. They were going to have oxtail soup with gnocchi, angel-hair pasta with clams, pimentos, and pine nuts, and a chocolate torte purchased at Lanciani's. Plus a couple of packages of cheese puffs ready to pop into the oven, for appetizers. Martin felt a treacherous spurt of jealousy, then pushed himself beyond it. Why not, after all? A young boyfriend coming to spend the weekend, Lewis's mothering instincts on tap, the desire to make his own meeting with Drew something special. The more he thought about it, the more touched he was. All this work in the kitchen was another sign of Lewis's welcome.

He himself had had a good week. He'd made contact with his old friends, friends he and Davey had shared, who were delighted he was back. And by a stroke of good fortune, he had been restored to his old job. The managing editor who had replaced him at the Tannenbaum Group hadn't worked out. Ted Tannenbaum, the publisher, gave him a big hug, ordered some herbal tea, and set before him an individual dish of trail mix. Things were still touch and go at all three mags—*The Hiker's Journal, White Water,*

Climbing for Fun—which meant he couldn't offer Martin more than his old salary. Martin was so glad to be back in familiar surroundings, to be treated as family by Ted and the others, that he didn't mind. He told Ted about his proofreading on the lobster shift in San Francisco. "When did you live your life?" Ted asked. Martin smiled ruefully. "I didn't—that's why I came back." Ted knew all about him and Davey.

Now, waiting for Drew to turn up, Martin reflected that his life was more or less in place again. He'd changed the things he could in the loft—dusting, tidying up—and accepted the things he couldn't. That meant adjusting to Lewis's ongoing messiness, to the rollaway bed, to the click of mice feet after dark.

"Can I do anything?" he hollered into the kitchen—that was another thing, you were always hollering here.

"Everything's under control," came the reply.

Drew turned out to be tall and blond, with a dropped chin like Fred Astaire's and a tight, sinewy build. He was wearing shorts, since it was September and still warm, and Martin noted bulging calves covered with curling blondish hairs. He swallowed once or twice—Drew was really sexy—then turned that off.

He wasn't surprised Drew felt at home—Lewis had the knack of making everyone feel at home—but he registered a dash of annoyance when Drew, after depositing his backpack in Lewis's bedroom, walked into his own little cubicle. He hadn't been invited in, but there he was, holding back the curtain, which didn't reach the floor, inspecting Martin's things.

"That your friend?" Drew motioned toward a photo of Davey.

"Yeah." His voice was sour—he couldn't help it.

"Nice-looking."

Martin cleared his throat. "He was very attractive."

Drew dropped the curtain and came back. He might have said lots of things, Martin thought, but there was no obligation. He'd no doubt heard the whole story from Lewis, knew dozens of situations like this, and figured words were superfluous. Still— poisonous thought—another person might have made some con-

ventional remark. Maybe they weren't going to get along all that
well.

Drew sat down, slinging one long, perfect leg over the arm of
the chair. Martin found himself staring at his crotch until he averted
his eyes. "I invited the Tissots to stop by tomorrow," Drew called
into the kitchen. "They said they were going to be in the city."

"That's fine," Lewis said, coming in with a plate of the cheese
puffs, now warm and delicious-looking. He put them on the little
table in front of Drew.

Drew turned to Martin. "I work with Brett Tissot—they know
all about me and Lewis. They think it's a hoot. Me and this lover
with a huge loft in Manhattan." He lowered his voice. "I didn't
tell them how old Lewis is."

"I heard that." Lewis, on his way back to the stove, turned
around. "You can tell them I'm your grandfather."

Drew burst into laughter. It was obviously a joke between them.
Martin glimpsed an easiness, a bond, that was greater than he'd
imagined. Drew was now gazing at Lewis with something like
adoration. He'd eaten two of the cheese puffs.

Suddenly, out of nowhere, Martin recalled his mother's cousin
Josephine. Josephine, who had never married, used to visit them
on Sundays in Cleveland. She was incredibly boring, telling long
stories about her awful boss, her girlfriends at the office, her vacation trips to a dude ranch. They were all warned to be nice to
Josephine, but it was impossible to be nice or nasty or anything at
all. They invariably forgot she was there. It was as if she had no
history, the material that would clot up in her veins, give her density
and importance. Now, watching Drew demolish the cheese puffs
without passing the plate, hearing him banter with Lewis, seeing
him stride to the kitchen for a drink refill, Martin couldn't help
wondering if he was simply invisible to the young man. If his veins
had failed to clot up with the substances that would make him
important.

When Drew returned with his fresh drink, Martin forced himself
to try again. He didn't understand about genetic engineering and

began to ask polite questions. Drew answered with more than politeness. He liked to talk about his work. He discussed falsifying data, sharing projects with other researchers, grant hassles, and his theories on why so many of the genetic experiments with the AIDS virus had failed. Martin found all this quite interesting, and it filled up the time before supper. After a while Lewis joined them.

The rest of the evening was not really enjoyable. Once Martin stopped asking leading questions, Drew lost interest in him. Several times Martin recalled Josephine. When a Woody Allen movie was mentioned at dinner—one Martin had seen in San Francisco—he chimed in with an opinion. As soon as Martin finished, Drew swung into another subject. For a dizzy moment Martin decided that Drew resented his presence. The next instant his mind cleared. That was ridiculous. There was plenty of room for both. But a doubt lingered. Was his own connection to Lewis, which was really a lifetime of good talk, less valuable than several months with a new lover? He recalled a Sartre remark to the effect that you can only share your deepest thoughts with someone you've shared your body with. Was it possible that, despite their three decades of friendship, their shared confidences and mutual support, he knew Lewis less well than Drew did? That there was a loving, surrendering, puppy side of Lewis he would never know because it only revealed itself in the sack? That Lewis's famous charm and good humor and erudite conversation were only the tip of the iceberg?

These thoughts made him so uneasy he hardly spoke for the rest of the meal.

When dinner was over and he had cleaned up alone, he headed for his cubicle. He meant it to be a sign—he was going to read and wanted some quiet. Drew and Lewis, after all, could retire across the central partition to the other bedroom.

But Drew had brought some cassettes with him, and the VCR was in the living area. Martin listened to the clicks and squeaks as the tape went in, then the gutturals of a German film. *Das Boot,* Lewis called, didn't he want to see it? No thanks. He gritted his teeth and read on. Impossible—the damned machine was just outside his bedroom. At last, seething, he got up and went into the living area. Drew and Lewis were cuddled together on the sofa. They weren't paying the slightest attention to the movie. Lewis had taken off his glasses, and from time to time Drew kissed him on the cheek and neck.

Martin sat stiffly, watching the film. It wasn't hard to follow but it was of absolutely no interest. His glance kept straying to the sofa. Why the fuck didn't they go into the other room?

At last, when the film ended with the submarine being blown up in a Mediterranean harbor, Lewis sat forward, found his glasses, and looked at Martin. "I hope we didn't keep you from whatever you were doing."

Martin glared at him. "How could you possibly keep me from that when you run a tape right outside my bedroom?"

Drew glanced at him nervously, but Martin saw, or thought he saw, a glint of satisfaction in his eyes. "Sorry about that," he said.

"It seems to me that the VCR could easily be moved to the other side of the loft."

"Well, there might be a problem with the cable line." Lewis got up, rather slowly, and lifted several lengths of cable. "I hadn't really thought about it. There might be enough extra."

"I think it would be an excellent idea." Martin knew he sounded petulant but he couldn't help it. He had just had another flash on Josephine. Whenever Josephine asked for quiet so she could read the Sunday paper, nobody had paid the slightest attention. Still feeling petulant and put out, he crossed the few feet to his sleeping area. He didn't say good night.

When Martin stumbled up for his two A.M. pee, he found the bathroom door closed. This had happened before—his bladder and Lewis's seemed to be on the same timetable—and he called out. Drew answered. A second later the door opened. Drew was nude. He looked at Martin, then stepped back to the toilet. Martin was now completely awake.

Drew gave off a golden glow. "Come on in," he said. He half turned toward Martin, who noticed that Drew was semihard. "You wanta see it?" Drew started pumping himself. He stared at Martin while he fibrillated his hand. His face was full of sly mischief.

Martin went into something like shock. At last he managed to say, "I'll wait," and backed off.

He lay in his cubicle, his heart whamming, until he heard the toilet flush and Drew's footsteps fade away. When everything was quiet, he got up and relieved himself. He had a lot of trouble getting back to sleep. Everything in the loft had changed slightly—moved or slipped downhill. He was embarrassed and excited. He also felt they had betrayed Lewis in some way. It was almost an hour before he finally slept. ·

The next morning Drew was cheerful and chatty. There wasn't a trace of embarrassment or remorse. Martin poured himself coffee, which Drew had made, and muttered answers. He was really feeling rotten. He hadn't slept soundly, and his face was tight with fatigue. He also figured he looked his age, which was always a depressing thought. Drew, on the other hand, looked brighter than ever. Almost radiant. He was wearing even shorter shorts this morning. Martin kept his eyes averted; he didn't want to be reminded of last night. Again he had the impression that everything in the loft had shifted slightly.

As Drew continued talking, Martin turned his mind away. Then he recalled a remark made by the leader of his grief group in San Francisco, a gritty, hard-talking black man who had clearly overcome a lot before getting there. One evening he'd listened to Martin talk about Davey, then had interrupted him in a harsh way. "You talk about your friend but you've still got yourself, am I right? You have still got *you*." Martin had nodded, going along with the verdict, realizing yet again that he couldn't be understood in this group or any group. The whole point was that he no longer had himself. It was his connection to Davey Frohmann that had given him his identity, the self this man was talking about. He had many theories as to why this should be so, but none of them really mattered. He and Davey had elevated each other into existence, and that was that. Whether it was the result of early imprinting or some chemical imbalance or romanticism or separation anxiety didn't matter. He wasn't quite whole without his friend; he was like one of those hermaphroditic souls in Plato, requiring a mate to be complete. He'd found a partner and lost him, and there was no cure in sight.

Lewis appeared, looking rumpled but serene. He'd slept like a log, he said. Martin glanced at Drew when he said this, but Drew's face was smooth, his manner calm. That little scene in the bathroom might never have happened. Martin knew he should forget about it, but he also knew he couldn't. He could use it in a dozen ways to crowd Drew out. Not that he would, of course—it was unattractive even to consider the possibility—but there it was. And then another thought struck him. Maybe Drew had set up the scene in order to crowd *him* out.

Now, watching Lewis putter around the kitchen, Martin found the loft, all two thousand square feet of it, impossibly small. Lewis and Drew would occupy it all day. He would be quarantined in his cubicle, or he'd have to spend the day on the couch, saying things he didn't mean. He had a view of a new kind of Saturday. In the old days, with Davey, it had been a precious time, a chance for renewal after the obligations of the week. But this Saturday wasn't like that. It didn't even belong to him; it belonged to Lewis and Drew, who were just letting him watch.

He observed Drew pour himself more coffee. Was it possible the guy was some kind of fraud, using the loft for a crash pad while he whored around? Was he just playing on Lewis's vanity and neediness? Then a more exciting thought hit him. There was the faint chance that Drew found him, Martin, attractive and had grabbed the opening: he really wanted to get it on with him. Taking a good look at Drew's figure, his splendid legs and cocked ass, Martin found his pulse speeding up. Maybe he'd missed an opportunity. The next minute he dismissed the idea. What nonsense. Either Drew was trying to make trouble or he had no loyalty at all. Both ways spelled trouble.

When Martin announced he was leaving a little early for his lunch date with Helena Bundy, they hardly looked up.

He was more than an hour early, but he'd kill time walking around. Even on Saturday morning at eleven o'clock the Village was alive with cruising men. A line from a Doric Wilson play came to him: "You people are indefatigable." That was before the epidemic, and they were still indefatigable. The men who passed checked him out with a sliding glance that betrayed nothing. He walked down to the river and back, vaguely aware that one or two glances had rested on him significantly. But what was the point? Everyone in California, in the groups and bars, had advised him that a new lover was what he needed. The advice never quite reached him; it just dangled in the air in front of him. A new partner was out of the question. Not only would it be impossible to find a replacement for Davey, but even if he did, what about the risk of losing him again? How would he survive that?

Helena was looking madly chic when she walked into the Minetta Tavern. She was tall, ruddy, with flaming red hair and generous features—a little on the horsey side but handsome. She ran a small press, Dionysos Books, mostly as a tax dodge.

After she described her latest troubles with the IRS, Helena turned her green eyes on him. "I told you not to go to California, but you wouldn't listen. Some people are like wines—they don't travel well."

Martin thought of telling her about the moves of his childhood, the constant uprooting which had destroyed the fragile webbing of his social life at two-year intervals, but checked himself. They were both too old for that kind of psychological fix. "It seemed like a good idea at the time." They looked at each other and smiled.

"So do a lot of things. That's no reason to do them."

"Well." He shrugged. "Here I am anyway."

"How are you getting along at this loft?"

"Lousy. I don't have a real bedroom, just a curtained-off cubicle. Sort of like a bathhouse I went to in London once."

"You need your own place. This is just a stopover. A caravanserai."

He began to talk about Lewis, about how long they'd known each other, the depth of their friendship. "I was hoping," he finished, "this would be a new home in Manhattan."

Helena shook her head. "What are those birds that build homes in other birds' nests?"

"Cuckoos."

"Well, it never works. It's a question of power. You give up power when you move into someone else's house. It's what happens to babies and aged parents, and you aren't either one."

Martin stared at her, denial forming on his lips. It was different with Lewis. They'd lived together before. There was no power imbalance. Sure, they'd had their ups and downs, their cycling and re-cycling, but there was a bond, a deep and unbreakable bond.

"Just keep your mind open," Helena said, motioning for the waiter, "and remember what happened to King Lear after he moved in with Goneril and Regan."

After lunch they went gallery-hopping in SoHo. They didn't talk about Martin's domestic problems anymore, which was a relief. He was sick of the subject. The afternoon became more fun as it went on. At certain times, when he was especially carefree, he felt that Davey was with them—going into the exhibits, making snide comments on the artwork. He mentioned this to Helena, who seemed pleased with the idea. "He liked anything as long as the colors were bright," she replied.

Martin had to laugh. Davey had been like a kid with a finger-painting set. He loved sharp, smeared colors. Then it came to him that as long as he had people to remember Davey, to talk about him, he wasn't gone. He could be brought back alive, shimmering in his tastes and prejudices and fancies. Maybe that was what he'd missed most in California—people to talk about Davey with.

He took Helena's hand and squeezed it. "What a great afternoon it's been."

She gave him a quick look of affection. For an instant he felt magically linked to her. The next moment they untangled their hands and he sensed the river of air separating them. But in that instant they had released their love for Davey, launched it into the air of West Broadway, and he was content.

When Martin unlocked the front door of the loft, he heard voices in the living area. He felt a wash of irritation—he'd forgotten about the visitors from Pearl River—then assumed a frozen mask and walked in. Drew and Lewis were on the couch. Opposite were Thea and Brett—Drew's friends. Thea was blond, slightly overweight, a full-blown rose with a kind, open face. Brett was tall and square with a ginger beard flecked with gray.

Lewis, helpful as usual, remarked that Martin had just returned from the Coast. It turned out that Thea had gone to Berkeley and stayed on after graduation. Martin, aware that her face was shining on him like a spotlight, didn't really want to talk about Berkeley right now. He didn't want to chat about tubbing or Telegraph Avenue or Chez Panisse. He wanted to think about his lunch and about Davey. Above all, he didn't want to deal with Drew, who, thank goodness, was wearing long pants.

But Thea started talking about a friend who had died of AIDS. Obviously she'd been primed. Martin listened. When she paused, he didn't fill the gap.

Her kind blue eyes remained on him, and he found his resistance increasing. She wanted him to make an effort, help the party along. But what could he tell her, despite her California openness, her eyes like the sky over East Bay, her tie-dyed skirt and scarf? Could he tell her that he still missed Davey every day, that he'd made a mistake in taking up residence here, that her friend Drew was waving his dick at him in the john after midnight? What could she make of all that? He flashed back to his experiences in California. They were the kindest people in the world and they forgot you instantly.

He looked at Drew, who was bantering with Brett. His irritation thickened into anger. Drew had usurped his place in this house.

Had made him feel unwanted, a Josephine. Maybe he was just doing what attractive young men always did—grabbing off as much attention and power as possible. It was up to him to fight back. But Lewis—who was sitting quietly in rumpled dignity, as if he had invented them all—Lewis had aided and abetted Drew. Had lured Martin back from California and now that he was on the premises, trapped in that hateful cubicle, had switched sides. Or maintained neutrality, which amounted to the same thing.

"It's a name out of mythology. I had a Greek boyfriend and he called me that."

The conversation had changed without his noticing. Thea was telling Lewis about her name. Her real name, she said, was Betty Jean, which she hated.

Martin felt Drew's eyes on him. He turned his head slightly. Yes, Drew was smiling at him, a golden smile. Martin looked away, then back. His resistance melted. Drew was a magnet hung in the air. Every square inch attracted him.

They continued to stare at each other. Drew's smile was fixed, his eyes level. He's inviting me to meet him tonight, Martin thought. He became so confused he lowered his eyes. Had a signal been sent? Impossible. The notion was obscene. The next instant he noticed that Lewis was observing him. He'd been alerted to something. Had Drew told Lewis about the scene in the bathroom? Had Lewis found it amusing because it confirmed his views of fidelity, of human nature? Had he seen something in it that Martin could scarcely imagine? For one disorienting moment he imagined that Lewis had sent Drew to the bathroom to meet him.

Martin stood up and went to the kitchen. His head hurt. He didn't like living this way. He wanted—it came to him in a burst of light—he wanted home to be a changeless place. He and Davey had made it a structure to withstand sieges, temptations, ambiguities. Their home had protected them against the chaos and disorder of New York. And now there were two homes bumping around in his head—the one he lived in and the one he had lost. He was stuck somewhere between the two.

He made his way back from the kitchen slowly, holding a glass of apple juice like a shield. The conversation had shifted to dinner plans. Ethiopian food was suggested. Drew looked at him during the discussion. Martin felt a tingle in his groin, and his throat went dry. The downhill slide to the loft which he had noticed last night returned. He said he was too tired to join them for dinner.

After they left, he went to his cubicle and lay down. He was exhausted. Yes, he hated change and now it was unavoidable again. He'd have to leave. This place was finished. He closed his eyes, reaching for an image of Davey, but Davey was nowhere to be found. And then he understood that he'd been wrong about Lewis. Lewis was his friend, but friendship was a conditional relationship, a contract full of escape clauses and provisos and stipulations.

A shudder ran through him, a shudder that combined self-pity and self-hatred, and he understood that he had come back here looking for love—not companionship or shared history or good talk but love. He'd expected too much from Lewis, expected him to replace Davey. He had failed to see the limits of their bond, the limits of all friendships. It wasn't Lewis's fault, it was his own. He had distorted things out of his private need.

And then, opening his eyes, he looked around the little bedroom. He hated everything in it—the drapes that didn't reach the floor, the bed that walked, the clothes that didn't have a closet, the peeling bureau, the ratty lamp. He had put up with all of it in hopes of being given something more important, but now he knew that nothing more important would come his way. He would always have to compete for Lewis's attention. If it wasn't Drew it would be someone else. He closed his eyes quickly. If he wasn't careful they would seep, and he hated feeling sorry for himself.

A couple of hours later he was awakened by Lewis and Drew coming in. Even though their voices were low and they kept to the other side of the loft, he stayed awake. He had to make sure of one last thing.

Around midnight he heard Lewis go down the hall to the bathroom, his heavy tread unmistakable. After that, Martin dozed.

When footsteps sounded again—soft and pattering this time—he checked his digital clock. It was 2:23. He heard Drew clear his throat.

He lay in bed fighting his lust, quieting his body, which was ready to be strummed like a guitar, until 2:43. Then he heard the footsteps return and fade away. At once he masturbated silently and furiously, aware that this particular orgasm, for all its delirium, marked a return of control. It was time to create his own life, for better or worse. Nothing else could do it for him—not travel or grief groups or reminiscences of Davey or childish dreams of love.

In the morning he hardly looked at Drew. He spent the hours before noon circling apartment ads in the *Times*. Then, still saying little, he went out to see what he could find.

When he told Lewis, a few days later, that he had found another place to live, Lewis didn't seem perturbed, but that was his way. He merely remarked, "I knew you wouldn't stick around very long, Martin. This place was never cozy enough for you."

Martin didn't bother to reply. Maybe they would discuss the whole thing in a few months, maybe even make amusing, insightful comments about the limitations of friendship and the charming treacheries of young lovers, but not now. Not yet.

Country People

I had misgivings the minute I walked in. The classroom was too small, the desks were for kids, and the blackboard was on rollers. When the first students turned up, my worries increased. I knew that adult education courses tend to attract the odd and the lonely, but this bunch looked more displaced than most. Taking the enrollment slip from a large, sad woman in her midforties, I wondered if my job was just to keep them occupied till they found what they were missing.

The woman's name was Emilia Quinn. She was wrapped in yards of yellow fabric like a sari. Her dark hair was in a tangle, but her eyes were beautiful. She gave me a wounded smile and took a seat by the window.

It had started with Ray Stonington last month, August. Ray had been in one of his mild, helpful moods, which should have warned me. We were sitting in his dining room, the candles illuminating the pine table, the Dutch corner cabinet, the spinning wheel in the corner. The dinner had been superb, as elegant as this eighteenth-century tavern in the Hudson Valley which Ray had converted to a residence.

He had spoken too casually: "They're looking for someone to

teach a night course in literature for adults." Ray named the college, one of those two-year affairs that Governor Rockefeller had sown around the state—an institution without the distinction of Vassar or the sectarian rigor of Marist or the blue-jeans cheerfulness of Bard. "Why don't you ring up the dean? He's a friend of mine."

I shook my head. I was through with all that. Twenty years in the New York City public-school system was enough. "Why do you think I moved up here?"

"This won't be anything like New York, Michael. One night a week, no knives, no drugs, sweet country people." I looked skeptical, and he continued. "It'll help with the shop."

Ray was manipulating me, but I fell for it. Since retiring from teaching, I had been living out a lifelong fantasy—running an antique store. The hardest part of selling antiques is finding the damned things. Suddenly I could imagine the students inviting me over to look at Grandpa's sea chest, at Great-aunt Laetitia's sewing dummy. I gave a reckless laugh.

"The only course I'd consider teaching would be a gay-lit course. That's what I couldn't do in the city."

Ray had given me another mild look and changed the subject.

A young man with fluffy sideburns under a blue Civil War cap handed me the class chit. The rest of his outfit was also vaguely military, though I spotted the edge of a beaded vest. He looked at me with wide brown eyes, unsmiling. *This* country person didn't look so sweet, though he gave off a sexy glow. His name was Cornelius Graef.

Yes, I'd proposed the course as a lark, an after-dinner joke, but a few days later Ray had called back. "I talked to John Sterling at school. Would you write up a proposal for a gay-lit course? He'd like to get it approved—on a non-credit basis."

I hung up the phone quite stunned. I'd meant it when I said I wanted to get away from all that—not only from teaching but from the old preoccupations. Too much despair, too many deaths. Besides, a new literature was being born, post-AIDS, coming from the generation after me. Did I really have anything to say about it?

Daniel Boone was standing in front of me. Where did these people get their clothes? Maybe I should expand the antique-clothing department in my shop. ("Care to see something in a designer deerslayer, sir?")

Daniel Boone's name was Nicolas Hillebrant. He was seriously handsome, powerfully built. "Question, sir." Greenish eyes played over me, calmly judging.

"Have a seat, Nicolas, we'll have questions later."

He didn't stir. He was beyond taking orders from teachers. "I have no money for books. I hope they won't be required."

"We'll discuss that in a few minutes, if you don't mind."

Nicolas turned at last, looking disgusted, and sat down next to Cornelius. They were friends apparently. I felt an old vulnerability stab at me—if I wasn't careful I'd give them too much attention, work for their approval, even flirt with them. My palms started to sweat. There were unexpected pitfalls in teaching a gay class.

The rest of the students straggled in. There were two more women—Millie Herkimer and Teage Dane—looking butch and paired, in short hair, work shirts, slacks. There was Israel Solomon, an elderly man with a pouter-pigeon figure and clouds of cottony hair. He took the front seat eagerly—a red-hot, as we used to say in grad school. The remaining two—William Astbury and Bradford Gower—were pale youths, no more than twenty, both afflicted with shyness. They slunk, more or less, to the back seats.

I waited for more latecomers. Eight pairs of eyes studied me. Not friendly, not unfriendly, just waiting. Maybe the sweetness would come later, I thought.

I began the introduction as planned. Michael Littman, formerly of New York, now of Livingston. Please call me Michael. I had never given a course like this. I owned the Den of Antiquity on Route 22. We would explore together. I would need their help. We would be reading and discussing selections from several thousand years of gay and lesbian literature.

I paused for questions. Nicolas Hillebrant spoke up. "I have no money to buy books, Michael. Neither does he." He jerked his head at Cornelius. A few others murmured in agreement.

"I'll either circulate my own books, borrow extra copies, or make Xeroxes. You won't have to buy anything."

A little relaxation—legs spread forward, sighs released, glances exchanged. It had been a problem for everyone. "Let's talk about the material," I began. "Also what periods interest you—classical, medieval, nineteenth-century, modern." I paused. "I'd like to make the course as democratic as possible."

Cornelius Graef spoke up. "Did any of them write about war, comrades-in-war, that stuff?"

I mentioned Whitman and the Civil War diaries, *Billy Budd*, then worked back to *Amis and Amile* and the Theban Band. Cornelius's face lit up. "You're gonna give us all them?" He smiled at Nicolas. *They're lovers,* I thought.

Millie Herkimer, the older of the two butch women, asked if there were stories about women living in the countryside. At first I could think only of May Sarton, then recalled *Patience and Sarah*. I sketched the tale, and her eyes glittered.

Gradually everyone spoke up. Their interests varied. The Bible, Oscar Wilde, Sappho, South Sea natives. The women liked poetry; the men wanted true stories. Only Israel Solomon was interested in political essays.

At last, when we had more or less settled on the shape of the course, which would meet once a week for twelve weeks, I asked them why they had signed up. Their reasons tended to be vague. Indeed, many of their comments were bewildering.

"People around here won't talk." Emilia Quinn shifted her bulk in the ridiculous child's seat. "Pretend they didn't hear you and clam up if they do."

William Astbury in the back spoke up. "We hear things've

changed, but you'd never know it in the valley. They keep us in the dark."

I wondered who was keeping whom in the dark, but I said nothing. Millie Herkimer took her girlfriend's hand. "We want to borrow some of that pride."

We broke up early. Israel Solomon walked me out to my car, informing me that he hadn't sat in a classroom for forty years, had run the apothecary shop in Livingston all his life, and was now retired. The shop, he said, had been founded by his grandfather. Israel had modernized the place but finally sold out to August Hardwick, the present owner.

He hesitated, shuffled, leaned into the car after I got in. He wanted to tell me something else but couldn't quite manage. Well, there'd be plenty of time. I'd probably hear everyone's story before we were done.

As I drove off I saw them all standing in a knot by the road in front of the building. When I waved, eight hands shot up. A surge of hope and, yes, sweetness barreled across the space. A ball formed in my throat. There were pitfalls, but there were pleasures, too.

During the following week, I looked up every time my shop bell jangled, hoping it would be a student, but no one showed. In fact, the bell rarely rang. My one sale consisted of a pine blanket chest, the milk-based paint still intact, which brought $135 from a New York dealer.

Only one event reminded me of my class—near Putnamville I saw a sign pointing to the Herkimer School. Ray Stonington informed me it was a home for problem kids—part reform school, part psychiatric hostel. No doubt a member of Millie's family was involved in some way.

The following Tuesday six Bibles were produced on my instructions—most of them small, old, and giving off musty smells. We started on Genesis 19, which most of them knew. After we got through with the fire and brimstone, I started on some of the new theories. The sin of Sodom might be inhospitality to strangers. "That we may know them" could be interpreted in many ways. The dogma of several thousand years was being questioned nowadays.

They hardly stirred as I spoke, their eyes wide. When I finished, Israel raised his hand. "They taught us that if a man lieth with another man as with a woman, that's an abomination."

Cornelius sputtered. "That's just a slander."

"There are no Sodomites," Nicolas chimed in. "There never were."

"We need new words then," Teage Dane said.

"Let's call ourselves squinchies and frimsters." It was Bradford Gower in the back row. Everyone hooted.

By the time the discussion ended, we were one awareness, one crew aboard the good ship *Revision*. The notion of unlocking minds had lured me into teaching twenty years before, but I had never released excitement like this.

After class, everybody bustled into the hall with me, still throwing out ideas. Emilia Quinn took my arm—her eyes fiery, her hair damp across her forehead. "You should have come up here a long time ago, Michael. Everything would have been different."

"A lot of things had to happen first."

"Well, thank God they did." She squeezed my arm.

I left them, as before, in a knot in front of the building. I wondered if they would walk home. More likely a van would pick them up. Livingston was loaded with vans.

As I drove home I speculated about their living arrangements. The class chits hadn't listed home addresses and we hadn't given any personal histories yet. A new thought struck me. Could there be a commune tucked in the hills around here, something left over from the sixties? That would explain the costumes, the occasional swap of odd decorations. It would also explain their ignorance. I pictured them reading *Godey's Ladies Book* and Mark Twain by kerosene lamp—an oddly gratifying image.

My thoughts moved on to the Herkimer School. Millie said her father's sister, her aunt Millicent, had started it as a seminary for young ladies. Millie didn't seem surprised when I told her about its conversion to a home for juveniles—her family had sold it years ago. She only smiled when I informed her I was going to take some of the school's antique fixtures on consignment. She said they should fetch a good price.

Now, turning into my own driveway, I was filled with contentment. I recalled my old habits, lying awake in the New York night, converting the screech of fire engines and ambulances into something more harmonious—the rattle of coaches, the echoes of post horns. Those fantasies always produced sleep. Now they were all around me—in my shop, the countryside, the classroom.

I unlocked the front door. I had just four rooms on one floor, not fully furnished yet, but I was more settled than I had ever been on Thirteenth Street. For a moment, coming in, I had the crazy notion that some of the original air from 1819 had been trapped under the floorboards and I was actually inside the last century. Then I laughed, fixed myself a drink, and flicked on the TV.

Nobody had bothered to read the *Symposium* clear through, despite the trouble I had gone to in Xeroxing it. In fact, nobody even brought a copy to class. When I asked why, they got fascinated with the dust on the floor and molding on the walls. At last Emilia Quinn spoke up. "We like to hear you preach, Michael."

"She means lecture." Nicolas laughed. "You do really fine at that."

I started on responsibility, the contract between student and teacher, then decided to can it. If they didn't want to read I'd preach. They must have seen the surrender in my face, because they settled back, grinning.

By the time I got into my favorite passage, everyone was paying close attention. "For they love not boys, but intelligent beings," I read from the Jowett translation, "whose reason is beginning to be developed, much about the time at which their beards begin to grow. And in choosing young men to be their companions, they mean to be faithful to them and pass their whole life in company with them, not to take them in their inexperience and deceive them. . . . And observe that open loves are held to be more honorable than secret ones, and how great is the encouragement which all the world gives to the lover."

A pause. The words, so simple and so radical, did their work. I could feel a chunk of the twentieth century breaking off and dissolving.

"That's very interesting, yessir." Israel Solomon was mashed down, quivering, in his seat. He half turned around. "Some of you remember David. David Whitmore." He looked up at me again, breathing hard. "He was just that, my companion for life. But he didn't realize it." A strange sound came from his chest. "I'm not sure I did either."

I put down the Plato. Here it was.

Israel and David had been classmates in Albany, both studying pharmacology. Then they had worked together in the drugstore founded by the first Mr. Solomon. But in a long lifetime Israel hadn't told his friend how he felt. "There was once," he said, "when David was sick—meningitis, very common in those days—when I almost did tell him. I thought it was my last chance. But his wife came in, and I lost my nerve." Israel studied his hands for a moment. "If I'd known about Plato, I could have quoted him. It would have made everything, well, respectable."

He closed down. Heavy, unsaid things washed around the room. I let the silence lengthen. Wasn't this why we'd come together— to know our history, to make sure it didn't happen again?

At last Emilia spoke softly. "It's never too late to mend things, Israel."

He didn't reply. There was a scuffling of feet. Time to move on, I thought. Nothing can be changed, only corrected in the mind.

Israel came up after class and finished the story. David Whitmore hadn't died of meningitis but of a fall two years later while climbing

Overlook Mountain. "So I had a second chance," he concluded, "but I didn't have the nerve then either. I sold the pharmacy. I didn't want to work if David wasn't there."

I patted him lightly, resisting the urge to hug him. There's nothing wrong with hugging, but it can't undo a lifetime of secrecy. "Try reading the Xerox," I said as I got into my car. "It'll help." He looked pleased and dubious at the same time. How could Plato help, really?

The drive to the Herkimer School took me through the center of my town. Downtown Livingston is only a few blocks long, but it offers all your basic services. I was interested in some extra-strength Tylenol. Last night had not been one of my better nights—due more to financial worries than to Israel's history, however. The drugstore—now the Hardwick Rexall—had been established in 1912, according to the script on the window. I stepped back to check out the brick building. I wasn't surprised to see a familiar name stamped on the iron plate just under the eave. *Solomon.* And below it, 1868.

A middle-aged man in a pharmacist's jacket sold me the pills. "Mr. Hardwick?" I asked.

"That's me, John Hardwick."

I introduced myself. He had heard about the Den of Antiquity. He was glad to make my acquaintance. I started to tell him that I knew Israel Solomon, grandson of the Solomon upstairs, then checked myself. Hardwick might ask how we met. It wasn't my job to yank Israel out of his hometown closet. I thanked him for the Tylenol and left, with a final glance at the plaque up top.

The Herkimer School was a rambling building in the Dutch style. Now it showed signs of abuse—torn screens, tar-paper patches, dying shrubs. It was as mismanaged as the lives of the boys within, I thought. The manager, an Irishman named Scully, with a varicosed face and a slight limp, turned me over to the caretaker. As we descended to the basement of the main building it occurred to me that my antique hunting always took me to places where people no longer lived.

The gem of the collection was a pewter chandelier, eight-branched, in good condition. I put the date at 1780–1790. There were also some light fixtures—tulips of amber glass, three to a stem, with rotted wiring, and an imitation Tiffany table lamp. Not a bad haul, I thought as we lugged the stuff upstairs.

I was waiting for the manager to reappear to sign the consignment papers, when I noticed the founder's plaque to one side of the front door. *The Herkimer Institute for Young Ladies,* read the florid script—an incongruous touch, considering the male adolescent snarls coming from upstairs. The first name on the plaque was faint, oxidized, but I managed to make it out—*Millicent Herkimer, Headmistress.* I pictured her as a tall maiden with a spine like a ruler and an immutable sense of right and wrong. Nothing like her confused niece. My eye ran down the names of the original faculty—each introduced with a cursive *Miss*—but I was interrupted by Mr. Scully. We chatted about the fixtures, my job being to keep his expectations low. Most people who consign antiques think they'll make a killing.

Again that night I had trouble getting to sleep, but not because of financial worry. I had convinced myself by bedtime that it was unrealistic to expect a shop to turn a profit the first year. Something else was tugging at a corner of my mind. Finally it let go of me, and I drifted off.

The class began to go more smoothly, even though their reading was patchy. I had the impression that one of the women—Emilia or Millie—read the text and did summaries for the others. We progressed from the Greek poets to the medieval ones, from Michelangelo to Shakespeare to Byron and Edward Carpenter. We managed Emily Dickinson, Radclyffe Hall, Djuna Barnes, and Gertrude Stein.

It was hard to catch them at their goofing off. At least one member of the class was always up on the homework. Sometimes I caught references to materials not under discussion, which made me wonder if their reading was wider than they let on.

But one night, when it was apparent that only Teage Dane had read the Willa Cather story and that everybody was taking cues from her, I recalled my commune theory. "Do you all live together or something?"

Cornelius, usually so guileless-looking, coughed and turned away. Nicolas filled in. "We've known each other a long time."

"It's not a commune, is it?"

Emilia stared at me hard. "How did you know?"

I tried not to sound pleased. "It wasn't that hard. The clothes, the way you always leave together, somebody does the coaching for the next class. Where is it?"

"Just off Sisleytown Road," she replied.

I paused, expecting an invitation to visit. A slight unease swept through the room. "What do you grow?" I asked finally.

William Astbury piped up. "Timothy, sorghum, alfalfa, blue-grass." He laughed briefly. "Plus a lot of weeds."

"You sell it to the dairy farms around here?"

He nodded. "Or they pasture right on our land, though it's against the bylaws."

Well, that explained it. It might explain some other things too —their insularity, their timidity. "Don't you miss traveling, seeing the cities?"

Millie Herkimer replied in a reproving voice. "Americans are one thing today and another thing tomorrow. We prefer a settled life in one place."

Who was I to blame them? Hadn't I taken refuge in the past, which was a community of sorts? The room was quiet. They were waiting, slightly embarrassed. I got the clear message that their urge to include me in their lives had been neutralized by something else. Were they growing a secret cash crop on that land of theirs?

They wouldn't be the first around here. Well, I might or might not find out eventually.

In the meantime, "Paul's Case" by Willa Cather was waiting. They took a dim view of Paul's suicide, once they heard about it.

Little by little, as the weeks went by, their stories came out. I kicked things off with my own. I told them about teaching in New York, my increasingly desperate search for a lover until, ten years before, when I was thirty-three, I'd met Tom Ritenour at a bar in Greenwich Village. They listened as I told about setting up house, our five years of fidelity, the difficult "open relationship" that followed, Tom's illness and death.

After this had been absorbed, Millie had a comment. "Maybe if you'd lived in the country, you would have been more content with each other." She glanced at her friend Teage. "Not so many temptations."

"Maybe so," I agreed. It was a moot point, and it didn't matter anymore.

Emilia Quinn weighed in next. She had lived with her mother. They took in summer guests—city people mostly. "So you see, Michael," she scolded, "we weren't as isolated as you like to think." She had a lover, a woman neighbor who managed her own farm and raised her children alone. But it had been difficult—not only the fear of gossip but the presence of the children and the elder Mrs. Quinn. At last her lover's farm had failed, the furnishings auctioned off, the place repossessed, and the woman herself committed to the state hospital at Wingdale.

"Our difficulty," Emilia said finally, brushing the tangle of dark hair from her eyes, "was fear. They were all lined up against us. We didn't know there had been others before, just like us."

I got a bright idea. "Why don't you bring your friend to class next week? If she can get a day release?" Emilia looked shocked. "She might learn something, feel better about herself."

Emilia took a deep breath. "It's too late for that, Michael." There was so much death in her voice I let the matter drop. Everyone else chimed in to cover my stupidity.

It was the week we were doing *Maurice,* near the end of the course, that Nicolas, looking mischievous, produced a photo. He waved it around. "Recognize him?" I had no trouble. It was a sepia print, mounted on cardboard, of Cornelius Graef. Cornelius, a bewildered eighteen, was posed in a fake Civil War uniform, with a fake musket in his hand. I turned the photo over: "W. A. Reed, Artistic Photographer, Copying a Specialty, Negatives Preserved."

Nicolas let out a teasing chuckle. "We took it in Rensselaer one afternoon. There's a photographer who lets you strike old poses."

I gave the photo back. Nicolas kissed the bewildered young face. "I think he's embarrassed," he said.

Cornelius sank down in the seat, pulling the cap—maybe the same one—over his face.

"Try to think of Plato," Israel remarked. "An open love is more honorable than a secret one."

"Shove off, Israel."

"If Plato is beyond your grasp," Israel went on, "try to think about Edward Carpenter and George Merrill. Or Gertrude Stein and Alice Toklas. Or Maurice and . . . what's his name."

Millie Herkimer clucked. "Cornelius, you were always a bad sport."

"Yeah?" The cap came off. "Why don't you tell your happy story, Millie?"

Millie flushed and turned away. But everyone was waiting.

"I was a teacher until a few years ago," she began.

"Like your aunt Millicent," I added.

She nodded. "A family weakness. But at school I met another teacher who forced me to face certain things." She reached over and touched Teage's hand. "I wasn't made for marriage, children, all that. It was my antagonism toward the opposite sex." She smiled apologetically. "Toward some of them anyway. We . . . this other teacher and I . . . wrote several letters. The letters were discovered; we were both discharged." She paused. "So here we are, trying to understand what happened."

"The heterosexual dictatorship," Bradford Gower remarked. He had become quite fond of that phrase.

"Also the male dictatorship," Millie amended. "They often go together."

Nobody disputed that.

We broke early that evening. *Maurice,* for all its Edwardian passion, had paled beside the pain in the classroom.

When the final session rolled around, we were deep in December. The fields were rusty, the trees like frozen bolts of lightning. We had all pulled closer, huddling around the lives we discussed, drawing warmth from old passions. I hoped I had given them more than literature, though—courage maybe, or freedom. I asked for comments, suggestions, evaluations. But for some reason the old reserve was back tonight. The course had been "interesting," "informative." My suggestion that we all repair to the Maverick Inn for a last drink was met with an embarrassed shuffle. Finally, irritated, I asked point-blank what they'd gotten out of the course.

Bradford Gower broke the silence. "Now I won't be ashamed if people call me names." A nod from William Astbury. "We won't run away."

Emilia spoke next. "You've given us ammunition, Michael."

"Pride too, I hope."

Cornelius started to speak. I could feel the words forming, wild things under the moon, but he beat them back. Pride wasn't in his vocabulary—at least not yet—but he had tried.

When the class ended, each student filed forward to shake my hand. Teage Dane kissed my cheek, then pressed a few strawflowers in my hand—dry and lavender. I laughed and thanked her.

Outside they huddled against the cold, knotted up as usual, as I struggled with my ignition. I let the engine warm up as we traded a last long look. I was full of sadness. We would never be a group again, never merge into a whole, examining prejudice, hunting justice. We might run into each other at fairs or auctions, but we'd never be a family again. It was the nature of every enterprise, I reminded myself, and might stand for the impermanence of all human connection. Still, as I drove off with a final wave, I felt a lash of the old rage. Why must all meetings end in parting? This was another, muted version of Tom's death. *Goodbye,* I thought, is the saddest word in the language.

I was due at Ray Stonington's for dinner the next night—a small celebration to mark the end of the course, he'd said. I was grateful. Even if the students had vetoed the idea of a party, Ray had come through. I really didn't want to be alone, not even inside my favorite year, 1819.

I drove carefully into Ray's driveway—he'd just put in more bluestone. Maybe, I thought, heading up the walk, I'd give the course again. Do it better next time—different selections, sharper commentary. But, luckily, I spotted this as a fantasy, a bad habit from the old days. Courses often got worse instead of better. And these students, for all their quirkiness, had given all they had to give. I had no complaints.

Ray had other guests: a young stage designer visiting for the week; the real-estate agent who had sold Ray his house; an assertive middle-aged woman named Jane Snow, who was helping Ray plan a garden of eighteenth-century produce—not an appetizing idea, I thought, unless you liked gourds.

We talked a little about my course. Ray had filled them in before I arrived. "You were right," I said to Ray at one point. "They were sweet country people. But it was harder to get to know them than I thought."

"That's often the way." Ray removed his glasses and rubbed one eye. "But once you know each other, it's for life."

I laughed. "I hope so."

It was a typical evening at Ray's—good food, good company, and everybody had to wear a lady's hat to dinner. "That's a Lily

Daché," Ray said approvingly when I chose a snappy little number in black velvet with an eye veil. "It would have cost you a fortune in 1940."

We were still at table, lingering over coffee, when Ray passed around his latest treasure, found in a box of miscellanea purchased at auction. It was a photo of his own house, before the north wing had been added. "I can date it quite easily," he said. "About 1895. They'd already cleared the land for the new wing."

It was sepia, with a familiar border. Something stirred in me and I turned it over. "W. A. Reed, Artistic Photographer, Copying a Specialty . . ." and the street address in Rensselaer.

I let out a whoop. "One of my students just had his picture taken there."

Ray looked disapproving. "Somebody's pulling your leg, Michael. That place closed fifty years ago. There's a Burger King there now."

The next instant a shudder went through me, and the knowledge uncoiled from the place it had been waiting. *Teage Dane's name was on the founder's plaque at the Herkimer Institute.* I had seen but not seen. Everything else fell into place. Israel Solomon had sold his store to the Hardwick family in 1912, the year his friend David died. The farm woman at the state hospital couldn't visit our class because she was no longer there. Cornelius Graef had been snapped in a studio by a photographer who mounted his pictures in the style of the day.

I tried to pay attention after that, but it was difficult. My head was buzzing, and my palms were wet. I left as soon as I could, apologizing for my behavior. "That's okay, Michael," Ray said at the door. "We know you teachers are hopeless when you lose your precious students."

I drove the little car as fast as it would go. A half-moon was climbing as I parked on the shoulder of Sisleytown Road. Luckily, the stones faced west. I'd be able to read them.

It took me a while, but finally I came to the last row. I had collected them all, every one. "Okay," I said aloud, the wind whipping my voice, "why didn't you tell me?"

I walked back to Cornelius's grave, then ran my hand over the granite marker, touching the dates. All except Emilia and Israel had died young. Why? Suddenly I knew—and also why they had disapproved so harshly of Willa Cather's Paul.

Snow began to drift down. *They died of the plague,* I thought, *and the plague was ignorance.* Maybe that was the worst of all, because it brings darkness to a living soul.

Snow settled inside my collar. I hunched down, into myself, as far as I could go.

But they had overcome it, because all plagues end sooner or later. There's no telling how or when, but they end.

It was too cold to stay out now. I turned and walked back to the car. The moon shone through the brightness, illuminating the stones. I got in, started the engine, and drove home, thinking about the course I would give next time.

A Good Deed

Greetings to you, Uncle Nanda!

We have arrived safely after a thrilling flight, and Auntie is so happy she hugs us every minute. I think, in spite of her letters, she has been a little lonely. Her house, on a quiet street in a section called Queens, is too big for her. Now that Anita and I have arrived, she says the house is smiling.

Our first weeks have been full of marvels, including our first ride on the underground, a visit to the World Trade Center, and our first barbecue in Auntie's back yard. A barbecue is the roasting of beef—yes, Uncle, a cow—over an open fire, so you can judge how far Auntie has strayed from her roots.

We have met all of Auntie's friends, mostly other doctors from the hospital and their wives, who have made us feel welcome. They were all born elsewhere—Dr. Emil Kieffer in Germany, Dr. Loretta Wu in Shanghai, Dr. Mario Jiménez in Argentina, etc. Not being Americans by birth binds them together, I believe. New York is full of people from elsewhere. It is an exilic city.

The one exception to all this foreign birth is a man named Francis Molloy, who is Auntie's favorite. He was born in a place called

Shaker Heights, which sounds very unsafe to me (it is somewhere in the west). Mr. Molloy is unmarried and not medical. Auntie calls him twice a day, fusses over him constantly. He joins us for dinner every Sunday, after taking Auntie to Mass.

Anita says that Mr. Molloy is Auntie's son, the one she never had. Perhaps he is also her ghost-husband. At any rate, Mr. Molloy, who is tall, thin, pale, and tints the top of his head so that it looks as if a mongoose has died up there, is a regular member of our household. Anita and I, of course, make ourselves agreeable, out of love for Auntie, who has not only brought us to America but more or less adopted us.

We are already enrolled. Anita is going to the nursing school connected to Auntie's hospital and I am at secretarial school in Manhattan. I take word processing, also Decorum and Manners. My experience in Mr. Devananda's office in Bombay has taught me everything else I need. We have already set up a little shrine to Saraswathi in our bedroom. The goddess of learning will help us.

Now you are acquainted with our situation. But you mustn't think we have forgotten you at home. We talk of you constantly, wondering if Bissoon has passed his entrance exams, if Mali is back from Ceylon, and a thousand other things. But until we hear from you, please accept the devotion of your loving nieces.

Suri and Anita

Jackson Heights
May 8

Dear Uncle Nanda,

It was good to receive your letter and hear that Bissoon has passed his exams and that plans are going forward for Ambika's wedding. The groom sounds very modest, which is a good sign. (Auntie says, "Shake a full bottle and it makes no noise.")

Everything goes well here, though I find the other girls at the Bondi Institute less than friendly. I believe it is the British influence, with its emphasis on complexion, though Auntie says I am too sensitive. At any rate, I work hard at my word processing, also at Office Decorum and Telephone Manners, which are informal to the point of rudeness in America. I look forward to getting my certificate.

Auntie has not been feeling well—a fact she has kept secret from everyone for a long time. She goes for tests tomorrow. She says that whatever happens, her Christian faith will see her through. She is wonderfully serene. Her goodness shines through.

Do you know, when the subject of Adolf Hitler came up at a party recently, and someone gave thanks that he was dead, Auntie reprimanded him? She shook her head and said, "If Hitler did not have the chance to repent and do penance before he died, it would be better if he were still alive." This statement shocked the guests, who do not understand the depth of Auntie's goodness. Then she launched into a story about a prodigal son, which was to prove that all sins may be forgiven if the urge to repent is sincere. To my mind this only confirms the weakness of Christianity. For all action there must be consequence—isn't that what the great wheel of karma stands for?

Yesterday we celebrated the fiftieth birthday of Francis Molloy. Yes, Uncle, fifty—an age not much junior to your own. But instead of celebrating a rebirth into honor and wisdom, everyone assured Francis he didn't look fifty, to which he replied that he certainly didn't feel it, and it became clear as the afternoon went on that he wasn't going to act it either. I regret to say that Auntie laughed and giggled as if she were the mother of a newborn boy—which, in a way, she was.

The party was held at Francis' apartment, which is very large and overlooks the Hudson River from both its floors. He is the owner. Besides Auntie's friends, his own attended. These were mostly men. As the afternoon continued, I recalled the old Pro-hibition Laws in our own country—two years in jail if you were caught with alcohol on your breath. You will understand how Auntie has changed if I tell you she mixed whiskey drinks for Francis. The party was made interesting for me because of chats I had with some of Francis' friends on the subject of Italian opera. They all seem to be experts.

When we arrived home, having given alms to all the vagrants and mendicants on the way as propitiation for our good fortune, Auntie came into our bedroom for a chat. She was in a good mood, which, I have noticed, always follows seeing Francis. At one point she remarked that Francis had filled her life with happiness and it would give her great pleasure to attend his funeral. At first I was surprised and confused. Was she wishing for his death? Only gradually did the truth reveal itself. To give him a funeral, perfect in every detail, including interment, would be the last, best expression of her love. She had seen him through hepatitis, kidney stones, and a coronary attack. Also a two-month stay in a hospital for alcoholics. When Francis needed her, she was there. And her last duty was obvious—a funeral mass and a costly coffin.

It soon became clear that she was expressing her disappointment. *She would not be here to perform these services for Francis.* Anita and I got very upset, of course, and accused her of hiding the truth about her health. It came out slowly. Although the test results won't be ready until next week, as a doctor herself she knows what they will show. This led her to thoughts of Francis.

Anita and I had a great deal to discuss that night. At first Anita thought Auntie's wish was morbid, arising from the religion she has adopted in America. But as we talked it over, we decided it was another example of her saintliness. By giving her friend the last rites of the religion they share, she would give him eternal life—or so she believes. It would be the final expression of her love.

I will close this letter, Uncle, with renewed expression of my obedience. Anita joins me in this.

Your faithful niece,
Suri

Jackson Heights
May 15

Dear Uncle,

I am writing to tell you of two crises in our lives. The first concerns Auntie. Yes, the news was bad. She suffers from adenocarcinoma, or tumors in both lungs. These have travelled from her breast cancer of a few years ago (you remember how we worried about that). She is now taking treatment once a week— treatment that leaves her ill for several days. But she never complains. Nothing disturbs her serenity. I believe that she has accepted everything, whether because of her old faith or her new I cannot tell. But Anita and I believe that Vishnu the Protector and Siva the Destroyer are still dancing for her soul. Unfortunately, she has refused all my suggestions for fasts, ritual baths, clothing, etc. Instead she goes to early Mass every day. She is losing her beautiful hair.

The second crisis concerns Francis. You probably have a certain picture of him as a man corrupted by meat, wine, and women. I can tell you that this picture is only two-thirds correct. Meat and wine, yes, but Francis is not inclined in the direction of women. Rather the contrary.

This will shock you, dear Uncle, but remember that here we are at the ends of the earth. Americans have little sense of family. In fact, family is something to be ignored or divorced—and if that is impossible, killed off. The approved way is to run over them with a car, which combines the two national pastimes, driving and killing. (No blame attaches to the assassin.) So Francis is not unusual in being without family. However, I have discovered reasons for this other than selfishness or laziness. My discovery came about during a visit to his apartment. Auntie had an attack of dizziness and Francis insisted that she lie on his bed for a while. She dozed off while I watched.

And then, quite by chance, I noticed a group of magazines on the desk next to the bed. I won't offend you by describing them, except to say that they showed in detail why Francis had never married. Naturally, I put them back and said nothing. But when we departed, Francis, who is very sensitive to moods, asked me if I was disturbed by anything.

Anita and I stayed up late that night. Anita, who is very kindhearted, pointed out that people like Francis can be ignored because they are not mentioned in the epics. Not in the Gita or the Vedas or the Mahabharata. They have been excluded from history because they are counterfeit men.

I agreed, adding that Americans have so many stories that they cancel each other out. No one has a guide to proper behavior. It is the chaos of the West.

From this we went on to Auntie. She is very attached to the old stories, since she was raised on them, despite her new devotion to the Christian saints. This former attachment explains her interest in Francis. He has given her a part to play—mother, bride, consort. However, now that we have discovered his true nature, isn't it possible that Auntie is playing a wrong part? Living a falsehood? How could she be the consort or widow of such a man? It struck me that Auntie is in danger of losing her place in the story too.

Then Anita and I recalled how Auntie came here after she was refused admission to the Royal College of Medicine. How her years of study brought professional success (with help from home). We remembered how our father used to say, "Many careers are open to women with character—look at your Aunt Chandra." It was the refrain of our childhood. What right do we have to force Auntie back into the old ways, into a history she has rejected?

On the other hand, don't we have a responsibility for her spiritual welfare? Doesn't exile create freedom while destroying the soul? And weren't her deepest wishes told us in a moment of frankness after the birthday party? And as her new daughters—she recently changed her will to include us—isn't our family obligation doubled?

As you can imagine, our heads were in a whirl that night. Finally we decided to ask you, as head of the family, for advice. What should we do, dear Uncle?

> Obediently,
> *Suri and Anita*

> Jackson Heights
> June 1

Dear Uncle,

Thank you for writing so promptly. You say that Francis Molloy's actions are not shameful to *him*. And you are right, though that runs the risk of individualism and anti-social behavior. There is even a political movement here which tries to justify tastes like his. But if such actions were truly useful, would they have to be defended? I concede that if Francis dressed in women's clothes, became a *hijra,* devoted himself to the Mother Goddess, spent his days singing and dancing and begging, there would be no cause for alarm. He would have a place in the story—a very humble one, but still a place. He would be defined by what he was excluded from. But of course all that is unthinkable here.

If you doubt the seriousness of our debate, let me tell you what happened two days ago. We went on an excursion with Francis and some other friends to the park in the center of Manhattan. We visited the zoological gardens, the obelisk from Egypt, etc. At one point Francis wandered off. We thought we had lost him. But, to Auntie's delight, he caught up with us an hour later—our progress was slow because of her wheelchair—and told us he had spied some friends in one of the wooded ravines. He had rambled off to greet them and lost track of the time. It was very apparent to me, however, and also to Anita, that he had been engaged in some kind of strenuous exertion. His face was red, his clothes were a little dishevelled, and he was panting. He excused himself and patted himself back into shape, but not before an almost unthinkable suspicion had inserted itself into my mind. Was it possible that Francis was using a Sunday stroll, a *family outing,* to indulge himself? He saw me studying him and became extremely nervous, laughing too much, picking some flowers, teasing Auntie. But there was a moment when my eyes met Anita's (we have the same eyes, flecked with gold, you remember) and we both knew what had happened.

That night, after we got Auntie to bed, we sat for a long time without speaking. An idea kept pressing against us, like a spirit in a *puja* room.

At last we began to discuss it openly, in spite of our reluctance, in spite of the wisdom contained in your last letter. There was simply no way to avoid it. First, I pointed out that we would actually be doing Francis a favor. We would lighten his karma. He would come back not as a rat or a crocodile but as something much higher—a neelkantha bird, for instance. We would end his other miseries too, including his financial worries. (He is an interior designer and has offended or lost most of his clients.) There was also the advantage that such action would make Auntie's dream possible—the dream she gave up the moment she confided it to us. This far outweighed, from our point of view, the fact that Auntie is Francis' heir. None of us needs a lavish apartment in Manhattan.

In spite of our long discussion, nothing was settled. We couldn't be sure that the spirit loose in the room was not an evil one, making a clatter, upsetting things. So we went to bed tired and unsettled. In the morning I realized that sleep is exhausting too—all those pumps and pulleys hauling oxygen and drawing blood, to say nothing of dreams, which can actually kill you.

In closing, I will repeat a conversation I had with Auntie a few days ago. She was cooking and talking about Francis as usual, though her energies are greatly diminished these days. I remarked that everything is kept for seven years, in case you find a use for it, but that she has kept Francis in her heart for much longer than that. And what was the use of him? Had he fathered sons? Had he accumulated virtue? Had he won battles? No—he had only moved furniture around. Wasn't it time to throw him away, like an old box or bottle? Auntie became quite angry and I thought she was going to order me from the kitchen, but then she laughed. "That is an old Tamil superstition, Suri," she said, "and we are in

America. Besides, friends improve with age." She looked through the window to where the barbecue machine sits, and added, "It was God's grace that brought Francis into my life, another proof of divine love." Of course, I had no answer to that.

Your distressed niece,
Suri

P.S. I have received my secretarial certificate. Dr. Loretta Wu, Auntie's friend, has found me a position with Sung Ware, which, despite the name, deals in shirts and pants. They are very polite—Mrs. Sung especially, who could teach that course in Decorum better than Miss O'Reilly did.

Jackson Heights
June 15

Dear Uncle,

Thank you for your letter, also the selection of prayers. Auntie is not receptive, but we are performing the rituals in our bedroom. Our minds are becoming increasingly clarified. As for your warnings, we have paid attention to those too. We know the dangers all too well.

I regret to say that nothing has helped Auntie's health, not our offerings to Ganesha nor Auntie's masses and candles. The malignancies have grown and she has become weaker, though not in spirit. She remarked recently, "I'm going to move out of this body, it's becoming uninhabitable." But she said this in the most cheerful way possible.

Francis, I admit, has been very helpful. He makes the trip here regularly to take Auntie to the hospital or to church. He had planned a trip to Cape Cod this summer but has cancelled it. Auntie, lying in bed last night after Francis had departed, told us we are to take care of him when the time comes. Yes, we are to look after him just as she does. She will train us, teaching us what food he prefers, what clothes and gifts, what restaurants and travel. We know all this already, but will let ourselves be instructed.

Naturally, Francis' strength has raised new questions. Is he redeeming himself? Accumulating good karma? At what point do kind actions tilt the balance? Is there a place for him in the story as nurse and keeper of the shrine? These are difficult questions.

There is another matter which I hesitate to mention for fear of being misunderstood (though I am sure, Uncle, as a businessman, you will grasp it at once). Francis has told Auntie that he plans to change his will. She will no longer inherit his apartment and we, as her heirs, will be left out too. This is of little interest to us, but isn't it true that the Catholic Church has enough property already? And what will they do except sell his flat to buy more crucifixes and stained-glass windows? Auntie told us this news with an expression of rapture on her face—I suppose it proves Francis' superiority of soul—and we responded as required. But we were not entirely pleased, if only because the Church is already the richest institution in America and gives nothing to the tax collector. I repeat, we have no need of a lavish duplex apartment.

So there, dear Uncle, you have our situation—at least until a few days ago. Last Wednesday, quite by chance, a new factor entered the equation, proving once again that everything was written ten thousand years ago and there is no straying from the script. But now I must digress to the subject of television.

Can you imagine how Gandhiji's power would have been multiplied if he had had his own talk show every week? Satyagraha might have taken deep root instead of touching only a few enlightened souls. The riots and deaths accompanying partition might have been avoided. His own fate might have been different (though this is doubtful). At any rate, in America, many sadhus and gurus and teachers use the screen to spread their spiritual wares, and collect money besides. But for every yang there is a yin, for every lingam a yoni, and at the opposite end of the spiritual spectrum are the criminal programs. Americans are fascinated with criminals—either real-life or fictional. Perhaps, in this casteless country, they fill some deep need. As you know, sects and groups are not watertight here—everyone floats around—but there is general agreement that criminals collect at the bottom, along with politicians.

Auntie is not immune to this addiction. It is her only flaw. She adores crime shows. And her tip-top favorite, the program she never misses, is called *America's Most Wanted*. The title refers to murderers and bandits who have eluded the Bureau of Investigation, which is the American version of Scotland Yard, and are being sought across the country. Viewers phone in with tips if they think they have seen them.

On the evening when *America's Most Wanted* comes on, Auntie sits spellbound. No one is allowed to talk. She presses her left side, then her right, to diminish the pain, and studies the photos as carefully as if she were peering through one of her old microscopes. When one of the escaped criminals is captured she is delirious.

Francis teases her about her attachment to the program. He says it proves she is essentially bloodthirsty. "It allows you to enjoy the violence and condemn it at the same time." This always makes them both laugh. I might add that as soon as the program comes on, Francis leaves for Manhattan.

The above is an introduction to an amazing event that took place two days ago. I was in Laxam's Spice & Curry Shop on Astoria Boulevard when a delivery truck pulled up and a man started unloading burlap sacks. He was balding, strongly built, in his sixties. There was nothing unusual about him except that when he came in the shop I noticed some markings on the fingers of his right hand. I looked more closely and saw the letters L-O-V-E tattooed above the second joint. Something jiggled in my mind and I glanced at the left hand. D-E-T-H was spelled out. A freezing shudder went through me and I understood that I was in the presence of one of America's Most Wanted. The tattoos were what they call identifying marks. The impossible had happened.

I said nothing, though my heart was pounding, and delayed my purchases until he had pulled away in his truck. I noted the lettering on the door—Montefiore Provisions. Laxam informed me that the man's name was Pops Pearson and that he had been delivering bags for about a year. The next instant I understood that all this had been pre-ordained.

Even so, when I outlined my proposal to Anita that night, the old doubts reappeared. Didn't the sages forbid us to hate? Wouldn't violence bind me forever to the wheel of rebirth? I thought of those holy men who won't breathe too deeply for fear of sucking in a gnat—where would I stand in that moral scale? And in your estimation, Uncle Nanda?

On the other hand, didn't we owe something to Auntie, our second mother? Hadn't Francis Molloy strayed irretrievably from the dharma, the path? And wouldn't it be presumptuous, even contemptuous, to ignore the god who had forced this new instrument into my hand?

As you can imagine, Anita and I discussed this intensely for several days. She had to be persuaded, her scruples overturned, though I knew I was really trying to convince myself. Finally we decided, without committing ourselves, to visit the Montefiore Provision Company (which we had ascertained was in another part of the city called Brooklyn) for a talk with the man of Love and Death. We are now waiting for the right time and a last sign from Siva, who must lead us onward.

Yours expectantly,
Suri

June 30
At the office during lunch hour

Dear Uncle Nanda,

I am sorry to report that Auntie is now spending most of her time in bed. She has stopped the treatment at the clinic, though not in time to save her beautiful hair. She wears a wig when visitors come. She is quite subdued, except when Francis arrives, usually on Sunday, to take her to Mass and join us for dinner. Then a change comes over her. She hums and laughs. She even finds the strength to prepare food for Francis—trays of sweets, coconut, fried tidbits, sugar crystals, jaggery, all that. She watches him nibble on these (never showing the least reluctance or requiring the slightest encouragement) with the old blissful expression on her face. She has signed some papers at the bank which enable me to draw money for household expenses.

Watching the two of them last Sunday, I reflected that both Auntie and Francis are displaced persons—she in external exile, he in internal. They have become each other's true family in America.

At dinner on this same Sunday, for which Anita and I prepared goat curry—you'd be amazed how hard it is to find the ingredients for this—Francis and Auntie made a surprise announcement. They are going to Lourdes in France! Yes! They bought tickets without telling us. They leave in two weeks. Auntie is hoping for a miracle and Francis will go along to take care of her. Francis asked me, quite insensitively, if I had ever heard of Saint Bernadette. Of course I had, but I had to keep quiet while Auntie compared the shrines and holy places at home with the power of a French peasant girl who had a vision in a cave. When I objected at last, she replied firmly that a Christian must go to a Christian shrine and that was the end of it. There was so much sorrow under her firmness that of course I let the matter drop. Before Francis left us that day, I overheard another item. He has made an appointment to change his will before flying to France. The Church will provide a lawyer without charge.

That night, as I got ready for bed, I heard a scraping noise, which I knew to be the scything of blades. The air quickened, I felt a rush of lightness, and the pictures on the wall began to scream. "Open your mind," a voice declared, and when I did a sharpness cut across it. It was Siva with his Sword of Decisiveness. When Anita came in from the bathroom a few minutes later, she found me in a trance. All doubt had ended. I had crossed over.

The following Saturday we visited the Montefiore Provision Company. This was in a part of Brooklyn filled with warehouses and parking lots. I wasn't frightened in the least, since I knew who was protecting me. In the front office we asked for Mr. Pearson and were directed around back to a loading area. He straightened up when he saw us, and watched carefully as we approached. I had the feeling he knew why we were there. I noticed that his head was shaven, not naturally bald, giving him a holy look, although his eyes were black and suspicious. "I remember you," he said. "You were at Laxative's in Jackson Heights."

"Yes, at Laxam's shop," I replied, "and we've come all the way out here to talk to you."

He studied me, then said, "Come inside."

He had a home on wheels, very popular in America, parked in one corner of the parking lot. This was where he lived. After we sat down in a tiny living area, he asked if we were Ricans—that is, natives of an island-colony in the Caribbean. Anita, speaking for the first time, explained our origins.

Mr. Pearson was wearing a red cotton shirt with a machine-gun printed on it. Underneath was the legend "Live Free or Die." These shirts with messages on them are extremely popular here and probably explain why America is a nation of speed readers.

As we talked of this and that, not wishing to rush rudely into things, he saw me glancing at his fingers. He tried to cover them by sitting on them, but finally held up both. "Which one you interested in, miss?"

"That one." I pointed to the left. "Though we spell it differently."

"That's what I figured. How do I know if I can trust you?"

The words furnished by my Protector came easily. "Because you will know about us just as we know about you."

Just then a large grey cat jumped on his lap. He stroked it with his right hand, the LOVE hand, and I could see that they understood each other. Then it occurred to me that last time he had been a powerful, predatory cat—a tiger perhaps.

He listened as I related our problem. I knew that a man of his background wouldn't understand the finer points so I put our errand in terms of a revised will and a lost inheritance. He strummed the fingers of his left hand, then asked where Francis lived and worked, what he looked like, and so forth. I supplied him with a photo and a schedule. He was especially interested in Francis' visits to St. Joseph's—not only with Auntie on Sunday but for bingo and other rites. It seems that he knew the church. "I've done work for the padre," he said, referring to the assistant priest, Father Falcone. "Him and Peanut."

I decided not to inquire further—he would have his own methods after all.

Finally the matter of money came up. I was ready for this, and was able to give him an advance payment, thanks to Auntie's trust in me. But it wasn't wrong to use her money. Wasn't Mr. Pearson about to provide an essential household service? He counted the bills quickly, as if used to handling large sums. Then he shook hands with each of us, using his left hand. That seemed to seal the bargain. After that he offered to walk us to the underground.

We chatted as we strolled. He told us that Father Falcone had been a prison chaplain and that he, Mr. Pearson, had been able to get him out of a ticklish situation. (Again, I didn't ask for details.) Now Father Falcone owed him a favor. As he spoke, I noted the cunning of the criminal mind.

"Even if he owes you a favor," I remarked, "it would be best to make him believe that in repaying it he will help in your reha-bilitation. That way he won't feel any guilt." He grasped my rea-soning instantly—more proof of his cunning.

We made a date to meet near St. Joseph's in a few days. By then all the arrangements would be made. He also said the rest of the fee would be payable then, but I stated firmly—Siva guiding my tongue—that the balance would be paid only on completion of the job.

So there you have it, our plan for Auntie's surprise gift. I might add that Anita and I were so exhausted after our visit with Mr. Pearson that we slept ten hours that night.

Your apprehensive niece,
Suri

Jackson Heights
July 4

Dear Uncle Nanda,

I am writing on a famous American holiday, their day of independence from Great Britain, much like our own. It combines political fervor with a kind of Holi—the triumph of good over evil, though they do not splash each other with colors. To tell the truth, the extra days of rest are welcome. Mrs. Sung, while courteous, is a slave-driver. Yesterday, as I was making tea on my little machine, she asked me why I stopped working while the water came to a boil. "Lost time can never be found again," she said sweetly. Only a husband can free me from Mrs. Sung, but of course that is slavery of another kind. My situation makes me a little envious of the leisure class in America, which seems to be everyone over fifty.

To continue our story. Mr. Pearson met us near St. Joseph's as arranged. With him was a boy of thirteen with spiky hair and a ruddy complexion. This was Peanut. He assists at Communion services. He was very nervous, darting about, mumbling when we spoke to him. I wondered why Mr. Pearson had brought a witness—especially a child—but it was too late to worry. Peanut, it was clear, would be part of the plan.

After Peanut ran off, as if chased by demons, we walked to Mr. Pearson's truck. There was room for all three of us in the front seat. There he told us that Father Falcone had been "brought aboard." By that he meant that the priest wouldn't interfere. He gave a mysterious smile and said that he had followed my suggestion. "He thinks I'm backsliding into some bad habits I picked up in the joint." I didn't want to hear any more details, but Mr. Pearson kept smiling. "I showed him that photo of your friend Molloy—after that there was no more trouble."

I didn't pursue that topic either, though I began to glimpse the ticklish situation from which Mr. Pearson had once extricated the priest. As I wrote to you earlier, Uncle, here we are at the ends of the earth.

Anita spoke up for the first time. "Do you think it's right to involve a child in this?"

Mr. Pearson's smile was unpleasant. "That kid was born old. Besides, what D.A. is going after an altar-boy with no previous convictions?"

I was learning a great deal about the American criminal system. "How can we be sure Peanut won't change his mind?"

"Father Falcone will see to that." He gave a chilling laugh. What awful events has Siva set in motion? But I couldn't resist asking when and where the deed was to be done.

"Better you don't know, miss, but you might want to go to Mass this Sunday."

He opened the door and we climbed down. I, who had hardly been on a street alone before coming to America, was now caught up in a deception as sly as any in thuggee. As Anita and I walked home, the old questions returned. Was it possible that Siva was merely tempting us? Acting out his bad nature? That it was our duty to resist?

My doubts intensified later in the day when Francis turned up unexpectedly. He said he had woken up that morning with a powerful summons—he was to visit his dear Chandra. He had cancelled his holiday plans and arrived on our doorstep right after lunch. Auntie received him in bed, not bothering with her wig. Francis knelt and put his arms around her. The room filled with love. I recalled that some of our oldest stories find a place for people, however undesirable, who are steadfast in loving. It is a purifying fire in which they are cleansed.

I have stayed up late to write you, Uncle, because I am sure that sleep will not come to my pillow tonight.

In sorrow,
Suri

Sunday evening
Astoria Hospital

Dear Uncle Nanda,

A terrible thing has happened. Auntie had an attack in church this morning as she walked back from the Communion rail. If Francis hadn't been beside her she would have fallen. They carried her to the choir room and called an ambulance. I am writing this from the emergency waiting room at Auntie's old hospital, where her friends on the staff come every few minutes to check on her.

Francis is pacing up and down, moaning softly. We have done him an injustice. Despite his failings, he is a good man. Auntie was never wrong about people.

As you can see, I have had a change of heart. Americans are always talking about pilgrims who go to the East for a mystical experience. I had to come West for mine. I am forced to conclude that our gods are lost in a new country where they don't know their way around. Francis Molloy is out of their jurisdiction.

Mr. Pearson was in church this morning. He was wearing a dark suit and tie and was sitting in the last row. When I came in he turned and squeezed his eyes at me. I pretended not to notice. But as it turned out, I might have smiled and nodded, not abetting evil, because the evil was thwarted of its own accord.

Auntie and Francis took Communion together as always, waiting until last, when the altar was empty, and they could kneel side by side. Father Falcone stood waiting, Peanut beside him with the plate of sacred wafers. Father Falcone started droning the words as soon as Auntie and Francis bowed their heads. I watched as he gave each a wafer and a sip of wine. I don't know what I expected, because both stood up, looking beatified, hands clasped, and made their way down the steps. It was then that Auntie had her attack —not unexpected when you consider her weakness and the stress of going to church—but still terrible to see.

A cry went up from the people watching—they all knew Auntie, of course—and several men went to help Francis. She was removed to a bench in the choir room and Father Falcone interrupted the service to say a special prayer for her recovery.

Dr. Wu, Auntie's old friend, has come into the waiting room just now. Auntie is being taken to Intensive Care. One lung has filled with water, a result of coronary failure. There is danger of death by drowning—not uncommon in cases like this. Francis, when he heard the news, stumbled. I caught him just in time, as he did Auntie in church, and sat him next to me. He is holding on to me as I write. We are united at last. I believe it is Auntie's gentle spirit at work, her last gift to both of us.

In peace,
Suri

The next day at home

Dear Uncle,

This might be the last time I write. The gods are raging. There is no way to placate them, no sacrifice great enough.

The terrible plan, the deception, was played out in all its immensity, though I didn't know it at the time. The true facts were hidden from me. Mr. Pearson had gone ahead as planned, with my misguided encouragement. There was only one flaw. The gods, in a final assertion of their waning power, made his plan go awry.

His idea was simple. When Auntie and Francis approached the altar there were two wafers left on the silver plate. One was stamped IHS, which is the usual lettering, the other HIS. Mr. Pearson had given Peanut the latter just a few minutes before the service started, together with instructions—to hold the dish so that IHS went to the lady, HIS to the man. This should not have been difficult even for a boy of thirteen. But by a destiny written when the stars were young, Peanut was distracted by a girl in the front row and spun halfway round. At that exact moment, Father Falcone reached down and *picked up the wrong wafer*. Peanut watched, saying nothing, as the priest gave it to Auntie. She swallowed it. Francis ate the other one. Both drank the wine. Auntie's subsequent collapse you know about.

Mr. Pearson revealed all of this to me, just after I returned home from the hospital. Peanut had confessed to him. But he told me we were lucky. Auntie was already sick. There would be no suspicion. We were "home free," as he put it.

What he didn't know—though I told him at once—was that Auntie had willed her body to the anatomy lab at her hospital and that Dr. Loretta Wu is an enthusiastic reader of mysteries. It won't take them long, I'm sure.

Mr. Pearson laughed when I spoke of fate. He said Peanut spun around at the wrong time because he is a dumb kid. "Do you think all this was written in the stars just so we could mess up in Astoria at eleven o'clock Mass on a Sunday morning?" I didn't know what to say so I said nothing.

As I sit here, struggling with the knowledge that I, of all people, have allowed the vengeful gods to shorten Auntie's life, my mind runs away with me. I imagine that one day Mr. Pearson and I will be featured on *America's Most Wanted*. Yes, Auntie's favorite program may show recent photos of her favorite niece, including identifying marks. If that happens, our chance of avoiding capture will be nil. Even in this huge country, a criminal band consisting of a bald man of sixty and an Indian maiden of twenty-six and her sister tends to stand out. My only consolation will be that Auntie would know I was only trying to do a good deed. She was too full of love to condemn anyone. I mean, if she could give Hitler a chance to repent, wouldn't she do the same for me?

I am waiting for the phone to ring now. I know I have misjudged everyone. I must try to hold my soul in peace, even as I hope for a miracle.

Suri

Being a Baroness

They went to see Wade Harlech on a Saturday morning. He was sitting up in bed with his old vain smile, greeting them as if they'd come backstage after a show. Ray was happy to see him like this, showing off a little. It was an old, comfortable pretension. After a while Wade pointed to a book on the table. Ray picked it up—the letters of Isak Dinesen—then showed it to his lover, Keith. "You know," he remarked, quite unnecessarily, "Meryl Streep, *Out of Africa*." Keith knew.

"The letters are marvelous," Wade said. "She wrote her brother back in Denmark, she told him . . ." He paused for breath while he smoothed the covers with a spectral hand. "She told him that it was worth having syphilis in order to be a baroness." His eyes, so large in his face now, widened further. "Her husband—you know, the baron, Klaus Maria Brandauer—gave it to her in Africa. She had it for years, died of it back in Denmark." The smile again, vain and ironic at the same time. Ray and Keith held themselves tensely.

"Don't you see?" Wade lay back against the pillows. "It was worth having this, all this"—he waved at the tubes and syringes and bottles—"to have as much sex as I wanted. With anyone. For years. All my life, really." He gave a little preening motion, touching his hair. "I always adored being a baroness."

Ray laughed dutifully, but he wasn't sure Wade meant it. Maybe it was a rationalization, or to make them feel better about his condition. Or maybe it was just one more role—his last impersonation. Something to carry off the visit, to dispossess the deadly presences in the room. Still, after they left, the words repeated in his head. Wade the baroness. If he'd been telling the truth, then he had no regrets. Wade was over fifty. He'd had three full decades of screwing around, all over the world, when there were no limits on what could be done.

They were quiet going home on the subway and after they got there. They probably wouldn't see Wade again. He'd been one of their outer circle, not a close friend but part of their lives. Actually, Ray had tricked with him ages ago, but when he settled down with Keith, Wade had dropped away. Keith didn't enjoy show-biz chatter, or the way Wade liked to stand in the middle of a living room as if he were onstage. Keith was a lawyer, a specialist in housing legislation, a quiet man.

Ray Stronson and Keith Anchises had met at Volunteer Night at the old National Gay Task Force on lower Fifth Avenue. Ray was stuffing envelopes, Keith was dispensing free legal advice at the housing clinic. They'd gone out for coffee one evening. Ray had liked the lanky, slow-talking attorney with the wide-apart eyes—almost his opposite, physically and temperamentally—and had been especially charmed with the suggestion they have dinner before Volunteer Night next week. The year was 1980. Ray wasn't in the habit of making dates like that. He usually rolled into bed and had dinner later. But this time he put his lust on hold. The delay of several weeks was worth it. When they finally hit the hay, it was like the last reel of a thirties movie. They had earned it and it was twice as good. Giggles of satisfaction and a fadeout. After a few more dates, each with a mischievous conclusion, Ray decided he had found someone special. Keith was looking for a steady partner. They were both in their early thirties—a time for settling in. Within a few months they had found an apartment in the Village. Their combined salaries—Ray was with a hotel chain, in charge of banquets and conferences—added up to a good sum.

They had three years of sexual ardor with only occasional quarrels. According to the *Times,* three years was the average period of intense romance for any couple. During that time they found other fits. They both liked to read, attend the Philharmonic, keep pets, go down to the Jersey Shore for bird watching. They worked hard at being friends, getting along. Sometimes Ray thought of his connection to Keith as a job, something that had to be tended and encouraged, couldn't be allowed to fall into disrepair. He knew this wasn't the immortal romance he'd dreamed about back in Minnesota. No, this was companionship, homemaking, and fun in bed. But he'd been around long enough to know how rare it was to find all those attributes combined in one person, so he was satisfied. Never mind the moon and the stars, he liked the way Keith analyzed things, the way he listened, the sight of his well-formed legs. Although they rarely discussed their feelings toward each other—the subject embarrassed them slightly and they were afraid of slipping into cliché—Ray knew that Keith found him equally engaging. Ray's quickness, his worldliness, his flair for domestic theater when things went wrong—all these kept Keith stimulated and laughing. They had a life together, rough around the edges where discontent or nostalgia abided, but better than being alone. And at certain times—over a cocktail or in a beautiful place, or in bed—love appeared, surprising them both, quickening things, making promises they succumbed to for a few hours or a few days, until other habits of mind reasserted themselves.

But, as luck would have it, their period of reliable excitement began to fade just as the plague became an unavoidable issue. They discussed opening up their bed to others, or opening up their relationship itself, but they were scared. Instead they tried to keep things going. They bought some sex films. Also some porno magazines and a few hot romances. They tried fantasies, though they were careful not to use them too often. These devices kept them going, though extra effort was required. It seemed a small price to pay for good health. Still, there were times when Ray almost gave in to temptation, usually on the way home from work, when the subway was full of young men who had had awful days at the office too, and who needed to release the tension. But he always managed to resist.

In 1985 the HIV test became available. They took it, with favorable results, then were extra careful for a few months and took it again. Negative a second time. They broke out a bottle of champagne that night and toasted each other with a kind of voluptuous virtue. They had come through, due partly to luck, partly to self-control. They had met on the cusp of the epidemic, fidelity had been maintained, and now they were home free. There'd be a cure pretty quick—everybody said so.

Also required was a little more imagination in bed. Ray in particular was having difficulties. Sex had always meant more than sex to him. It meant freedom from the Brethren in Minnesota, freedom from the repressions of his family. Also a wonderful chance to make new friends; most of his friends were former tricks. The adventure of having many partners was the greatest adventure of all, he liked to say, and the reason gay men looked ten years younger than they were. All those hormones surging. He got carried away by the notion of the intimacy of anonymity—scoring with dozens of strangers, a huge floating harem which you could endow with hope or romance or devotion—anything you liked.

After hearing the theory of intimate anonymity four or five times, Keith got irritated. There was no going back, he said. They'd have to be satisfied with each other. They were at Saturday breakfast— they usually had banana-and-yogurt pancakes on Saturday—when Ray aired his theory once again and Keith snapped at him. "For God's sake, stop whining. You're like a broken record." Ray sighed. Keith was right, even though he didn't really appreciate the depth of his, Ray's, needs. They were in the sixth year of their householding. Sometimes he felt split in half—the old explorer and the new prisoner. "Well, if you can do it so can I," he said at last. He only half meant it, or hated meaning it, but there was no other way.

They began to expand their sexual repertory. They bought more video cassettes, tried more fantasies, and experimented with various flavors of creams and oils. Sometimes their bedroom smelled like a drugstore. But even as they became technically more skilled the old thrills lessened. They talked about this and made plans to try another toy, another method, but next time wasn't much better.

And they heard about more delays in finding a cure. One prediction estimated ten more years. Another mentioned the year 2000. Ray knew that fucking only with Keith until the millennium was out of the question. And he was pretty sure that by then his own expanding form, with its wide hips and ample ass, would have lost what remained of its appeal. Still, they'd have to try. It was like the army. You didn't want to scrub down the barracks once a week but you did it anyway. If sex with Keith was turning into a GI party, he'd have to accept it.

In the meantime they continued their experiments. They built a big video collection. They went to a safe-sex club. They took trips to places where they'd had fun during their first years together— Key West, Puerto Rico, and San Francisco—and were able to ignite a bit of the old eroticism. They tried bondage and urolagnia, whips and tit-clamps. They used cowboy outfits, hard hats, and jockstraps. They read Pat Califia in the *Advocate,* Dr. Ruth, Rabbi Kushner, and Shere Hite. None of these, however, took the place of what they'd lost.

They also cranked up the fantasy machine. To their old staple, the gas-station attendant and the hitchhiker, they added a whole new cast. They experimented with drugs, though a little pot seemed to work best. As the closets and drawers of their bedroom filled up with toys and props, Ray recalled how simple sex had once been. You took off your clothes and grabbed each other, and nature took care of the rest. But that had been years ago.

Once in a while Ray thought about Wade Harlech, who had died a few weeks after their last visit. Maybe Wade had been right.

Maybe it was better to catch the virus than to go against the tide, against the male's inborn need for variety. Maybe that was an inevitable trade-off. Emerson's law of compensation, life as a zero-sum game. He wasn't sure—he certainly didn't want to die before his time—but mortality might be the price of freedom. He hinted at this to Keith, who reacted badly. "What are you saying, you can't stop acting out for a few years?" He didn't know where Keith had picked up that phrase—probably from one of the sex-addict groups that had been popping up like poisonous mushrooms, though neither of them had gone to a meeting. A whole world was implied in the term, a world of judgment and morality he thought they had left behind. He got angry the next time Keith referred to "acting out" and told him to drop it. Sex wasn't acting out. You bought the whole idea of AIDS-as-punishment when you used it.

From time to time they compared themselves to straight couples. How did those people manage? Ray knew by observing his parents, his brother and sister-in-law, his colleagues at the office. These pairs condensed, diminished. They became people of dull gaze, scaled-down vision. Improvisation disappeared from their lives, to be replaced by habit, children, gossip, squabbling, and an endless search for other kinds of diversion. "The whole idea," he snapped one night, "is to keep them from destroying each other before they get the kids out of the house." He knew this wasn't strictly true —his brother and sister-in-law seemed to enjoy each other—but it relieved him to say it. He also pointed out that every married couple, except the wealthiest, looked older than any faggot of the same age—at least in the old days. Keith, of course, objected to all this generalizing. He told Ray he was heterophobic. Maybe Keith had a point. Still, there were few lessons to be learned from that world. Whatever was to work for them would have to be theirs alone.

But by the late eighties, after the deaths of many friends, even their best strategies weren't working very well. Their bedroom, Ray thought, had an unexploded thundercloud over it, a discharge of energy that couldn't quite take place. Riding the subway one night, registering the tropical gaze of a young Latin hanging on to the next strap, he reflected that he and Keith simply knew each other too well. He'd seen Keith red with sunburn and gray with flu. He'd smelled garlic on his breath and sweat in his crotch. He'd heard him fart in bed and piss in the middle of the night. He knew Keith's body better than his own—it was what he saw most, after all. Far from being a sensual cue, Keith's bony frame, patched with occasional hair, now reminded him of an animal hide. It was always on the verge of breaking down. It required feeding, cooling, heating, and evacuating. Living with Keith's body was harder than taking care of a newborn baby.

And their friendship was deteriorating too. He had once found Keith's slowness, his deliberation, attractive. Not anymore. Half the time he didn't know what Keith was thinking, or if he was thinking anything. Why did he wait so long before opening his mouth? Was speaking an unacceptable risk? Were words land mines that would explode at some future date? Sometimes they sat all evening in front of the TV hardly saying a word.

And after the mayor appointed Keith a judge—one of the first openly gay magistrates—he got even slower. Also critical. He pointed out Ray's faults, that he was obsessive about food and had a chatterbox side that was getting worse. Hearing these comments—betrayals, really—Ray wondered if they could ever be undone. How did couples keep going after hurtful things had been said? Maybe he and Keith hadn't started out with enough love. Or was it possible that a deeper romance would have made their present hurts and disillusion worse? He wasn't sure. He only knew that they weren't enjoying each other's company much. They both made excuses to spend evenings, even weekends, apart.

On the few occasions when they managed sex Ray had to grit his teeth and imagine he was touching someone else. It wasn't all that great for Keith either—he could tell from the straining, the flinging away when it was over. They slept in separate beds now. The tensions at home had probably contributed to Ray's recent health problems. He had a swollen prostate and his blood pressure was on a permanent upswing. He decided that masturbation, which he'd never given up entirely, would be better for his health. Several times a week he locked himself in the bathroom. Keith's face, when Ray emerged, was a study in avoidance. They didn't even discuss their sex problems anymore.

And then, one Friday night, Ray fell. It happened when he was walking Batty, their basset hound. He'd noticed the guy before— another dog owner on the block—and even spoken to him. But tonight, a summer evening, the man looked really attractive. Sort of like Keith when they'd first met—lanky and slim, with wide-apart eyes and thinning brown hair. As they watched the dogs sniff, and chatted while waiting, Ray noted that the stranger had the same mild, soft-spoken manner that had first struck him about Keith. For a moment it made him think that no time had passed. But it was the prospect of freshness that tempted him most. A body he hadn't touched, whose shape he hadn't memorized. He recalled a painting by Magritte, a man with clouds for a face. Now his own face was turning into clouds.

He walked the stranger, who said his name was Scott, to his door on the next block. They traded dog chat on the way. At the brownstone Scott asked if he'd like to come up. Ray had been sure he would—Scott had seen the clouds too. Climbing the three flights, Ray tried to reassure himself. This guy was a dog owner, a neighbor, obviously reliable. And there was the physical resemblance to Keith, which somehow laid on a seal of approval.

Inside the apartment the dogs smelled and pawed each other as the two men sat on the couch. Ray felt himself relaxing—an iron thread letting go. This was home territory. He almost felt like smelling the rugs and chair legs along with Batty, to fix the place in all his senses. Then, looking at Scott, at his trusting smile, his wide-apart eyes, he was filled with tenderness. Why had he denied himself? Why had he been afraid for so long? Why had he de-monized everything outside their own bedroom?

Scott lived in one room, which made it a little awkward. Espe-cially since his dog, a German shepherd, starting whipping around in a frenzy. "He's jealous," Scott said. "I'll put him in the bathroom." He dragged the dog by the scruff of the neck. Batty barked several times; then both animals settled down.

When Scott came out, he looked slightly embarrassed. Ray wondered if the dog noises had thrown him off. Maybe he'd changed his mind. But no, he started to unbutton his plaid shirt. Ray began to do the same.

Scott finished unbuttoning but didn't take off the shirt, revealing a black T-shirt underneath. He paused. Ray stood up and slipped off his shirt. He wasn't wearing anything under it. Scott made no further moves. Maybe, Ray thought, he wanted some help—liked to be undressed. A turn-on from the old days. But when he reached out, Scott backed off. His embarrassed look returned. Slowly, half turned away, he removed his shirt. Underneath, the black T-shirt had cut-off sleeves. Scott had beautiful arms—white and sinewy. Ray reached out, skimming his fingertips along the skin. Scott turned to face him. They hugged lightly, not pressing hard, and Scott nuzzled his cheek. It was a familiar and delicious moment for Ray. Sex had its moves, like ballet—a part you learned early in life and never forgot.

Gently he began to tug at Scott's undershirt. A happy vertigo took possession of him. This choreography had been laid out by a master. He tugged some more at the T-shirt. Then Scott's hand closed over his. "I'm wearing a catheter," he whispered.

Ray stared at Scott's chest. He could make out tubing under the black cloth. He looked up. Scott was standing stone-still, his eyes wide and fixed. Behind him Ray heard Batty scratch. He had only a few seconds to make up his mind. Shapes pressed against him, dim shapes full of terror. Alongside these were Scott's luminous presence, the promise of his touch, the question in his eyes.

Ray smiled. "That's okay."

The undershirt stayed on as they settled on the couch. Ray rolled it partway up and stroked and licked the skin around the catheter tape without disturbing it. They nuzzled and hugged. They kissed each other's necks. When they were both ready, they nodded and finished off individually. After that they lay side by side embracing. Scott's lanky body, with its signature of bones, felt full of love.

At last they broke away, and Ray began to put his clothes in order. "I hear those things are easily infected." He touched, very lightly, the tube under the black T-shirt.

"Yeah. I've been lucky so far."

A dozen questions came to Ray's mind—questions to show his sympathy, curiosity, support. But he decided that asking them now would change the nature of their encounter. Maybe Scott didn't want that. He finally asked one question only. "I'm thirty-seven," came the reply.

After Ray was dressed, they hugged again. "I live right on the next block. I guess I'll see you around," he said.

"Yeah, I'm always walking the dog."

Neither said anything about trading phone numbers.

Ray gave a last look as he started down the stairs, Batty thundering alongside. Scott stood in the doorway, unsmiling.

Keith hadn't noticed Ray's extra time on the street. He'd been balancing his checkbook on his computer—a new and harmless hobby. Ray went into the bathroom, intending to wash thoroughly, but stopped himself. What was there to wash off, except the usual street grime? He soaped his hands, dried them, then went to the living room and turned on the TV. He watched, not really listening. Gradually he became aware of a shift deep inside him. He'd have to tell Keith what happened. He wasn't sure how Keith would take it—at least not at first—but there was no doubt in his own mind that he had resolved their old dilemma. He wasn't sure exactly how or why, but everything was going to be okay.

Avery Milbanke Day

The literature of hesitation, that's how one reviewer had summed up his seven books. Avery's forehead had burned and his stomach had churned when he read it—not in the *Times,* thank God, just in one of those little magazines that pop up suddenly like targets on a rifle range. He couldn't remember its title, though the critic's name stuck in his memory. Minna Kennedy Valletti, a curious amalgam of ethnic reference. It was easy enough to paste a label on any writer's output. He had done it himself, though always more generously, less reductively. Readers liked labels. The human mind required categories—only thus could it apprehend reality. Without categories the world was a jumble, incomprehensible. The trick, if you were affixed with a label, was not to be offended by it. To understand what prompted it. He had reminded himself of this at bedtime for several weeks after the article appeared, knowing that his dreams would be stormy, reflecting his hurt, but it hadn't helped.

Coleman gave a little moan and tried to throw off the covers. Avery quickly dipped the cloth in the alcohol and patted it around Coleman's head—on the chin, the cheeks. He hadn't been paying attention, had let his thoughts run away with him. Useless thoughts in a groove outworn. But it was so tempting now to review his setbacks in light of his new victory. To have the last laugh.

Coleman's eyes were open. Avery bent forward to hear any sound. He needed only a word, a syllable, to know what was wanted. They hadn't spent all these decades together for nothing. Coleman wanted water, because his right hand had cupped slightly. A gesture as good as a word. Avery headed for the bathroom.

Well, if his books were hesitant, that was part of their charm. He had been raised on the great Victorians, and they were nothing if not hesitant, although *moderate* might be a better word. Eliot and Thackeray and Trollope didn't go to extremes. The coin of human emotion hadn't been so debased that they had to scream and shout and tear off their clothes. The subtle interplay of thought and action, ambiguity and discretion—that had been the stuff of literature when he was growing up in Michigan.

"Coley," he whispered. He pinged the glass straw—it was bent and always represented sickness to him—against the rim of the glass. But Coleman had retreated to his dream state. Avery put down the glass. He would have to wait.

How different the bedroom looked now, with Coley so sick. The four-poster bed, the pier-glass mirror, the odd pieces of Queen Anne, Biedermeier, Second Empire, all picked up at auctions, no longer cohered. This room, the one they shared, the glowing core of the farmhouse, had lost its aura of intimacy, revelry. Now it seemed the outpost of a hospital. It had become a public room, where their friends and neighbors, Coley's brother Jonathan and family, doctors and nurses, came to stand around. On weekends former colleagues of Coley's from the museum and foundation world drove down from New York, bringing fresh air and gossip. Their space—to use a word he detested—had been invaded. Even now, when he was alone with Coley, at the very heart of the house, he felt accompanied. Sickness was no longer a private affair.

He had written about sickness in his first novel, the one that won the Harper Prize, establishing him as a new voice out of the Midwest. It had been the sickness of Grandmother Kean, alone in her big bedroom at the end of the hallway, soiling the bedclothes, erupting at all her orifices, burdening his mother, his sisters. But the doctor had come only once a week, and there had been no talk of putting Ganga in a hospital. She would die at home in her own good time. Nor had there been many visitors to the sickroom, the belief being that visitors merely added to the family's burdens. Instead food was sent—hams, puddings, fruit pies. The ordeal of the Milbankes was not forgotten, merely waited out.

Coleman's breathing was shallower now. Soon it would be time for the morning injection. Avery's glance moved to the syringe resting malevolently on the dresser. He had become an expert at that—squeezing the air out of the thing, jabbing Coleman's distended veins, sending in the Demerol. Dr. Hartington had hinted at an overdose. "You'll probably be tempted," he had said, and left it there, knowing Avery too well to believe the temptation would be serious. But he had suggested a part-time nurse for the hard, dirty work. Dr. Hartington thought he was too fastidious for bedpans and vomit. But then he didn't know about Grandmother Kean and watching his mother and sisters take care of her when he was twelve.

Too fastidious. The adjective brought that horrible article to mind again. What had she said? He searched his memory as if he were probing an old wound. *His work is marred by a fatal fastidiousness.* Yes, that's what she had written in that nameless publication. Coleman, of course, had advised stoicism. "She's just trying to make her reputation by destroying you, happens all the time."

Avery knew that—Coleman rarely said anything he didn't already know—and he hadn't found it helpful. The trouble was, he had expected praise. It was an occupational disease of novelists, and there was nothing new to say about it except to note that Truman Capote, whose death seemed such a mystery to everyone, had clearly perished for lack of praise. No matter how nasty your themes, you still wanted to be loved for them.

But he had slowly accepted, or risen above, his critical fate. He had acquiesced in the neglect, slowly altering his perception of himself, changing from writer to ex-writer, from voice to echo, from someone on display to someone out of print. But all that was changed now, he thought with a little smile as he removed the cloth from the alcohol again and squeezed it. Yes, all changed.

There had been Eudora Welty Day at the University of Mississippi—maybe that's where Midlothian had gotten the idea. Or maybe it was because he was a native of Wexford County and the school was trying to find a niche for itself in local scholarship, regional history, apparently the coming thing. Maybe it was— vexing thought—because his books lent themselves to academic exegesis. Well, it didn't matter why the college nearest the town of his birth decided to honor him. The point was that it had happened, would happen soon. In just six weeks, in fact. It was all set.

Coleman was still as death. Avery wondered when it would be and how he would feel when it finally happened. He had certainly accepted the medical reality. Metastatic cancer would not be impeded or reversed. It had gone from Coleman's prostate, via his lymphatic system, to his pelvis and colon. Now it was in the spine. The body's defenses had been overwhelmed after a lifetime of vigilance. Although he could picture Coleman dead, in a coffin banked with flowers, or cremated, and all the attendant ceremonies, he could not imagine his own life afterward. He didn't know if he'd be depressed, diminished, liberated, or numb. This house, which had been their weekend retreat for so many years and their full-time home for the last ten, might claim him for good or propel him outward into the world again.

The telephone in the hall interrupted him. It was Marilyn, her daily call, after which she would call Jonathan at his office at Rutgers. Avery filled her in. Then it occurred to him that Coleman's relatives still hadn't heard the good news. "I forgot to tell you"— he tried to sound casual—"I'm going to have a little affair in my honor at Midlothian College, back home."

Marilyn made the appropriate sounds.

He cleared his throat. "They're actually calling it Avery Milbanke Day, and they're trying to get the governor of Michigan to issue a proclamation."

This time her enthusiasm was unforced.

On the way back to the bedroom another thought struck him. Why wouldn't the Midlothian affair lead to a general revival of interest in his work? Maybe even a reissue in one volume of some of his shorter pieces—*The Best of Avery Milbanke*. It was an exciting idea and perfectly logical. He'd give Robert Straszheim a ring after lunch and see what he thought of it.

Jonathan Hollister was at the window, his favorite spot, looking out over the bleak meadows—tufts of brown grass, spikes of weeds. They had finished Saturday lunch. Marilyn was on the love seat, knitting. She looked, in her way, as remote as her husband.

"I've been reading . . ." Jonathan trailed off.

"Yes, dear?" Marilyn urged him on. This must have been rehearsed in advance.

"I've been reading about these hospices they have." Jonathan didn't turn around. "You know, the patients are usually quite happy. Given everything to make them comfortable."

Avery waited. It all seemed very predictable.

"Yes, Ave. They give them the medication they need, the painkillers."

Avery thought about his own doses. He measured very, very carefully.

"They can do things the family can't. No guilt involved."

"Do I understand you, Jonathan—"

Marilyn interrupted. "Don't jump to any conclusions, Avery. He's just telling you what he's read."

"Yes, it's the European way. They don't have this philosophy that suffering is good for you."

"I never believed that, and neither did Coleman."

"I'm just saying that patients are happier there. Especially the . . . um, very sick ones."

Jonathan stopped, his duty done, but Marilyn picked up. "Don't you see, Avery, this can't go on? It's taking a terrible toll on everyone. Especially you."

He noted her delicate features behind the horn-rims, the tinted chestnut hair, the long, beautiful fingers tapping the needles, the blouse and tweed skirt that showed off her slender figure, good legs. The younger brother's wife, not yet fifty, saying sensible things. But there was no way to talk across the years. He had come of age in another time. He closed his eyes for an instant and saw his mother coming out of Ganga's room, a huge bundle of soiled sheets in her arms. "Go in and hold her hand," she instructed him. "She's low this morning."

Marilyn was staring at him; Jonathan too. No way to transmit all that. "We're doing okay, Marilyn, as long as Dr. Hartington says so." Ganga had been in a state of near dissolution, oozing out of her flesh in all directions. She had been like the rest of them, big and rawboned, but now she had overflowed her boundaries. He had gone to the double bed and taken her hand—feeling the slickness of the gold wedding band, the crispy skin—and thought about pushing her back into the old familiar shape. But it was impossible. Even her hair, long and steel gray, had come loose in a terrible way. She wrapped her fingers around his, tightly, as if he might keep her safe a while longer, postpone the voyage. She had never clung to him like this—no one had—and he got scared, then angry at his mother. But something came to his aid—a squirrel in the elm tree outside. The squirrel stood, alert and poised, on the other side of the window, and he felt better. Stronger. He didn't know why.

"We only want you to think about it, Ave." Jonathan was a smaller, neater version of Coleman, but with none of his verve or jauntiness. Same dark skin, blue eyes, bony build, but a tidier package altogether. He taught history, Coleman always said, because he disliked clutter.

"We'll just go in and say good-bye." Marilyn folded up her work and put it in the wool bag she had knitted herself. "Then we'd better run. They're forecasting snow."

Coleman was awake when they went in, and asked to sit up. Jonathan cranked the bed. A general cheeriness appeared, as if Coleman had just made a complete recovery.

As they chatted, Coleman speaking softly but with a bit of his old snap, Avery thought about the homburg. When he first met Coleman at a gallery opening in New York—a George Platt Lynes show a few years after the war—Coleman had been carrying a homburg in his hand. It had seemed both rakish and correct, a faint parody of the formal world in which Coleman moved even as a young man, as well as a notice that he was quite at home in it. Avery had felt instantly drawn to this poised, snappy man with a hat that was a joke and not a joke, and accepted his invitation to dinner. A year later he wrote a story, "The Homburg," about a museum director who was able to seduce impressionable girls from the Midwest because they were charmed by his hat. Leo Lerman had taken it for *Mademoiselle*.

"We'll be back next weekend with a couple of films." Jonathan patted his brother's hand. "Anything in particular?"

"Doesn't matter." Coleman shook his head, the jaunty smile flashing for a moment.

"Get something British," Avery advised. "He likes those."

After they left, he went back to the bedroom. Coleman was still alert and asked for a cigarette. Avery hadn't been able to tell him about the Midlothian affair, but now Coleman seemed clear enough to be able to listen. Avery pulled a chair to the bed, suddenly happy, and began to talk in the gravely voice that he had accepted as another humiliation of age. It was always different telling things to Coley—part of their long, secret pact. They had known, shared each other's destiny. There had never been any doubt. Starting in 1948, they had moved gracefully, inevitably, into the places reserved for them. Coley had left the Met Museum for the Modern, then with Rockefeller help became head of the Beckwell Foundation, an influential spot in the art world. He himself had advanced his literary career, step by step, until time and taste had decided he was passé. But now, it turned out, rediscovery was part of his destiny too. The place that had been reserved was his for a lifetime.

Not that he had to explain any of that to Coley, who always grasped such matters instantly. Coley wouldn't have been surprised to hear now, this minute, that Avery had won the Nobel Prize. If he'd been able to respond, he would have flashed a smile and asked about court dress.

When Avery finished his little narrative, he sat back. The experience was now complete—more complete than it would be during the hectic weekend at Midlothian, when he might get rattled by all the new faces and talk. Coley was staring into space, the cigarette held dangerously close to the blanket. He wasn't sure if Coley had understood every word, but he had certainly gotten the drift. Avery Milbanke was still a figure in American literature. Coley hadn't made a wrong choice all those years ago when he asked the big pale youth who looked as if he belonged on a tractor to have dinner with him. Not wrong then, nor thereafter, when they had put their private and public lives together.

Fame. It was an ugly word, with overtones they had never liked, distorting more than it clarified. For most Americans it was a place—an estate or a party or a TV show or, God help them, a magazine cover. But it was nowhere really, an entity measurable only in pauses and nods and tones. And an idea of yourself, an idea you could hang on to if you woke up in the middle of the night, or noticed a new failure of the flesh. Of course, there were certain handy by-products—bigger advances on your books, higher lecture fees, grants and juries and honoraria—but these were not as important as the intangibles, the private satisfactions. Yes, he and Coley had both believed in their version of fame, and it had united them. Some people thought they were snobs—they had been caricatured in several novels—but that wasn't true. They had never cared about money or family pedigree. It had been the aristocracy of art, and if worldly advantages followed, they were strictly incidental.

He removed the cigarette from Coley's thin hand. He seemed to be nodding off. Avery watched his eyelids flutter down. What would have happened if he'd written about relationships like theirs? If he'd published something scandalously specific like *The City and the Pillar* or *A Single Man*? He would have been stereotyped, pigeonholed. He would have become a ghetto author. He would never have become the centerpiece of Avery Milbanke Day.

Of course, everyone knew about Coleman and him. They had been one of the most famous couples in New York. It was Avery and Coleman, no second names necessary—like Wystan or Morgan or Katherine Anne or Thornton, all of whom they'd known. There was no need for a proclamation, no need to wash that particular linen in public. But strangely enough, this was precisely what the young people wanted nowadays. One of them, a junior professor whose name he'd forgotten, had sent him a copy of a talk he'd given at a literary conference, in which Avery Milbanke and Coleman Hollister were mentioned by name. This child had told the assembled dons that in the middle years of the century it required little courage to present a male lover in the salons of upper bohemia. Such display was merely another form of elitism, like going to the Rue de Fleurus to look at the pictures or taking tea with Natalie Barney or driving to the Blue Nuns to cheer up George Santayana. These remarks had made his blood boil. What did these youngsters know about courage? What did they know about getting out of Michigan, which stuck up like a frozen haystack between two great inland seas, and learning to move through the gossip and back-stabbing of New York and London and Paris? What did they know about the snubs and slights, the condescension and charity? Or about the self-control that allowed them to keep going?

Coley's eyes were closed. Avery, aware that his blood pressure was up and his hand was trembling slightly, cranked down the bed and checked the condom catheter. A wonderful invention. He was glad to have something to do, to take his mind off all that nonsense. If Coley had been able to talk, he wouldn't have gone off on this tangent. Coley, with his wonderful sense of the world, had kept him steady, saved him from despair or worse over the years. He had a sudden view of himself as a wobbly ship, steering by uncertain stars. His powers were great, but it had been Coley who kept him on course. Again, he wondered what would happen after Coley left him. Would he go to pieces, become confused or paralyzed or alcoholic? He was seventy years old and his flesh hung down on him in folds, but inside he was still a rawboned youth with a tendency to let things run away with him. Whom could he trust after Coley? Who else would know about the place that had been reserved for him for a lifetime? Who else would hold the safety net under the golden illusion that was America?

Coley's darkish skin, which had always contrasted so beautifully with his blue eyes, was gray now, as if rubbed with ashes. Avery took his hand, feeling guilty. Why was he thinking about himself? Runaway mind, the Buddhists called it. At this point only Coley mattered. He tapped into the beat in the wrist. He knew all about pulses now. Coley's was weak but regular; he had gone to sleep. Avery sat for a long time, holding Coley's wrist. The steadiness of the beat calmed him. Coley was still here, after all, and in an hour he might open his eyes. He wasn't alone—not yet.

Robert Straszheim took him to an expensive café on West Eighteenth Street. Flat eyes in Pompeiian frescoes looked out from the walls. Robert had aged. The line of his jaw—a long, aggressive jaw—was sagging. It looked as if he had wads of cotton stuck in there.

"So, Avery, it's not the business I was trained for. The midlist book is gone."

As Robert explained what he meant by the midlist book, which apparently included anything not produced by a TV celebrity or a young man on cocaine, Avery began to feel mildly depressed. Why had he bothered making the three-hour trip to town? He should have stayed home with Coley, not imposed on Marilyn. What Robert was telling him, politely, was that an Avery Milbanke reader was not a good idea. No one was interested in reprinted fiction from the forties and fifties. And the Midlothian affair was local news, small potatoes in the imperial city.

As Robert went on, releasing the tones of Andover and Yale trapped in his chest half a century ago, Avery felt his spirits sag even more. All writers lose their audiences sooner or later—why had he thought he was the exception?

"Of course," Robert continued, "if we could get some decent coverage of your conference . . . Trouble is, they hate to leave New York. And it's a little late to try for a special."

Avery thought about Michigan at this time of year. The TV cameras would ice over. "Why can't we do some interviews here before I go?"

Robert looked uneasy. "They ask a lot of embarrassing questions these days."

"I've done interviews before."

"This isn't the *Paris Review*, Avery. They'll get personal. Is it true you've lived with Coleman Hollister for forty years? Why didn't you ever write about such relationships? What are your views on AIDS? That kind of thing."

"What does all that have to do with my novels?" A stupid question—he knew the answer already.

"Nothing. But unless they get interested in you, they won't get interested in your work."

Avery sat silently. He recalled seeing Isherwood on the *Dick Cavett Show* years ago. Chris had handled the ugly, probing questions with his usual aplomb. He himself could never do that, could never convert himself into a talk-show charmer.

"As I say, the rules have changed." Robert was trying to be helpful. "You've always been a private person."

Of course, if Coley were here, seated next to him, his response might be different. He would feel his strength, hear new voices inside him, tell Robert to arrange something. Suddenly he recalled the junior professor who had criticized him for being a snob, for refusing to be more political. Maybe the man was right. Maybe he had taken refuge in American house parties and European châteaux. He had a sudden unnerving view of himself as a careerist and a social climber.

"Well, there's bound to be *some* publicity, at least in the Midwest," he said at last.

"Oh, decidedly." And then they spoke of other things.

After lunch—they parted with false promises to do it soon again—Avery decided to walk up Fifth Avenue and from there to the bus terminal at Forty-second Street. Though it was chilly, the sun was bright, and he had a sense that he might put his thoughts in order by walking. This was where it had all begun, after all, in this shining city at the edge of America. New York, when he arrived, was not only the magnet, the arbiter of all things, it was also something more—the place to be free. That hadn't been possible at home. But here, right here on Fifth Avenue, which he was now striding up with his long steps ("For God's sake, Avery, slow down"), he had learned. It was difficult to slough off the Avery he had seen reflected in his mother's worried eyes, his sisters' quiet disapproval, the roll call of the neighbors, each with a different reservation about him, but he had done it. He had found and released his true voice in the novel that won the Harper Prize. And when he met Coley—he was near the Empire State Building now, where Longchamps used to be—he had not drawn back either. What they did, in Coley's studio apartment on East Sixty-fourth, at his own furnished room next to the old Whitney on Eighth Street, was the logical culmination of his new power, his new voice.

But it was still confusing. If what you did in private, if your appearance as a couple in public, proved you had conquered your fears, why was that no longer enough? Why did they demand more? He had never described the sex act, never given anatomical details, even when doing so meant an extra fifty thousand copies sold, as John Updike had proved ages ago. He simply didn't write about those things, with partners of either gender. Did that mean he was a prude? A coward?

How confusing it was. He had reached the library without noticing. The lions, Patience and Fortitude, sat on their pedestals, dreaming of stone savannas and endless prey. He had researched many of his essays here—Peacock, Meredith, Chatterton—and the marble facade, so deliciously overdone, a confectioner's master-piece, still charmed him. On impulse he turned and went up the broad steps, passing through the revolving door into the atrium. It was cleaner, brighter, and the old coat check was gone. He glanced up to his right. The gilt lettering of the benefactors had been touched up, no doubt at their expense. And straight ahead, a dim space that had always been closed off was now open. Gottes-man Hall. He might take a look there on his way out. But first he wanted to go up to the main reading room, the core of the building.

On the stairs he looked for his favorite painting, *Milton aveugle dictant 'Le Paradis Perdu' à ses filles*. It used to hang at the landing between the second and third floors. It was gone. He felt suddenly disoriented. Milton in his armchair, his blind face serene while his daughters waited for the next line—it was nineteenth-century kitsch of the noblest sort. Why had they moved it? Didn't they know they mustn't shuffle things around like a pack of cards?

Irritated, he moved toward the catalog room. Of course—com-puter terminals everywhere, young faces reflecting their greenish glow. The old card files, so hard to handle, so well thumbed, so full of exquisite calligraphy, were gone. Only electronic squiggles remained. His disorientation increased.

The twin reading rooms, just beyond, were unchanged, thank God. The same inefficient lamps, bow-backed chairs, general gloom. He stood for a while watching the book-retrieval lights flash on and off. How many hours had he spent on that bench, waiting for his number to come up? But as he stood there now he gradually became aware that someone was staring at him. He glanced at the first table. Facing him was a young man in a dirty hooded sweatshirt. Narrow blue eyes, pale skin, handsome in an undernourished way—Slavic, perhaps Polish. Avery was caught in the narrow stare for a long moment, then pulled himself away. He looked around. The room was full of derelicts, homeless people taking refuge from the cold, dozing behind stacks of useless vol-umes. This young man was one of them. He looked back. The man jerked his head and smiled. What did that mean? That he wanted to meet in the hallway? Avery responded to the danger and excitement even as he sensed that the man was in the same category as the missing Milton and the new computer terminals. There had been a shift. The library was no longer as before. Now it reflected the seams and secrets of the city outside. It provided sex as well as information. Maybe it was like literature itself—something new had been added.

He turned and walked out, aware that his pulse was pounding. Back in the main hall he saw the sign for the Berg Collection. They were having a Virginia Woolf exhibit. He headed that way.

She was laid out in a sea of mirrored cases—letters and diaries and photos and first editions. He had met her at a small affair at Victor Pritchett's in London. She had a very good opinion of herself—that was the impression he had taken away. Of course, she was quite celebrated and he was only a budding American writer. But now she was more than celebrated, she was the virgin queen of feminist letters. As he paced the aisles he found everything terribly familiar and rather boring. None of it was as exciting as the young man in the hooded sweatshirt. He thought of going back, following up the signal, meeting, talking, perhaps even arranging something. But even as he thought this he knew he couldn't—it was simply out of the question.

He made himself leave the exhibit and descend the main staircase. It was getting late; he wouldn't make any more stops. Marilyn would be fretting.

He was walking down Fortieth Street toward the bus terminal when the teenager spoke to him. He was standing at an entrance to Bryant Park, and at first Avery thought he said, "Smoke." But a second later he realized he had said, "Sex." He turned around to see the boy smiling and groping himself. His skin was the color of cocoa butter, but pearly and lustrous from the cold. Avery's heart speeded up as the hustler walked toward him.

"How ya doin', man?"

"I'm fine." He should move on, but he was rooted to the spot.

"Lookin' for some fun?" The boy's face was seamless and new.

Avery looked around. A few yards away, near the fountain that didn't work, a policeman was watching them. He didn't seem very interested. When he saw Avery looking, he turned and walked the other way. "No, I'm not," he said at last.

"Then how about you give me somethin'? To buy a token like."

Avery fished in his pocket and brought out some change.

"That all you gonna gimme, man?"

He muttered something in response and turned, moving rapidly. The boy hurled an obscenity after him.

He walked the rest of the way to the bus terminal in a state of mild shock. The sights and sounds of the city had not put his thoughts in order. Just the opposite. New York, the city at the edge of the continent, whose inhabitants weren't civil in the best of times, had taken another turn for the worse. Sex and rage and despair were out in the open. There had been a hernia in the body politic. The old city, the city of his success, had shrunk to a tiny fraction, a slit. He had been a fool to contact Robert Straszheim. Time had passed; it couldn't be turned back. There was nothing here for him.

Marilyn had supper waiting. It was kind of her—she might have slipped out the door with a word and a kiss. But he had begun to feel better as soon as he reached Berwick, seeing the town hall, being recognized by Merle in the parking lot, braking to avoid a doe grazing at the edge of the road. He was home again. There were his duties toward Coley, toward the house, toward Marilyn and Jonathan. New York was retreating. In another hour it would be gone.

He walked Marilyn outside after supper, standing in the driveway as she drove off, though he was wearing just his cardigan. He wasn't looking forward to the rest of the evening or, for that matter, the next four days. Coley had been deteriorating recently—that afternoon with Jonathan and Marilyn had been his last good day—and the Midlothian weekend was coming up. The closer it came, the more strenuous it seemed, and this afternoon in the city hadn't helped. Avery Milbanke Day now seemed more like a wake, an obsequy for his vanished talent, than a celebration. On top of that, there was his speech. He still hadn't written it. He'd tried, but it wouldn't come. There was too much to say and too little. The obvious things—his roots, his family, Michigan—didn't appeal to him. A talk full of literary anecdote would be trivial. And any general remarks on literature . . . Well, he wasn't sure he had anything new to say there either.

He went into the house, shivering. He could sense his confusions of the afternoon lying in wait. And at the other end of the house was Coley.

He went in there first to report Marilyn's departure. Coley was perfectly still. Avery touched his wrist. Just a flutter. "Coley," he whispered.

Coley opened his eyes. Avery knew every crack and gully in that face—had watched them take form, one by one, over the years. He was engraved with the sight of Coley. The same was true of Coley, at least until recently. They were engraved with the sight of each other.

And then he understood what his speech at Midlothian had to contain. He had to talk about Coley and their life together and the difficulties faced by writers of his generation who, almost without exception, had been unable to write of their own lives. He would point out that he was not one of the exceptions. He was the product of a particular time and place. All gifts had limits—the limits themselves gave shape to the gifts—and only certain words had been available to him. Perhaps he had cared too much about society or had feared ostracism. Perhaps he had really been a snob and had been fooling himself with his definitions of fame. But there was no way to change all that now.

Some people in the audience wouldn't like such a speech. They'd consider it too personal, but that wouldn't stop him. It would be like walking out of that exhibit with Coley and his absurd homburg back in 1948, despite the stares and clucking tongues.

He went back to the den for pad and pen. But he'd write in here, on the chaise longue, keeping an eye on Coley. That was one way to put it. Another was that Coley's presence would help, would give him courage. He chuckled as he began.

He was awakened at two in the morning, still on the chaise. Coley was on the floor thrashing. He hadn't heard him get up, had nodded off himself, the yellow pages scattered all around. He had warned Coley a thousand times not to get up, to call him. But Coley thought everything was possible.

He got Coley back to bed, gave him an injection, and stayed awake until early morning, when he called Dr. Hartington.

"Well, it might have been cardiac arrest, and probably will be next time," came the weary voice over the phone. "Maybe it's time we called Good Samaritan."

"I'll keep him here for a while."

"Up to you."

He hung up feeling guilty. The time had come but he was ignoring it. Did keeping Coley at home serve some selfish purpose, unknown to himself? He tried to be honest. Coley hated hospitals, had made it clear he didn't want to die in one. Coley's wishes had to be respected.

But behind this there was something else. He let his mind rove as he fixed breakfast—Coley could take only bouillon now—and put on coffee for himself. What was it?

And then, as he was helping Coley, spooning the liquid between his discolored lips, he thought of Ganga again. No, there had never been talk of putting her in a hospital. Home was where you died, just as home was where you were born. There were the church and grange for public affairs and home for private ones. And what could be more private than dying? That last morning had been clear and cold like this one, everyone sitting around her bed, saying anything that came to mind, all of them trying to be natural, to hold on to the little things in the face of the vast forces loose in the room. Mama dressed up in a shirtwaist and pretty plaid skirt, powder and rouge on her face, Ellen and Martha also in Sunday clothes, Uncle Orrie in his barn clothes but his face and hands scrubbed. And Ganga. A shapeless mass on the bed, her face jaundiced, her eyes closed, her spirit wedged between living and dying, staying and going. Mama had started some Psalms—she knew dozens by heart—and after that they bowed their heads and spoke the Lord's Prayer, each of them secret and alone, thinking thoughts they could never share—though he had taken the liberty of guessing them when he came to write the scene. And when they finished the prayer, there had been another pause, a long one; then Mama had said in a plain voice, "She's gone." Each of them had filed up to the bed and kissed her forehead, still warm. He had felt peaceful and relieved. They had kept Ganga company right up to the gates of death. You couldn't go any farther than that. They had all been strangely happy for the rest of the day, as if they had completed some difficult task, like washing down the milk room. They had hummed, told jokes, laughed quietly. It had been, he recalled, one of those days when everything was in place.

Now, watching Coley shrink after last night's fall, he wondered if it was nostalgia that made him want the same thing again. Coley wasn't Ganga. He should call Hartington now, ask for the ambulance.

But he was unable to go to the telephone.

He spent the morning typing and revising his talk. It seemed to have faded in the light of Coley's new trouble, but he was glad to have it down. He recognized his best writing style—hard, specific, dramatic. Amazing he had never been able to do this before.

Dr. Hartington arrived at two in the afternoon, examined Coley, left some new medication, and departed without mentioning Good Samaritan. Avery felt his disapproval and twice almost asked him to order an ambulance. But each time the words wouldn't come.

Over the next two days new shadows crept into the sickroom. Coley refused liquids, couldn't speak, couldn't even puff on the cigarettes Avery held to his lips. Marilyn spared as much time as she could, sleeping over one night, and Jonathan canceled a day's classes. Coley's new crisis posed another problem. Avery was due to leave for Michigan tomorrow, Friday. Arrangements had been made to pick him up in Detroit for the long drive upstate. If he was going to cancel, he would have to do it now.

It was unthinkable. He couldn't cancel. Too many preparations, too many people, too much at stake. And Coley, he thought, Coley wouldn't want him to miss this weekend, even if it had long since faded from Coley's mind. Affairs like this were part of their pact. Avery Milbanke Day was one of the things his life with Coleman Hollister had been about.

Marilyn and Jonathan arrived the morning of his departure, ready to spend the long weekend as planned. Avery watched them unload their Volvo. Their faces seemed harder, grimmer, as if this weekend was going to be the worst of all. And maybe it will be, he thought, going to the front door.

Jonathan was icy with detachment. He gave Avery's hand only the slightest pressure. And Marilyn, brushing against his cheek, struck him as utterly remote. He followed them into the spare bedroom. Perhaps they were merely tired, he thought. They went back to Coley's room, where Coley lay in a coma. Yes, worn out from all the chasing around (a two-hour drive from New Brunswick over bad roads; weeks, months of it and their fund of sympathy used up). He recalled the talk they had had about hospices. They hadn't forgiven him, probably blamed him for their fatigue, late hours, this weekend of full-time care. If Coley had been in a hospice, everything would be smooth, organized. They certainly wouldn't be staring at him over Coley's bed, their eyes glazed with resentment.

"Hartington's home number is by the phone. You can bypass his service if anything happens."

He saw them trade looks and he read more blame, more anger. He had set this up for maximum inconvenience, and now he was going halfway across the country for a weekend of banquets. He felt a new surge of guilt, a need to apologize. What was he doing? What selfishness was behind it?

And then the guilt was replaced by quiet knowledge. It had been a long time coming but it was here. It had arrived like the message from the squirrel in the elm, when he was holding his grandmother's hand. He turned and went to the kitchen. He dialed the college and asked for the dean. He explained carefully, taking his time, omitting nothing.

He had a hard time persuading Jonathan and Marilyn to leave. It was their turn to feel guilty. They had to be convinced that this decision had nothing to do with them, that he knew they didn't mind spending the weekend, and so forth. "It's just that I saw things clearly at last," he said over and over. "I'm sorry it took me so long." He didn't even try to explain. How could they possibly understand that he had written a speech to celebrate his connection to Coley and that staying here was the final truth of it, beyond any honor or acclaim? And that if the dean followed his instructions, this private act would become a public one? They did, finally, agree to stay for lunch, which made everybody feel better, although conversation was strained.

After they left, Avery went to the chaise in the bedroom. In one of his novellas he had observed that life was mostly perch, mostly waiting, and here he was, proving the truth of that. But now, instead of blankness and suspension, he had unusual views. He saw the winter sunshine on the crusty snow. He saw Coley's thin form hardening into a chrysalis. He saw his mother and his sister washing and dressing Ganga's body. He spent the afternoon on the chaise, waiting, as these sights unreeled in front of him.

Coley died at four the following morning—an hour, Avery knew, when the soul struggles hardest to escape its prison. He had been sleeping on the chaise, but a sound pierced his sleep. He went to the bed and stood quietly. When he was sure Coley was gone, he kissed him and stroked his hair. "Good-bye," he said, "good-bye." Then he knelt down and recited the Lord's Prayer. After that he walked through the house switching on all the lights. It seemed the best way to start celebrating Avery Milbanke Day, for both of them.

AUTHOR'S NOTE

I wish to point out that there are certain obvious correspondences between the life of Jelson Raines in "The Language Animal" and that of James Baldwin, whom I never met. My purpose is not to retell Baldwin's story—in fact, the character is a composite of several writers I have known—but to illustrate the dangers of literary over-compensation, the pitfalls of narrative, and the conflicts that arise during a long life spent describing things. A few well-known circumstances of Baldwin's life (and that of other imaginary lives) became a framework on which to hang a thesis.

Another story that needs explanation (or apology) is "The Jilting of Tim Weatherall." Some readers will recognize the title as a spin-off of Katherine Anne Porter's short masterpiece, "The Jilting of Granny Weatherall," which is also the final reverie of a dying person. My story is a relic of an old, ambitious project which I labeled "Tales from Literature." These tales would retell certain stories from a gay point of view, adding up to a book. In my first story collection, Couplings, I included three such tales, switches on stories by Henry James, Thomas Mann, and Joseph Conrad. That I got no farther with the project testifies to my common sense or incompetence or both. I trust that the present story will be the end of that particular urge.

A word about the title, *Fidelities*. As I cast about for a title, I looked for a common theme to the stories. It came to me early one morning that most of them dealt with constancy of one kind or another—perhaps my favorite virtue. They describe constancy in relationships over a lifetime, in ethnicity, in attention to the usable gay past, in sexual enjoyment, even in resentment. One story, "The Temple of Aphaia," gives the destructive underside of loyalty. It was just a short step from this realization to the title *Fidelities*.

I would also like to use this space to thank my editor, Edward Iwanicki, for the professional guidance and encouragement he has given me at every step—not only with this collection but with my novel *Family Fictions*. I have been extraordinarily lucky indeed.

R.H.